FORGOTTEN KINGDOMS

OF CLAWS & CHAOS

USA TODAY BESTSELLING AUTHOR
M. SINCLAIR

Copyright © 2024 by M. Sinclair

M. Sinclair reserves all rights to and/or involving this work as the authors. This is a work of fiction. All names, characters, places, incidents, and dialogues are products of the author's imagination or used fictitiously. Any resemblance to actual people either living or dead, or events is purely coincidental. No part of this book may be reproduced in any form or by any means whether electronic or mechanical, including information storage and retrieval systems, now known or hereinafter invented, without written permissions from the authors, except for brief quotations in a book review.

Cover Artist: Stef Saw of Seventh Star Art

Title Page/Page Header Artist: SamaiyaArt

Character Art: Lumie.Art

Map Artist: Elle Madison

Editor: Refined Voice Editing & Proofreading

❦ Created with Vellum

FORGOTTEN KINGDOM COLLECTION

Eight women.
One sacrifice to save their kingdoms.
A chance to reclaim the love they lost.

Forgotten Kingdoms is a collection of full-length stand-alone fantasy romance novels with fated mates and a guaranteed happily ever after. With vampires, fae, shifters, and everything in between, each book features a unique heroine and her epic love story that can be read in any order. All relationship dynamics are M/F.

Novels within this set include:

- Of Blood & Nightmares by Chandelle LaVaun
- Of Dragons & Desire by GK De Rosa
- Of Death & Darkness by Megan Montero
- Of Shadows & Fae by Jen L. Grey
- Of Elves & Embers by Elle Madison & Robin Mahle

- Of Mischief & Mages by LJ Andrews
- Of Serpents & Ruins by Jessica M Butler
- Of Claws & Chaos by M. Sinclair

Series link to the Forgotten Kingdom Collection: https://mybook.to/ForgottenKingdoms

Forgotten Kingdoms
Pronunciation Guide

Terrea — TER-AY-UH
(World Name)

Havestia — HAV-EST-EE-UH
(Festival when the veil between worlds opens)

Aelvaria — EL-VAHR-EE-YA
Ember — EM-BURR
Hadeon — HAY-DEE-ON

Draconia — DRUH-CONE-EE-UH
Saphira — SA-FEE-RUH
Ryker — RYE-KURR

Isramaya — IS-RUH-MY-UH
Rhodelia — ROW-DELL-YA
Varan — VAIR-EN

Isramorta — IS-RUH-MORE-TUH
Morgana — MORE-GONE-UH
Avalon — AV-UH-LAWN

Magiaria — MAYJ-AIR-EE-UH
Adira — AH-DEER-UH
Kage — KAY-J

Sepeazia — SEH-PEA-ZI-UH
Stella — STELL-UH
Brandt — BRAN-T

Talamh — TAL-OV
Alina — AH-LEEN-UH
Kieran — KEER-AN

Vargr — VAR-GURR
Evera — EH-VEER-UH

Court of Moon and Stars
Kingdom of Fuoco
Kingdom of Eyre
Kingdom of Terre
The Never Court
Kingdom of Aquos
Draconia
Ael
Kingdom of Nightfall
Kingdom of Eventide
Sacred
Vargr
Isle of Wildcrest
Court of Blood
Kingdom of Kropelki
Kingdom of Ognisko
Court of Nightmares
Sepeazia
Isramaya
T E R

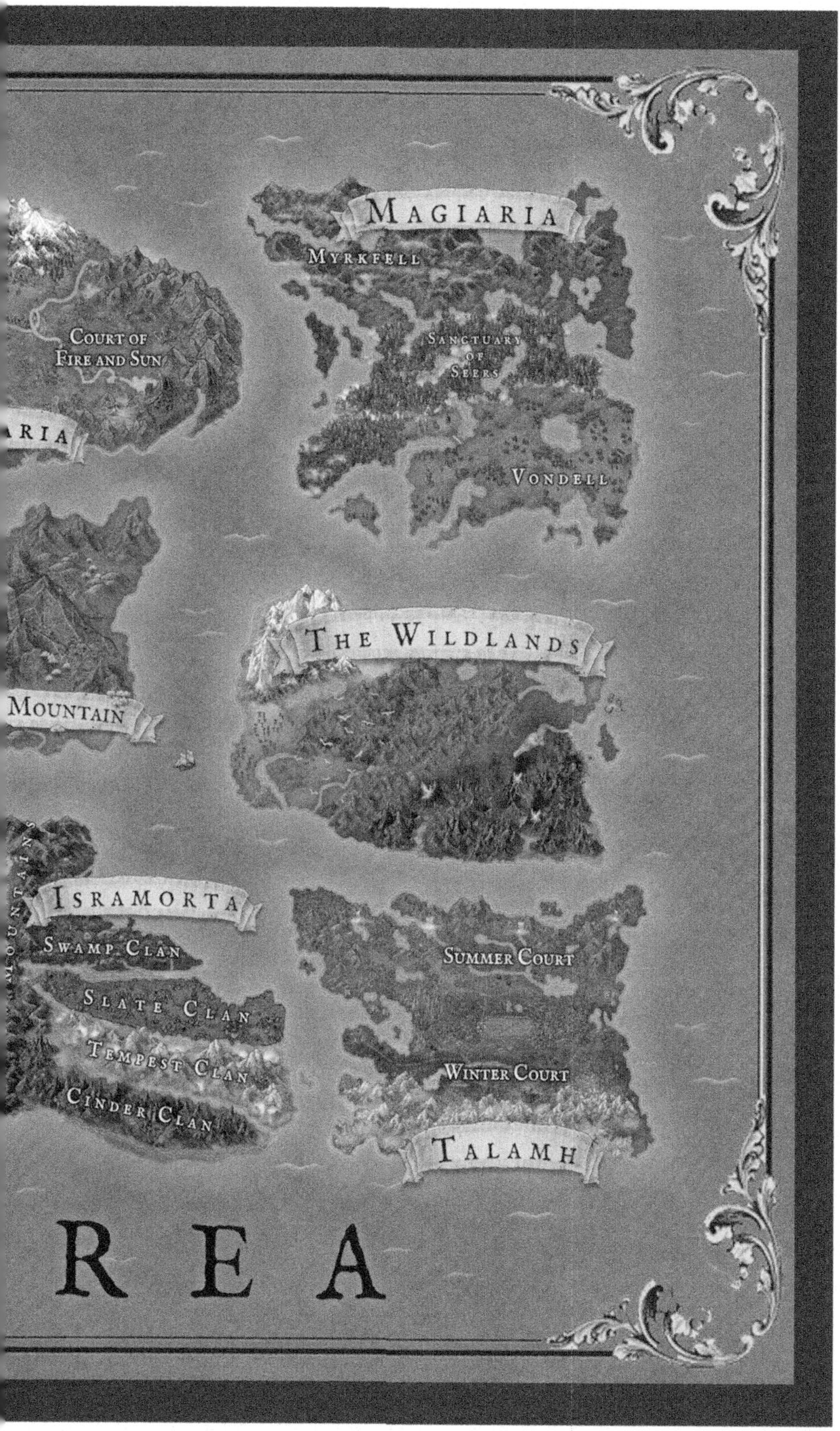
Magiaria
Myrkfell
Sanctuary of Seers
Vondell
Court of Fire and Sun
aria
Mountain
The Wildlands
Mountains
Isramorta
Swamp Clan
Slate Clan
Tempest Clan
Cinder Clan
Summer Court
Winter Court
Talamh
REA

Kingdom of Nightfall

Midnight Keep

Darkridge Mo...

VARGR

Kingdom of Wolves

Castleridge Keep

Kingdom of Eventide

Isle of Wildcrest

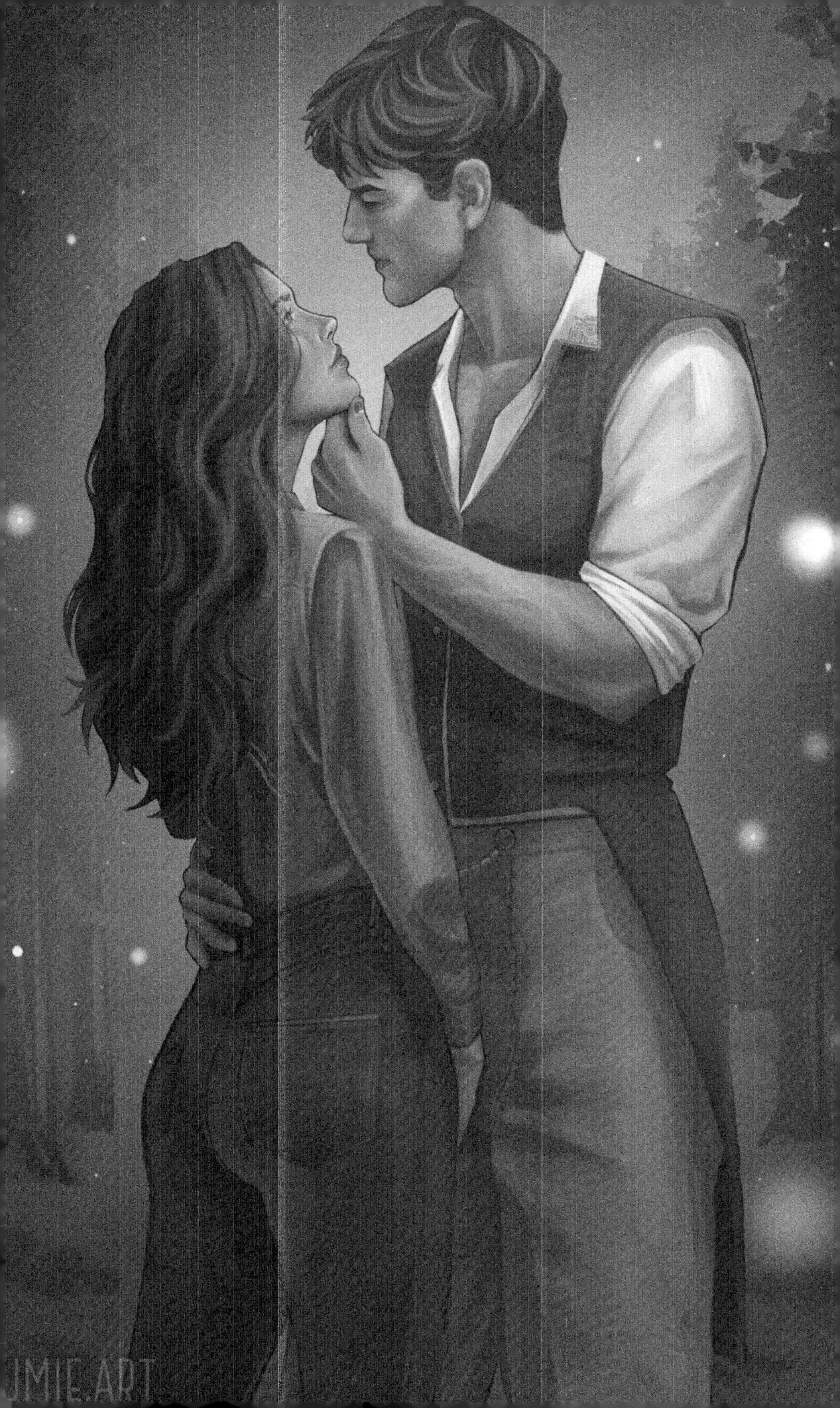
JMIE.ART

The Union of Love & Madness

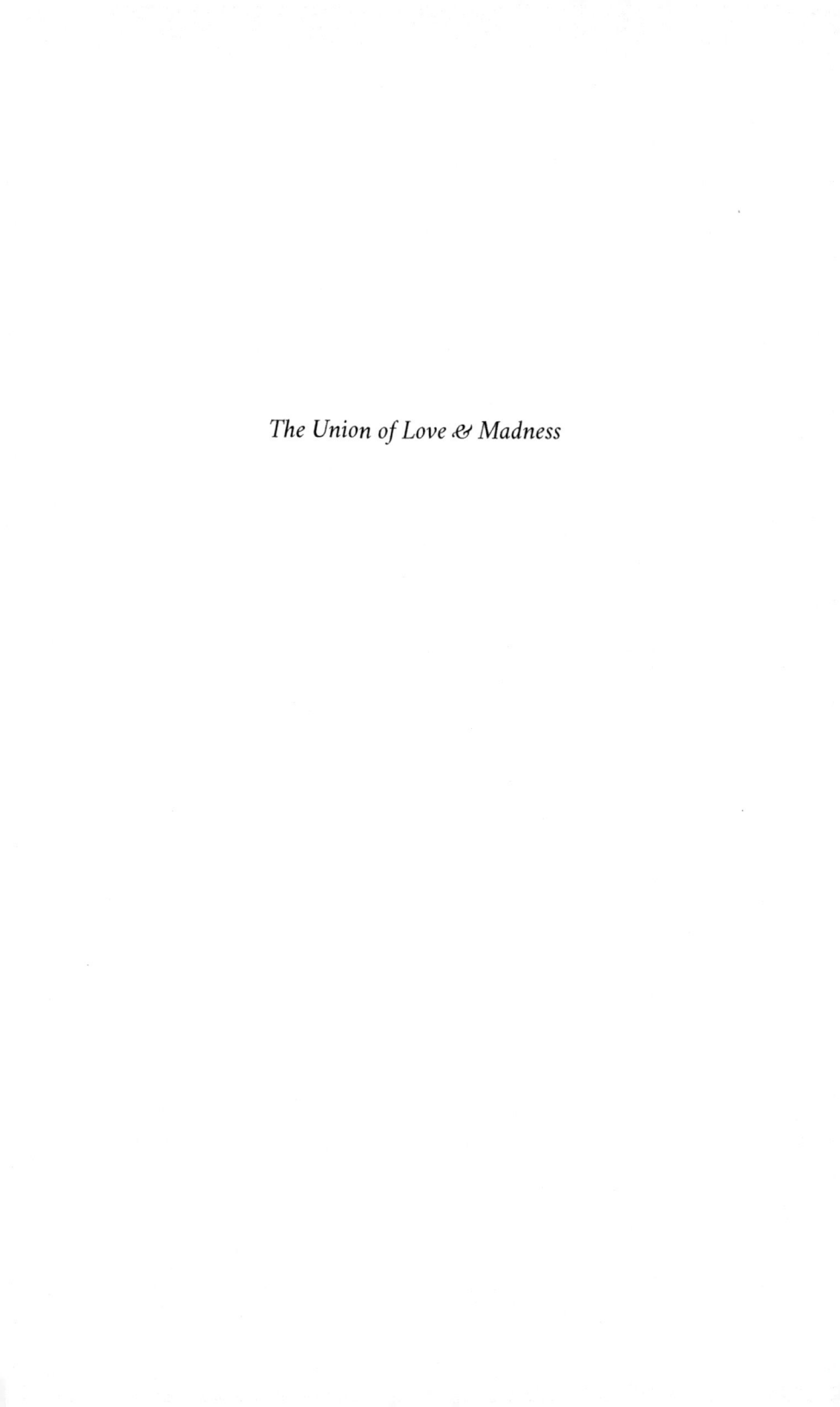

To my two beautiful daughters. You inspire me every single day to continue crafting stories and building imaginative worlds for others to enjoy.

DESCRIPTION

A forsaken wolf princess.
A new king risen to power.
One opportunity to unite their broken lands and love.

Overcome by the exhaustion of her monotonous day-to-day life, all Evera wants is one fun night out. A chance to escape a rigorous work schedule that drains her of all semblance of happiness. When a mysterious portal consumes the air before her and an enigmatic, intense man pulls her through, she wonders if her wish is being granted.

As she's swept into a foreign, magical land she doesn't recognize, Evera finds herself separated from the man who pulled her there—a man who not only knew her name, but seemingly everything about her.

Completely alone, Evera treks through a mountainous landscape to reach the Kingdom of Nightfall. With each step, she encounters its foreboding and mysterious qualities, making it clear that she's not on Earth anymore.

Arriving in Nightfall brings more questions than

answers, though, as she discovers that not only does she have royal blood, but there's a primal magic running through her veins that allows her the ability to shift into a wolf. What startles Evera the most to learn is that she had a life in this world before—with the very man who stole her through the portal: Axel, the King of Nightfall.

Memories begin to resurface, and she quickly recalls that Axel had been the only person she trusted—the only one standing between her and the darkness of her parents' rule. But has time changed the man who once swore to protect her?

A war is waged between two kingdoms upon news of her return, and Evera is the prize.

A single question wreaks havoc in Evera's heart: Does she want to belong to anyone at the end of this?

Author note: This book contains a sweet but strong female lead, a growly alpha wolf that would burn the world down for her, and a love so deep it will mend the rifts of their kingdom. High spice. Content is intended for mature audiences and 18+ recommended.

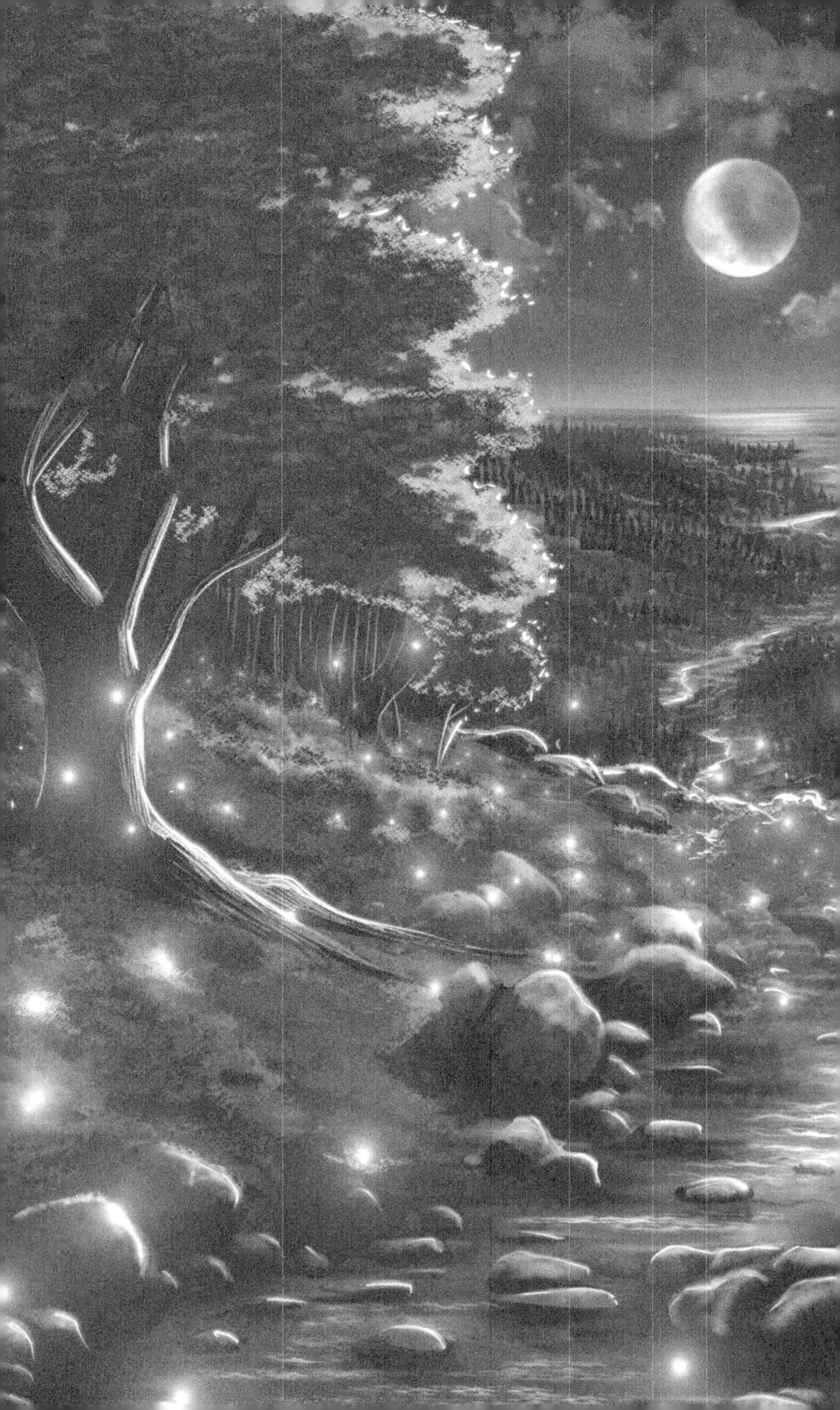

CHAPTER ONE

EVERA

Everything about this place was an illusion.

I stood, tray against my hip, waiting for a set of drink orders as I eyed the casino floor, my chest squeezing uncomfortably with the knowledge that *I* was part of that illusion. It was early evening, but in this building it was permanently night, the twinkling stars replaced by glittering chandeliers. Wealthy, luxuriously dressed clientele weaved in and out of tables, placing bets and throwing around money I couldn't even conceive of. The lack of windows, pounding EDM music, and heavy smoke only added to the blanket of haze that coated the scene.

And here I was, watching all of it, feeling…feeling detached. I shouldn't have. In fact, after everything I'd been through today, I should have been fed up. Angry. Maybe it was the long work hours, or maybe it was that my toes were numb from the stilettos I was forced into, but I just couldn't find it in me to muster the energy.

"Evera." Christina appeared next to me, looking chipper and well rested before her shift. "You can go home. Doug wants to talk before you leave, but I'm taking over twenty minutes early. He said to not worry, that it won't affect pay."

"What pay?" I murmured. Her lips pressed up knowingly, and she took the tray I offered. Letting out a small sigh, I made my way across the expansive floor of the casino, to the hallway that led to the staff dressing room and Doug's office. To say our floor manager made me uncomfortable was the understatement of the century.

I really hoped the reason he wanted to talk to me had nothing to do with going out for dinner. I had used every excuse in the book so far, not wanting to outright reject him in fear of losing this damn job, but I was growing limited in options.

Deciding to get it over with, I approached the door of his office, pausing only momentarily to knock before stepping into the darkened space. His office was as eccentric and obnoxious as he was, filled with dark leather furniture and posters of naked women on the walls, as if flexing that his ability to openly objectify whatever and whoever he wanted made his position enviable.

To be fair, it wasn't that far off base, considering his wealth and power.

Almost immediately upon entering I had to moderate my expression, my nose twitching in discomfort. Doug was more than occupied, it appeared, a woman with bright pink hair positioned on his lap, completely naked from the waist down. Her words were cut off as she let out a shocked sound and nearly fell off his lap, scrambling to cover herself before darting towards the bathroom.

"Evera wouldn't have minded!" Doug called out, offering me an amused look. "Or maybe you would have."

"None of my business," I said quietly. His gaze narrowed

on my expression before darting down my frame, openly staring at every curve of my body. Which considering my lack of groceries or any real meals outside of when I worked at the Daily Egg Diner each morning, weren't very obvious.

Even my uniform seemed to fit a bit looser now that my rent had increased. The once tight leather skirt and matching corset half-top now felt a bit more comfortable, despite showing the same amount of skin.

"It could be," Doug offered. "And it sounds like you need it."

"What do you mean?" I demanded, crossing my arms defensively. I may have noticed the differences in how I looked, but I hadn't thought others could.

"The chefs told me you've been taking leftovers home."

That would explain it.

Shame and embarrassment pressed heavily onto my chest and caused my cheeks to flush. It had to be Tony who'd opened his chauvinistic mouth. He was pissed because I'd rejected his offer to make sure I was always well fed with his—

I inhaled, not wanting to go down that particular memory lane as I tried to read Doug's expression. It was cocky and amused, not an ounce of sympathy to be seen. As if he liked that he was backing me into a corner.

Steadying myself, I shrugged. "If the food is just going to be tossed at the end of the night, I don't see an issue. It's damn good food; someone should eat it."

Doug's smile turned dark. "The food here is fucking awful. I think your situation is worse than you let on, Evera. It sounds like you need help."

Not from him. Never from Doug.

"I promise I'm good," I said, trying to infuse indifference into my voice, "but it won't happen again."

"Be sure it doesn't, or else we may have to do something about it." He nodded towards the door. "That's all."

My jaw tightened as I turned towards the door and slipped out. I hadn't wanted to be there in the first place, but being so summarily dismissed stung, and it wasn't long before tears of shame and frustration filled my eyes.

Mostly because Doug wasn't wrong.

Even with two jobs and a studio apartment in a converted motel twenty minutes away from the strip, I was barely making ends meet. Most nights—hell, most *days*—I barely ate, and sleeping was damn near impossible with the array of stuff happening outside my door.

From a couple that liked to screw right against the railing of the balcony in front of my door to gunshots and police sirens that sang through the night in mockery of a lullaby, I rarely was able to relax enough to sleep. I spent most of the night tossing and turning, waking up exhausted around three a.m. to get ready for my eight-hour shift at the Daily Egg and then coming here to work six more.

It was little wonder I looked like crap.

Pushing into the dressing room, I went to my locker and stripped out of the dumb uniform, trading it for a pair of oversized jeans and a hoodie. I didn't pause to look in the mirror before pulling on my sneakers and my threadbare backpack—I didn't want to see the truth in my dull gaze, the thought that was plaguing me and making my soul so damn heavy I could barely breathe.

I couldn't do this forever. But I didn't have any other options.

Now that I was out of uniform, I wasn't allowed on the casino floor, so I made my way down back hallways to an exit. As I cut through the kitchen, which was mostly empty right now, I narrowed my eyes at Tony, who offered me a dark smirk from where he stood across the room talking to one of the servers. I was tempted to flip him off, but I knew it wasn't worth it—he had a bad temper, and one I didn't want to ignite.

I'd seen the girls he dated. I'd also noticed when they disappeared, just never coming into work one day.

Breaking out of the exit and into the warm evening air, I shielded my eyes from the hot sunlight bearing down on me, the dry heat oddly soothing against my skin.

Tightening one hand on my backpack, I slid on a pair of dollar sunglasses and made my way towards the bus stop. The traffic was heavier than normal today, and I had to dodge a lot of people dressed in costumes…what the heck was going on? Seeing people dressed up wasn't an uncommon occurrence in Las Vegas, but this many was odd.

When I reached the bus stop, it came to me—Halloween.

It was Halloween. Something I had completely blanked on considering the majority of my shift at the casino had been spent in the VIP room, where the individuals wouldn't be caught dead in costume. It also explained why so many of my coworkers had been talking about going to parties tonight. Swallowing down the bitter reminder of how many of them had completely normal lives, I made myself comfortable on the bench and began to list all of the things I was thankful for.

It was something I did when I felt desperate. When I felt hopeless.

Luckily, by the time I'd listed out what felt like a fairly small collection of blessings, the bus pulled up and I joined the ten others boarding. I threw myself into one of the worn plastic seats and let my eyes close, planning to take advantage of the twenty-plus minutes until we arrived at my stop.

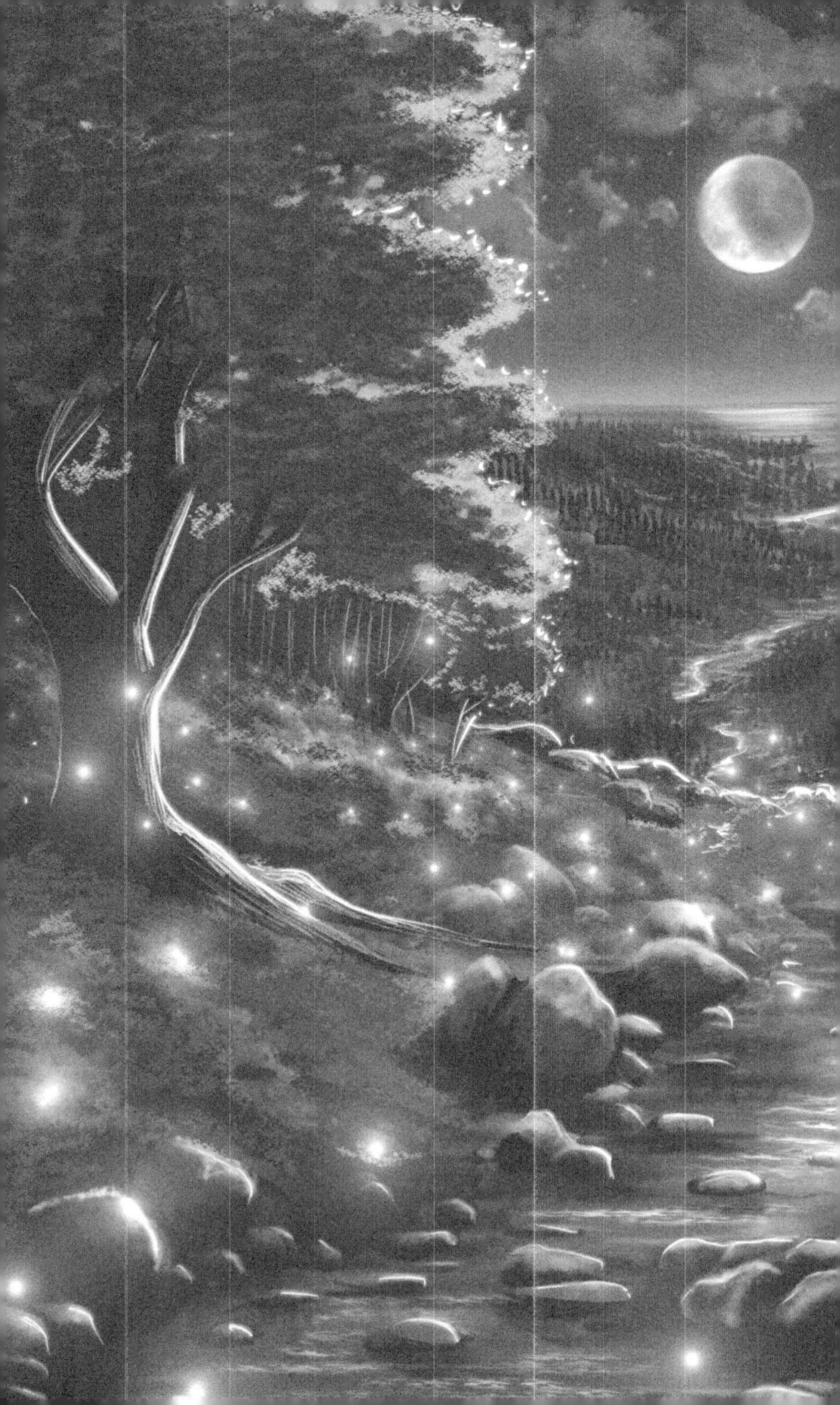

CHAPTER TWO

EVERA

Maybe I'll try to go to bed early tonight, I thought as the bus began rambling down the road. If I got in bed right when I got home—before people went out, let alone came back and caused absolute chaos outside my door—maybe I could actually get some sleep. Biting down on my lip, I considered one of the very small reasons that sounded so appealing right now. Other than the exhaustion, of course.

My dreams—well, specifically the dream from last night.

It wasn't concrete enough to replay it in my head; I couldn't grasp onto anything besides the feeling I woke up with, the imprint it left on my soul that gave me a sense of warmth, security, and safety. There was one visual that stood out, though—a pair of dark eyes that seemed to track my every move, the sensation of rough hands catching my waist. They left a fiery trail along my skin, and when I woke up this morning, chills and a flush covered my body, making me feel almost breathless.

So maybe I was hoping for a repeat of that. Maybe I was hoping for more detail.

"Broadway and Clark."

My eyes snapped open, and I stood and grabbed my backpack as we approached my stop. Offering the driver a nod, I hurried down the steps, glad my bus fare had already been paid for the month. After all, if Doug continued on this path, I would probably be using it to go to job interviews.

As I trudged toward the flight of stairs that would take me to my place, I looked around the converted motel buildings that now served as studio apartments, all surrounded by parking lots that were either in horrible disrepair or held cars in a similar state.

Three stories up, the iron rail of the motel balcony was painted a tangerine orange, standing out against the stained yellow building. I ignored the group of men and women gathered around an expensive car in the parking lot, the stairs squeaking as I climbed, probably drawing attention. Luckily, no one said anything to me as I reached the door —*345*.

Pulling out my key, I looked around to make sure no one had followed me, not feeling safe until my front door slammed shut and I flipped the lock. You could never be too careful.

Throwing my backpack to the side, I collapsed onto the couch, letting out a long exhale and lifting a hand to massage the tension from the base of my skull. The buzzing in the back of my head was a tell-tale sign of an approaching migraine.

They were something I'd had since I was very young, a product of stress and exhaustion made worse by my fear of the unknown, which I'd developed as I was passed from foster home to foster home. I couldn't remember a time when I'd had any level of stability before my eighteenth birthday, when I'd been cast from my house and moved to the strip to find work.

Now, four years later at twenty-two, I didn't regret my choice in the least. Life may not have been easy, but it was *easier* when I had control over my day-to-day, something I'd lacked growing up. Opening my eyes, I found the singular personal photo I had sitting on my small console table.

Laurain.

She'd been in her mid-fifties, her house filled with cats rather than children. She'd been so sweet and so incredibly kind. I hadn't lasted there very long before my social worker realized I wasn't enrolled in school, let alone that the house wasn't fit for a child...but the months I did spend there were incredibly peaceful. I'd been heartbroken when we were separated.

It wasn't until three years later when I was fifteen that I saw her obituary. The picture on my console was printed from that, but instead of making me sad, it made me happy knowing that she was loved enough, had enough friends in her community that someone had held a funeral for her. It meant that someone would miss her.

Before I could let my mind wander too far, a piece of paper on the ground caught my attention. Frowning, I crouched down and unfolded the paper, which someone must have slipped beneath the door. It was a flyer for a Halloween party at a place called *The Portal*.

A small smile tugged at my lips. Something about it appealed to me, and I wondered if maybe, just for once, I should just go out. To just let go a little bit. Hadn't I just been lamenting the fact that my coworkers had been invited to parties and I hadn't? Grabbing my phone from my bag, I pulled up the number of one of my only true friends. She moved around a lot but often came to the area around this time of year.

We'd met at a restaurant a year or so back when she was working seasonally, and while we didn't work together anymore, we talked often. Dialing Stella's number, I put the phone on speaker and stared up at the popcorn ceilings, noticing a spider in the far corner of the room.

"Evera?" she asked on the third ring.

"Hey," I drew out, looking down at the sheet before asking, "How do you feel about going out tonight?"

"Go out?" I could practically hear her brows scrunching together through the phone. I nearly laughed, but considering most of our hanging out revolved around watching movies and relaxing at my apartment or at the diner I worked at, her reaction wasn't surprising.

"It's Halloween, apparently. I got this invite to a party at The Portal."

"I haven't heard of that place before," she murmured. "What time is it?"

"It doesn't say," I said, turning the paper in search of something I'd missed. "I don't know...later? Like in an hour or so?" I laughed at myself. "I don't know; I don't party."

"So just show up and hope for the best?"

"Yeah, just show up." I could only imagine how crazy I sounded considering her laughter, so I added, "I really need this."

Stella's laughter trailed off, emotion flooding her voice in response. "Same, actually."

Somehow it made it a lot less lonely knowing we both were in a tough place.

"I'll send you a picture of the invite, but let's say two hours?"

"This should be interesting," she said, sounding nervous.

"It'll be fun," I tried to reassure her, adding, "Don't forget to dress up!"

I smiled as I pressed the end button before she could respond. Now I just had to figure out what the hell *I* was going to wear.

Despite my lack of actual space, I liked to consider my apartment well kept and clean. It was only one room, much like you would imagine in a motel, with an attached bathroom. The front of the room near the window held a sofa that pulled out into a bed, and the back of the space had a kitchen—right next to the bathroom. I had never decorated or really put any effort into making it feel cozy, but after a few years it had started to feel like home. Or at least what I assumed home would feel like.

Pulling off my clothes, my blinds already closed from being gone all day, I put my jeans and sweater on top of the small table near the kitchen as I passed it to get to the bathroom. After sending Stella the details from the flyer, I felt a small thrill of excitement at the prospect of going out. I desperately needed a break, and at least this would ensure I would spend the night doing something other than worrying about where I'd get my meals from now that Doug had put his foot down.

My apartment and my dreams would be here when I got back, that much I was sure of.

Turning on the shower, I let it heat up to steaming before slipping into it and letting out a groan of relief as the hot water cascaded over me. Washing off the 'work' from the day, I felt a lot better once I stepped out. When I cleared the fog off the mirror, the small smile tugging at my lips did a lot to make me look more alive, less downtrodden. I knew something needed to change in my life, but it was hard to change anything when you felt like you were living the same day every day, barely managing to survive.

I put in a fair amount of effort getting ready, more than usual, meticulously applying my dollar store products and darkening my green eyes with mauve shadow. My skin was still tan from the summer, and my hair, which I blow-dried to lay flat down my back, had a hint of gold. Happy with my hair and makeup, I opened the small chest that worked as my wardrobe.

I grumbled under my breath as I dug through the garments—how could someone who got by on so little have accumulated so much? I knew what I was looking for, but it'd been at least two years since I'd been to a Halloween party—dragged there by one of the girls from work—so it was probably buried at the bottom...

I breathed out a sigh of relief as I finally spotted it—a red velvet cape. I think I'd originally bought it at a thrift shop, but I honestly couldn't remember. Pulling it out, I sorted through my day-to-day clothing options before choosing a pair of over-the-knee black socks and a little black dress that fit tight at the waist and flared out mid-thigh. It was my play on Little Red Riding Hood—a simple costume comprised mostly of things I could reuse and wear throughout the year.

"Shit," I muttered as my phone alarm went off while I was in the middle of pulling up one of my socks, and I hopped across the room to stop the shrill sound. I quickly pulled on the other, slipped on my red and black sneakers, then clasped the cape over my dress. Grabbing the small black purse I rarely used, I threw in my cell phone and wallet before eyeing the room one more time. I felt a weird sense of apprehension come over me and I briefly worried, not for the first time, that someone would break into my apartment while I was gone.

Glancing at the picture of Laurain, I decided to do something I'd been mulling over for a while now—I removed the picture from the frame and tucked it into my wallet. It was my only possession I was truly sentimental about, and I felt a hell of a lot better having it on me.

Satisfied with my decision, I stepped outside and promised myself that tonight would be different. I *needed* it to be different.

I needed something to change.

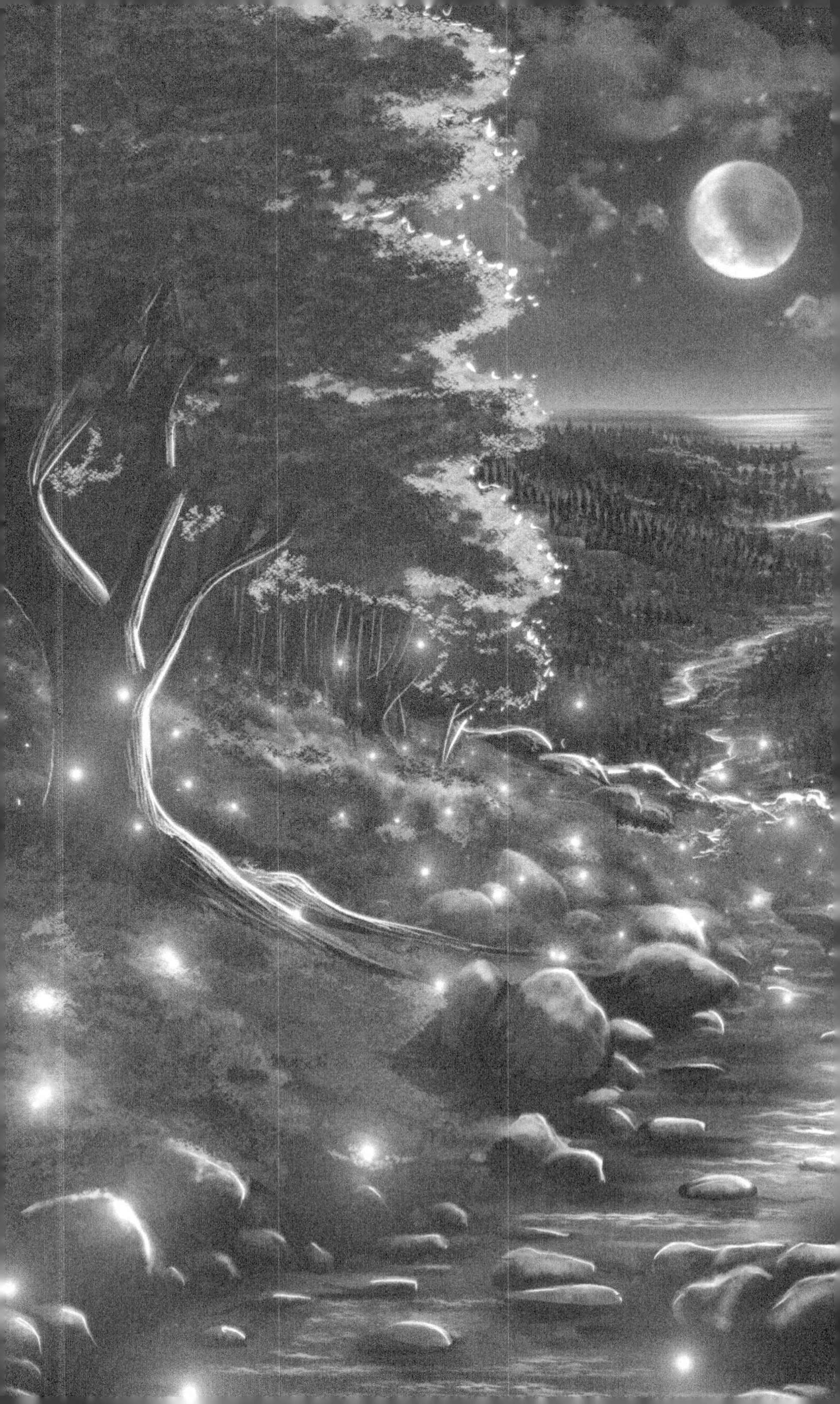

CHAPTER THREE

EVERA

"This is The Portal?" I asked the taxi driver, having decided to splurge on the ride. I hadn't loved the idea of taking a bus in the outfit I was wearing, and the looks I'd gotten waiting for my ride just right outside my building confirmed the decision was a good one.

"That's what it says on my GPS," the woman replied, eyeing the building in concern. It wasn't that it looked particularly run-down or abandoned—rather the opposite—but it wasn't nearly as crowded as the other places, and the luxury it exuded looked almost...dangerous. If that made sense.

After paying for my ride, the woman offering me a few words of warning, I quickly discovered why there were no crowds lingering outside—*everyone* was already inside.

The glass and gilded gold doors were opened for me by not one but two doormen, and once inside I stood in awe of the spectacle ahead of me. The lobby and casino floor seemed to stretch on forever, like some type of illusion, and my eyes instantly caught on the mosaic tiles that lined the floors. The smoky, dark atmosphere was only broken by the glittering chandeliers, but instead of feeling suffocating like it did at work, here the opulence of the place made it feel elegant. Piano music played in harmony with the ringing of the slot machines, and a distant, deeper thumping bass could be heard from a club within the hotel.

My gaze darted around the space, almost overwhelmed by the amount of people in costume. How the hell was I going to find Stella?

Spotting a bar positioned to the side of the lobby, I decided to start there and sighed in relief when I immediately caught sight of my friend. Stella stood out amongst the crowd for two reasons—the first being her awesome costume, a fuzzy gray triceratops hoodie with bright, patterned leggings, and the second because of her light blonde hair. She was objectively stunning but completely unaware of it, her attention down on her sneakers. Men in the bar were sneaking looks her way, and I would have found it funny if I knew it wouldn't make her uncomfortable.

"Stella!"

Her head snapped up and a bright smile lit up her face. "Hey!" she chirped, immediately standing as I pulled her into a hug. "You didn't mention how huge this party would be—I mean seriously, it's like *everyone* is here!"

"They probably dropped a flyer under every possible door." I shrugged. "I'm surprised you didn't get one."

"Maybe they weren't doing the motels? They might have only done the hotels on the strip," she responded, but the hesitation in her gaze made her answer feel a bit off.

Brushing the thought aside and putting on a brave face, I pulled her toward the bar. "Come on, let's grab a drink. I need one after this week."

The bartender appeared as soon as we squeezed into two seats that were miraculously free amongst the sea of patrons crowding the bar.

"How can I help you ladies?" he asked, his genuine smile relaxing me a bit. My eyes flickered down to his name tag as I offered a smile. *Carlos.* He was handsome, his dark hair styled away from his face and coming to rest right at his bright white collar, and his teeth were so incredibly white that the man could have easily been in a toothpaste commercial. It was impressive.

"My friend and I will both take a glass of champagne—we're celebrating."

"We are?" Stella asked.

"Anything important? Or just life?" Carlos asked, grabbing for a bottle that looked a bit too expensive for my taste.

"Just enjoying a night off from work and being with friends," I explained, keeping it simple.

"Well that deserves several drinks on the house," he mused, sliding two glasses across the lacquered surface before placing the bottle in an ice bucket in front of us. "Cheers, ladies."

As Carlos disappeared, Stella stared at me in confusion. "Do you know him?"

"Nope," I admitted, "but he could probably tell we needed a drink." I was mostly teasing, but I didn't hesitate to tip back the glass of bubbly as Stella did the same.

"What's going on?" she asked, her eyes shading with concern.

I could have lied or refocused on the celebratory mood, but I wouldn't—it felt good to be able to tell someone about what was going on. To confide in a friend.

"Honestly? I'm consistently working over sixteen hours a

day, I'm making almost no money because rent has gone up, and my boss is an absolute creep." I took another sip of my drink. "Lots going on, and none of it fun."

Stella sighed. "I'm sorry; that sounds horrible and I definitely understand...Honestly, I'm out in some cheap motel until I figure out where to go next. I only headed out this way recently since it's been warm here consistently."

My eyes widened. "Shit, you should have called me! You absolutely could have stayed with me."

Stella took a long sip of her drink and shrugged, though she smiled. "You're a great friend, but I don't want to be a burden. It sounds like we both have a ton of stuff going on. Besides, I'm trying to figure out what I'm really looking for, you know? Everything just feels...off. Maybe I'll head toward the ocean. Anyway, I'm just glad we were able to meet up."

A smile tugged at my lips, understanding that sentiment completely. "You're right—you're completely right, and this bottle is *not* going to finish itself. Drink up. We can ignore all of our problems until tomorrow."

A plan I fully intended to stick to.

Apparently, life had other plans.

Two hours later, I was more than a bit buzzed, walking what felt like circles around the casino as I tried to figure out where Stella had gone. I'd lost her after going on a little side quest—or at least that's what I was calling it—trying to help a woman find her sister. I also had a bad habit of stopping at each of the tables I passed, wanting to watch how easily people threw around money for the sake of playing with pure chance.

Normally I found it exhausting and frustrating to watch, but tonight after a few drinks I was viewing it in a different light. It was almost mesmerizing, and I found myself wondering what it would be like to live life like that...to live so freely.

A sudden change in elevation had me letting out a startled cry as I nearly fell down a set of stairs that led to a lower level of the casino. Catching myself on the railing, my cheeks flushed pink as I looked around to make sure no one had noticed. Luckily, the costumed patrons seemed so focused on their own nights that I was able to coast down the stairs and pretend like it had never happened.

Which was fairly easy because the next level of the casino was busier than the first. I allowed myself to get lost in the crowd, still searching for Stella as I watched people feed countless dollars into slot machines, slide piles of chips across the velvet tables, cheer as luck struck...until it all became too much.

More than a bit overwhelmed, I made my way towards one of the long hallways that branched off the casino floor. I had no idea where I was going, but the longer I walked down it, the quieter it grew, until I finally reached a pair of glass french doors. Peering out into the night, I saw a garden pavilion on the other side.

I pushed through the doors, letting out a pleased sound as the warm air ran against my skin, combatting the chill of the hotel despite my cloak. Above me the moon shone brilliantly, and I tilted my head back as if I could absorb its rays like the sun. Letting out a long sigh, I found a bench to sit on and ran a hand over my face, feeling my mood dip.

It was a hell of a lot easier to be celebratory when I was surrounded by people.

The sudden creak of the french doors opening had me snapping my head up, and I frowned at the way the heavy wood swung in the wind—a wind that had *only* just appeared. A chill rolled over me as I got the strong sensation that I was being stalked, a long-buried predatory instinct inside of me taking hold and telling me to run. *But from what?* My vision was a bit blurry from alcohol, but my muscles locked in apprehension, my body going on high alert as my senses became much more keen.

Standing, I turned sharply towards the garden, and a startled cry caught in my throat—one that I refused to release. I hadn't been wrong—there was someone stalking me, watching me. The lean, muscular body stepped out from the shadows and into the light of the moon, causing my stomach to tighten uncomfortably.

"Evera, it's good to see you again."

My brows drew sharply together. *I had never seen this man before in my life.* If I'd met him, I wouldn't have forgotten such a handsome face, or his bright red hair and vivid green eyes that stood out under the moonlight. But there was another reason I wouldn't have forgotten him—everything about him made me extremely uncomfortable.

His costume made him look like he belonged in the middle ages, but the way he slowly walked towards me, like he was trying to appear relaxed and harmless, was completely lethal. My body broke out into a cold chill, as if it remembered this man and not for a good reason.

"I have no idea who you are." I swallowed, shifting back on my feet but not turning to run. Something told me running would be really bad.

His chuckle was authentic as he tilted his head. "Now I

don't believe that—you may have lost your memory, but I can't imagine you forgot about me. About *us*."

"Us?" I crossed my arms protectively over my chest as he stepped even closer, and his scent hit me. It wasn't a pleasant scent—well maybe it should have been, faintly smelling of pine—but something about it made my stomach roll. I was nearly sick as the visceral imagery of him wrapping his hand around my throat played across my mind, but that had never happened before. He'd threatened, though. I *couldn't* let that happen, couldn't let down my guard around him—

What the hell was going on?

"Yes, us." He appeared right in front of me, taking advantage of my distraction. "Us and our future together—a future that is about to come to fruition."

"What the hell are you talking about?" I demanded.

"Fifty years," he mused, his eyes glinting cruelly. "I've waited that long, and your ignorance isn't going to have me waiting any longer."

Without a moment of hesitation, he caught my arm and pulled me roughly against him, a surprised scream escaping my throat. His hand clasped over my mouth and I bucked against him, my strength absolutely nothing compared to his. Tears crowded my eyes as he dragged me towards the shadows he'd appeared from.

Somehow I knew that if he got me there, everything would change.

Before I could let out another scream, the space around us shook. The man holding me hostage froze and the ground beneath us trembled, stones scattering as the winds picked up. Above us the moon appeared to grow larger, and unexplainable relief like I couldn't describe flooded my chest.

A flash of silver light flooded the shadows, and what could only be described as a portal grew larger and larger—until it was the size of at least three of me. *Holy crap. Was I imagining this?*

Before I even had time to contemplate the possibility, a figure emerged from the portal. The man holding me hostage cursed in anger, his grip on me tightening to bruising. He didn't move forward though, and my body went slack in his arms.

Not because I'd lost the will to fight, but because I couldn't focus on anything else but *him*.

I'd never believed in the supernatural or anything of that nature, but the aura that this man carried, enhanced by the silver light highlighting his massive muscular frame, was otherworldly. The scent of cedar and smoke filled my senses and I nearly whimpered in relief, knowing instinctively that despite appearing more threatening, that this new man was far safer than the one holding me hostage.

It didn't explain why every ounce of fight seemed to drain out of me at the sight of him, though. I'd always been a fighter. I wasn't loud, but I wasn't passive either. I would fight for my survival. But in the face of this man, I wanted to...

What did I want to do?

Run into his arms and feel his touch on my skin, his lips against my neck.

It was the oddest sensation that laid at the root of that impulse, not just desire but pure belonging.

"What are you doing here?" the man holding me hissed. The new man regarded him with a dismissive disdain before his eyes moved to me.

All at once it felt like something fissured inside of me. I gasped against my captor's hand as my knees nearly broke, those eyes catching me off guard completely. *Obsidian.* They were like the void of night without the moon, his gaze holding me captive just as much as the man behind me.

I felt nearly out of breath, and I couldn't help but let my eyes scale over his nearly six-foot-five frame and golden skin, his dark brown clothes and velvet green jacket making him look like a king among men. His hair, a rich chestnut color, was shorter on the sides and longer on the top, making me wonder what it would be like to run my hands through it. The man was effortlessly powerful—I could feel it radiating off of him from here. Despite not knowing anything about him or his name, I couldn't help but dub him as a 'king,' and not only because of how he was dressed.

"The better question is why *you* are here, Reynor," he said, moving forward slowly and purposefully, "and why you have your hands on her." His voice was a deep rumble, and something inside of me shifted against my rib cage as if trying to break out.

"I already told her about *us*, about how she's going to marry me," my captor hissed, and disgust curled in my stomach.

The king chuckled, a hard edge to his laughter. Still, when he finally reached us, I felt much safer as his gaze darted down to me once more. Flashes of images I didn't understand played before my eyes, and at once I recognized the man.....*at least I thought I did.* I couldn't grasp onto anything substantial; just the strong feeling of recognition you got when you saw someone out of place.

"I don't care what claim you think you have on her," he said softly, "you have one chance to let her go."

Reynor tightened his hold on me. "Over my dead body."

A snap sounded, and I let out a gasp of surprise as the

hand over my mouth was literally broken, the king's larger hand darting out and breaking the wrist of my captor. I could barely react before Reynor shoved me back with his other hand, snarling as he crouched into a defensive stance in front of me.

"Move."

"Never," Reynor countered, his form seeming to grow larger.

A deep rattling noise, almost inhuman—scratch that, *completely* inhuman—left the king's chest. Reynor's body locked up, allowing the other man to move past him with ease. Chills rolled up my spine, and I slowly stepped backwards, tripping and landing on my ass. I scrambled to regain my footing, my fight-or-flight instinct overruling what my heart was telling me.

It didn't matter if this man was saving me—he was a lethal predator. Chancing a glance behind me, I started to turn—

"Don't. Don't run from me, *çiçeğim*."

The way his voice softened made me feel less threatened, but only moderately. *And what was with the last word he'd said? Che-chay-him? What did that mean?*

"Who the hell are you?" I demanded. The king's eyes shot down to my feet as that sound rolled through the space again. My toes curled, and I took another step back. Whatever power that sound seemed to have over Reynor clearly didn't affect me.

"I can explain everything once we leave." He stopped, extending a hand. My own twitched, as if I was supposed to take it. "I don't want to force you, but we have limited time."

"Leave here? The hotel?" Did he know how insane he sounded? "Why would I leave with you? I don't know you."

"I know you don't remember, but I need you to trust me —" Thunder cracked in the clear sky and the ground shook again, a deep rumbling sound emanating from the silver portal door. "Evera, we don't have much time. Please." The soft tone of his plea nearly convinced me to grab hold of his hand. I hesitated, those obsidian eyes capturing mine again—

Reynor appeared out of nowhere, a dagger slicing through the air at the king's side. Before Reynor could slice again, the king was suddenly across the garden, seeming to have disappeared into thin air. The action broke the spell, and I felt dizzy from trying to track the fast movement.

I paused to regain my bearings, reassessing my situation. I needed to get out of here, needed to escape what was becoming an increasingly dangerous situation.

In my moment of hesitation, Reynor grabbed me by the arm, lodged a dagger right against my ribs, and began dragging me towards the portal.

"Let go!" I hissed.

Reynor chuckled, ignoring me, and called out to the king. "I'll gut her if you try to take her from me. You know I will."

"You *will* regret this," the man warned. Reynor scoffed, throwing me behind him so that I was stuck between him and the portal. His body shimmered with an emerald mist and his skin seemed to shift, his frame growing larger and larger...

I rubbed my eyes, but I wasn't imagining things—bright red fur sprouted on his arms, his clothes ripping at the seams.

"Back up, Evera, as much as you can," the king said, moving with lethal intent towards Reynor. My survival instincts had me looking around while they were distracted, desperately trying to find a way out of this.

If I backed up much further I'd step through the portal, so instead I started edging to the side, careful to keep my distance from Reynor. But it became harder and harder to do, the space closing as Reynor retreated from the king, the liquid mercury of the door right within reach. If I could just—

The king suddenly surged forward with a roar, and Reynor's monstrous frame slammed into me, pushing me right to the edge of the portal. I teetered for a second, refusing to grab onto Reynor for balance...

And fell.

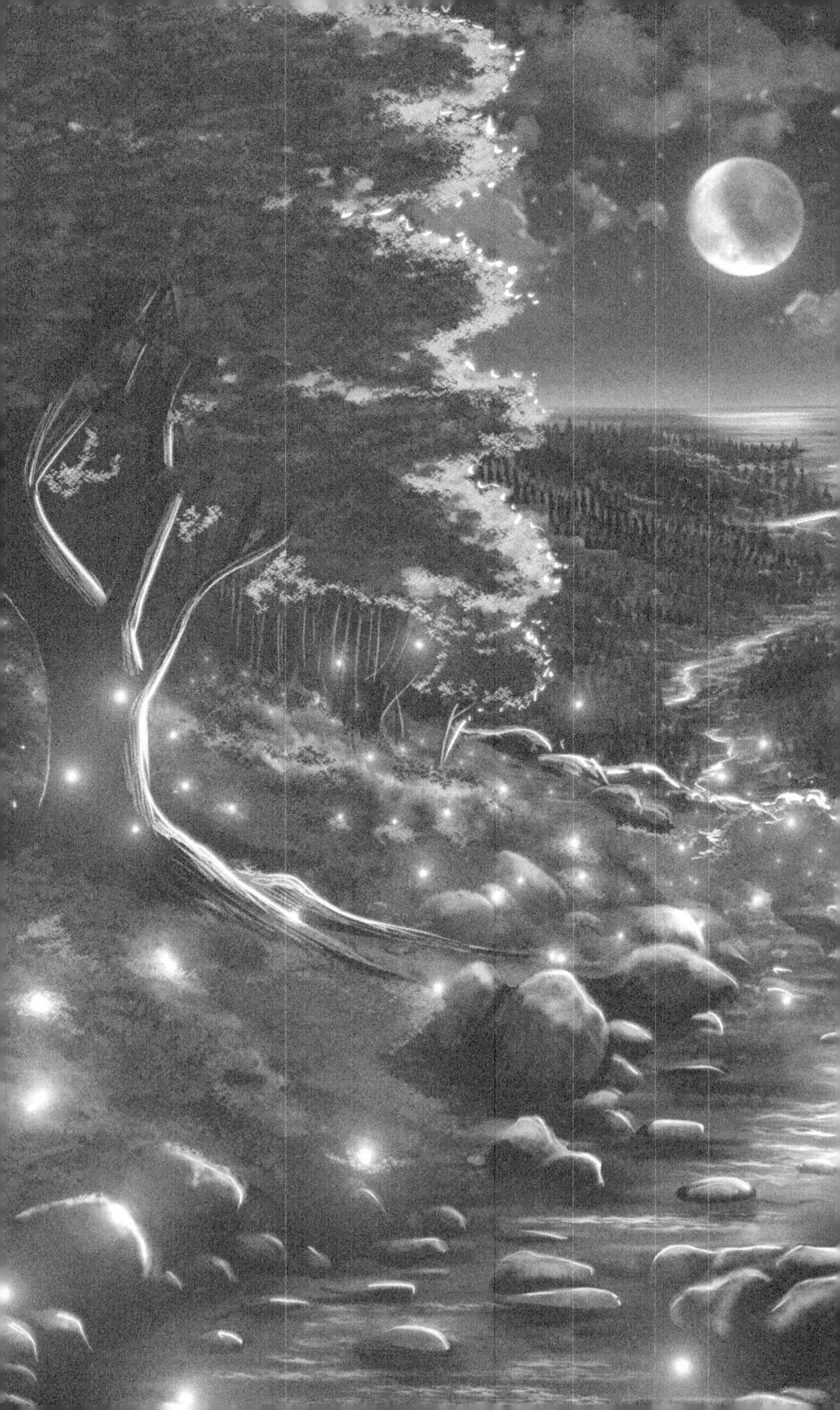

CHAPTER FOUR

EVERA

I opened my mouth to scream, falling at what felt like light speed, but nothing came out. An animalistic snarl vibrated the space around me, accompanied by a shadowy figure plunging in after me, the king and I leaving Reynor behind.

Rough hands wrapped around my waist and I let my head fall back, the king's dark eyes holding me captive. I couldn't speak and didn't have a chance to try as everything went blurry around me, a vision flooding forward, almost like a memory I didn't realize I had.

Heavy familiar footsteps followed behind me, and a smile tugged on my lips. My plan was working, though it was a risky one. I easily navigated the gardens, avoiding any pathways that would lead to a dead end. I held my skirt at my ankles, my bare feet carrying me nimbly across the manicured lawn. Exhilaration coursed through me, and I couldn't help but smile at the energy reaching out to me from behind—he was getting closer.

Slowing just a bit, I turned the corner into my favorite section of the garden and let out a small scream as a hard, muscular arm caught me around the waist. This time I didn't sink into the sensation or relish in it; this time I took action, turning towards my would-be captor and bringing my hands up to his jaw in a soft and purposeful gesture.

His gaze, which was predatory and lethal—his creature tracking my every expression—softened at the realization that I hadn't been truly running from him. His hand tightened on me in an almost bruising way, possessive and protective, and I swallowed down the emotion that clogged my throat.

Despite my original plan, I found myself hesitating in the wake of his dangerous gaze. But I shook those thoughts away, allowing my eyes to dip down to his lips. I wanted to be very obvious about what I so desperately wanted from him.

"Evera." His voice was rough and warm, causing my toes to curl.

"Please?" I hated the idea of begging, but I couldn't help it. I wanted to...well, I wanted a lot of things with him.

"You know we can't." He pressed his forehead against mine, and a frustrated sound left my throat as I gripped his shirt tighter. I didn't want to believe that we couldn't be together or that he didn't feel this connection between us. I refused to believe it.

He stepped away from me, his dark eyes filled with regret before his expression completely closed. "We need to get back. Your parents have called for you."

"Why?" I whispered, ignoring my parents' summons. "Why can't we—"

"I said no, çiçeğim."

I flinched at his tone, tears welling in my eyes. Fine. I brushed past him, promising myself that I wouldn't do this anymore. I had *given him a chance, and instead...well, it seemed he didn't care what we both wanted.*

His throat produced a low rumble, and I felt even more betrayed knowing that his creature felt the same about me. That didn't matter though.

According to him, it couldn't matter.

Nothing I did would ever make him realize the truth. It was hopeless.

When my eyes opened again, I could still feel the intense sadness and pain, the longing for the man in the dream—the man who was holding me. *So I did know him.* But that didn't make sense. Never in my life had I been to that place with the gardens, and I'd never known my parents, so how could they have summoned me?

Blinking, I focused on my savior, his expression conflicted—*and then he was gone.*

Something cracked in my chest, and all at once a power pulsed through my center. I screamed as unbearable heat and pain expanded from within, pushing at my skin until every nerve ending was on fire and I thought I would burst. My ear drums nearly split as tears welled in my eyes, waves of agony, unexpected and unstoppable, tumbling over me again and again.

My body slammed into the hard ground, my hands shooting out just in time to brace for impact, but barely.

I groaned as I collapsed into the grass and dirt underneath me, my head pounding and body shaking as a wave of nausea rolled over me. I had no idea what was going on— where that weird silver portal-like door had taken me, or why I felt like I'd known that man.

Especially since the man in the dream was different from the king in the pavilion. I mean, they were *literally* the same man, but also very different.

The man in the vision wasn't as intense, his darkness and lethality softened. The man in the pavilion had been truly dangerous whereas the other felt softer, more comforting, and familiar...and how had my brain even conjured that other man? Was I still drunk?

Rolling onto my back, I kept my eyes closed and took stock of my body. Everything hurt from falling, but my brain felt sharp. I didn't feel under the influence at all, but my skin still stung, that pulse of power having left a lasting impression on my nerves.

Maybe I would open my eyes and find I was in my bedroom—that everything, from the portal to those men, had been a dream... Or maybe I would find myself face-planted on the floor of the casino or something embarrassing like that. That would make far more sense.

Instead, as time ticked forward and nothing changed, I felt stunned and confused, the king's dark eyes flashing across my memory again and again. Every time, the feeling of wanting to run into his arms and melt into his embrace slammed into me, like in the memory but so much more intense. There was a darker edge to the feeling now and it felt like the start of a fraying garment, the one disturbed thread begging me to pull—even if it was connected to a web of something dangerous and possibly disturbing.

Shaking myself, I opened my eyes and sat up. I couldn't lay here forever.

The space around me spun, and I found myself looking around for Reynor or the king, each for completely different reasons. But no one greeted me. I was completely alone, and

I was *not* where I'd been when I started the night—the casino garden was completely gone.

I hadn't had the opportunity to travel a lot outside of moving from foster home to foster home, but almost immediately I immediately knew I wasn't anywhere close to Las Vegas…honestly, I wasn't sure where I was. It wasn't like anywhere I'd ever seen in pictures, instead appearing as something out of a fantasy realm.

I found myself in a forest clearing in the dead of night, the *two* moons shining high above catching my full attention. They were beautiful, glinting like gemstones—one diamond, one a smoky quartz—in a midnight sky. The breeze rolling over me, while slightly chilled, had me feeling even more alert than before.

Even the colors around me, from the grass to the night sky, seemed richer, more pigmented. The leaves were dark green, almost emerald, and I could feel eyes on me as if something was watching from the edge of the clearing. It didn't make me feel nearly as uncomfortable as I would have assumed, though—it felt natural to the space. I inhaled and tasted the purity of the air, making me realize how long I'd been breathing in polluted air—far too long.

Standing up, I brushed the dirt from my clothes and wrapped my cape tighter around me—suddenly very glad that I wasn't in heels and had something that would provide a little bit of warmth. Rubbing the center of my chest, I felt an uncomfortable ache, and a weird energy rolled over my skin in response. It was like an electric field was causing the hair on my arm to stand upright.

I pulled my hand away instantly, completely freaked out. *Not going to do that again.*

"Where do I go now?" I asked out loud. My eyes darted

around the space, finding a singular break in the trees. The portal, that odd silver door that had taken me here, was completely and utterly gone. As if it had never existed. Muttering to myself in confusion, I walked towards the break in the trees and was instantly shrouded by darkness as the trees closed around me.

Yet...I found I could see. Not as well as in the light, but much more than I could normally see in the dark. I'd never had particularly good vision—I mean, I had a freaking pair of reading glasses at only twenty-two! That didn't seem to be a problem now though...

As if waiting, the minute I was covered by the tree's shadows, the wildlife around me exploded back into action, noises filling the space in a comforting effect. I couldn't tell you how long I walked, glad once again I'd decided to wear sneakers, but by the time I reached another separation in the foliage my limbs felt used and the muscles stretched. Not in a bad way, but like I'd done a workout.

"Shit," I murmured as I stepped through the thinning trees, my steps leading me to the edge of a cliff that overlooked a vast landscape lit by the dual moonlight.

Looking behind me, I realized I stood on the slope of a mountain near the base, the tree-covered slopes of the rest of the range extending to either side. Below me a vast river surged through the valley, hugging near the warm lights of a town before disappearing between the peaks in the distance.

The thing that really caught my eye, though, was a structure near the river that stood above the rest like a glowing beacon, the white stone reflecting the dual moonlight. Candles floated around it on the ground level, or at least I assumed they were candles by how they flickered. But then I realized I was seeing people—lots of them.

The soft breeze carried the sounds of celebration and the scent of a bonfire. For a long moment I was mesmerized by the sight, my heart thumping loudly...and then I reminded myself that I was stuck on a cliff in a place I didn't recognize and seemed a lot like another planet.

Which would make sense since I fell through a freaking portal.

I nearly groaned at how ridiculous that sounded, but at the same time, it felt *right*. Or maybe I'd been reading too many books lately. After all, if there was one thing I would find money for, it was books on my phone. Probably not the best use of my limited funds, but it was a small pleasure I afforded myself.

Shaking my head and refusing to let my imagination get ahead of me just yet, I looked over the ledge to see where the nearest town was. A small breath of relief escaped me as I realized that the drop wasn't as steep as I'd originally thought, and there was a grassy path littered with trees that slanted gently toward the village. I had no idea what I would face there, but it had to be better than just standing here.

I pushed forward and began to make my way down the mountain. After about five minutes of carefully choosing my steps, I tripped over my own feet and hit my knee on a stone, the sharp edge feeling like it struck bone. "Shit," I hissed, holding my knee and feeling blood soak through my sock.

Refusing to look at it, I wiped the blood off of my hands on my black dress and continued forward, but the coppery scent was almost impossible to ignore. Ever since I was twelve, the sight of blood brought on a feeling of queasiness I'd never managed to get over.

. . .

"You're being ridiculous," Rebecca hissed over my shoulder, rubbing her arms to stave off the cold. "We'll wash it off and move on."

"I can't even get it out," I growled at my foster sister, tears streaming down my face. My arm was stuck in the metal fence of the school yard, the rusty metal cutting my exposed skin and causing blood to run down my hand. Why had I thought it was a good idea to reach through it?

"We have to go inside." She tugged on my waist as the school bell rang, and I cried out as the metal cut deeper into my skin. Instantly, she let go. "Fuck this—you're on your own."

And I had been on my own. Completely.

No one had noticed me missing in the classroom, not even my teacher. I'd been stuck there until a teacher found me after school, nearly frozen from the autumn wind. For hours, all I'd been able to focus on was the rusted metal and the blood that continued to drip slowly down my arm. They had called the fire department to cut away the metal, but the damage had been done. A scar permanently marked the incident on my left arm.

After that, the sight of blood filled me with unease, but I'd done my best to learn to live with it since it was impossible to avoid. I would admit, though, that in the moment I did my best to not focus on it.

When I finally reached the base of the mountain, the grassy path turned into a dirt road that led to a small town only about twenty yards away. I instantly felt more on edge as it came into view because it was yet another reminder that there was *nothing* familiar about where I was. Honestly, it reminded me of the Renaissance Faire I'd been to before.

I walked through the streets on the outskirts of town,

making my way to what appeared to be a central hub, hoping to find someone that could help me figure out where I'd landed myself. A market square glowed with hanging lights in the autumn night, highlighting the cobblestone roads. The square held small shops with handmade signs advertising their goods and services—thankfully in English—the paths between them made for pedestrians and not vehicles of any kind. In concentric circles leading out of the town square there were houses lining dirt roads, and as I neared I could see light shining through the windows, signaling that someone was home.

There was one thing that stood out to me though as I looked around the square...it was completely empty. My gaze fell on one of the largest buildings in front of me, two stories tall. *Lorie's Inn.* Music drifted from inside, and voices were audible underneath the harmony, making it clear a large group was gathered inside. A perfect place for finding aid. I didn't love the idea of going door to door as it was, so this seemed like a better idea.

Straightening myself up and summoning some bravery, I approached the stone building. The windows were plastered with posters for musical performances as well as advertisements for stouts and bottles of ale sold at the pub within, the warped glass underneath nearly completely covered.

As I reached the wooden door, I could hear laughter inside, and the sound warmed my chest. I turned the handle and decided to take the risk, praying this was a good idea... not that I had many options.

As the door opened, my hand released the knob... and I realized I'd made a mistake coming here.

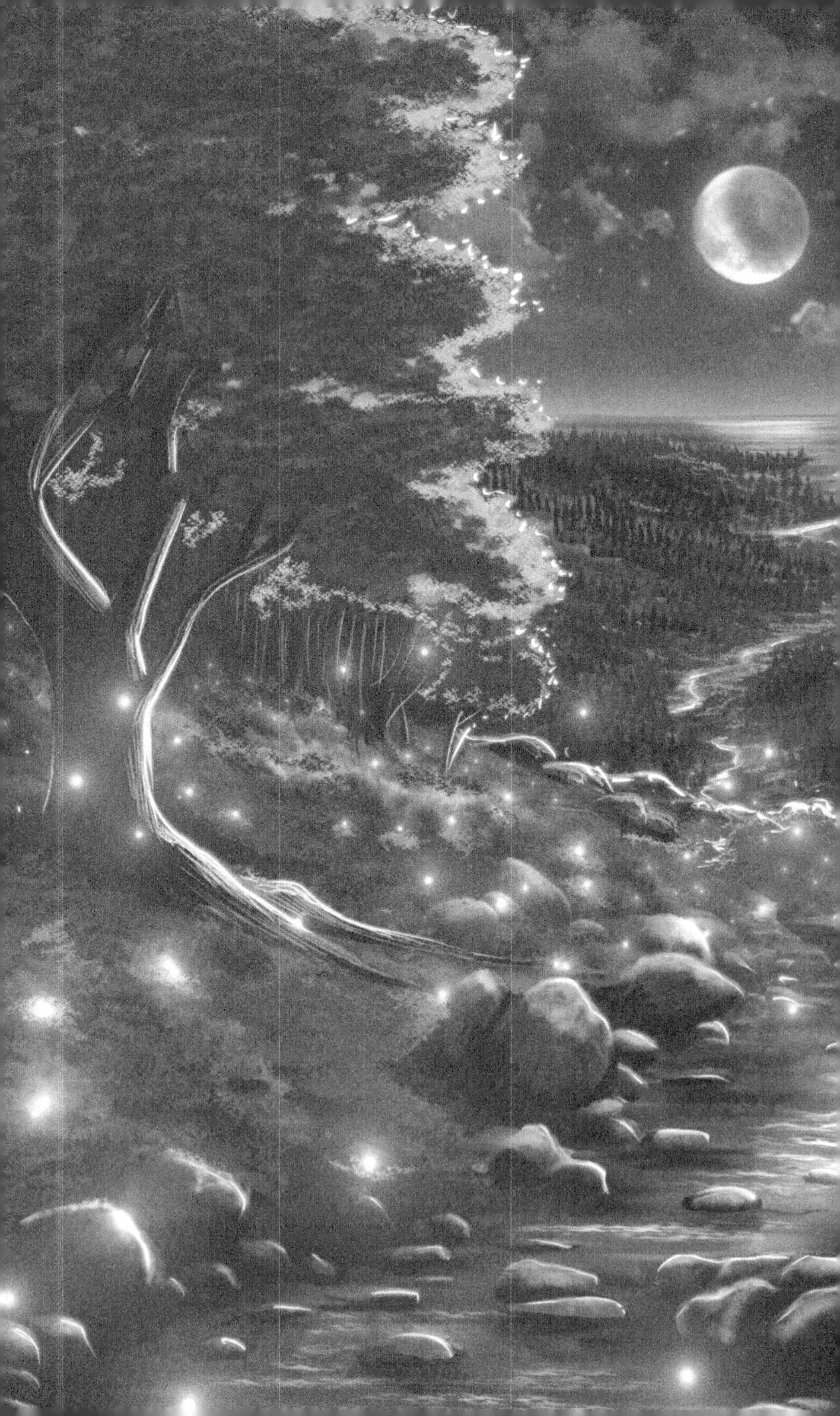

CHAPTER FIVE

EVERA

The door creaked open, immediately silencing the celebratory mood in the pub. I shouldn't have opened the door—hell, I clearly shouldn't have been here at all. I mean seriously, this was like some scene from a fantasy novel, and one I did not belong in.

My eyes widened as I looked around at the stone walls, windows covered in tapestries, and the muted but richly colored outfits that every person in the place wore. All of their gazes were fully focused on me. I knew I stood out. Mostly because of the costume I was wearing, sparkles and smoke from the casino no doubt lingering on me. That wasn't even including the fact that I probably looked a mess following the fight, the portal, and then my trek down here...

"Toto, I've a feeling we're not in Kansas anymore," I murmured, trying to break the mounting anxiety in my chest. Unfortunately, the joke wasn't even funny to me, let alone anyone around me.

Knowing I couldn't leave now without causing even more of a scene, I tugged the cape further around me and made my way towards the bar, voices picking up slowly. I felt myself shifting nervously, my nails digging into my palms so hard I knew they'd leave a mark. Intertwining my fingers so they couldn't do as much damage, I sat on a barstool and tried to get the attention of the bartender on the other side.

Which shouldn't have been hard since she was looking at me, but her conversation was with the man across from her, their heads close together—probably talking about me.

"Passing through?" a masculine voice inquired. I snapped my head to my right, the thick beard and dark hair of the man sitting next to me a bit unexpected considering how young he appeared. He couldn't be more than eighteen, if that.

"Something like that," I said awkwardly as I continued trying to wave down the bartender. "Honestly, I don't even know where I am."

Had I just admitted to a strange man that I was lost and alone? Had my sense of self-preservation gone out the window? I ran a hand over my face. I needed rest and food. Until then, I would probably continue to make stupid mistakes.

"You don't know where you are?" the man inquired, looking confused.

No sense in trying to backtrack at this point. Plus, the man wasn't giving me any creeper vibes, and his gentle disposition encouraged me to answer honestly.

Or maybe I was just thrilled to be talking to someone who potentially had answers.

"Yes, I woke up in a clearing on a mountain—"

"Mom!" the man called out, interrupting me. The bartender snapped her gaze over, offering him a concerned look before offering me a disapproving one. Clearly I'd done something wrong in her eyes—-apparently she didn't appreciate me talking to her son.

As she slowly walked over, I noticed how her eyes scanned over my outfit, their dark brown shade matching the eyes of the man next to me. In fact, now that I was paying attention, I could see the resemblance in everything but the woman's silver-streaked hair that was tied back in a loose bun.

"You know we don't allow kingdom dwellers here," she said, her gaze on me with full disapproval now. "You won't find any men here willing to buy your services. It's a family establishment."

Her words took a moment to sink in, but when they did I snorted, covering my mouth in surprise at her insinuation. This woman thought...well, she thought I was a sex worker.

Shit. My outfit was a bit shorter than I would normally wear, but it wasn't exactly scandalous by any means... although I suppose it was compared to what everyone else in here was wearing.

"Oh no. I'm sorry, I know my clothing looks weird, but I'm not here to sell anything...especially not myself." My words seemed to instantly relax her, her gaze taking on a more curious quality.

"She's not from here, doesn't even know where she is," the man next to me explained, "and she's bleeding. Her knee, I believe—I can smell it."

He could smell that? Usually I was the only one...but the woman didn't question his words, giving me another glance and nodding in understanding.

"Well, don't you worry—the people of Ashlayton Village are friendly if nothing else. We'll try to figure this out. You are more than welcome here. Now follow me." The woman's tone had completely shifted, morphing from wariness into an easy acceptance and willingness to help that seemed more natural to her. The sudden change had me momentarily stunned, but then I quickly stood to follow her, my knee throbbing in pain. I offered her son a thankful smile as I rounded the bar, catching up to the woman as she walked through a wooden archway that led further into the inn.

I should've been far more worried about trusting strangers, but two factors had me facing the unknown. The first was that I didn't have any other option, which was a pretty good motivator. The second? I usually had really good instincts about people, and this woman seemed completely sincere in her concern for me. It also helped that the inn as a whole exuded warmth.

The place was comfortable and cozy, the hallway lined with a worn runner made of intricately woven colored threads, lamps lining the wall every few feet. They had electricity here, the light bulbs flickering in and out, but I got the feeling that it might be the extent of the technology here. I hoped they had indoor plumbing because a hot shower sounded really nice right about now…

I was more than curious to learn more about the odd mix of technology and medieval aesthetics here.

"My name is Lorie, by the way, and that was my son Stephen," the woman said as we stepped into a commercial-size kitchen, the burners low and pots simmering on the iron stove.

Lorie—like the inn. She motioned for me to sit at the wooden table, its mismatched chairs multicolored much like the cabinets and other decor in the place.

"Evera," I introduced myself. Lorie smiled softly and motioned to my knee. "I fell," I explained, then wanted to roll my eyes at myself for giving such an obvious answer. I rolled down my sock to my ankle and hissed, realizing the injury was more substantial than I'd been allowing myself to think it was.

"Good thing we have medical supplies here," she said as she rummaged through a cabinet. "Ashlayton isn't the most advanced town in Vargr, but we manage just fine."

"I've never heard of Vargr before…in fact, I'm not really sure how I got here. I've been trying to piece it together, but…" I motioned uselessly with my hand, not sure where to start.

"Well, you know your name, so that's a good start," she said as she sat next to me with a box of bandages and ointments. "Why don't you tell me what happened?"

"Alright." I intertwined my fingers as she organized the supplies on the table. "I was at a party—a Halloween party at a casino in Las Vegas."

Her brows drew together. "Las Vegas? That must be a city in one of the other kingdoms. And Halloween…is that what you call the harvest celebration? I've never heard of that before."

"We have states, not kingdoms…" I hesitated before taking an alcohol swab from her. "Maybe if you told me about your kingdom it'll help me figure out what happened? I have a feeling that what I remember may just confuse things."

I highly doubted that anything she said would help, but I had a bad feeling about this and wanted to go ahead and get it over with.

"Right," she said as I began to clean my wound, my jaw tight as I ignored the way my stomach churned at the sight of blood. "As I said, you're in Ashlayton in the Kingdom of

Eventide in the land of Vargr. There are two kingdoms, ours and the Kingdom of Nightfall, but that's on the far side of the Darkridge Mountains. Nearly unreachable."

Good lord, I felt like I needed to grab my phone—not that it was working—and start taking notes, but I managed to sort through the information sufficiently and decided on a question I figured would be telling. "How many 'lands' are there? If this one is Vargr."

"In Terrea? Eight, not including the land of the Sacred Temple."

Was that the large building I'd seen? Come to think of it, it did have the feel of a religious monument, the way the people were circling it. But the way she spoke of the Sacred Temple, saying it was on a different piece of land, made me question myself—the building I'd seen wasn't that far away.

"I see." I nibbled my lip. "Are any of the Kingdoms named Earth?"

Her eyes widened. "Oh no, Earth is in the human realm. Their kind can't travel here unless they use a portal when the veil is lifted and that…well, that isn't possible with any normal level of magic." A dark look filled her face with sadness before she fixed me with a concerned dip of the brow. "Why do you ask?"

So we weren't on Earth…because Earth was for 'humans.' Did that mean the people here weren't human?

I probably should've been freaking out, but my lack of surprise made me realize that I'd been preparing myself for that exact answer. It actually gave me a sense of validation, to know that I wasn't crazy. I mean, the possibility that this was a dream wasn't completely off the table, but this felt far too real to be a dream.

"Can I trust you?" I asked.

Lorie straightened in her seat. "Yes, Evera. You can."

"I'm from Earth. I was taken through a portal by two men—well, I was pushed in while they were fighting, and I landed in the mountains right above here. I came down them and found my way here...wherever here is. Apparently Ashlayton."

"That's...that's impossible," she murmured, shaking her head as she stood and examined my head, tilting my chin. "I worry you've hit your head. Are your memories intact? Maybe you've heard one too many tales—"

"Lorie, I promise you that's not the case," I said softly.

Her gaze searched my face, and when she saw how serious I was, she turned and began searching for something on a low shelf. I wouldn't lie, her reaction was confusing, and not clarified much by her following statement. "I want to show you something, Evera. Because what you're saying... well, it would only be possible if you were...I just don't see how that could be."

Her mumbling left me anxious as she opened a large book, her voice dipping out of my range of hearing. Lorie leafed through several pages as she slowly made her way back to the table, turning the book towards me when she found the one she was looking for. My eyes narrowed on the portrait, my stomach tightening nervously and a cool sweat breaking across the back of my neck even though I didn't recognize the two people pictured.

The woman's severe face and pursed lips conveyed her distaste, her eyes a very similar shade as mine. Her golden hair was perfectly curled and styled away from her pale skin, and she wore a deep copper colored dress that managed to make her come across as even more intense. On her head was a bold crown of gold and diamonds.

The man next to her was nearly a head taller than her, his hair dark with golden streaks. His eyes were a rich brown, and his skin tan. By all accounts he should have had a warmth to him—I almost imagined a smile on his face. Instead, he looked painfully upset, his eyes narrowed in a way that made it seem like he was actually looking at you, judging anyone who had the misfortune of looking at the portrait. He wore a crown as well, his coat a deep purple that complemented the woman's copper dress.

"Who are they?" I asked.

"Our king and queen," she said, a distinct bite to her tone.

"You don't like them."

Her eyes went wide, and she looked around the room, checking for anyone who might overhear. "I wouldn't...I wouldn't say that."

"Are they assholes?"

"Yes," she said reflexively before clenching her jaw. She closed her eyes and took a deep breath before speaking again. "You'd think I'd be better at holding my tongue after all these years. I blame the distance from the castle; it's made me lazy."

"Why did you show me that?" I asked as she closed the book and returned it to its spot on the shelf. Sitting down, the woman folded her hands and offered me a bandage for my knee, which I'd forgotten about.

"Fifty years ago, when the veil was last lifted, one of the rulers of Terrea committed a terrible atrocity to the land while he thought everyone would be distracted. His actions sparked a war that brought monstrous creatures and ruin to Terrea. In order to right the wrong that led to the conflict, eight women sacrificed themselves—or so the story goes." She paused, considering her next words. "It happened on

Havestia, the goddess's day—fifty years ago exactly. Which only adds to the mystery of you being here."

"You think this involves me?" I asked, trying to piece together where she was going with this.

"Possibly," she murmured. Lowering her voice, she added, "I tell you this because while the crown was always corrupt and horrible, they only grew worse following that incident."

I blinked in confusion. "Why?"

"Because one of the women who sacrificed herself was their daughter, the princess of our lands and the only true heir. Because of her, the story of that night and its sacrifice has been told wide and far." Her eyes filled with sadness. "She was loved by everyone, and when she was lost—even though it was a noble sacrifice—it was a loss for everyone."

"I see."

"It was prophesied that the princess would return fifty years later…" She squeezed my hand. "And here you stand, tonight of all nights, from the human realm."

The breath whooshed out of me. She had so much hope in her eyes, and I hated to squash it.

"I'm not a princess." In fact, I was the exact opposite of royalty, an orphan who struggled her way through life.

The light in Lorie's eyes dimmed, her gaze downcast. "I suppose it's more likely that you suffered an injury while in the mountains. Maybe you're remembering tales of Earth—many children here are told them."

That didn't ring true either though. I could remember everything about my life in Las Vegas. That hadn't been some insane dream. All of the work I'd done to build a life for myself—working to afford a place of my own, finding ways to feed myself—all of it had been very real. I mean, hell, look at my clothes—those, if nothing else, told the story of my life on Earth.

"You said humans can't travel here if the veil isn't lifted?" Because I was definitely human…right? What else could I even be? How would I know?

"It's possible you're from another kingdom, that they stole your memories—I've heard there are creatures that can do that."

Creatures? To this point I'd only been imagining other types of people lived here—fairies, magic users, something like that—but *creatures*? I was starting to get overwhelmed.

"Maybe. Either way, it makes blending in kind of difficult," I murmured, deciding that for now I wouldn't ask any more questions. I wasn't sure I could handle it.

"Let's do something about it then," she said, composing herself and motioning for me to follow. "I always have a spare room available—you never know if someone will need a place for the night. You're more than welcome to use it, and I'll bring something you can change into. Whenever you're ready, come downstairs and I'll have a meal prepared for you."

"That is incredibly kind," I said, my heart softening at her generosity. "You don't have to do all of that for me."

"I know." She offered a small smile. "But this is what we do here."

I didn't bother arguing with her, and when we reached the small room, I instantly felt at ease with the simple furniture and comfortable bed in the corner, a fire going in the fireplace. She pointed towards the door. "The bath is through there, and I'll put clothes on the bed for you. I know you may need a moment. Maybe…maybe some memories will come back to you and we can figure out where you're from."

"Maybe. Thank you, Lorie. For everything."

"My pleasure, dear."

The moment she was gone, I sank to the floor, pulling my knees against my chest and resting my head on them, letting out a frustrated groan. My head was starting to pound. I was tired, I was hungry, I was hurt, and I still couldn't quite comprehend where the hell I was. After a few minutes of feeling sorry for myself, I stood and made my way towards the bathroom, relieved to see that they not only had a bath—with indoor plumbing—but also a shower.

Deciding to shower rather than take a bath, I quickly cleaned off, blood washing down the drain as the stones under my feet grew wet. Once I was done, I dried off and stepped out, wrapping myself securely in a towel. The vanity was empty, clear of personal belongings, but I dug a comb out of the bottom of my purse and brushed out my hair in long strokes.

When I returned to the bedroom, the wardrobe door was open, displaying a simple deep-blue cotton dress that Lorie must have brought while I was in the shower. Having no other choice, I put my same undergarments back on before slipping into the dress and tying the matching blue sash beneath my breast. The fabric hung to the floor, covering the sneakers I'd had to put on without socks.

Not my best—I would still stand out, but at least I wouldn't stand out quite so much as before. I took a long breath, looking out the windows at the light rain that now fell, then left the room and made my way slowly downstairs.

A weird sense of foreboding washed over me, and when I reached the central room of the inn I realized why. Everyone in the room sat in tense silence as they watched purple-and-navy uniformed soldiers flood inside.

The men were huge, their frames dwarfing even the largest men in the room, and I came to a startled stop in the shadows of the hallway. The soldiers had arranged themselves in formation, and upon an unspoken command split to create a path for a man more intimidating than the rest. *I recognized him.* How was that possible?

"Citizens of Ashlayton, we are in search of an individual who goes by the name Evera."

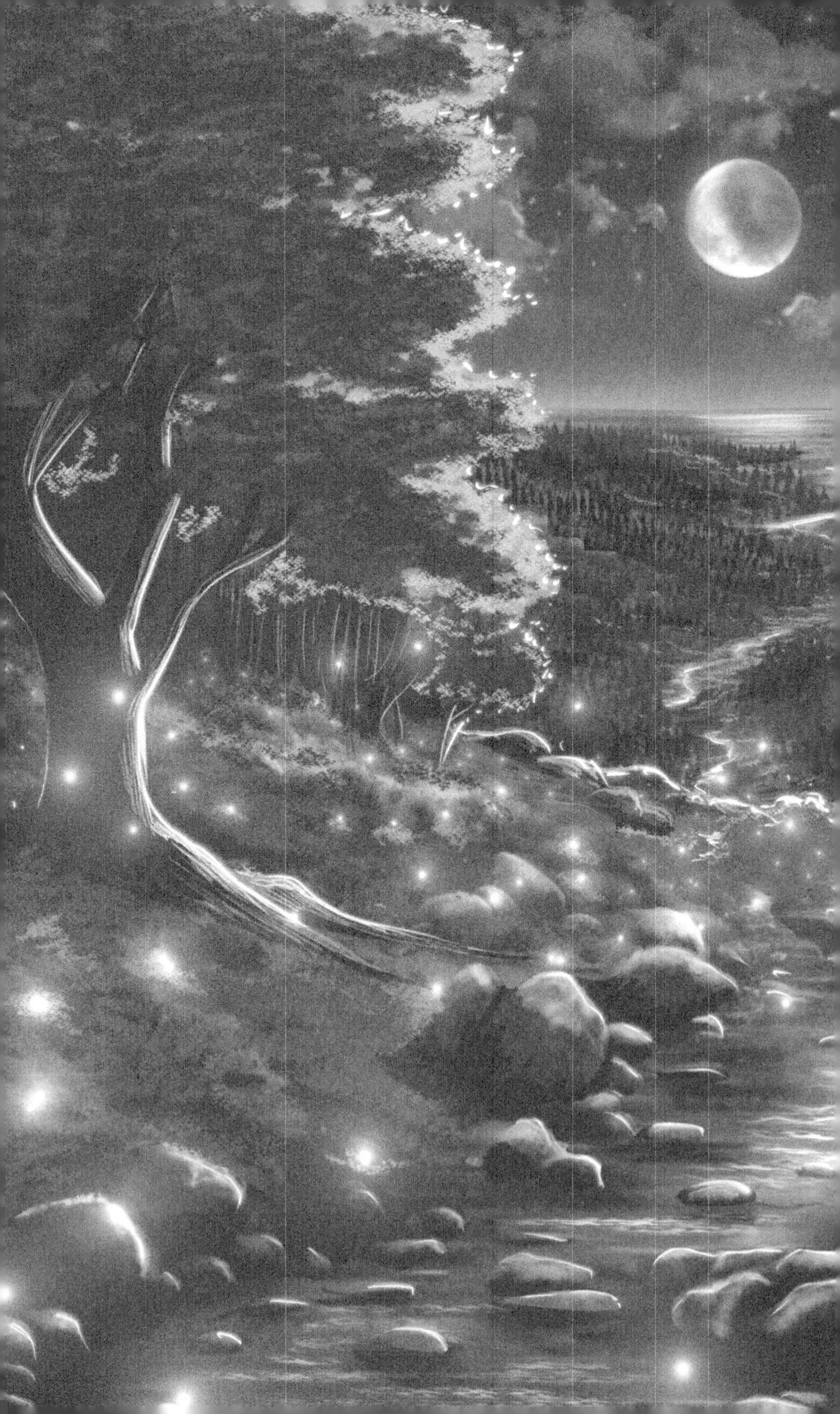

CHAPTER SIX

EVERA

I stood frozen in the shadows as an uneasy feeling sank through my bones. With short blonde hair and dark eyes, the officer's face felt familiar, his uniform decorated with more medals and pins than those of the men around him. Even the way he held himself made it clear he was higher in rank than the others—more important and more dangerous. Yet I didn't feel the instant recoil I'd felt when I first saw Reynor…and for sure not the intense sensation I'd felt upon seeing the king.

Instead, there was just that nagging sense of misplaced familiarity.

"Don't be nervous," the officer said to the crowd. "Evera isn't dangerous, but she is *in* danger, and the crown seeks to ensure her safety."

The pub's patrons shifted uncomfortably, not quite looking at one another but not quite looking at the officer either. I stepped forward, not because I particularly believed the man, but because I had a way to ease the disquiet. This was one of my fatal flaws—I was always trying to make those around me a bit more comfortable. It was why working in the service industry came naturally to me. Though I did have my limits.

As I stepped out of the shadows, all attention was diverted towards me. The officer looked at me wide eyes before looking…disappointed to see me? A polite smile was painted onto his face.

"My name is Evera," I offered, and whispers broke out in the room.

The officer nodded sharply, completely unsurprised by my proclamation. "We're glad to see that you're safe. Is it possible for us to speak outside?"

"You can talk in here," Lorie interjected, arms crossed. "But your soldiers can wait outside." She wasn't intimidated by them like the rest of us, her protective streak making me like her ten times more than I already did. Now I understood why she'd chided herself for needing to hold her tongue—I had a feeling she rarely did.

"Of course." The officer turned towards the soldiers, nodding for them to file out the door. "Evera, my name is Captain Oliver," the man said as he stepped towards me. "I'm glad we were able to locate you."

"How do you know my name?"

"This way!" Lorie called out, eager to get us in private. I felt comforted by her presence, but I didn't forget that Oliver hadn't answered my question. Lorie led us into the kitchen, and I sat at the table once more.

Lorie offered me a serious look. "I will be right outside the door; all you need to do is call."

"Thank you," I offered her a tight smile as she disappeared and left me with Oliver.

Almost instantly his face transformed as he sat back in his

seat and offered me a frustrated look. "What the hell are you doing here, Evera? You should be far away from the Kingdom of Eventide."

What?

My mouth popped open in surprise. "Do we know each other?"

The answer was *no*, for the record, but he clearly remembered me.

His stare sharpened. "You didn't get back your memories when you came through the portal? I don't understand why you wouldn't have."

"How could I get back something I haven't lost? I have all my memories." Though I was honestly starting to doubt it. "What does that even mean?"

"Fuck." He ran a hand roughly through his hair. "I guess that explains why you aren't already far gone. He's probably looking for you, though; we're going to have to figure out a way so I don't have to bring you back to the castle—"

"Wait." I put up a hand, cutting him off. "What the hell are you talking about?"

"Right, okay." He inhaled and sat forward, fixing me with a look. "Might as well get right to it. Long story short—your parents, the rulers of this land, knew you would return tonight because it's been fifty years since—"

"The sacrifice," I murmured thinking of Lorie's words.

"You remember?"

I shook my head, dashing yet another person's hope. "Lorie was telling me about it."

"Ah, right...well, they sent your half-brother to grab you from Earth, but something clearly went wrong. He was back at the castle licking his wounds and telling us that we needed to find you. That you were here in Vargr."

"Reynor? Is that who you're talking about? Or are you talking about the other man?"

"Another man? I can't imagine Reynor bringing anyone with him...but yes, you are the princess of Eventide. It was foretold that you would return tonight—your parents were banking on it. They were not happy that Reynor came back empty-handed."

"Okay," I murmured after blowing out a long breath, shifting back in my seat and intertwining my fingers. "I have no idea what to even say to this. I mean, what you're suggesting is insane—"

He motioned to my hand, the action effectively cutting me off. "He's going to kill me for even touching your hand, but let me try to show you."

Before I knew what was happening, his hand clasped around mine and a surge of magic—a fine black mist—sparkled along my skin, a howl vibrating in my ears before the world dimmed.

"Sit up straight—now." My mother's cruel voice had my spine straightening. I offered a terse smile and forced myself to look at the scene below.

It didn't surprise me that my parents were putting someone to death—in fact, it was almost a weekly occurrence—but I was surprised they were making me watch it. Reynor, whose gaze I could feel from here, always went willingly, but I always chose not to.

Which of course is probably why they wanted me here, always claiming I was too soft to ever be a ruler. I was heir to the throne, but I knew that they wanted Reynor to rule with an iron fist instead. I was waiting for the day that they suggested I marry my half-brother. It wouldn't be the first time it had happened in our kingdom's extensive history, but I would sooner throw myself off this balcony than to ever stand next to Reynor, let alone as his wife. Disgusting.

Luckily, my bodyguard served as a shield between him and me...except for today. I wasn't sure where he was, and that worried me for several reasons...one of which being that I liked to be around him. The other because I knew that Reynor didn't like how protective he was over me, so he would no doubt take advantage of his absence.

Oliver was watching out for me today instead—which I didn't mind, exactly—but it wasn't my preference.

"Ah there he is. Evera, look." My father's voice had my gaze moving to where four individuals were lined up to have their throats ripped out. I felt my stomach drop, seeing that he was down there. Axel.

His massive frame was turned towards the people who were awaiting the executioner, but his gaze was on the balcony. On me.

"Why is he down there?" I asked, trying to keep my voice light and curious.

"All of the head guards take turns as executioners. Today is his day," Reynor mused.

I knew Axel was more than capable of killing. As it stood, he was feared by many, not only for his actions but his words. I'd seen him cut others down with his sharp tongue...but not towards me. Never towards me.

I'd known Axel for three years now, ever since he was assigned to my guard when I turned eighteen and began to have more freedom. While he had many years of experience in the royal guard, decades no doubt, he had never spoken about what he'd done before he was assigned to me personally. So while I knew he had probably killed before, I didn't want to see him do it now, and I knew he didn't want me watching him do so either.

"I'd rather not watch the man who protects me kill four people," I said evenly. "You know I don't like blood."

My father sneered. "You will watch."

And I knew I didn't have a choice.

Axel took one more look up at me, his regret-filled eyes making my stomach clench. Then the shift overcame him. His skin sprouted fur and broke, his human form exploding to release a creature nearly nine feet tall and standing on two feet. I shivered, wishing that he'd chosen his other form—the one that was more wolf-like, the one that we sometimes spent time together in.

But this hybrid form was why he was so powerful, so strong. A creature that even my own father feared. Tears gathered in my eyes as he approached the first prisoner. I wasn't sure how I would feel about Axel after watching this...

No, I knew. Nothing could change the way I felt about him.

Yanked hard out of the vision, a gasp left my throat as tears welled in my eyes, fear causing my heart to palpitate. But before I could ask about any of the details, including my past and the creature that Axel had shifted into, I was hit with a realization.

Axel...the man from the hotel and the vision...they really were the same. *Holy shit.*

Acute sadness swelled inside of me, the loss of him radiating through me, the tears now streaming freely down my cheeks. I couldn't remember how I'd lost Axel, but I had. One moment he'd been there, and the next we'd been separated—ripped apart.

Intense pain and betrayal washed through me. I had

lost...everything. I had given up everything. Because of the sacrifice, or something more? I couldn't remember.

I'd lost a part of myself that was filled with magic, and now the silence inside of me caused me to panic. There should have been something more there, another voice—another source of energy.

My wolf.

What did that even mean?!

Why did I grow up on Earth? Why had I been taken away from all of this?

Nothing I had assumed was real was real. My whole life. I mean, it existed and was real, but I'd never been part of it. Not really. I belonged here. This was my truth, and the rest, my entire life in Las Vegas, had been pure illusion.

The thread had been tugged, and now I was caught in the web of Oliver's magic. Because that's what it was—true magic. The facade of my life on Earth had started to unravel, memories trickling in as I viciously yanked at the thread in my mind.

"She's asleep for the night. I made sure to lock the doors—I'm not letting her do this," Axel's low voice rumbled, making my heart hurt.

I was far from asleep, and my sensitive hearing picked up on him talking to Oliver in the hallway. The two of them were like brothers, united in their efforts to protect me. I trusted Axel with my life, and he trusted Oliver, which meant I trusted Oliver...but neither of them would be able to stop me from what I planned to do tonight.

It was the only way. The only way to save everyone.

Axel would be livid, but I couldn't live my entire life in this state of war, knowing my people were being killed day by day. My family may not have minded—they may have even enjoyed the monstrous slaughter—but I cared for the people of this land...and I would give everything for them.

I didn't know what the high priestess would require from me, but I planned on answering her call. The red light I'd seen only two hours ago, its pull so intense it felt wholly unnatural and powered by magic, told me I needed to go to our temple. I had a feeling the high priestess, Abba, would be waiting for me there.

I may not have understood what waited for me besides that, but it was the answer to fixing this.

Suddenly, the door opened and I turned my head into the pillow so my expression wouldn't reveal that I was still awake. I heard only one set of footsteps, which meant that Axel, as he did most nights, planned to sit in the armchair far into the corner of the room, keeping an eye on me as Oliver stood guard outside the door.

The man was overprotective to a fault, and maybe I should've found it invasive, but after Reynor's attempts to find me alone again and again, to pester me about marriage, I didn't mind in the least. Plus, despite not admitting it out loud, the idea of Axel watching me all night caused warmth to infuse my body and desire to dance across my skin. I wished I was bold enough to call him to my bed.

With how today had gone in the garden, though, I wasn't going to risk it—he'd outright rejected me.

When his footsteps stopped at the side of my bed, I wondered if maybe he would join me. I nearly smiled when the bed dipped slightly and he sat on the edge, his rough fingers running through my hair as his familiar scent wrapped around me.

"I know you're awake, çiçeğim."

Lifting my head up, I offered him a narrowed look, and his lips pressed into a knowing smile.

"How did you know?"

"I saw how determined you were today. You think I believed you'd just give up without a fight?"

Sitting up so that I was nearly nose to nose with him, I spoke honestly. "I have to do something, Axel. Everything is telling me that I have to go."

"No, you don't. This isn't your fight." His jaw clenched. "Promise me you won't, Evera. Promise me you'll get that fucking idea out of your head."

"I can't make that promise."

His hand grasped my chin and tilted it up. "I don't care what you think you'll find at the temple, the price is too high. It's not happening. I will tie you to this bed before I let you go tonight."

Biting my lip, I took a chance and leaned forward, brushing my nose against his. "I don't believe you."

Axel stilled as his other hand caught my waist, probably to stop me moving closer. A grim satisfaction at being right filled me. The man wouldn't even let me kiss him; there was no way he'd tie me to the bed.

"Don't—"

"Don't what?" I demanded softly.

Hesitation filled his gaze as his body grew even more tense. "You know what."

Sighing, I sat back and closed my eyes, "I know, I know. Goddess forbid you ever touch me—"

"Axel!"

Suddenly I was tugged forward onto his lap, and I let out a soft surprised sound as his lips grazed the corner of my mouth. It only lasted a moment, though, before I was deposited back on my bed and he disappeared out the door.

A smile pressed onto my face. That counted as a kiss right? Maybe not fully, but it was something...

I was still going to the Sacred Temple tonight, but maybe when I returned there could be something more between us.

Maybe.

My eyes slowly opened this time, and Oliver's expression was grim, having extracted his hand from mine long ago. "It worked? It helped unlock some of your memories?"

I opened my mouth and then closed it again. "How did you know that would work?"

Oliver spoke quietly. "Axel possesses magic that not all of us have. It's why your father feared him and tried to keep him under control. He transferred some of his power to me, and when I touched you his magic connected with yours to jumpstart those memories. I have a feeling he was aware that this would happen."

"Right, magic...and Axel. And you were with him. You worked together for my parents. God, they seemed horrible, and Reynor even worse. And then I was at that execution and they were making me watch, and Axel, he turned into this creature—"

"Wolf shifters," he explained. "We shift into wolves, and some of us have larger humanoid forms as well called half-shifted forms. All of us have some level of magic, but Axel has more than most. So do you."

"I'm supposed to have *magic*," I said softly, wistfully. I was supposed to shift into a wolf.

This was insane.

"You said that when Reynor came to get you, he brought someone with him. Who was it?"

I blinked, realizing I had allowed my thoughts to stray.

"Oh, Reynor didn't bring anyone. Axel showed up. That was the other man."

Oliver went completely silent, his eyes widening before he chuckled, running a hand through his hair. "That doesn't fucking surprise me in the least, impatient bastard. Also explains why Reynor didn't want to search the kingdom for you himself. Coward. He must have been terrified to see Axel."

"I don't understand. I mean, I understand why he's afraid of Axel, but why isn't Axel here with you?"

"Things changed after you sacrificed yourself," Oliver said, his eyes going distant. "Axel no longer works in the castle...

"He knew you'd be coming back, I just didn't realize he'd attempt to use the portal. It means he's coming for you, already searching for you."

Oliver suddenly cursed, standing from his chair.

"What?" I demanded.

"You need to get over the Darkridge Mountains before he tries to come this way. You don't have much time at all—and you can't come back with me to your parents' castle. What waits for you there is far worse than anything you'd face in the mountains. The other soldiers have probably already made the crown aware we found you, so you have to find a way to get out of here without my aid."

"Reynor? He's part of the threat?"

Oliver tilted his head a bit, equivocating. "A very *small* part. I don't know what your parents have planned, exactly, but it's not good—it's not fucking good at all."

"How do you know?"

"Whispers, rumors," he murmured. "Hearsay from trusted

sources. Now that you're here—the true heir—your parents' connection to the land will fade along with their magic as yours grows. But they want that power for themselves, forever. They will do anything to maintain control of the kingdom, and if they can't control you they take more drastic measures."

Unfortunately, that tracked completely with what I remembered about my parents.

"I have no idea where I'd go," I said. I'd only just gotten here, and already I was being shooed away. I tried to rack my brain for any other possible options, but I was drawing complete blanks from the limited scope of my memories. Outside of the Kingdom of Eventide, there was nothing.

"You'll find a safe place through the mountains," Oliver promised. "Axel is there. We just need to figure out how to get you to him."

Axel. I craved to find my way back to him.

Lorie appeared, slipping through the door with a knowing look in her eye—one that was victorious at being right. "I can help with that."

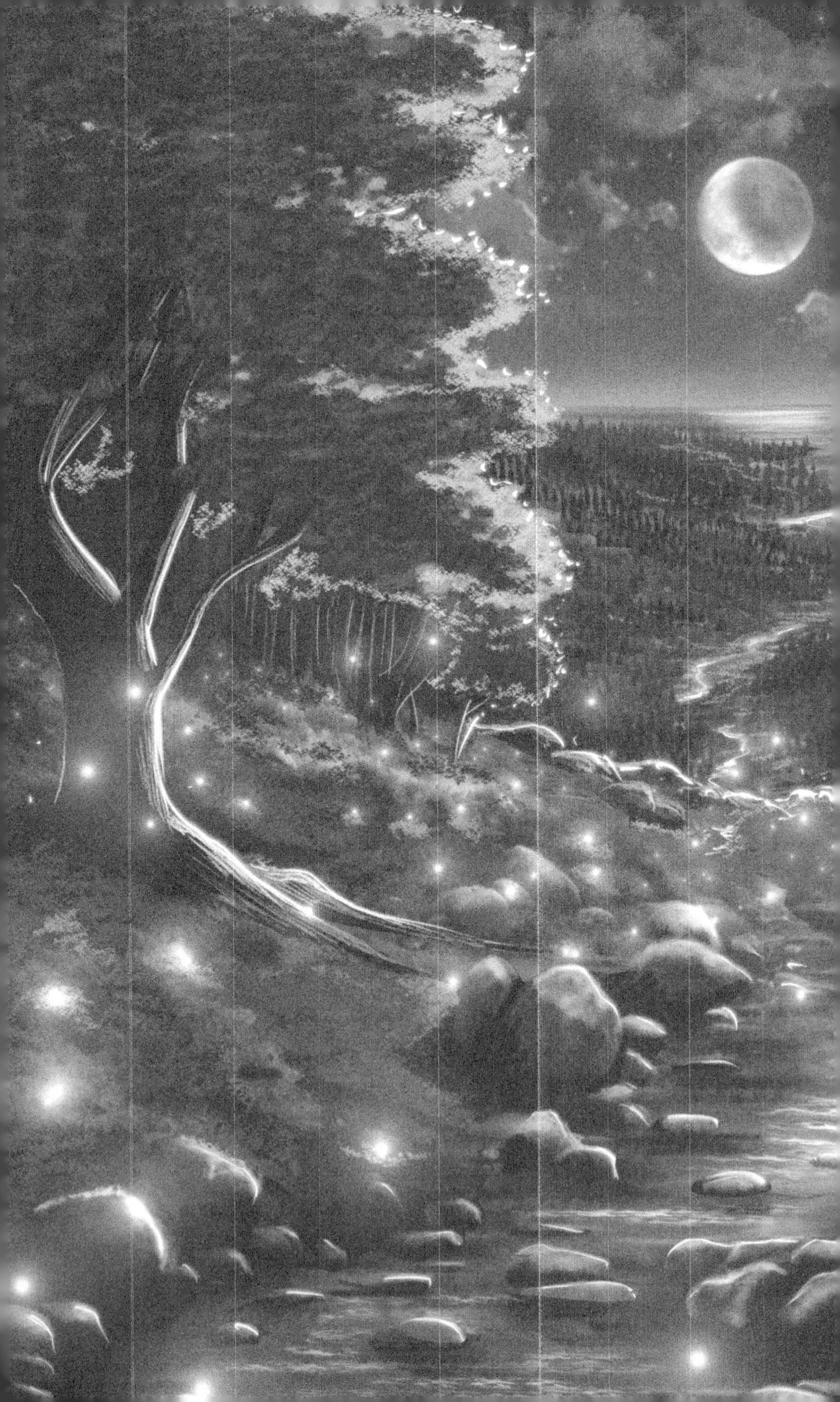

CHAPTER SEVEN

EVERA

The cold wind rustled over my skin as I pulled the straps of my bag to secure it. I knew it was going to be a long night—Lorie and Oliver had said as much. Memories lingered on the edge of my consciousness, the vast sea of them just out of reach, taunting me. But I remembered enough to know that Oliver's warning that I couldn't return to the castle I'd grown up in should be taken seriously. A darkness waited for me there, and Oliver was confident that traveling over the mountains was the better option.

I had to place some trust in him, if only because of the place he held in my memories. Mainly because of the trust Axel seemed to have in him.

Lorie hadn't disagreed, though the mention of going through the mountains filled her with fear. She pinned Oliver with a long, penetrating look before agreeing to his plan.

Oliver had distracted his men while I snuck out the back with a pack of supplies, a travel cloak, and a few other things Lorie had given me.

I'd already made it a few miles outside of the town, but I was so eager to get out of here that I felt like I was moving too slowly.

My gaze darted ahead to the river rushing towards the west, my eyes following it to the place where it cut through the mountain range. I swallowed down my nervousness as I hummed softly to distract myself, refusing to fear what waited for me in the mountains. It would be fine.

I attempted to pull at my buried memories a bit more, but the exhaustion from the day was catching up to me. My chest seemed to vibrate with energy once more, giving a little painful electric shock each time I tried. I knew it was something to do with magic long-buried, but without the feeling of my wolf running under my skin—something I'd started to remember—it felt hollow and empty. The small surges of power caused heartbreak more than anything.

While I couldn't remember everything about being a wolf shifter, I could pull on the few memories I did have: the sensation of magic under my skin, seeing Axel shift into such a deadly creature, the knowledge there was another more 'natural' form to our wolves. But it wasn't enough. I needed more information.

In the distance, a howl broke through the night, followed by several more. They were far away, but the sound still made shiver. The idea of such a dangerous predator out there, human or not, spurred me to walk faster.

I was so trapped in my thoughts that I didn't even realize I'd been walking along the riverbank until the shadow of the mountain began to cover the light from the moons. I probably should have been more scared now that their light was gone, but I felt more and more secure in every step I took away from the Kingdom of Eventide, especially now that I was hidden in shadows. After a while, even the howls in the distance didn't scare me anymore—they were probably celebratory in nature.

I found myself almost disappointed that I couldn't celebrate with them—that I couldn't release an answering call. *What a weird thing to even consider.*

Maybe when I was reborn I'd become truly human and lost my wolf? The idea filled me with an intense sadness and longing that made me dizzy. I stopped for a minute, steadying myself, as I took a deep breath in before slowly releasing it. Unfortunately it wasn't enough, causing my knees to break as darkness slammed into me, another stone falling and revealing a memory—

My wolf carried me across the dark grass towards the temple, crossing the bridge that my parents had constructed to unite the lands of Eventide that were separated by the large river. I could feel the priestess waiting for me, and I didn't hesitate to shift back into my human form as I reached the temple, my breathing rough. Axel would soon realize I was gone and begin to chase after me.

He could find me after I did this. I had no idea what the goddess would ask of me, but I was willing to give it for the sake of our land and the people.

Screams echoed in the distance, the roar of the monstrous creatures released on our land growing in response. Tears welled in my eyes as I pushed through the temple door. It had been dangerous for me to travel here, but not everyone had the luxury to hide behind the castle walls or find refuge here at the temple.

The cold stone room had a spiral staircase, and as I began to climb it, the air shimmered, the ward releasing to reveal a beautifully lavish space with several 'floors' that all looked down on a center column to the first floor. The temple was sometimes left without a caregiver, so a spell had been placed on it to protect the knowledge and artifacts it held. Yet it revealed itself to me so quickly, making me feel welcome.

When I reached the final platform, I was greeted by a portal, and I knew without a doubt that I was meant to go through it. Before doing so, I sent up a prayer to the goddess that Axel would forgive me for doing something so reckless.

Icy water engulfed me, and I realized I'd tumbled right into the damn river. A gasp had me opening my mouth and sucking in water, and it felt like shards of ice were piercing my lungs. My survival instincts kicked in as the water tried to strangle me, and I began furiously kicking my legs, fighting against the current. My limbs started to numb, their movements slowing, but all I focused on was going up, fighting to break the surface.

Right as I managed to, choking on the water in my lungs, I hit a rock so hard that it had me gasping in pain. I could feel the bruise it would leave on my torso, and my head spun. I was being swept further and further towards the mountains, and as I tried to gather my wits about me, the current pulled me under right as I'd managed to gain some semblance of control.

My lungs felt like they were about to burst, like millions of pieces of me were going to go flying like shattered glass.

Pushing towards the surface, I tried to reach for the moonlight breaking through, but I couldn't do it, my strength weakening. I thought for just a moment a flash of dark eyes appeared in front of me, but that was crazy—my eyes were closed, unable to open under the assault of the icy water.

The world began to grow smaller as my brain began to repeat the same memories again and again, flashes of Axel being the only thing I could see. The only thing I could focus on.

I was going to drown. After everything I'd been through tonight, everything I'd learned, I was going to drown having never seen him again.

As if hearing my internal thoughts, the stone wall holding my memories back began to rumble and shake, and I wondered if in my last breath I would see everything I'd truly lost.

But then something I could have never expected happened. Howls echoed in my ears, and my body trembled as if I was on the verge of something…something that propelled my body towards the surface with the force of a rocket.

I broke through the surface with a scream of relief, coughing and choking as I grabbed my pack with clumsy hands and brought it forward, using it as a floatation device. My body was trembling, but something had been unlocked, released—and while I couldn't focus on it, it was flooding my body with power. I didn't fight the sensation, hoping it would grow and reveal itself.

I gave into the water, letting it carry me forward, though it threatened to pull me under at every turn. I knew I needed to swim to the side, to crawl on shore, but there was no shore to be seen—only sheer faces of rock.

I felt like I'd been stuck floating for hours when I saw the sides of the mountain growing closer together, the river growing more narrow.

"Finally," I groaned, grabbing onto a rock and using the last of my strength to pull myself into a small alcove in the face of the stone. There was nowhere to really go besides back into the river, but it was enough for now.

I poured the excess water from my backpack and sighed. "Now what?" I murmured, talking out loud in an effort to not feel so alone.

I fell onto my back and looked skyward. At least in this small alcove I was protected from the wind. I wasn't protected from all the elements, but if I was going to rest, it would be here. The energy inside of me was restless, but my body was so tired that it didn't matter, my eyes falling closed before I could stop them.

The power that had exploded out of me extinguished all at once like a blown out candle.

It was nearly dawn when I woke up. I was sore. Uncomfortable. Starving. Exhausted. I couldn't risk staying here to rest any longer, though. I had to get to the other side of the mountains, where Oliver thought the threat from my parents would diminish. I was thankful for the advice because I couldn't remember anything being on the other side of the mountains, so I probably would've gone to my parents. A clearly horrible idea.

So I trusted my instincts, feeling a draw to the other side of the mountains, and walked along the narrow ledge between the river and the mountain that was now visible in the light of day. It took what felt like forever before I reached the end of the pass, the land dipping and the faintest light on the horizon highlighting the expanse before me. I observed the barely lit landscape with wonder, the sight making me feel like all of this was worth it.

The landscape was far more hilly than the other side, the river extending out towards the edges of Vargr, and in the distance I could see the gleam of the sea. Everything was already so vibrant under the dawn light that I couldn't imagine what it would look like with the sun high in the sky.

My gaze moved to the left where the largest mass of land was, and on the shoreline in the distance I could see a castle standing proudly within another smaller mountain range, the fortress dark and dangerous against the morning sky. Yet somehow it didn't have the intended effect on me; rather, I was drawn to it.

Was this a secondary castle for my family? I didn't remember that being the case, and I doubt I'd feel so drawn to it if that were true. Maybe it was abandoned?

I remember being told that at one point there had been two kingdoms, long before my parents' reign...or maybe I was misremembering that. I suppose it didn't matter. All I knew was that my entire body was urging me forward, telling me *that* was our goal.

I wouldn't be able to make it in this state, though. The blisters on my feet, which had emerged not long after I started my journey sans socks, were growing worse now that my feet were wet. I hunched forward and slowly followed the river down the mountainside. My heart was beating fast and laboriously, and I was nearly out of breath as I saw a fortress in the short distance—a military structure. I made *that* my goal instead of the castle, not seeing any towns before it.

My head pounded so hard my vision blurred, and my

stomach cramped painfully. When was the last time I'd eaten? At work, maybe? *That seemed like a lifetime ago.*

As I reached the base of the mountain, a weird sensation came over me, and I pushed through what felt like an invisible web. One that caused a 'pop' to sound before the sky above me lit up in a brilliant spark. I muttered a curse and hurried forward. While I couldn't remember all the magic associated with our land, I knew that had been some type of warning signal—and I didn't want to stick around to see who would come to check it out.

My plan to move forward quickly didn't work out very well, though, because in my exhaustion, I fell forward and nearly hit my face on a pile of rocks, stopping myself at the last minute with my hands, my wrist radiating pain.

Groaning, I righted myself and looked towards the keep. *So close.* Maybe a few miles at most….

Suddenly, a vicious howl tore through the air, its deep, reverberating bass causing me to still. My exhaustion tore away as adrenaline coursed through me. The sound was so familiar. I snapped my head around, looking for the source as it called again, my body propelling me forward without my consent.

Was it Axel? Was that possible?

I began running. I had no energy, yet I pushed forward trying to find…something. *Him.* So many things were pulsing through me at once, and some of them were confusing. My teeth hurt, my body pulsed and trembled, and I found myself craving a vicious, predatory hunt. That last one scared me the most. I began to hear and smell everything around me, from the deer to my left, to the heartbeats in the keep I was approaching.

The howl sounded again, and I dropped to my knees with

a groan. It felt like the sound was tugging at something in my chest, pulling viciously, but whatever it was was stuck behind the same wall that held back my memories. I let out a sob as I made it to the military keep, stopping a few feet outside the door to collapse on the ground, unmoving. I knew someone would find me passed out—drenched, freezing, and injured—and the security of that thought was enough for my body to finally give out.

As my eyes closed, though, a vision flashed through my mind. A massive black wolf stood watching me, its howl echoing in my ears, and I whimpered, wishing I could see the wolf in real life. *Finally*, my body succumbed to unconsciousness.

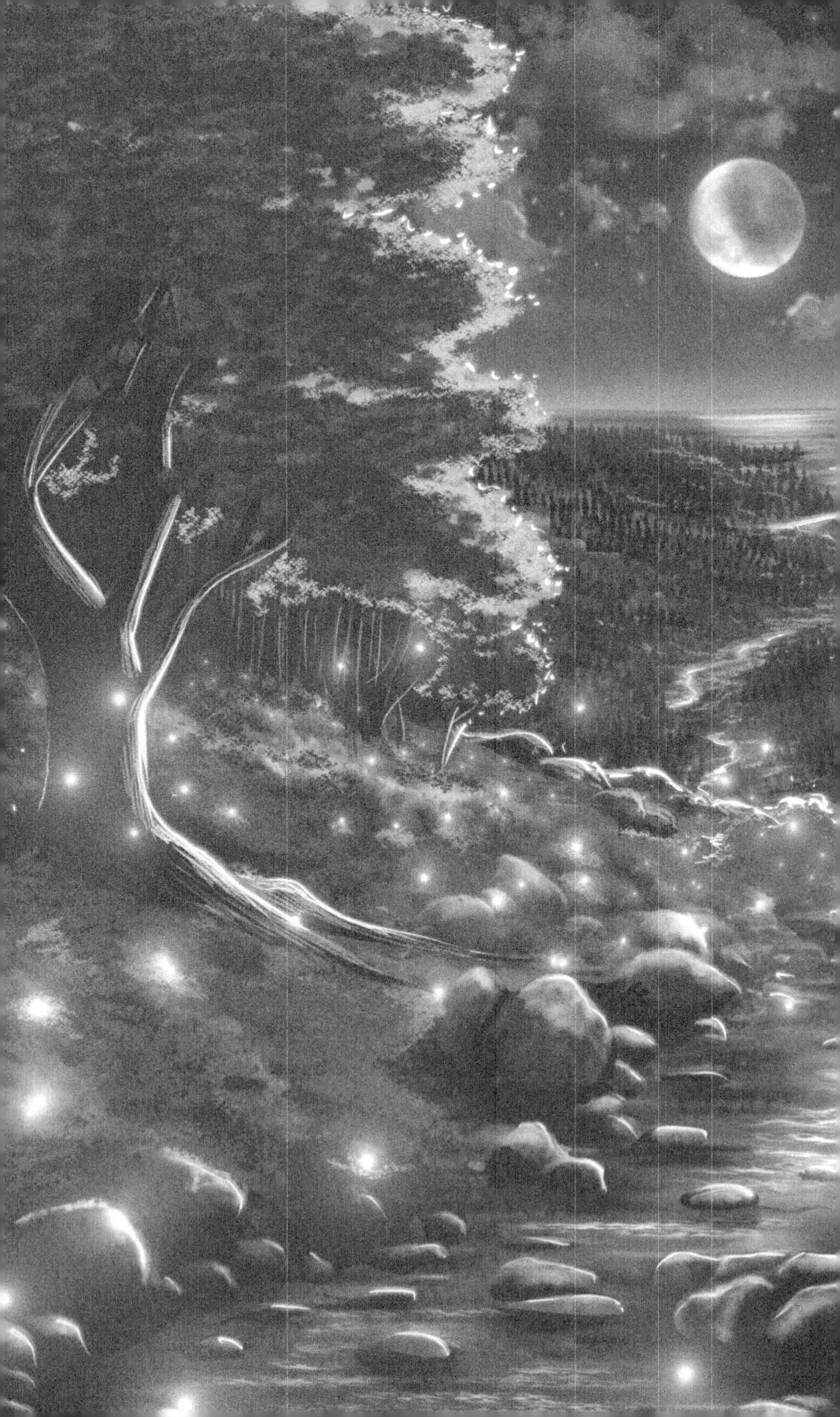

CHAPTER EIGHT

AXEL

"I want every single available scout searching our lands for her. Now."

Arnoux's second-in-command nodded sharply and left the room. I turned my attention to the captain, who'd been standing next to him. "We may need to go to the kingdom of Eventide come morning, especially if she landed on that side of the mountains. Allow the soldiers to celebrate Havestia until dawn, then prepare them for travel. I don't want her stepping foot inside their castle."

We *had* to intercept her before that. It wasn't a fucking option.

"Understood." He turned on his heel and walked out of the strategy room, leaving me alone in the vast stone space. My attention turned towards the open balcony, and I surveyed my land. In the distance, I could see the Darkridge Mountains outlined in the dark, the moons causing the river to glint like silver coins. My jaw clenched as I resisted the urge to shift, knowing I needed to be able to communicate with my men if I wanted to find Evera tonight.

My fists tightened on the railing as the concept of Reynor or her parents finding her first played through my mind—it was an absolutely unacceptable possibility. I knew they would take advantage of her confusion, especially if the portal travel and arrival in the realm hadn't restored her memories.

No. I refused to consider that possibility. I'd already waited fifty years for this day; she *had* to remember me. Remember us.

I thought I'd seen recognition when I grabbed her as we fell through the portal, but something had caused her magic to rupture under her skin, releasing in a powerful blast that kicked me from her portal stream and landed me back in my own damn castle. I would've found it impressive if it hadn't meant losing track of her.

"Both orders have been placed, according to the captain," Caz announced from the door, his normally stern and collected mannerisms disjointed—probably because tonight had gone nothing like we'd planned. It should have been simple. I should have been able to bring her safely through the portal *with* me. I should have been able to bring her home.

But Reynor had gotten there first—I should have known they'd have something planned.

"Should we prepare anything else?" Caz prompted.

I turned towards him and shook my head. "Everything else has been prepared; we just need to find her."

I was relieved when he said nothing else, my hands spread on the railing of the balcony as I let my head fall, trying to fight for a semblance of control. One I never struggled with normally, except when it came to Evera—*çiçeğim.*

And she was *my flower*, but she was so much fucking more than that.

"This could mean war."

Nevermind. Apparently, Caz was still here.

"It could," I murmured, turning to face him. "I imagine that no matter what we do, it will result in war. When Evera is brought here, the Kingdom of Eventide will deploy every measure possible to get her back. We cannot let that happen. If they have access to her magic, they will drain this land of magic, taking it all for themselves—we'll be worse off than we were five decades ago."

Caz nodded, seeming to hesitate in what I knew he wanted to say.

"Say it," I demanded.

"Do I need to be prepared for her *not* wanting to be here? I know we prepared everything for her as if she wanted to live here, but if she doesn't…"

Caz stopped at the vicious sound that left my throat. He may have worked for me for over three decades now, but even he knew that certain subjects were out of bounds—like anything having to do with Evera.

"Go."

My response was harsh, far harsher than I normally spoke to him, but he left immediately without question. I turned back towards the scenery, shaking my head and refusing to entertain his question. Memories or not, I could tell that Evera remembered *me*. Maybe not who I was, but the sensation of our magic connecting. I could see the flare of recognition, heat, and trust dance in her gaze when I first stepped out of the portal.

It had taken every single ounce of willpower to remain focused on Reynor and the threat he posed rather than her.

It had been fifty years, but Evera was exactly as I remembered her...yet also different. While she looked very similar, no doubt close to the human age of when I'd lost her, there were differences.

The woman I'd protected for three years had an air of innocence that clung to her. She'd been sheltered in a protective cage because of who she was, placed on a pedestal. There had been a lightness to her gaze and an easy smile, always.

The woman I'd come across in Las Vegas had been hauntingly beautiful. There was a darkness to her gaze that hadn't been there before, but more than anything, a strength. I saw it in the tilt of her chin as she challenged me, bravely questioning my motives even though she'd been scared. It had not only impressed me, distracting me from Reynor's cowardly knife attack, but turned me the fuck on.

That wasn't surprising though. I had always found her drive to disobey my orders, especially while trying to keep her safe, both frustrating and in the same breath admirable. Especially when she tried to run from me.

Even more, because the idea of disciplining her was so damn appealing.

It had taken every ounce of willpower to deny myself her, but no longer. Things were different this time, and I planned on taking Evera and showing her exactly what these years had created inside of me. A deadly storm filled with rage and mourning, one that could only be quelled by her touch.

If she didn't want me, I feared for the realm. I knew neither myself nor my magic would take her rejection well.

A flair of power against our wards had me stilling. I was intrinsically tied to this land, having claimed it as my own. My eyes snapped shut, and I inhaled sharply, smelling her sweet honey scent as her mere presence called to a primal need inside of me.

Evera.

My eyes opened as a cosmic light show flashed against the mountains, signaling what I'd already felt. *She was here.* Before I could inform anyone—although they would be able to figure it out fairly quickly—I shifted.

My wolf form—the more natural one—took over, and a growl rumbled from my chest. Even as a wolf I was tall enough to stand at the balcony and look over the land, my snout above the railing. The two moons called to me, and the dawn light highlighted the break in the mountains where she must have crossed. Before I could stop myself, I let out a howl.

My magic was calling for her, beckoning her towards us. Her magic was faint and barely there, but I could still feel her clawing at my consciousness, trying to get my attention. Wanting to connect as we had before.

Where was her wolf? Why couldn't I feel it? And why did her magic feel so weak? What changed?

Images of her staring at me with large eyes, clothed in that human costume, played through my head. I wanted to be able to touch her again, to pull her to me. To feel her skin against mine, to demand a kiss from those lips, to pillage her mouth until she begged for more.

Another howl broke from my throat, and two more after. I couldn't stop, the release enough to keep me from running towards her. I needed her brought to me. I didn't want to scare her, and I knew I would with my intensity and her lack of memories. But at the same time, I needed her to understand how different things were now.

Because of her...for her.

How had I denied her a kiss so many times before? My willpower was far weaker now, and I'd long ago accepted that. I'd been trying to protect her. I'd been alive for nearly four hundred years when I was assigned as her personal guard, so I thought nothing of it—until I saw her. Until I caught her scent. Heard her contagious laughter. Saw that flash of defiance and passion in her eyes.

I'd known I was fucked, but I didn't realize how hard she was going to make it for me to ignore those feelings. Evera had never been shy about her attraction to me, but she hadn't realized what she was asking for—why it was wrong that she wanted me when she had an entire future ahead of her.

A princess did not mate with a guard.

And I knew if she had ever pressed those lips to mine, I would pin her to the ground like a feral animal, marking her until she was completely and utterly mine in every way possible.

Then I'd lost her. She'd sacrificed herself, given everything to the realm, before I had a chance to stop her. My only solace had been in knowing that she would return, and I spent the past five decades ensuring that when she did come back, things would be far, far different.

A princess couldn't mate with a royal guard...but she could mate with a king.

"Your Majesty."

My head snapped over to find Captain Arnoux standing in the door. How long had I been trapped in my own thoughts? I immediately shifted back and stood to full height. "You saw the wards?"

He nodded sharply. "We've already received news from

the Midnight Keep. She was found unconscious steps away from the door. She's being transported to the castle now, along with a medical team who's monitoring her."

A breath hissed out of me. Wanting to go down to the Midnight Keep myself, I grabbed a jacket and went to the door, the captain stepping out of my way. I knew it wouldn't be long before they arrived, but it wouldn't be soon enough. Especially now that I knew she was injured.

I strode through the halls and jogged down a set of stairs, everyone moving out of the way for me. The citizens of the Kingdom of Nightfall lived a peaceful and safe existence, one that I monitored constantly. I'd promised them safety from the Kingdom of Eventide, mainly the King and Queen who didn't give a fuck about anyone living under them.

With that being said, I was well aware of how feared I was, and it was a reputation that I had earned. The only enemies I hadn't cut down, slaughtered in cold blood, had been Evera's parents and Reynor.

The first because I knew they still would mean *something* to her, at least until she said otherwise, but Reynor because what I had planned for him was no quick death. I wanted him to be drained of every ounce of willpower before I granted him the mercy of an end. It was what he deserved for thinking he could have my woman. *My flower.*

"Prepare my horse," I called to the attendants stationed within the doors of the castle. I would've shifted to travel, but I didn't want to scare her, and a bear-sized wolf was intimidating, even to other shifters.

"King Axel!"

I stopped in my tracks. There was only one person who would raise their voice like that to me, and unfortunately he had the right to do so. I turned sharply to the small elderly man who approached, regarding me with disappointment.

When I'd brought on several older members of the community to serve as an advisory board, I had no idea how much I'd come to regret it.

"I don't have time, Marx."

"Do not go to the mountains. If they sense you are near they will use it as an excuse to start a war—one I assume you are trying to avoid. Don't be the first to mess up."

I clenched my jaw and tried to not sound too harsh because I respected the old bastard, even if he was damn nosey. "I appreciate your advice, but she's—"

"Already on her way," he said simply. "Do not go, Axel."

Running a hand over my face, I contemplated ripping his throat out. The captain appeared next to me, announcing, "Five miles out."

"Fuck," I growled and shook my head. "Has the medical team reported back?" I hated the idea of anyone touching her, but I *loathed* the idea of her being injured.

"Not yet. I did advise them to not touch her unless absolutely necessary. The same goes for my men, of course."

Nodding, I opened the doors of the castle and willed the carriage to come into view. I didn't care how intense I seemed over this, or how eager. *Five fucking decades* I had worked to build the Kingdom of Nightfall—all of it for her.

I was a king in my own right, a threat to the Kingdom of Eventide. A force to be feared in Terrea. But none of that mattered when it came to her, the woman I belonged to.

When I heard the clomping of horse hooves and the clattering of carriage wheels, my attention sharpened. My queen was coming home to her kingdom, and I would do absolutely everything in my power to ensure she never left. I wasn't sane when it came to my flower—anything but—and I relished in it.

Evera was the *only* one that could satisfy the desperate need inside of me. A need that twisted violently and coiled around my heart, demanding every ounce of my attention.

No…*çiçeğim* couldn't escape me this time.

I would own every inch of her and make her mine.

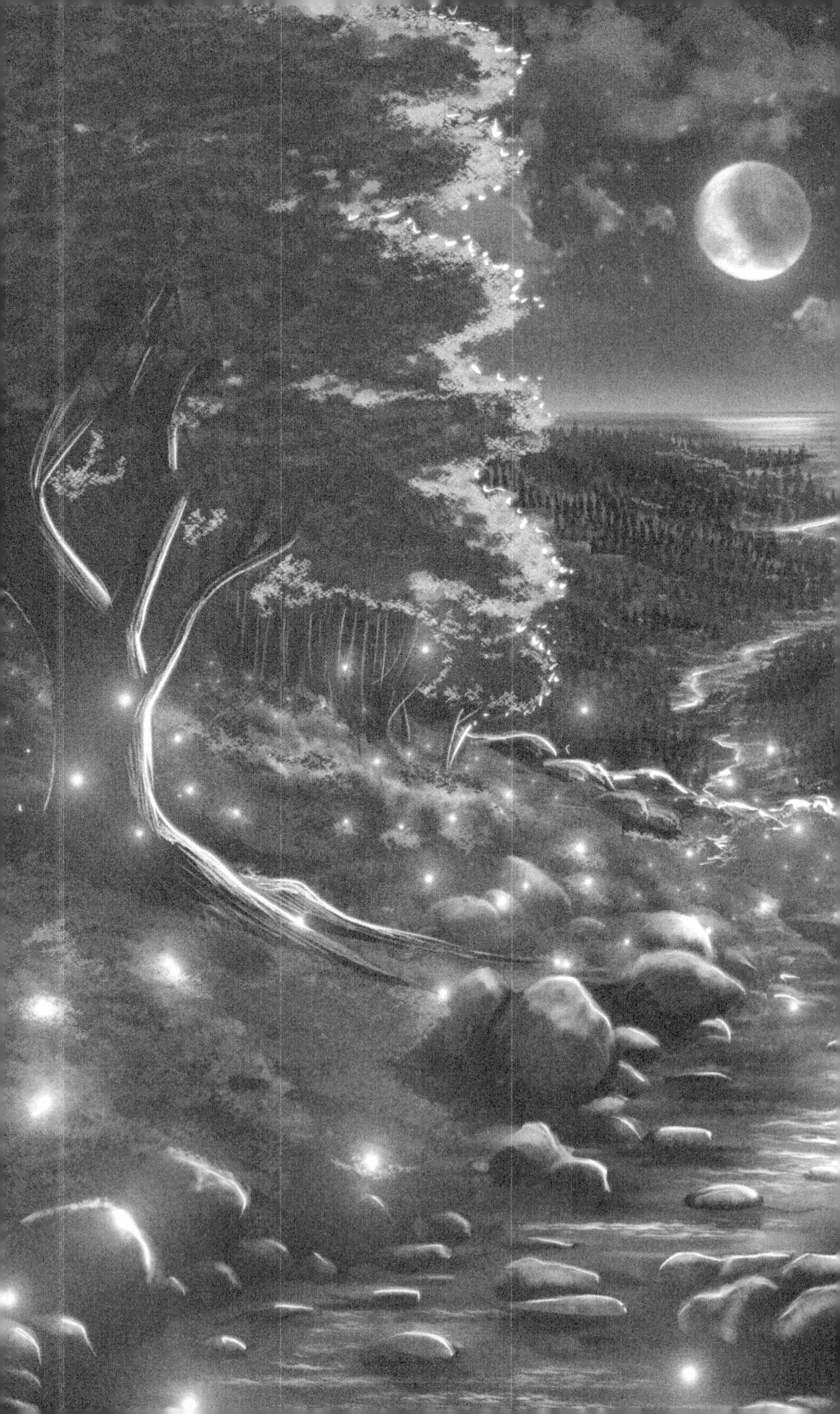

CHAPTER NINE

EVERA

A sudden jolt of the carriage had me nearly rolling off the bench and faceplanting onto the ground. My eyes were heavy and my vision blurry. The only reason I even knew I was in a carriage was because moments ago I'd woken to the sound of horses neighing and the continuous bump and sway of the road.

I steadied myself and attempted to sit up, my body feeling lethargic and my chest aching with pain, like I'd broken a few ribs or something.

"This isn't good," I whispered to myself, taking stock of things. I was the only one inside the carriage, and I was glad to see my pack on the floor. The water had drained out of it, and while it was dry, it was looking rather…limp. Everything inside was probably ruined.

At least the carriage was nice—simple and luxurious, understated, with its dark walls and velvet-lined seats. It was little comfort, though, considering the questions plaguing me.

Who had put me in the carriage to begin with? Were they

friends? Enemies? I'd made it through the mountains, where Oliver thought I'd be safe, but what if he was wrong? What if the military fortress had been home to my parents' soldiers? This was far from an ideal situation.

The power surge I'd felt in the river was buried now. I couldn't even feel it, making me wonder if I'd imagined it. And I had absolutely no way to find Axel. Even if I did, it had been five decades—the man I knew was a distant memory, literally, and had been replaced by someone far more dangerous. Someone I wasn't sure I wanted to come across again...or maybe I did. I honestly wasn't sure.

A shiver of fear at the unknown rolled over me, wondering if I had traded danger from my parents for something far worse. Had I imagined the safety I felt in his presence? Had I sought his protection only because I'd been so scared of Reynor, or was it something more?

"John! Good to see you. News reach the kingdom yet?"

My ears perked up, and I leaned towards the window. I couldn't see past the heavy curtains, but I didn't want to disturb them and alert the individuals outside that I was awake. Hopefully they wouldn't dampen the sound too much.

"Yes. Make haste, though—apparently he's impatient, especially after hearing the medical team had to treat her for injuries."

Her? Clearly they were talking about me.

My brows dipped as they said their goodbyes and the carriage surged forward. I could hear the sound of footsteps around me, and I briefly wondered if we were being accompanied by walking traffic as we made our way into the kingdom.

My biggest question? Who was 'he'? Someone who was clearly impatient for me to get there.

Also, the medical team had treated me? That explained the bandage on my head and the wrapping I could feel on my ribs when I took a breath. My knee had been rewrapped as well, and numerous bruises along my arms and legs had joined the injury. My body had apparently gone through hell, and I hadn't even realized it—being too tired, too scared to stop and take stock, too frozen to feel anything.

Wiggling my toes, I also realized that they'd wrapped my blistered feet and replaced my sneakers with boots—and socks. I was thankful for that. At least it seemed that wherever the hell I'd landed myself, the people wanted me well.

"Make space! Make space! We're trying to reach the castle," someone barked, and that nervous unease filtered through me again. The noise around the carriage grew, the sound of doors opening and people talking crowding the space. Their words glazed over my ears, but I did catch interest and curiosity in their tone.

Suddenly I felt trapped. I rubbed at my eyes with the back of my hand, trying to keep back the tears that threatened to spill. I needed to get out of this carriage, run away from these people. It would be dumb to stay here and passively wait to see what fate awaited me.

At the same time, I was still so damn exhausted I wasn't positive I *could* run right now.

I was so caught in my thoughts that the sudden jolt and stop of the carriage caused me to nearly slam into the side wall. Groaning, I put a hand to my ribs and grabbed my backpack, holding it protectively against my chest as I anxiously waited for the door to open.

The doorknob began to turn, and I clutched my pack

tighter and plastered myself against the seat as much as possible—as if the millimeter of extra distance would do any good. An older man with gray hair and shrewd dark eyes stood in the doorway, his stiff stature and uniform filling me with an unexpected amount of relief.

Not a single speck of navy or purple in sight—we weren't in Eventide, then.

"Evera, I assume?" The man's voice was calm and collected. I nodded but didn't move forward, his brow dipping at the death grip I had on my backpack.

"I'm Caz, the Crown's executive officer. If you can follow me, you'll be presented to the king—"

"Oh stop, you're going to scare her," a woman's voice interrupted. She shoved past Caz, shooing him until he stood a few feet back from the carriage.

Now that his frame wasn't filling the doorway, I could see we were in a courtyard of some sort. The tall walls that enclosed it were manned with soldiers walking atop them, but the sunlit greenery and happily chirping birds softened the image. Not that it made me feel much better.

"You look terrified, honey," the middle-aged woman said as she offered me a hand. "I promise you have no reason to fear us. I'm sure you've heard horror stories of the Kingdom of Nightfall, but we don't wish you any harm. I do want to make sure you're okay, though. My name is Vanessa."

She was right—I was scared, and in pain. But more than anything, I was trying to decide if I needed to fight or run for my life. I'd never heard of the Kingdom of Nightfall, and while I was beyond relieved we weren't at the castle in Eventide, it still wasn't very comforting.

Vanessa, though, exuded a maternal warmth that had me

slowly nodding. I loosened my grip on my backpack and began to shift forward in my seat—

"Marx is barely restraining him," Caz said to Vanessa. "I would hurry."

My eyes widened at his terse tone, and Vanessa shot him a scathing look that softened as she returned her attention to me, beckoning for me to come out. "Don't listen to him, our king is just eager—"

"Impatient," Caz corrected, looking amused.

A dangerous noise echoed through the air, the sound propelling me forward. It should have scared me, but instead it intrigued me—much more than anything they were saying.

I ducked my head as I jumped out of the carriage, immediately regretting the decision as I landed. I hunched over in pain, grasping my ribs and shifting on my sore feet. I drew the fresh air of the courtyard into my lungs as I tried to recover, quickly becoming distracted by an alluring scent it carried.

I stood straight, suddenly alert, trying to locate the source of that scent. Sunshine shone on about half of the courtyard, which was mostly empty aside from the soldiers, the other half cast in shadow by the dark castle that soared above me. My eyes traced over every element of the building before finally landing on the stairs.

Oh.

Everything froze. My eyes widened, pure desire spearing me as a pair of midnight eyes held mine from across the distance. I gasped as my heart began to beat double-time, and my legs nearly gave out, the wind whipping around me as the world seemed to tilt. Large arms wrapped around me, and I was suddenly lifted from the ground, my face buried against a massive, muscular chest, a booming heartbeat right underneath my ear.

"Axel." My voice was a whisper as his hand slid into my hair, holding me captive against him. I could feel eyes on us, and when I finally managed to open my own, I was completely surrounded by the feel of his magic and the soft rumble that left his chest, warming every part of my body.

"Çiçeğim."

His nickname for me. How had I forgotten about that?

"I didn't think I would find you," I expressed softly, my vulnerability slipping through. His expression was unreadable, but the grip he had on my frame was anything but. It was possessive. Protective.

I absolutely loved it.

"You remember?" he asked, his rough voice rolling over me in the most appealing way possible, causing my body to heat.

"Not everything," I whispered, "but some."

Before he could respond, Caz cleared his throat. A change came over Axel, his eyes hardening into obsidian stone and his grip on me turning possessive. The warmth I'd felt dimmed, and a panicked sensation rolled over me as I realized I was in the arms of a man I literally didn't know. At least not anymore.

"Your Majesty, I would suggest we take this inside."

"Your Majesty?" I whispered, my eyes searching his face before flickering up to his dark hair—*where a crown sat.*

Suddenly, the darkness I'd seen from him in Vegas seemed to take over, extinguishing the sunlight around us. It felt like his shadows were wrapping around me, and the howl of a wolf from somewhere inside my soul had my heart beating faster. It was both thrilling, adrenaline pushing through my very veins, and terrifying.

The crown on his head was as dangerous as the man himself and fit him perfectly the copper metal mirroring the jagged peaks of the Darkridge Mountains and featuring a crescent moon in the center. At the same time, I wasn't sure I liked it on him.

My Axel hadn't been a king. He had been my protector, my everything. He'd never been wrapped up in the court politics that my parents played, the ruthless games that turned everyone around them into pawns.

"I don't...I don't understand."

I could tell he was confused by the slight shift in his brow, his eyes sharpened on my expression, but before he could respond, another voice chimed in.

"Fifty years can change a lot, Evera."

The deep voice put me on edge as Axel's jaw tightened. He gently placed me down and stepped in front of me, shielding me in the most casual way possible. I came to his side, though, and laid eyes on someone who I had no recollection of—though he looked very similar to Axel.

"I didn't think you would join us," Axel said casually. The leaner, shorter individual appraised his brother—at least I assumed he was Axel's brother—before looking at me with amusement. There was nothing outwardly wrong with the man from what I could tell, but he made me feel...off.

Had Axel ever told me about his family? I couldn't remember.

"Well, considering I never met her back when we were lowly peasants, I figured late was better than never." Offering a polite smile that didn't match the malice in his gaze, he motioned to the castle. "Come brother, at least bring your guest inside—everyone is very curious about the person who's placed our king in such emotional distress."

"Watch it, Xakery," Axel warned, his voice like rolling thunder. I looked between the two of them, swallowing nervously. I was getting far too caught up in this situation, and I really needed to try to figure out what type of danger I was in before I fell back into his arms...so why did that feel impossible?

Everything about the man was distracting, from his possessive hold to the aggression that rolled off of him, his magic clutching me close. I hadn't realized it, but I could feel his wolf, and he seemed to be searching for my own. I didn't think he would find it. I worried that I had no magic anymore, that somehow the explosion in the river had expended the small amount I had left from my previous life.

Would fate be so cruel to bring me back to a world filled with magic but leave me with none? Now that I remembered my magic and my wolf, I mourned the loss of them.

"Welcome!" Another voice filled the space as we stepped into the massive foyer of the castle. It was bustling with people, most of whom had come to a stop to watch us. Soldiers, castle staff, court members—everyone was staring at me and Axel.

I knew how it looked with the way he was holding me, his arm wrapped around me protectively and hand splayed on my waist possessively...and that wasn't good since the man had barely uttered two words to me and I had no idea where we stood. Yet I didn't move out of his embrace.

"Marx," Xakery sighed. "Always so loud."

"Fuck off," the old man said nonchalantly, and my eyes

widened. Axel's lips pulled into the slightest smile as Marx approached us, his brother sneering and walking away.

Marx couldn't have been more than 5'2", but his presence was huge. He was dressed in gorgeous robes that followed him across the floor, taking up space that no one dared invade. His eyes were a milky white, but he looked right at me, smiling warmly.

"Always been a little shit, from the first time I met him." He sighed and turned his attention to Axel. "I'm waiting on the day you expel him. I mean, truly, Axel, I understand family loyalty..."

"He hasn't done anything." Axel's body was rigid with tension as he looked down at me. "Yet."

"And you, dear—you must be Evera. I've heard so much about you."

"You have?" I felt my voice pitch higher before looking up at Axel. "Listen, this is a lot. All of this. I don't understand... you're a king now? Why? More importantly, *how*?"

"I'll explain everything," he promised. His expression implied that there were things he wasn't comfortable discussing here in front of the crowd. My gaze darted around, wondering what threats waited for me here—especially if the king himself was concerned.

"I always say to listen to your wolf in times of confusion—they're usually right," Marx advised.

My chest squeezed, and I kept my eyes on Axel, not wanting to miss his reaction. "I haven't connected back with my wolf. Or my magic. I thought I felt it, but now it's just...gone."

Axel's eyes flashed with concern. "You don't feel your wolf?"

I looked away, unable to hold his gaze any longer. How

had I forgotten the intensity of it? "No, but that may have to do with my memories."

Why did I suddenly feel like I'd revealed something terrible? Marx stayed silent, but out of my peripheral vision I could see the way his brow dipped, the subtle action broadcasting his concern. Axel's reaction was far larger, looking at me in alarm before turning his eyes to the room and everyone's attention on us.

Had they all heard my admission? Suddenly, Axel looked angry. I tried to remember when I'd seen him angry before, but nothing stood out to me. I began to try to tug my hand from his, uncomfortable with the way this was going. I needed to get away from all these people.

Without a second of warning, Axel lifted me into his arms and strode from the room. I bit down on my lip, unsure of what to say or do, feeling conflicted and more than a bit out of place. After we'd traversed three long hallways and a set of stairs in silence, I began to feel like I needed space.

"Axel, can you put me down?"

"Never."

"You seem really upset about this magic thing. I barely have my memories back, so it doesn't surprise me—"

My back hit the wall of the hallway, and his large body completely eclipsed me. His hand wrapped around my throat in a firm but soft grip as I let my head fall back. Holding my gaze, the man's control seemed to slip as he surged forward, my eyes shutting as Axel kissed me.

It was tentative and soft for a mere second, then everything exploded around us.

The walls trembled, and a howl seemed to vibrate through the halls of the castle. My hair stood on end, and my body lit up like an electrical outlet. I gasped against his lips as he pressed harder against me, devouring my mouth. I let out a whimper of relief at his touch, my hands grasping his shirt to pull him tighter against me, loving the feel of his hard body against mine.

This was the kiss I had wanted for so long.

Axel ripped his lips off mine, breathing hard. I stared up at him in shock, desire rolling over every inch of my body. His hand tightened on my throat, making my nipples harden, and I pressed my legs together, feeling an ache of frustration.

"I'm sorry for this, *çiçeğim.*"

Axel's words confused me—until his magic surged through me, hard and fast. Lethal.

I let out a bloodcurdling scream as the steadfast wall in my head began to crumble, pain and agony like I'd never experienced lighting up every single nerve...before lights exploded behind my eyes.

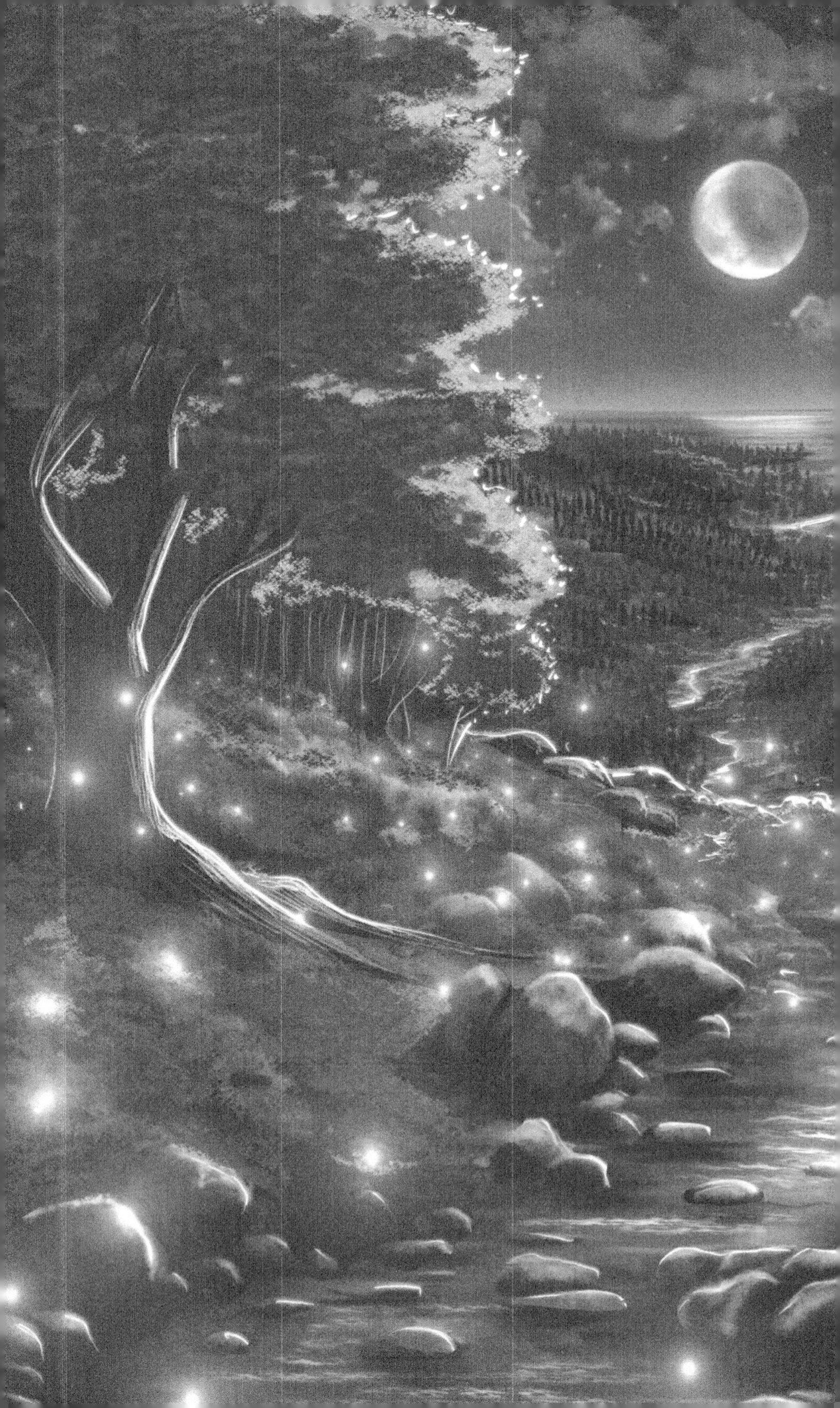

CHAPTER TEN

AXEL

"No head trauma, just the physical injury. We've cleaned and wrapped it again, but she also has several bruised ribs, blistered feet, and a cut on her knee that appears to be a day old. We expect her to recover within a few hours, assuming her magic is up to its usual standard," the medical attendant said, her eyes running over her clipboard.

I crossed my arms, tension running through me. I didn't like this—I fucking *loathed* this.

When I'd seen my flower in the human realm, she'd looked scared and tired, possibly tipsy, but now? Now she looked far too delicate, her skin ghostly white and her entire frame wrapped in bandages. She was laid out in bed, her damp hair spread around her like a veil. Her slow, relaxed breathing was the single tether to my sanity right now.

Vanessa was brushing through her hair, having managed to wash and change Evera's clothes before the medical attendant arrived. I nearly shook my head, remembering how she'd had me leave the room—insisting that she deserved some sense of privacy.

I didn't disagree with the sentiment, but what Vanessa didn't realize was just how obsessively focused I'd been on Evera—I had every inch of this woman memorized. I'd spent years simply watching her. So while I understood what she was saying in theory, it drove me crazy to have her out of my sight, even for the few minutes it took for Vanessa to help her change clothes.

It was unneeded. Pointless. There was nothing I didn't know about Evera.

And that wasn't even including all the fucked up shit I'd managed to justify in the name of protecting her. I shook myself from those thoughts as I tried to refocus on the medical attendant, glad that Caz was here as well, listening to every detail and notating it. I hadn't been the easiest to deal with today, but he'd never strayed from my side.

Honestly, I wasn't positive what I would do without him or Vanessa, the pair of them working in tandem. They were two of only a few individuals I could trust without a second thought, including my own brothers.

Of those, Xakery was the one with the largest agenda by far.

"We'll be sure to give her the herbal remedy when she wakes," Caz assured the medical attendant. I refocused, examining the bottle she handed him. I would be the *only* one giving her anything, let alone medicine. I breathed a small sigh of relief when he handed it directly to me, and I placed it near her bedside.

"Of course," the woman replied. "I'll be back to check on her in a few hours. Don't hesitate to call me back if you sense anything has changed or her state seems to worsen."

"Thank you." I rarely offered gratitude, and I could tell it surprised her, but she simply bowed her head and walked out, leaving the four of us in silence. I would say 'thank you' a million times over if it meant Evera received the best medical attention in Terrea.

Stepping towards the bed and rounding so I was on the opposite side of Vanessa, I reached out to intertwine my fingers with Evera's, running my thumb over her soft, delicate skin. Her hand was dainty and elegant, her long fingers a point of fixation for me—having wanted to put a ring on one specific one for years.

"She's going to be recovering from the bruised ribs for longer than a few hours," I told the others. "She has no connection to her magic or her wolf."

Vanessa inhaled sharply, and Caz's silence said everything.

"How is that possible?" Vanessa asked. "Especially when you're still experiencing—"

"I don't know," I admitted, refusing to go down the path of examining why I was feeling the effects of our closeness but she wasn't. This connection between us was *everything*, running over my skin as I tightened my grip on her hand.

"Regardless," I continued, "I want her to be as comfortable as possible. The two of you should arrange to have everything she needs brought here. I don't know when she'll wake up, but I'll be by her side until then."

And every moment after.

"Of course. I'll get started on that immediately," Caz said, striding from the room.

Vanessa finished brushing Evera's hair, remaining silent for a long moment before admitting, "There are rumors circulating through the castle about her connection to her wolf and magic. Be prepared, Axel—there's already talk, and there's no point in hiding it."

"I could never hide her."

"But you can't take her as your queen or form a bond if she doesn't have magic."

The fuck I can't. Tightening my grip on her hand, I refused to respond to Vanessa for a long moment, knowing my temper wouldn't serve me in this situation. The citizens of Nightfall could believe whatever they wanted; it didn't matter to me. The fact was, there was only one truth, and that was that Evera was mine. "I'll make sure to get her everything she needs," Vanessa said as she stood, squeezing my shoulder in passing before she left the room. "I'm sure everything will work out."

I would absolutely ensure it worked out. There wasn't another option.

I looked down at Evera, my gaze running over every inch of her beautiful golden skin, her damp brown hair. I knew once it dried there would be golden streaks in it, spread around her like rays of sunshine. There was a warmth to my flower, and it radiated from every part of her, down to the golden circle that surrounded the dark emerald of her eyes. I had memorized every freckle on the bridge of her nose and the way that her body moved, elegant and graceful. It didn't matter that she'd been reborn or had been raised outside of the castle—she had an innate sense of self that would shine through no matter what plane of existence or time she inhabited.

This woman had been my ruin from the beginning—from the moment I first saw her. I had never coveted anything in my life, never wanted anything as my own, until I stepped into her presence. Guarding her had made me realize how many men wanted what was mine, what was destined to be mine—not that I'd ever let myself give into my need for her. At the time, I fought it, again and again.

That was over. I'd lost her once, and I would never make the mistake of squandering my time with her again.

Until she woke, I wouldn't know if the magic I'd surged through her had helped. I hadn't wanted to do it, but I'd felt something there before, and I refused to believe she'd lost all of her magic. Especially when my wolf was so damn insistent that her wolf was there, right underneath the surface.

Her wolf.

I could remember exactly what she looked like shifted, a mixture of brown and gold. My wolf nearly forced a rumble from my throat, wanting to shift together like we had before. To run and hunt together. Closing my eyes and pushing for control, I hoped like hell that he was right, that her wolf really was there.

I would take her as my mate and my queen...but that could only happen if she had magic to form a bond with not only myself but the land. I could claim her as my own, mark her from head to toe, but unless she had magic, we would never be considered official mates. There would also be a part of me that would be terrified she could be taken from me, especially with no mating mark to adorn her pretty little neck.

A knock on the door had me turning my head, and it creaked open to reveal my younger brother. I relaxed, though only moderately. Where Xakery had an alternative motive for everything—usually fairly harmless, if annoying—Rhaegal was the exact opposite. He was straightforward and blunt about what he planned to do, if he chose to talk at all.

Sometimes I rathered he didn't, honestly.

While he didn't play games like Xakery, he was my second-in-command for a reason. His penchant for violence was known far and wide. I killed when needed, *often*, it felt like, but I didn't take exceptional enjoyment in it. The same could not be said for Rhaegal.

"She's here. Xakery said she'd arrived, but I needed to see it for myself."

"Now you have." My jaw clenched, knowing Xakery had probably already taken the rumor of her having no magic and ran with it. *I'd* been the one to claim this kingdom; *I'd* been the one who built it from the ground up. But despite the place I'd given him in court, he was spiteful of not being king. We'd grown into strangers over the past few decades, and he'd certainly become a pain in my ass, but he hadn't messed up enough to warrant removal.

Yet.

"What do you plan to do?" Rhaegal asked.

"Do?" I offered him a dark look. "What's it to you?"

"You have a kingdom that's loyal to you, Axel. You brought a human woman to our lands and are acting as if she's your mate. People will talk. They don't realize who she is, not yet, and her lack of magic doesn't help," he explained simply. "You need a plan."

"What I need is for her to wake up," I admitted softly before offering him a dark look. "Get the fuck out. Now."

And he did. Rhaegal was a lot of things, but he'd said his piece and now he would leave it be. Which meant I could focus back on my flower.

My hand came up, one knuckle brushing against her cheek as a soft sigh left her lips. Thinking of her in my memories and seeing her here in my bed were such vastly different experiences. I felt intoxicated by her mere presence, and I needed her to wake so I could experience more. I savored every reaction from her, from the surprised sounds that left her lips to the way her eyes widened when her body reacted to mine.

I knew she was confused, scared, and not completely comfortable with me yet. I knew I was different than before, my magic tainted by the blood I'd spilled to build this kingdom. I didn't regret it for a second, but it was also why her hesitancy didn't surprise me. Her body and soul may remember me, but her mind was telling her—rightfully so—that she should be scared. Considering how I want to devour her, the sentiment wasn't completely wrong.

The slightest movement had me snapping my gaze up. Evera's eyes blinked open, and as she looked around the room, I tried to imagine what she was seeing. My suite was the largest in the castle, naturally, but I'd kept the stone walls simple and unadorned. The bed was large and comfortable, all the normal aspects of a suite present, but after all this time it still didn't feel lived in.

I think I hesitated to ever truly make it mine without her here. Now I was wondering if I should've put more effort into it.

When her eyes found mine, I realized I had absolutely no idea what to say to her. I had a feeling she would have questions, and as I watched her wake up, I could practically see the doubts and concerns flooding in all at once.

"I passed out," she whispered, licking her lips. "What happened?"

"I surged my magic into you, hoping to wake yours. Do you feel any different?"

Rubbing her chest, she frowned. "I'm not sure. I don't feel my wolf like I used to in my memories, but I feel something behind that wall. I feel like more knowledge and memories are slipping in, but I'm not sure my magic is."

Disappointment filled my chest, but I refused to show it. "It's been less than a day; I'm sure it will return."

Her eyes flickered down to where our hands were connected, tensing slightly. "Less than a day, and I found you. I didn't realize...Oliver didn't tell me you were king."

Because Oliver knew how much she hated court politics and knew it would make her uncomfortable. I wouldn't lie—while it was absolutely necessary to have his eyes and ears inside that damn castle, I missed him. The man was more of a brother to me than my real brothers were. Soon enough, I hoped he would be able to end the charade on the other side.

I knew what kept him there. Oliver was determined to protect the Kingdom of Nightfall, even if it meant playing such a dangerous role. His loyalty was something I would never question.

"I know this is a lot to take in—"

Evera pulled her hand back, pulling her knees to her chest. "A lot? I'm being flooded with memories from a different life, emotions from a different life—this isn't me. I grew up in the foster care system on Earth. *With humans.* Not as a princess in some damn castle. This has to be a dream or something."

The foster care system? I wasn't familiar with that, but the concept of her living anything but a perfect life made me extremely uneasy. Had she been suffering the entire time we were apart? The concept caused my chest to seize, realizing that this entire time she had been left wholly unprotected on Earth.

Evera had always been so damn strong. I knew she didn't view it that way, but her ability to navigate life in Eventide while maintaining her positive outlook was a strength on its own. Now, though, I could see a different type of strength radiating off of her, and I hated to think about the reason it needed to be there in the first place—what she'd gone through to gain it.

My hand itched to reach for her, but she shook her head. "I can't think when you touch me, and I need to be able to think. Desperately."

"Do you?" I murmured, lifting my hand to her cheek anyway and gently running my knuckle along it once again. "I know you feel the connection between us."

"One that shouldn't exist without magic, but I don't have magic or a wolf," she hissed, her eyes filled with confusion and sadness I wasn't sure she even understood.

I could tell she was resisting this—resisting *us*. I didn't want to scare her, but I also knew that the two of us were inevitable. We always had been.

"And what's the big deal about me not having magic?" she continued. I inhaled sharply, moving my gaze down to her lips, because that was not a conversation we needed to have right now—but Evera was perceptive and had no doubt felt the tension in the room at her announcement.

For now, though, the conversation needed to wait. It would lead to questions about why I hadn't acted on our connection before, why I'd refused her when she offered herself to me back when I was her guard—when I was certain she didn't understand what she was asking for. I'd been bad at expressing myself to her even then, and after years of turmoil within our realm, I was even worse now despite knowing exactly how I felt about her.

"Oh, now you don't have a freakin' answer," she growled.

"Not an answer you'll like," I admitted, standing and

running a hand through my hair. I didn't trust myself on the bed with her, especially as she stared at me with fire in her eyes, daring me to tell her no. Daring me to admit what I should have long ago, even if she didn't realize it.

"It doesn't matter if I don't like it, Axel." She pulled the covers off herself and sat forward. "You kissed me. You freakin' kissed me! I practically begged you in my last life to do that, and nothing. From what I can remember, you rejected me again and again, but now you kiss me?"

"You should stay seated, you're injured," I insisted, not allowing myself to respond to her question. My flower was going to find out real fucking quick how often I'd almost kissed her before. How often I did a ton of shit to quell the beast inside of me that demanded we claim her.

"Whose bed is this, even?" she huffed, sitting back. My jaw clenched as I removed my crown and set it on the table, not wanting a reminder of the weight it carried right now.

"It's your freakin' room, isn't it!" She growled when I didn't immediately answer, a noise that I swear was supposed to be intimidating. It was cute as hell.

"It is."

"So you've kissed me, and now I'm in your bed. What are you playing at, Axel? You never wanted me before, but now that you're king you want me here? Oliver said my parents wanted me for my magic and to gain more power in the realm. How do I know your intentions aren't bad like theirs?"

I snapped.

I was across the room, pinning her to the bed, in a second flat. I was careful to not press on her delicate frame, but I completely covered her, one arm braced above her and the other grasping her chin so I had her full attention. Fear and excitement jumped in her gaze, and it nearly had me groaning as I tried to look past the red I saw at the mention of her parents.

Her fucking parents.

"Evera, my intentions are as different from your parents' as you can possibly imagine," I said, my gaze turning cold and my voice sounding detached, even to myself.

"Why should I trust you?"

My chest tightened. I'd once had every single drop of her trust, back when she'd entrusted me with her life. How could she now, though? With only some of her memories—she wouldn't.

I pulled myself off of her and grabbed my crown, placing it back on my head. "I'll show you that you can trust me."

"How?"

My voice was soft and lethal as I looked her in the eye. "By slaughtering the two individuals you call your parents. I'll paint the streets of their kingdom red with their blood and then give it to you as a present. Then you'll understand how different I am from them."

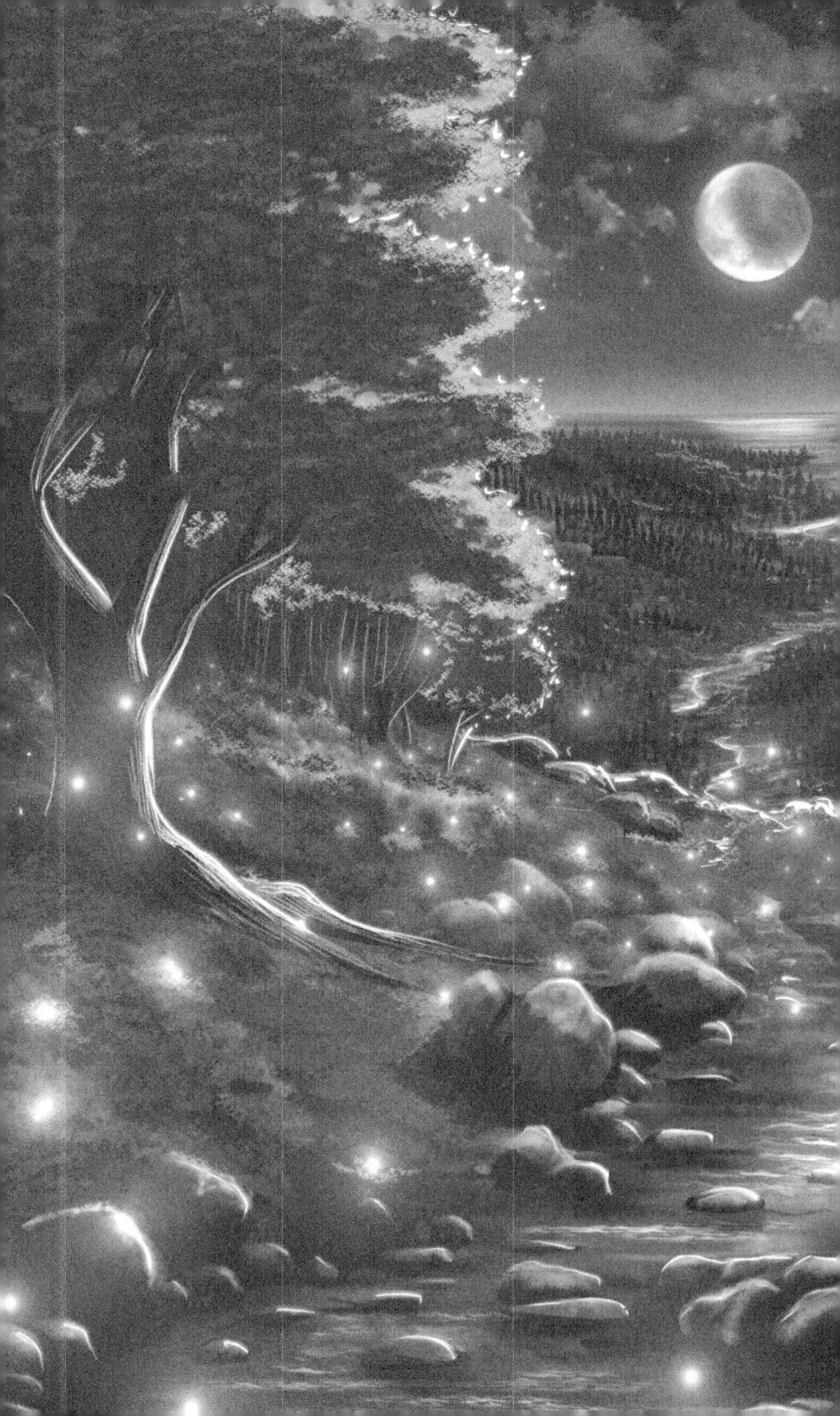

CHAPTER ELEVEN

EVERA

The door slammed shut as Axel stormed out, clearly very determined and more than a bit pissed. I nibbled my lip, hating the guilt I felt for questioning his motives, while also recognizing that the question was fair.

Why, now, did he want me? Had it been the time apart or something more?

Though the larger question playing on my mind had to do with my reaction to his threat—the promise, practically a vow, to spill my parents' blood as a way to show I could trust him. Honestly, the more I remembered of them, the more I recognized that wouldn't be a loss for anyone. My eyes closed as one of the newest memories revealed to me stood out in bright vibrant colors.

"Evera." My mother's voice drew my attention from where I sat on a lesser throne to the right of my parents, Reynor absent from his mirrored position on the left. I turned to look up at her as she offered me a pointed and disappointed look. I knew it was because

of my expression, which showed a mere ounce of sympathy towards the family they'd just sent away.

They'd come to us seeking help, worried their food stores wouldn't make it through the winter—and my father had laughed in their faces, telling them that they should've worked harder. I made note of their faces and promised myself that when I was done for the day, I'd have one of my trusted handmaids track down the family and deliver several large rations of wheat for the winter months.

My parents would never notice anyway.

"Right, onto the next point of business." My father stood and whistled, and a squad of guards strode through the doors, most of them individuals I recognized. Except for one.

Straightening my posture, I focused on the dangerous man—the largest of them all—standing in the center. His uniform was pristine, and though he appeared to be in his late twenties, the energy and authority he exuded belonged to someone several hundred years old. My body heated as I took in everything about him, and my wolf yipped happily in my ear, enough that I had to press my lips together so no sound escaped.

I didn't think it worked completely, because his dark eyes snapped towards me—and I absolutely melted. The breath whooshed out of me, and I leaned back into my throne as my father began talking, his words going in one ear and out the other...until he said his name.

"Captain Axel, you requested that your position be shifted from the battlefield to domestic endeavors?"

"Yes, Your Majesty. I've served the crown for over three hundred years. I want to ensure my focus stays sharp, and I think a change of environment could help that."

"I agree." My father smiled. "Luckily, I have the perfect job for you."

"Really?" my mother asked.

"Really," he confirmed, a devious glint in his eye. Returning his attention to Axel, he announced, "You will be Princess Evera's personal guard now that she's eighteen. Good luck."

Delight filled my chest as a small smile tugged at my lips. I knew my father had meant it as an insult, a punishment, but I felt like it was anything but...until I met his gaze. Axel looked far from happy—he looked furious.

I never fully understood his reaction that day, and I had never worked up the nerve to ask, worried that I'd hear something that would break my fragile heart. Now I wondered if his reaction was to my father's snide commentary and the derisive looks he gave me—it made a bit more sense considering how protective he'd been from the start. He was like a silent shadow, reacting to threats before I even knew they existed. I'd absolutely loved having him so close, and I mourned the loss of our familiarity.

But now he was king.

In theory, it made sense—he was an amazing leader. But I'd watched my parents rule for my entire life and knew firsthand how the throne corrupted—how it twisted everything. I didn't want that for Axel, and I had a feeling that the more my memories returned, the stronger I would feel about that.

"Whatever," I murmured to myself, trying to shake away the horrible habit of overthinking. I swung myself out of bed, wincing at the pain in my ribs. My body was still drained, but my mind was on high alert. There was absolutely no way I would be able to stay in this room all day, though it was a perfectly welcoming space that was grand in size yet simple in style.

The stone walls and floors weren't adorned with any art or sculptures; the large windows and curtains surrounding the glass balcony doors to the far side were the only decoration needed. The bed—nearly double the size of a king size bed, which made sense considering Axel's size—was centered in front of a fireplace, and the sheets were so incredibly soft, much like the rug underneath my feet.

The entire place was so comfortable, and in theory I could have easily stayed in here buried under the covers—if I wasn't feeling so uneasy about everything going on. I peeked inside the wardrobe, not surprised to find men's clothing. Though it was inconvenient since I was already wearing an oversized men's shirt, my other belongings nowhere in sight.

A knock on the door announced Vanessa's entrance into the suite, a stack of clothing in her hands. She stood within the receiving room, surprised to catch sight of me from the other side of the living room positioned between us.

"You're up!"

"I am...I have a lot on my mind," I explained, feeling the need to excuse why I was snooping around and not in bed.

"I'm guessing it has something to do with Axel storming angrily down the hall?"

"I felt like it was more of a determined stride, but yes—he did seem pissed," I grumbled as she handed me clothes, her eyes sparkling with mischief.

"Everyone bends over backwards for the man, a little push won't hurt him," she said before moving on. "Now, I have some clothes for you here. You're not supposed to be out of bed because of your injuries, but I won't stop you from leaving. I know when my mind is on the run, it helps to walk around. Just make sure you're careful, and if you start to feel bad, come back so we can call the medical staff. Understood?"

"Yes," I agreed, finding her calm yet no-nonsense demeanor very relaxing. It reminded me a bit of Laurain.

Oh my god—Laurain's picture! It was in my wallet...I needed to find that backpack.

"Your things are being dried out and will be returned promptly," Vanessa said, as if reading my mind. Which, come to think of it, was probably part of her job—predicting the needs of others. "Do you want to eat before you go out?"

"I'm not super hungry." I nibbled my lip in thought. "I don't even know where I'm planning to go, to be honest."

"You could walk the gardens, go to the library—"

"Library," I said immediately, thinking that it would be a fantastic place to gather information on how Axel had seemingly founded a new kingdom following the war...and maybe more information about the events that led to my sacrifice. I was positive the details would come back to me over time, but time didn't really feel like something I had a lot of right now. Not if I wanted to have all the pieces of the puzzle to work with when it came to the state of Vargr, and more importantly, my parents.

"I'll have food brought there; how does that sound?"

"That would be amazing, thank you."

Vanessa's eyes twinkled with warmth before she turned and left the room. Now that I had a plan, all I needed to do was get dressed.

Sorting through the clothes she'd brought, I was relieved to find a pair of soft brown suede pants and a loose-fitting shirt that not only fit the fashion around here, but also wouldn't restrict my injuries or hang awkwardly around my bandages. Vanessa had even included fresh undergarments, and I couldn't find it in me to care that the bra and socks were a little too tight. My boots were near the front door, at least from what I could see, but I would leave those for last.

Slipping into the en suite, I combed through my hair with my fingers and looked around for a toothbrush, finding a collection of toiletries in a bag on the counter—probably from Vanessa as well.

Once I'd washed my face and brushed my teeth, I strode across the suite to put on my boots. I momentarily wondered if the guards would stop me from leaving, but when I stepped out of the room, they all looked away without a word. Thank goodness.

I floated past them, but when I heard two sets of footsteps start to follow, I grimaced. Call me crazy, but I had a feeling that there was no point in asking them not to follow me. In the few times Axel had left my side in my past life, he had ordered his squad to tail me, so he probably was doing the same now.

He should have been here himself, though. I shook my head at that thought. We had a connection I couldn't deny, but that was all I knew for sure right now. *So why was I acting so attached?*

Turning, I fixed both of them with a look. "If you're going to follow, can you at least tell me where the library is?"

The younger one offered a sheepish smile. "Two lefts, down a staircase, and then a right."

"And we do have to follow," the other explained, apologetic. "Crown's order. We promise you won't even notice us."

I found that hard to believe.

"Right." I sighed and turned around, deciding to ignore them for now. It ended up being far easier than I assumed, much like the guard had promised, as I explored the beautiful halls and admired the views out of the large windows that decorated the bridges that connected different sections of the castle, revealing lands blooming with life and full of sunshine. It was like Axel had taken the darkness of the land upon himself and left only beauty for his people to enjoy.

As I made my way down a set of stairs, I looked around the main floor, noticing a few more people moving about than when we'd arrived. I was glad that most didn't pay me any mind—it was obvious the reason they'd been staring before had nothing to do with me and everything to do with who I'd been with. In a way, it was really nice being able to move throughout the castle as if I was simply a staff member. If you ignored the guards behind me, of course.

After another right, I found myself smiling at the massive archway at the end of the hall. I quickened my pace and felt my mouth drop as I entered the library—although I wasn't sure you could call it something so simple.

A pure masterpiece, that's what it was.

The room was a massive circle, the ceiling domed and covered in artwork depicting beasts and creatures of all kinds, a dual moon at the very center. Pearly white bookcases and shelves soared four stories into the air, each and every shelf filled with books.

Thin long windows let in a ton of lights from between each set of bookcases, making the space feel light and airy. I ran my eyes over all of it, and the gold ladders accompanying each shelf made me want to go to the very top to see what secrets lay there.

It was only when I looked toward the center of the room near a grouping of couches and tables that I realized I wasn't alone. My eyes widened at the three people there, mostly because they seemed trapped in a glaring contest—well, at least the two I didn't recognize were.

"Ah, the lady of the hour," Axel's brother, Xakery, chimed. He sat away from the other two individuals, reading a large book. "I'm surprised he let you out of the room—he should learn to keep his pets reined in."

"Excuse me?" I growled, narrowing my eyes on the man, who I was really starting to hate.

"Shut it," the woman snapped, breaking her glaring contest with the other man. "What are you even doing in here, Xakery? Don't you have somewhere to be?"

"I despise you," he noted indifferently, not looking at her but instead holding my gaze. Then, without any fanfare, he stood and walked out of the room, brushing past me completely.

"Ignore him. He's not worth the energy," the woman advised, rounding from where she'd been perched on the back of a sofa. My gaze darted over her, and I felt a moment of insecurity because she was objectively stunning and completely at ease with herself.

Her black hair was long and straight, down to her waist, and her golden skin appeared to almost sparkle—the white dress she wore enhancing the effect. Tall and statuesque, the woman looked like some figure from Greek mythology.

"He seems...*interesting*," I noted quietly, not positive who the other man was or who she was and if I could trust them —but mainly I didn't want to say anything bad about Axel's brother and come to regret it. Then again he was such an asshole that I would be pissed if Axel did agree with his commentary.

The man made a sound of agreement, but his gaze was still on the woman facing me. I was struck with the realization that the man was probably related to Axel as well, his brown hair and dark eyes nearly the exact same—but he was taller and leaner than Xakery—dressed in all black military gear. A long scar broke from the top of his eyebrow down to his jaw.

"Evera, right? Axel's guest?" she asked, drawing my attention back as I nodded. Her smile was soft and authentic, "I'm Clarissant, or Clari. Whichever you prefer."

"Wonderful to meet you, Clari." I offered my hand in greeting, which she immediately met.

"And that is King Axel's younger brother, Rhaegal." She motioned behind me. "Although, as I suggested with Xakery —not worth the energy."

Somehow I didn't believe she meant that.

Rhaegal narrowed his eyes on her. "We still need to talk."

"Nothing to talk about," she shot back. "You made your priorities clear—service before self-interest. So have fun on your scouting trip. I'll just go with Vox to the—"

"I will kill him."

Oh my. Clarissant's smile grew, her back towards him so he couldn't see. She put a dismissive hand up, waving him off, and he shook his head, walking towards her until he stood right behind her. My eyes widened, suddenly feeling like I was part of a moment I wasn't supposed to be.

"I will kill him, Clarissant. You decide his fate."

And then he was gone, storming past and leaving me with Clarissant, who sighed happily after a moment. "The man is absolutely psychotic."

"Are you happy with what he just said, or…" Because when Axel threatened to kill my parents, it didn't bother me nearly as much as it should have. I wondered if she felt the same in this situation.

Her eyes flashed with a bit of darkness. "I hate Vox, so it's no loss. He knows that. It's a little game we play—just like the one where we won't admit we're mates."

Mates. That's right, our kind had mates—*fated* mates, if I remembered correctly. Did that mean Axel had a fated mate? I couldn't remember if that was something I had thought of or that had bothered me in my past life.

"I'll leave you to your plans, but I'm sure this won't be the last time I see you," Clarissant said, squeezing my shoulder in passing. "It'll be nice to have another girl around."

I watched her walk away, the library suddenly silent. I exhaled slowly, feeling like I'd just been thrown into the middle of a soap opera. Needing a moment to recover, I made myself comfortable on one of the couches and looked at the books already laid out on the nearby table. I needed to search the shelves for the history I wanted, but I could take a moment to be nosey first...

"Hello, dear," Vanessa chirped, wheeling in a cart of food with Caz in tow.

"King Axel mentioned you shouldn't be out of bed," Caz drew out, looking faintly amused. Though the amusement was in his gaze, not his expression—that was stoic.

"Then he shouldn't have stormed from the room," I said pointedly before looking over the food. "This looks amazing. Do you want to join me?"

"Work to do," Vanessa sighed, shaking her head. "You are so sweet, though, to offer. Eat up and relax—if you're looking for anything specific, just use that book over there to find it."

Caz was already halfway across the room, and Vanessa turned to follow. My chest squeezed a bit as they both left me, not liking the feeling of being so alone. Deciding to make myself a plate of small sandwiches and pastries, I set it out on the table before walking over towards the index she mentioned. When I looked over it, though, my brow furrowed. It was full of blank pages, a quill sitting next to it.

"You have to write what you want to find." The older man from when I first arrived materialized next to me with his casual statement, causing me to tense in surprise. He motioned to the book, tapping it with a finger before walking to the couch and grabbing a plate, making himself at home.

Looking down at the quill, I decided to try out his method and wrote what I wanted to know: *The History of the Kingdom of Nightfall.*

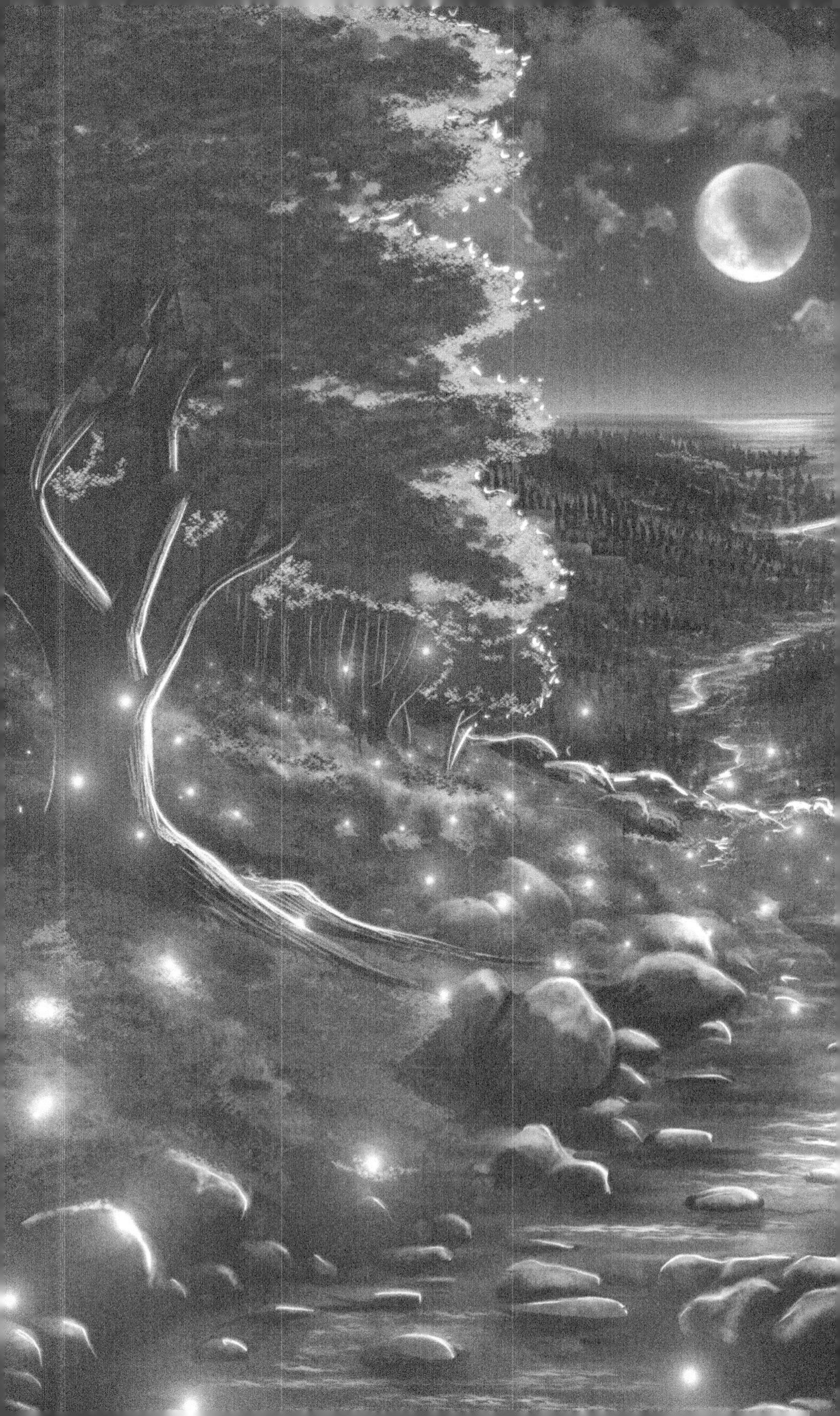

CHAPTER TWELVE

EVERA

As the ink dried on the paper, a faint wind rustled through the space, lifting my hair and shifting my shirt against my skin. Wind chimes sounded in my ears, and the shelves sounded like they were moving, rearranging themselves, though they appeared to remain still. When the building started to creak and the floor began to rumble, I started to worry that I'd done something wrong, that I'd somehow broken the library—

Suddenly it stopped, a singular book floating toward me.

It landed with a soft thunk on the podium, on top of the index-book. I lifted the navy blue and gold leather book, and my eyes must have been as wide as saucers as I carried it to the couch. I knew there was magic here—I'd felt it—but actually seeing it...

"That was really wild," I said to the older man, who watched me expectantly with a sandwich stuffed in his mouth.

"This is one of my favorite places in the castle," he agreed, leaning forward to pour himself a cup of tea. "I spend most of my time here, when I'm not sorting out some type of drama within its walls. I swear, everyone has a problem nowadays."

"I don't think I caught your name earlier," I said.

"Marx."

I nodded, remembering Axel calling him that. "So, Marx, is that what you do here? Help people with problems?"

"Part of the job, but in the official capacity, I'm a Council Advisor—there are four of us, and Axel comes to us for advice," he explained. His eyes moved to the book in my hand. "I'm guessing that you're here looking for information on the Kingdom of Nightfall?"

"Yes." I hesitated before saying more, but then decided to be honest. "I'm not sure how much you know about my situation—"

"Mostly everything," he admitted easily. "While those around the castle don't realize who you are yet, King Axel has made it no secret over the years that he was waiting for your return. It's probably why the rumors are running so rampant, because without your magic, no one can tell if you're the woman he's been waiting for."

There was something to this magic thing that was far bigger than I'd initially assumed. More and more it seemed that not having it was a much larger problem than Axel was letting on.

"I see." I folded my hands. "Well, because of that and our joint past, I'm trying to figure out how exactly we got here. How Axel went from being my guard to ruling a kingdom that didn't even exist the last time I lived in Vargr."

"It's all in there." Marx nodded at the book. "But I can probably answer most of your questions, especially if you're willing to share your lunch with me."

My lip twitched as I looked at his half-eaten sandwich. "I feel like it might be a bit late to tell you *'no'* now."

Marx flashed me a smile before taking a sip of his tea. "Right. Well, let's start at the beginning then."

"The night that I sacrificed myself?"

"Yes, but before that as well—what do you remember about the war leading up to it?"

"I remember some things about my parents and their kingdom, and I remember that a red light appeared into the sky and called me to the land of the Sacred Temple…but outside of that, most of my memories revolve around Axel," I admitted, the last part causing my cheeks to flush.

"Your parents." Marx heaved a sigh, his expression turning solemn. "As you know, you were the only true heir of the Kingdom of Eventide. Your half-brother Reynor was a spare heir but illegitimate, the result of one of your mother's lovers. They tried to hide it, but it was pretty obvious since you two look nothing alike."

I tried to repress a shiver, not wanting to think about Reynor. I knew he posed a threat, I could feel it in my bones, but I didn't know how much of one or what he'd tried to do in my past. I wasn't sure I wanted to remember.

"The Kingdom of Eventide, for as long as I can remember —which is a few thousand years—has ruled Vargr with an iron fist, instilling fear in generation after generation. Your parents aren't an exception, and their rule is even more bloody and ruthless than others'. Our magic is primal in nature, vicious and predatorial, and that's something they celebrate.

"However, before the war, they still indulged their citizens with small moments of reprieve, like the sacred day. Havestia is a celebration of the goddess that takes place every year throughout our realm, but it takes on a particularly special note every fifty years, when the veil lifts. It was always considered a day of festivities and good cheer, but those years filled the air with a different type of power, reinvigorating our territory as a whole."

"You said it 'was' always considered a day of celebration? What changed?" I asked, having a feeling that despite the festivities at Lorie's Inn the night I arrived, the day was no longer celebrated in full spirit. The land had been far too quiet for the night of the *sacred day* celebration—the candles by Vargr's temple coming to mind.

"Here in Nightfall, we celebrate. I've heard that in Eventide there are small, intimate gatherings, but the castle refuses to endorse it...all because of what happened five decades ago.

"On that day, when the veil was lifted, King Valandril of Isramaya took his new queen and her dying sister to the Sacred Temple where a pool existed that was said to have the power to heal. Healing wasn't his *true* motive though. While he was there, he cut a root from the sacred tree and brought it back to his own kingdom in hopes that it would grant him limitless power—not an entirely shocking move, if you knew him."

"Limitless power to take over all of the kingdoms?" I asked, remembering Lorie had mentioned there were a fair amount of them. It was a complete guess on my end, but why else would you need that much power?

"Yes, to become the King of Terrea, but also to march through the veil when it opened in another fifty years and take over the human world."

My eyes widened at that. *Talk about ambitious...*

"Some of the kingdoms joined him, understanding what

he planned to do and wanting to have access to this power—including your parents."

That didn't surprise me in the least.

"It didn't go to plan, though, and when he planted the root, it caused a chain reaction that shifted everything in Terrea at once. A plague wrecked our land, instantly destroying the beautiful expanse of natural wildlife and resources we benefited from, even poisoning our water. Not only that, but creatures that had once lived natural lives in the forest became mutated and monstrous, searching out our kind for hunger. The screams rang through every house as the beasts tore through village after village—"

My skin broke into chills, remembering the screams I heard as I ran toward the temple.

"For two weeks, our realm faced war on a scale that no one had ever seen before. Man against monster, man against man. It decimated so much, left so many dead…we feared nothing would end it."

"But something did." I nibbled my lip, realizing where this was going.

"Yes. You, Evera, took part in ending it—you received a call from the high priestess and went to the Sacred Temple. You decided to make the biggest sacrifice one could ask, giving your own life."

"I didn't realize when I went there that I was going to have to," I murmured, not wanting him to think I was some kind of martyr. "I don't remember exactly what happened, but I have to assume they told us when we got there."

"We were told of your sacrifice—of the sacrifice of the eight women who saved our realm—and that when the veil reopened, you would return. I think many assumed it was metaphorical, but because you were the princess of the realm, many wanted to believe it was real, and Axel kept that thought alive—vehemently."

I swallowed down my emotion and nodded, pouring myself a cup of tea. "What happened after the war?"

Marx picked up another sandwich, and after a bite, continued. "Everyone found out about your parents and what they'd done—how they'd sided with King Valandril. Axel was livid. He gathered the soldiers that reported to him and tried to seize control of the castle. But as its rulers, your parents' magic was intertwined with the land, and eventually he had to retreat."

Had he tried to kill them because of the war, the lives lost? Or had it been because of my sacrifice? I would never assume the latter, but something told me that the Axel I'd known would have been...I'm not sure what he would have felt at my loss, but something big for sure.

"But it wasn't only Axel that retreated—half of Eventide left with him. I don't think he planned on becoming a king, but when the group of them crossed the mountains, it was the start of the Kingdom of Nightfall. Your parents greatly underestimated Axel and what he would do when he left—what he was capable of.

"For the past five decades, he's been expanding and creating this kingdom," Marx said happily, leaning forward and tapping the book. "It's very interesting. The man is persistent, if anything, and he was able to take an uninhabitable land and form it into the home of a flourishing society. His success is something your parents still find threatening, which is why they're constantly trying to wage war against him."

"I'm glad I didn't go there—to their castle," I admitted. "I don't know what they would've done, but from what I can remember, our relationship was far from good."

"As the true heir to the Kingdom of Eventide, you hold the most power—especially since as time goes on, your parents' hold on the land loosens. It's normal, a natural progression of the transfer of power from one ruler to the next. *That* is why they want you back."

Who was the true heir here, in Nightfall? Did my power extend here? Was that why Axel wanted me, or had he claimed this land fully as his own? Not that I had any magic to begin with—not anymore.

"Thank you so much for explaining all that," I said after staring down at the book for a long moment. "I hope to remember all of it myself, but it helps to get a bearing on everything that is happening."

"Of course." Marx stood and brushed crumbs off his robes. "Now, I must be going—I can practically hear Caz complaining about something."

Smiling, I watched him walk away before running my fingers over the book on my lap, letting it fall open to the first page. I was thankful Marx had laid such a good foundation of information, because without it I probably would've been overwhelmed as I started to read.

Flipping through the gold scripted pages, I came across a map of the Kingdom of Nightfall. The Darkridge Mountains marked the eastern border, and near them stood the Midnight Keep. That must've been the military fortress I'd stumbled to when I first arrived. It was strategically positioned near the river to monitor for anyone crossing through the mountains —mainly my parents and their soldiers, if I had to assume.

So much of the kingdom, though, seemed unexplored and

looked to be uninhabited, beautiful in its sprawling hills and craggy mountains. I examined the body of water that led out to the ocean, realizing that behind this great fortress, in the distance, would be the ocean as well. I had no idea if the ocean was swimmable or anything like that, but I would bet it was beautiful.

Looking towards the windows at the blue sky, I found myself wondering if exploring the landscape would be a better way to spend the afternoon. It could be dangerous, though—if I was even able or allowed to leave. Axel hadn't said I was trapped here, but he also had soldiers following my every move, so it was a bit hard to not view it that way.

Returning to the book, I got lost in the text, flipping from one page to the next and reading a full-length edition of exactly what Marx had summarized. My fingers traced over the detailed drawings of the monstrous creatures that had terrorized our lands, and I was almost glad I didn't remember everything about that time. A faint echo of the guilt I'd felt in the dream—for my people—was still there. It was what had pushed me to go to the Sacred Temple to begin with.

I only broke out of my trance when the sound of voices intruded on my concentration. Two young men, probably around my age, and an older woman whose face was set in a stern tone were talking in a low whisper to the guards.

"What do you mean we can't go in there?" the woman demanded. I could practically feel her annoyance.

"The library is currently occupied—"

"They can come in," I called out. "I'm going to head out soon anyway."

I realized with a start that I'd basically just issued orders to the guards. I hadn't asked, I hadn't wondered if I was allowed, I hadn't been unsure at all—I'd simply given them instructions. I may not have actively remembered my time being princess, but some part of me did.

"Thank you," the woman said as the guards let her pass. She strode to the opposite end of the room, one of the men following her.

The other walked over toward me, a smirk on his admittedly handsome face. I arched a questioning brow as he stopped in front of the food cart, his hands in his jacket as he surveyed everything on the table.

"You're new here," he said—not a question—as his gaze ran over my face. "I would have remembered seeing you."

"I am," I agreed. I didn't have a reason to dislike the guy, but he didn't seem very friendly—it was like a guise of civility existed on top of something hollow. Something that contrasted his pretty boy appearance—the man's lashes were nearly longer than my own.

Also, that emptiness I saw there? It wasn't something I was interested in discovering.

"What's your name?" he asked, rounding the couches and coming to sit next to me. I nearly cursed—couldn't he have chosen one of the many seats across from me? I turned to face him nonetheless, wanting to keep my eyes on him.

"Evera."

A flash of recognition shone in his gaze. "That would explain the guards."

"What do you—"

An electric sensation ran up my spine as my chest squeezed, and a shadow fell over me as a low rumble vibrated the air.

"King Axel." The man shot to his feet, his skin paling as he shifted backwards, almost like he was going to run.

"Alezar" Axel's voice was smooth and dangerous as his hand slid over my shoulder and wrapped around my throat in a delicate but possessive hold. A wave of desire threatened to drown me, my nails digging into my palms as I tried to control the urge to turn and throw myself into his arms. "What do you think you're doing?"

"She let us in here. I was just coming to thank her, I didn't realize…"

"Yes you did." Axel's voice turned cold. I wanted to see his gaze, see how dark his eyes were and what they were expressing, but the way he held me meant I couldn't move. "Go. Now, before I decide I don't need you or your brother."

Without another word, Alezar ran towards the door, the woman and his brother following close behind.

The guards closed the doors behind them, making it clear that Axel had every drop of power in this situation. His hand fell from my throat, and I chose not to examine the disappointment I felt at that.

Axel came to crouch down in front of me, shifting the coffee table away with a simple push of his hand.

"You're back," I said, still a bit pissed at how he'd run out on me. His dark eyes examined the text I held, seeming to gather all of his thoughts before he snapped his gaze back to mine.

"And you're out of bed—injured and walking around. What are you doing, *çiçeğim?*"

"I'm perfectly fine," I insisted, "and not that it's any of your business—"

"Everything you do is my business."

"Right." I narrowed my eyes, trying to not blush. "Well, if you wanted me to stay in the room then *you* shouldn't have stormed out."

His eyes sparked with a simmering heat that had me swallowing nervously, his hand moving forward to remove the book from my lap. "So if I stay in the bedroom with you, you won't leave? Ever?"

"Obviously not ever," I huffed, "but you declared you were going to kill my parents and then left—what am I supposed to do with that?"

His jaw tightened, and he wrapped a hand around my thigh, smoothing his fingers over my suede pants. "Believe me. Trust me. I plan on showing you that you can...although instead of asking me your questions, I find you here. Talking to Alezar."

"He was being friendly," I said, not bothering to explain that Marx was actually the one who'd provided the most useful information.

Axel chuckled, his smile absolutely dangerous and causing me to stare wide-eyed, awestruck by how handsome he was. *Did he always look like that when he smiled?* If so, I was completely screwed. Axel was lethally attractive, but when he smiled, it was something completely different.

"Friendly? Sure. But being friendly isn't the problem—it's the fact that he was looking at what's mine. Coveting what's mine."

"I'm supposed to take that as meaning that I'm *yours*? Even though you never wanted me before—"

Like the predator he so clearly was, his rough hands darted out and tugged my hips forward. I nearly fell back, having to catch myself with my hands. Leaning forward, he grasped my chin in a firm hold, my legs parted on either side of his muscular torso. *Holy shit.*

"Listen closely, *çiçeğim.*"

How could I not? That commanding tone was doing absolutely too much to me. I could barely focus.

"Even without your memories, you know you belong to me. You always have. It was never about me not wanting you—it was more complicated than that," he rumbled.

But did I believe that? Did I trust him?

"What was it about, then? Because Marx told me that after my sacrifice—"

"Your death," He bit out, his jaw so tight I worried it would shatter. "Your *death*, Evera."

"After my death..." I waited for his nod of approval before I continued, "Marx said that you tried to take the castle of Eventide and kill my parents because of how they endangered the entire kingdom—"

"That wasn't why I did it."

Axel's voice was eerily calm, his gaze clear and completely focused on me. The face of a man who was telling the truth. So I decided to ask the question that was practically begging to be asked.

"So why did you?"

"For the same reason I plan to kill them even now —*because of you*, Evera. *For* you. Because I place blame for your death solely and completely on them. I lost you because of them, and for that they will pay with their lives."

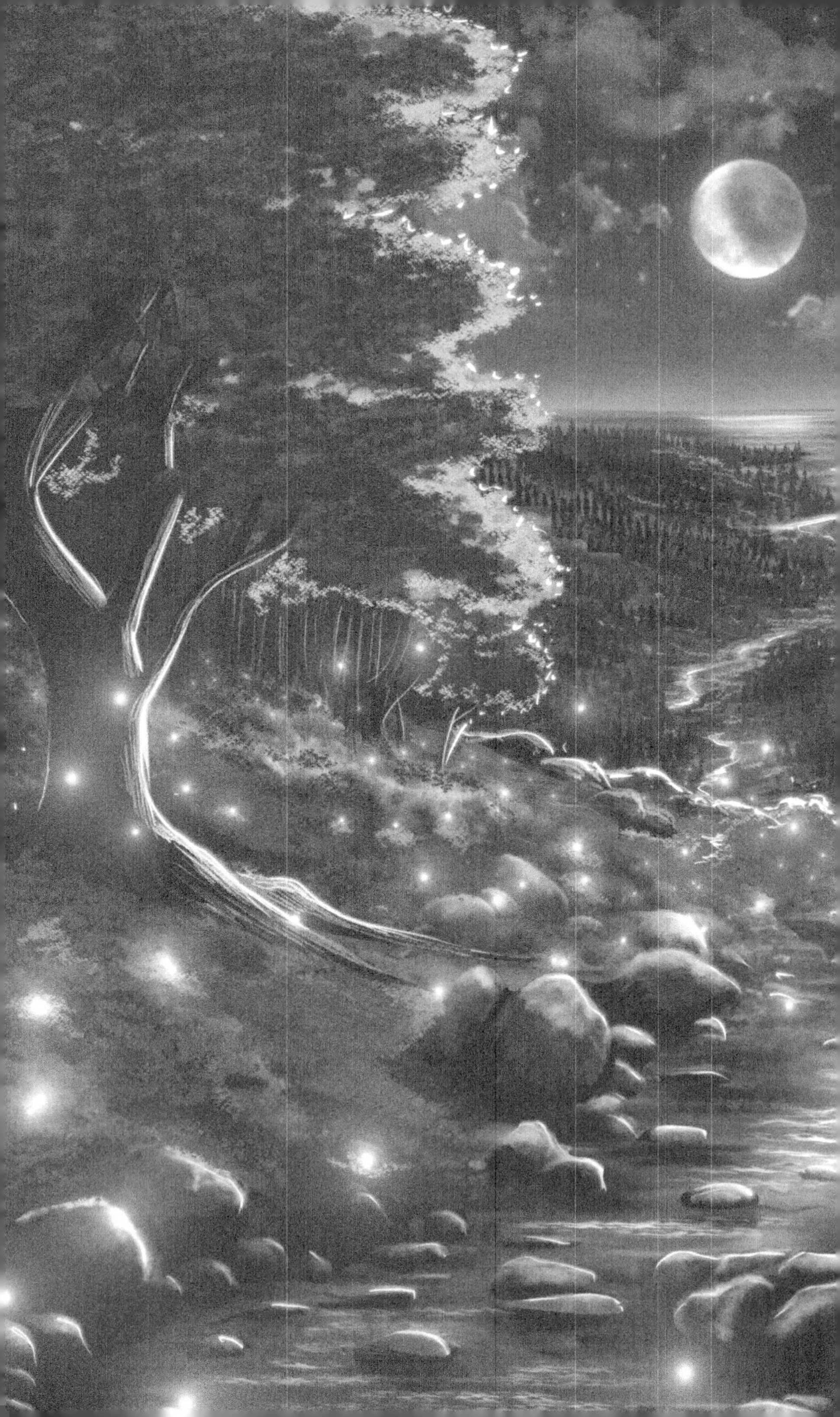

CHAPTER THIRTEEN

EVERA

Axel's threatening words heated my body in a way I could have never expected, causing chills to break out along my skin as my toes curled inside of my boots. I couldn't turn my head or look away, captured by the intensity of his midnight gaze.

He knew it, too, his chest producing a deep rumble that vibrated down my spine. My nipples tightened against my bra, my legs trying to press together for some type of friction. His broad, muscular chest didn't allow for it, and the faintest smirk appeared on his lips.

"If I didn't know better, *çiçeğim*, I would say my threats turn you on." Axel's words were soft and spoken between us, but they caused a blush to bloom across my face as if he'd shouted them. I suddenly felt the faintest sense of embarrassment that I was so easily readable.

Hadn't that always been the problem between us, though? I'd shown him everything and received nothing in return.

"You have no idea what you're talking about." I swallowed

nervously, trying to tug my chin from his grasp—although it was a failed effort.

"Liar," he growled, one hand tightening to almost bruising on my hip. "Little liar. I can scent how wet you are, and I know if I stripped you of these pants and buried myself between your thighs, I'd find proof of that."

"Axel," I whispered, squirming under him as victory flashed in his gaze.

"Tell me what you need, Evera." His lips brushed against my own in a bare whisper of a kiss as my hands hesitantly slid onto his shoulders, loving the feel of them under my fingers. I wanted to rip his jacket off, to feel his warm skin, but in the face of his overwhelming charisma, I felt shy and not nearly as bold.

"I don't know," I said, meaning it in more than just a physical sense—I literally had no idea what I needed from this man. I had no idea what he was willing to give me.

"I do, though." He nipped my bottom lip, and I let out a surprised gasp that turned into a moan as he sucked on the sensitive skin. "Just say you need me, and I'll take care of it. Trust me."

Was it even a question? I may have been confused about a lot, but not my desire for Axel—my need. Trust was another matter though.

"I want to trust you," I said as his eyes darkened. "Tell me that you don't want my magic for yourself, Axel. That you don't need it for land. Tell me and I'll believe you."

"All the land over the Darkridge Mountains is mine. Your claim as an heir is not valid or useful here," he said, his tone softening the harsh words. It was exactly what I needed to hear.

Staring into his gaze, searching his expression, I realized...I believed him. Wholly. Which meant there was nothing holding me back, nothing stopping me from fully enjoying this moment and giving into it...

"I need you, Axel."

The air between us crackled and sizzled with tension, and I saw the snap happen—the moment when Axel went from the master of self-control to a man wild and unrestrained. Something I'd never experienced before; something that called to a base part of me.

His hand slid from my chin into my hair and he yanked me forward, hard enough that I gasped—a sound that was completely absorbed by his mouth as he seared his lips to mine. I whimpered as his hand tightened in my hair, heat exploding over every inch of my body. The tether between us, the string of energy that vibrated there, seemed to explode with fire, and I moaned at the sensation of his lips moving against mine. The hand that had been on my hip moved to my ass, where he gripped me so possessively that it caused my legs to open further.

"Those fucking sounds," he groaned. "Those are only for me."

I'd never heard them leave my mouth before, a whimper of need leaving my lips as the world shifted around me and I was suddenly pressed against the couch, my body cushioned by the soft velvet pillows. His massive frame was over me, and my hands greedily explored every hard line of his chest. When he pulled his lips away, disappointment slammed into me.

"Tell me."

"Tell you?" I asked, feeling dizzy with need.

"Tell me that they're *only* for me," he growled.

Of course they were only for him. Even before I remembered our past, I'd never given them to anyone else.

"They are," I whispered. "Only for you."

"Good girl."

A sudden ripping of fabric had me looking down at where he'd torn my shirt, his shadow completely covering my frame as he ran his gaze over my skin. I felt a bit shy about my body, knowing it wasn't nearly as curvy as it had been in my memories, the image not helped by my tightly wrapped ribs and light bruising across my skin.

Luckily, he either didn't notice or didn't care, his need overshadowing his attention to those elements. A pained sound left his lips as he ran a hand over his cock, my attention straying down to where his hard length was pressed right against his pants...

Holy shit, he was huge.

Apparently it was obvious where my focus had gone, because his hand came to my chin as he brought my gaze back to him. "Don't worry, *çiçeğim*—we're in no rush."

"That's not true." I squirmed underneath him. "I need you, Axel. I really need you."

As his lips began to trail down my throat, placing kiss after heated kiss, I felt my frustration grow. I needed attention *everywhere;* my body ached for him. When I tried to roll against him, tightening my legs around his waist, his chuckle was dark and sexy.

"We will not rush this, Evera," he warned, the humor fading away. "Do you understand me? I plan on savoring this. I want you begging for my touch before I give it to you completely. Five decades I have waited for your return. Five decades I have spent every damn night in torment. I am going to enjoy every fucking moment of this."

"Axel." I whimpered as his head dipped once more, his mouth trailing between my breasts. My nipples tightened painfully, begging for his attention. When my hands tightened on his shoulders, my nails digging into his skin, a deep rumble left his throat, making me wonder if I was hurting him.

But he didn't ask me to stop, instead pulling one cup of my bra to the side, exposing my breast. The instant assault of his lips wrapped around the sensitive peak had me nearly climaxing on the spot.

Shit. I was so screwed—his touch was absolutely *everything*.

"Fuck, your skin tastes perfect. You're so damn soft," he rumbled, returning to teasing my nipple before switching to the other. My moans echoed through the room and the throbbing between my legs only grew, the position of him between my thighs finally giving me the friction I needed.

Right when I could feel my climax growing, though, he shifted. I let out a sound of frustration, feeling his smile against my skin. He loved this—he loved that he was working me up so damn much, and it made me both hate and love him.

Wait—love him?

Those thoughts came to a hard stop as I was suddenly flipped onto my stomach. Axel carefully lowered me, his lips brushing over the bandages around my ribs before lifting my hips. I nearly asked what he was doing, but a pillow was wedged underneath me and his rough fingers were tugging my pants over my hips in a second flat.

I turned my head back in surprise as he held my gaze in a challenging way, almost like he thought I would tell him to stop.

"What happened to not rushing?" I teased, loving the way his eyes ran over my ass before he finished bringing my pants to my knees.

A small smack to my ass had my eyes widening as I gasped in surprise. Axel leaned forward and brushed his lips against mine, and I shivered as he whispered, "I have to taste you. Now. Tell me I can do that, Evera."

It was a demand that I absolutely wouldn't think of saying no to.

"Yes."

With a sharp tug, he pulled my panties down before smoothing a hand over my ass. A frustrated sound left me as another smack to my skin had me jolting forward, my nipples brushing against the velvet of the couch teasingly.

Axel's chest produced a sound that didn't sound human as his fingers ran through my wet heat, and when I heard him suck it off his fingers, my head spun. I was so close to coming, the first orgasm I'd have by anything other than my own hand, so when I felt his breath against my center I wanted to beg him to run his tongue against my skin—or to slide himself deep inside of me. Just *something*.

"Fuck," he rumbled, "you taste so damn sweet—"

His words were cut off by the moan that left my lips, his tongue running along the seam of my slit as if he couldn't bear to wait another minute. I whimpered his name as he began to tease and lick the delicate skin, stiffening his tongue and dipping it inside, causing my legs to tremble. When I felt him suctioning his lips around my clit, I knew I was absolutely done for.

The world around me detonated.

My skin turned into fire and my insides molten as pleasure blasted from my clit through every nerve ending of my body, causing spots to form before my eyes. It was the most intense orgasm I'd ever had, and my body was absolutely liquid as I sank into the cushion, my throat hurting from crying out his name.

"Goddamnit," Axel growled, pulling back. I turned to look at him, and my eyes widened at the sight that greeted me. Axel's massive hand was wrapped around his cock, the hard length pointed right at me. My center tightened, wanting him between my legs. It was such an intense urge that I pushed my hips back so that his cock brushed against my wet heat, his eyes flaring so intensely I felt the urge to submit to him.

I didn't understand it, not completely, but I almost wanted to bare my neck to him…

"Fuck—" His voice turned rougher as he came, his seed covering my ass and pussy, my entire body melting at the feel of his hot release against my skin. It felt so primal, and both of us were left breathing roughly as he stared down at me, looking completely unraveled. His crown was thrown aside and his hair was messy, his shirt open and his cock still out and hard. It was so hot I was at a complete loss of what to say or do.

"Axel," I breathed, trying to sit up, but he quickly captured me against the couch, his large frame creating a cage.

"Don't run." He nipped my ear. "I don't trust what I would do."

Axel's fingers ran against my slit as he pumped them into my tight channel, and I shivered at his touch on my sensitive skin. Then he smoothed his fingers over my ass, collecting his cum, and did it again.

"What are you doing?"

"Marking you everywhere, *çiçeğim*." His voice held a lazy

threatening note that somehow turned me on more than it should, causing me to squeeze around him.

"Exactly, just like that," he growled before pulling back and putting himself away.

I laid there, an absolute boneless puddle, as he slowly turned me over and adjusted my clothes. As he lifted me into his arms and carried me from the library, his jacket draped over me, I stared up at him, wondering what the hell we did now.

"I'm the only one naked here," I grumbled as Axel slowly washed my hair before moving onto my body. He massaged each limb carefully and kissed where I was injured, having removed the bandages himself. It wasn't until then that I noticed that my bruises were healing faster than normal. It made me wonder if my magic was acting without me realizing it…or maybe that was just naive hopefulness.

"I'm nearly naked, but I love the disappointment," he murmured, my gaze darting to his boxers in frustration. He was completely focused on his task, and I thought back to what he'd said about waiting five decades for this moment, for what passed between us in the library. I knew it wasn't about my magic, but that still left questions unanswered.

"Axel…" I hesitated as he stood, completely shadowing me in the corner of the shower.

"Yes?"

"Why now? Why after all this time? What's different?"

He smoothed a thumb over my lip in thought, his lack of an answer making me anxious. So naturally, I began rambling.

"Was it the time apart? But you said you went after my parents because of me."

"Correct."

"So if you felt that way before, why...why did you reject me again and again? I don't get it. I threw myself at you, Axel." I crossed my arms over my chest, hugging myself in an effort to soothe the hurt.

His eyes darkened as he brushed his lips against mine. "And resisting you was pure torture."

"I don't get it." I didn't want to be having such a serious conversation, especially in the glow of what had just happened—but I also knew we had to. We couldn't ignore it.

Pulling back, he let out a deep rumble. "The difference is that I'm king now."

"So?" I felt my brow arch.

"That's the difference."

The lightbulb finally went off in my head. "Axel, I *never* cared about any of that. I never cared that you were my guard and I was a princess. I didn't want to be a princess! You knew that. I just wanted *you*."

Something about what I said erased the softness and warmth from his face. His eyes went hard, and his fingers tipped my chin up as he spoke in a hard tone. "I know you didn't care. I cared, though. I cared enough for both of us."

Anger slammed into me. "What the hell is *that* supposed to mean?"

Axel shook his head and stepped out of the shower. Turning off the water, I grabbed a towel and followed him into the bedroom. "I'm serious. What do you mean by that?"

"Doesn't matter," he growled, running a hand through his hair before disappearing into a small side room that I realized was his closet. I watched as he walked out, got dressed for the most part, and slipped on his shoes—all without saying a word. All I could do was just stand there and gape at the sudden change of pace.

"I don't get it—where are you going?"

"I have to handle some shit," he murmured. "Stay here. Promise me."

"I am not promising that."

Axel's eyes flashed with heat. I whimpered as he slammed his lips onto mine and then just…left.

What the—

The door slammed shut, and I let out a groan. Axel had always had a gruff nature, but this was on a different level, more confusing than I'd been prepared for. It was clear that Axel had some misconception of how I felt in the past. I'd been obsessed with him, but somehow he believed that it wasn't enough? That he had to be king before he was 'worthy'? I groaned again, falling back on the bed.

What was I going to do with the man? If things were supposedly different now that he was king, then why did I still feel like there was a wall between us?

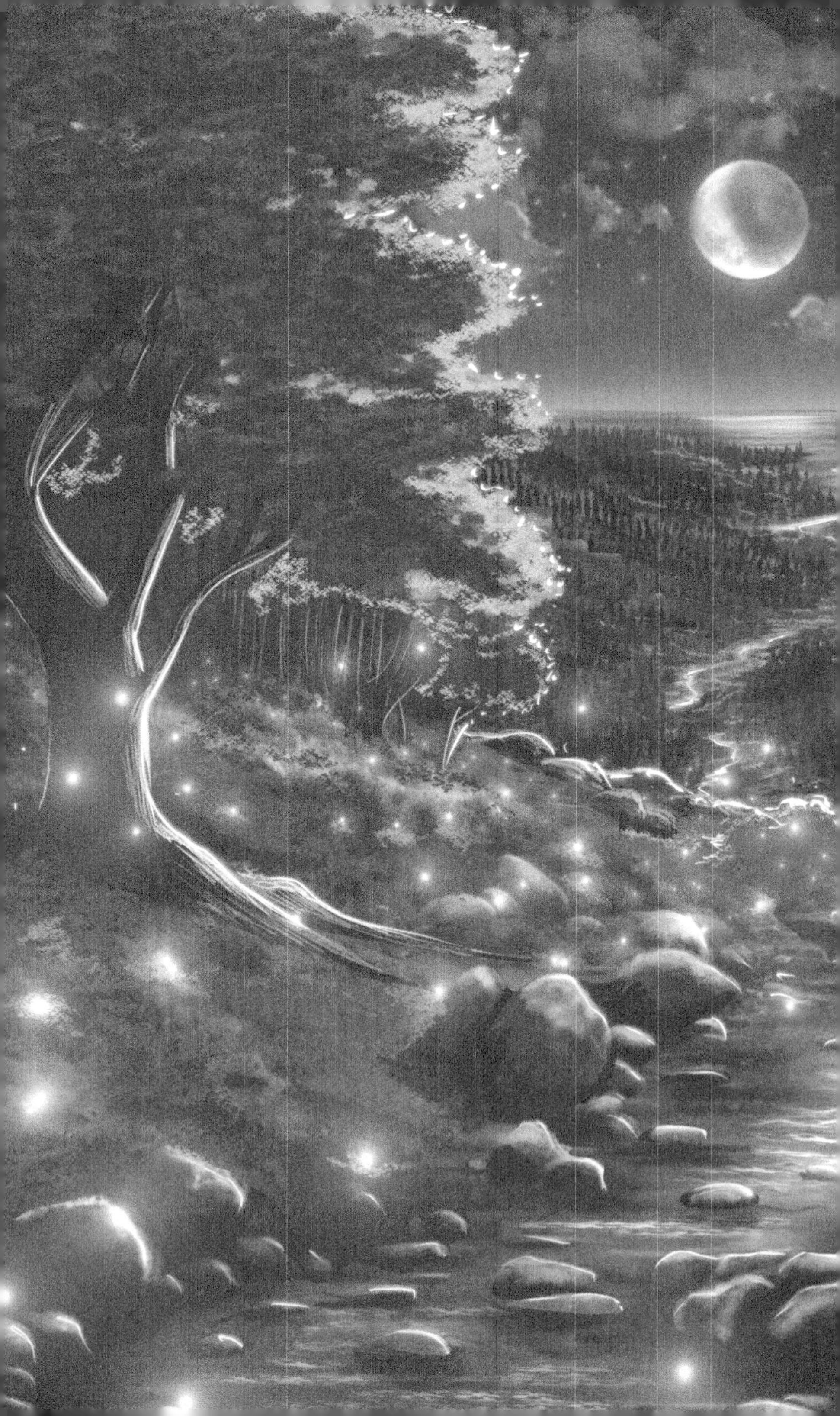

CHAPTER FOURTEEN

EVERA

"Our land has been plagued with darkness, saturated with the blood of innocents—take mine to cleanse it."

Those were the words I had spoken before drinking from Abba's chalice alongside the other seven women bearing witness to the sacred tree's pain and impending death. It was the reason we'd been called here—to save her.

All because of him. King Valandril.

I felt justified in my choice to come—I would willingly sacrifice everything my parents would never give to save our people—even if it meant losing everything I loved. It would be worth it to save those my family was supposed to lead, supposed to protect.

Even though I now understood that this would be the end of the line for me, I felt calm and centered. My only possible regret was that I'd leave Axel behind, though I didn't try to stop myself from thinking about him. If anything, it strengthened my resolve, knowing he would make the same choice. It was the only solution to the disastrous consequences of Valandril's actions.

Snarling and thrashing brought my attention from the roots of the tree to where King Valandril was strapped to the trunk, his *expression monstrous. He'd returned in an attempt to take more from the sacred tree in his unending pursuit of greed.*

I felt no sympathy for the man.

The silence beneath his screams was deafening as all eight heiresses walked forward. Warm, wet soil greeted my feet as I entered the pool surrounding the tree, the eight of us spreading out so that we circled around it. My gaze moved past the man responsible for this, my chest aching for the sacred tree. Its once vibrant, colorful bark and leaves were now a dark grayish blue. Not for much longer, though—we would fix this.

We had *to fix this.*

I stood proudly next to the other women, feeling stronger and braver knowing they would be doing this with me. I may not have met each of them individually, but I could feel the strength they radiated—the complete resolve.

This was what it meant to be a leader. To be part of something bigger than yourself.

Pointing the sharp tip of my blade at the tree, our voices sounded clearly through the night as we chanted in unison.

"BY MY BLOOD, MAKE THEE WHOLE. SEVER THE BONDS, CLAIM HIS SOUL."

Valandril let out a panicked gasp, his skin turning white as snow. He thrashed harder against his bonds, looking like trapped prey.

"BY MY BLOOD, MAKE THEE WHOLE. SEVER THE BONDS, CLAIM HIS SOUL."

Violet mist coiled around the king's hand and filled his palm. The same power was echoed by his queen, Rhodelia, who stood next to me—a dark smile of victory on her face. My eyes widened, realizing just how powerful this woman was, but my head snapped back to Valandril. I wanted to see every ounce of his suffering. It was only fair for all the death he caused—I wanted to bear witness to his punishment.

"BY MY BLOOD, MAKE THEE WHOLE. SEVER THE BONDS, CLAIM HIS SOUL."

Following the others, I brought my blade up and dragged it across my palm before doing the same to the other hand. My wolf howled inside of my chest, trying to break out in an effort to protect me from my own actions. Once the cut was complete, my blade turned to dust, scattering into the pool of water at my feet as the sacred pool began to ripple and pulse with power.

"BY MY BLOOD, MAKE THEE WHOLE. SEVER THE BONDS, CLAIM HIS SOUL."

Grabbing the hands of Stella and Rhodelia, our blood mixed as my body burned with the power of the magic surging through it.

"BY MY BLOOD, MAKE THEE WHOLE. SEVER THE BONDS, CLAIM HIS SOUL."

Blood burst from between our grasped hands and a pained sound left me, my vitality and magic flowing from my veins and to feed the tree, our blood tinting the water of the sacred pool pink.

My blood shifted and shimmered in the water as the shadow of my wolf ran across it like a phantom, followed by others. Tears welled in my eyes at the sight of Axel's wolf, and somehow I knew he could feel my pain. I hoped it wouldn't last for long.

"BY MY BLOOD, MAKE THEE WHOLE. SEVER THE BONDS, CLAIM HIS SOUL."

Our blood hit the trunk of the sacred tree and all at once—it came to life.

The roots rose from the depths of the pool, coiling around Valandril to squeeze him tightly. The sound of his bones snapping filled the air, his bloodcurdling screams accompanied by the roots digging deep under his skin.

"BY MY BLOOD, MAKE THEE WHOLE. SEVER THE BONDS, CLAIM HIS SOUL."

Inhaling sharply, I closed my eyes and drew Axel to the front of my mind for what I knew would be the last time. This was almost the end, and I needed his strength, his memory, to push through the agony that awaited. I wouldn't give up now; we'd almost done it.

"BY MY BLOOD, MAKE THEE WHOLE. SEVER THE BONDS, CLAIM HIS SOUL."

Pain like I'd never experienced before shot through me in agonizing waves, jagged roots shooting up through the water and spearing my hands, digging into my veins. Sharp points tore up my arms as the roots ripped flesh from my body, blood pouring from me as I screamed silently.

"On the night The Veil shall open, Nightmares claim thy sacred tokens," Abba chanted loudly. "But magic stolen comes with a cost, For by His hands blood will be lost. Bound in war, triumph is hopeless, Thy future lies In death and darkness."

I rose into the air as roots tore through the bottom of my feet and through my bone. My body was numb with agony, but I didn't break my hold on the other women's hands. Bright golden light surrounded us as the tree devoured our life force, roots and branches slithering across our skin and cocooning us so that we were one large mass feeding the tree. Water rose around our bodies, and my breath stuttered to a stop as I trembled against the force of it. But my resolve did not falter.

"Yet on the Eve thy battle ends, eight fierce souls will make amends," Abba continued, louder. "Hand in hand they shall unite, A pact in blood, heiress to fight."

The tree was taking back what Valandril stole, draining the life and magic from his soul before swallowing him whole, consumed by the trunk of the tree, until there wasn't even a whisper left of him. Tears of happiness broke through the pain, overpowering it, as the world around us trembled with power. The pure force of the tree affected everything, flashes of color lighting up the sky and its leaves shimmering in shades of red, pink, blue, and purple.

It was beautiful. Absolutely beautiful.

"When gifted power pays sacrifice, Mother Terrea shall repay the price." Abba's voice was strong, and it pushed me to hang on. I could feel my life force fading, and I knew this was the end. This was it.

Axel's howl echoed in my ears and I trembled, wishing I could've seen him just one more time.

"Blessed be her soul reborn, Seek from where the Earth was torn. To bring peace to all lands that burn, In fifty years eight heiresses will return. The lines of fate have been spoken, On the night The Veil shall reopen."

My last breath whooshed out of me, and for just a moment I thought I heard Axel bellow my name. It was the last sound I heard before everything went dark.

I woke in a cold sweat, my heart pumping so hard that it felt like it'd soar out of my chest. I stared wide eyed at the fireplace, crackling away as if I hadn't just been hit with a memory that resurfaced some of the worst pain I'd ever experienced. My nerve endings were alive with acute agony at the feeling of the tree spearing me, its roots delving under my flesh...but none of that was as intensely painful as the moment I arrived at the Sacred Temple and realized what the high priestess was asking of us...when I realized I would never see Axel again.

Even now, tears ran down my cheeks in hot streams, my heart aching painfully for everything I'd lost.

Axel—I needed to see Axel. I needed to make sure I hadn't

imagined that he was within reach, that we were back within the same realm.

My gaze fell on a chair near the bed, empty and cold. Reminded of the way he'd stormed out on my yesterday —*twice*—I resisted the urge to go find him.

But maybe…maybe if I told him about the memory of the sacrifice, it would help. If I explained how I'd felt realizing I would never see him again, that my sacrifice was going to be the end of it all…

Or at least I'd thought so.

Groaning, I shook my head. No. No, I wouldn't do that. I had to maintain some level of pride right now. Pushing that idea from my mind, I slipped out of bed and went towards the bathroom, finding a pile of clothing on the counter along with a note.

Evera,

The closet now has clothing of all kinds in your size. I figured this selection would be the best for wandering around the castle unnoticed.

Vanessa

I smiled at that, feeling like she already knew me so well. I had no idea what would be in that closet, but I wasn't ready for anything crafted from the fine materials that Axel wore. Not only because it was so different from my modern clothing, but because back in Las Vegas, I never would have worn anything so extravagant.

Sorting through the pile of clothes on the counter, I picked out a simple green dress that was made of a cotton material, throwing a sweater over it. I brushed my teeth quickly and washed my face before tying my hair back into a loose braid. Happy with my appearance in the mirror, I pulled on a pair of wool socks along with my boots.

Making my way towards the door, I passed a tray that had been set out on a cart in the living room, the silver domes making me think it was possibly breakfast. That wasn't what fully caught my eye though. No, it was the flowers that were in a vase on top of the tray—a bouquet of white morning glories. I didn't need to wonder who they were from—there was only one man who knew that was my favorite flower, and he'd often gone with me to pick them from a field near the castle in Eventide.

This was why it was so hard to stay mad at this man—he could be so sweet.

As I left Axel's room, taking a moment to eat some of the fruit and pastries left for me on the tray, I greeted the guards good morning and set off. As I passed the windows in the hallway, I realized that I must have slept in, the amount and angle of the light coming in suggesting it was early afternoon. The memory of the dream still hung onto me like a dark shadow, and I didn't even know where I was going until I heard a familiar voice. *Axel.*

Clearly something had led me here to him. Convenient. Or maybe not, since I probably should've been avoiding him.

Stopping outside a set of doors, his rough, deep voice carried into the hallway. "You have no idea what you're talking about."

"I do," Xakery insisted. "The entire kingdom is talking about her."

How much did we want to bet that *her* was me?

"Let them talk," Axel said dismissively.

"With the current state of things, you can't take her as queen," Rhaegal pointed out. "Nor your mate—but you know that."

"You'll have to choose someone else," Xakery concluded. A growl echoed through the room, and I took a step back at the sound of something crashing to the floor.

Choose someone else? And why couldn't he take me as queen or as his mate? Not that he'd mentioned that to me.

"Leave. Now."

"Just remember what I said," Xakery drew out, growing closer to the door. "Your people expect a queen and heirs. She can't do either of those things, Axel. Not now."

The door opened, and Xakery's eyes clashed with mine. A smile pulled onto his lips as my gaze darted to where Axel stood over his desk, head hanging as his younger brother talked to him in low, sharp tones.

"Why hello, Evera," Xakery drawled. "You move so quietly I didn't even realize you were here—listening."

Axel's head snapped up, his expression livid.

"Axel," Rhaegal warned.

"Evera, come here," Axel said quietly.

Xakery's smirk widened, looking downright delighted at the turn of events. "Just remember—he didn't deny it," he said in a quiet whisper before striding down the hall.

My stomach plummeted as I realized he was right. I stood in the doorway, frozen, as Rhaegal moved past me as well, silently and without voicing his opinion on the matter.

"Evera." Axel's voice was softer this time, a complete contrast to the way he was rigidly holding himself in place. It was almost like he was holding himself back.

"I came here to tell you about a dream I remembered—of the sacrifice—and to ask why you never came back," I murmured, rocking back on my heels. "But it's clear that I still don't have a grasp on everything going on here."

His gaze tracked my movement. "What you heard is far more complicated than Xakery would lead you to believe."

"Then explain it, Axel, because you didn't deny that I couldn't be your queen, or more importantly your mate." Axel's jaw tightened as I spoke. "Do you plan on taking another?"

Fated mates were something that couldn't be denied, and I'd always thought that we were...something special. But now that I didn't have magic, I didn't know what to think.

"Absolutely not," he said vehemently. "And neither will you."

I tried to not find his possessive words appealing as I crossed my arms and shrugged. "I mean, if we can't be mates, I don't understand what we're doing—

"Axel!"

My back was suddenly pressed against a wall next to the door, Axel lifting me and slamming his lips against mine. I whimpered, letting out a soft moan as he gripped my hair.

"You're mine, çiçeğim. That's all that matters—no one else is involved in this."

My chin tilted up. "Then what are you hiding?"

His gaze darkened. "It's not a matter of what I'm hiding. Just trust me that nothing else matters—the queen or mate element. We'll figure it out."

Letting out a slow breath, I tried to hide my annoyance. I could tell once again that he truly believed what he was saying, but it didn't make me want to know what he wasn't telling me any less.

"Put me down."

Axel let out a low rumble but let me slide down his body.

"I want to know everything, Axel. I don't expect you to tell me now, but this isn't going to work if you're keeping secrets."

I pulled away from him and turned on my heel, feeling confident in my decision. It stung, though, when he didn't follow me out the door.

A breath of relief filled me as I stepped outside into the fresh air. My guards followed quietly behind me, as usual.

Enough of that.

I turned and walked backwards, examining their neutral expressions—though the younger of the two began looking unsure at my sudden attention on them. "Okay—if you're going to be part of everything and see everything, I should know your names."

The younger man offered a bright smile, completely friendly. "Arthur."

"Nice to meet you, Arthur," I said, returning his smile before looking towards the other man. He scowled at Arthur, making it obvious he didn't consider it professional. "What about you?"

"Balon."

"Well it's wonderful to meet both of you," I offered before turning around, feeling a bit better. I had no idea what was happening with Axel, but maybe I could find some friends here—build normal relationships. Something I hadn't gotten to do as a princess, not that I'd had the time.

My dream of normalcy was dashed, though, when I

turned a corner and found myself on a training field. Everyone froze, their eyes moving towards me in shock before quickly looking away. *Of course.* My very presence made them uncomfortable.

I nearly groaned but simply continued on, trying to brush it off.

"They're just being respectful." Clari walked down the path the opposite way, a woman in uniform standing by her side. Was that her guard, or a friend? The way she offered me a bright smile, I was going to assume the latter.

"Respectful?" I asked, coming to a stop.

"Axel let it be known far and wide who you belong to," she mused. The girl next to her smiled, looking amused by the concept. Despite her uniform, she had a softness to her, her golden hair falling down to her waist and her nails painted a lilac color.

"Maybe he should act like it then," I grumbled.

"Men rarely have an idea what they want, or better yet, *need*," Clari pointed out, her eyes shading dark for a moment before she returned to her bright smile.

I think Axel knew what he wanted, but he wasn't good at telling me—although I was pretty sure she was talking about Rhaegal.

"By the way, this is the Kingdom of Nightfall's Great Prothonotary. She does all the important stuff that no one has the patience for—announcements and treaties and the like."

"Great to meet you. I'm Evera." I offered my hand, and she immediately met it.

"Kathleen. We were actually going to do some light training if you're interested. We'll be mostly shifted, so no need to change."

"I could try," I said, admitting, "I haven't shifted yet since returning."

Clari's eyes darted around as she squeezed my hand. "Keep that quiet for now. Let's do it somewhere more private."

I didn't have an opportunity to ask why, though, before a demanding, powerful voice filled the space.

"Kathleen, what are you doing out here?"

"Goddess," the woman groaned, my gaze darting behind her as a massive man approached.

Unlike her, he looked exactly like he belonged in the military, his jacket covered in medals and pins and his face severe. His dark hair was short, and his bright green eyes were solely focused on her.

"Training, since I'm in the military," she drew out. Turning to me, she said, "Evera, this is Captain Arnoux."

"Nice to meet you," I said. Captain Arnoux offered me a nod in greeting and then literally picked Kathleen up over his shoulder and strode towards the castle. She gave us a small wave before hitting his back and voicing a series of half-hearted complaints that didn't deter him.

"Mates," Clari sighed, shaking her head. "I think she comes out here just to mess with him. She never ends up getting to train, especially when other men are around."

"So you both have mates?" I asked hesitantly. Her gaze darkened, and she shrugged.

"I know Rhaegal is my mate, yes."

"But..."

"A story for another time," she promised. Though she spoke to me, her gaze was narrowed on a spot across the field. Everyone out there was a man, just like she said, except for one group of women. One of whom was staring right at me.

Clari clucked her tongue in annoyance. "Ignore her. Actually, ignore most of these assholes—but particularly Dallina."

"Interesting name," I murmured.

"Not an interesting person. A bully, honestly," Clari said. "Now come on, let's go shif—"

"You must be Evera!"

The minute we turned our backs, Dallina ran up to us, her group of comrades watching with interest. Unlike Dallina, whose cruel gaze regarded me with disdain, the other women seemed friendly—or at least not so immediately judgemental. That was a start, I suppose.

"And you really have no reason to be talking to us," Clari responded dismissively.

"Just figured I'd introduce myself to the individual our king is so captured with." She offered a tight smile, her eyes momentarily narrowed on Clari before moving back to me. "I wanted to invite you to come train with us—we're about to go on a run."

"She doesn't need to train with you. She's far above any of you," Clari said defensively.

"Maybe another time," I offered.

Dallina's expression turned dark. "Will it be another time?" she asked loudly. "Because I heard that the king's mate can't even shift. He waited for you this entire time, and now you don't have any magic to speak of."

My cheeks heated, and I noticed my guards tense. I gave them a small shake of my head, asking them to not intervene, as embarrassment flooded me.

"How is that any of your damn business?" Clari demanded.

"It's everyone's business if the king can't take a mate and produce heirs, especially when there are so many other women who could give him that."

Her jealousy was beyond blatant, and I felt pain in my chest at the idea of Axel mating with anyone else. But I was gathering fairly quickly that all of this was highly dependent on my magic.

"Like I said, I appreciate the offer, but I'm going to go shift and train with Clari." I turned and walked away without waiting for her reaction, Clari admonishing Dallina once more before following me.

"I hate her," Clari growled. "She's mad because she's always wanted Axel."

"She's right, though—I can't shift, and I'm guessing that means I can never be his mate?" Something she had essentially announced to everyone.

"Hey." Clari pulled me to a stop and spoke softly. "You have been back here for two, maybe three days—it will come back to you eventually."

"I hope so," I whispered.

"We'll just train every day until it does. I know that your ability to shift causes complications…but I don't think that's going to change how Axel feels."

Axel said as much, but something would always be missing between us. Despite my limited memories, I could feel the absence of the connection that existed between our wolves. Similar to how I missed the feel of my own magic, I missed the ability for us to connect on that level.

Our kind had fated mates, but until the act of mating and the placement of a mating mark occurred, it was only a connection. It wasn't official, and they could choose someone else to mate with—even if the connection would never be as strong.

As much as I hated it, Dallina made sense. If I had no magic I couldn't be Axel's mate, whether we were fated or not. And any children we had wouldn't be true heirs.

"Why wouldn't he tell me?" I demanded softly.

"Probably doesn't want you worrying about it." Clari shrugged. "Honestly, who the hell knows? Like I said before, men never know what they want or need."

"I just need to clear my head," I said, rubbing my hands over my arms as a chilled wind brushed over me, still feeling insecure.

"How about after training, we go out tonight with Kathleen. A local village, the one she grew up in, is holding a festival. It'll be really fun, and we can worry about all of this tomorrow."

I loved that idea.

"Sure."

Although, the last time I'd gone out for a night, I'd landed myself in a different realm...so who knew what would happen.

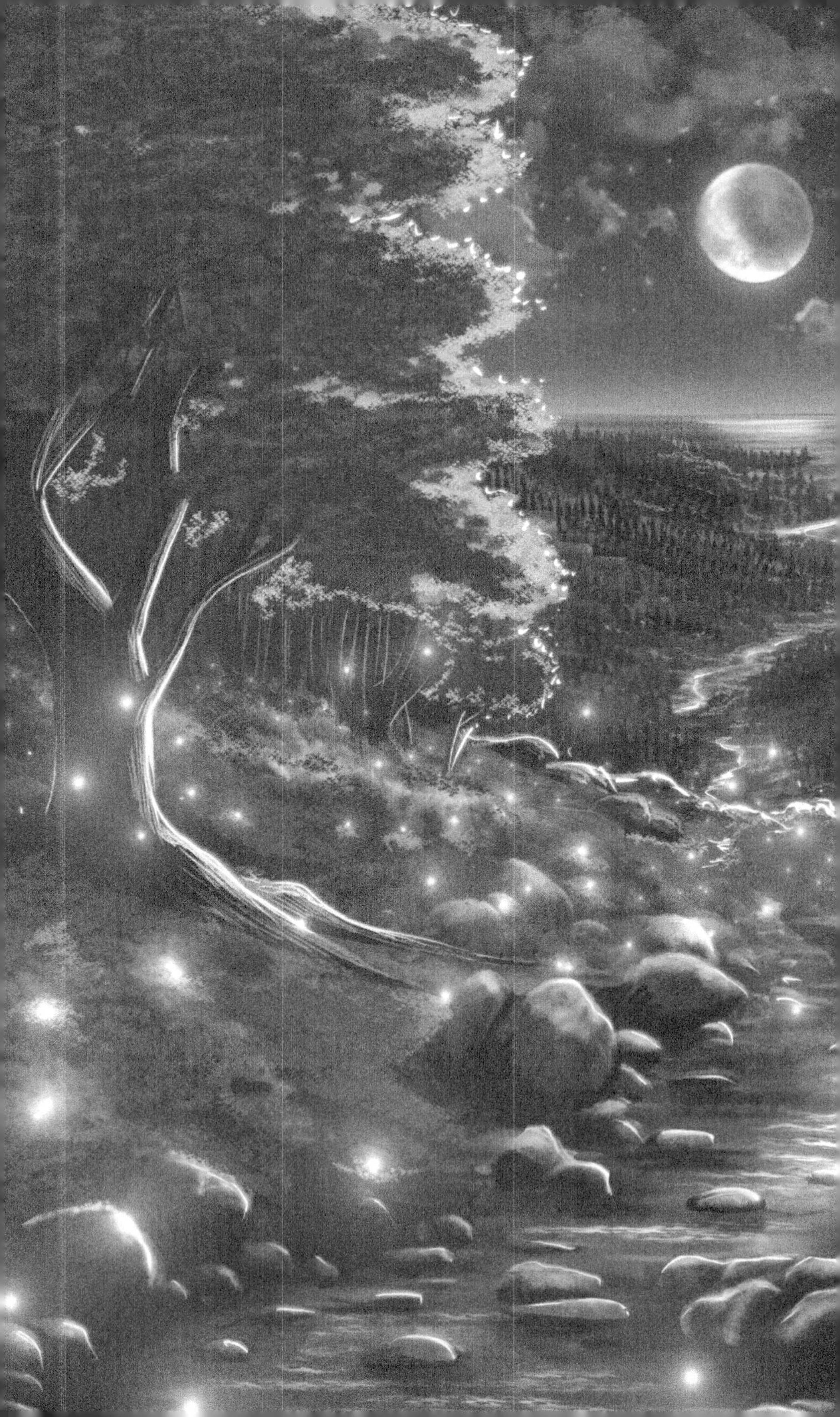

CHAPTER FIFTEEN

AXEL

I hadn't thought it was possible for today to get worse, but I was being proven wrong at every turn. It had been hours since I'd seen Evera, and every second that passed created an anxious void in my chest. I wanted to leave this damn office, but unfortunately I was stuck. I was still the King of Nightfall, which meant I was responsible for addressing every single threat that faced us.

It would be all too easy to ignore them, though, especially after last night. And if Evera's safety also hadn't been in question...well, I would have happily buried my cock between her legs and forgotten about everything for weeks. And with how easily her body had responded to my touch, she may have just let me...if I hadn't fucked it up.

I'd only ripped myself away from her afterwards in the shower because I couldn't bear to admit the reason I hadn't acted sooner in her past life, the truth that she would realize sooner or later: that I simply wasn't good enough for her. I'd returned to the bedroom after she'd fallen into a deep sleep, watching and standing guard over her like I'd done from the moment I first met her. As I watched her peaceful, steady breaths, I realized I needed to tell her why I hadn't done anything before—the full truth. Because after what happened between us, I didn't want any other walls to exist. Nothing to separate us.

Everything about the experience in the library had drawn out a primal and possessive urge that only existed when I was near Evera. I'd wanted everyone to hear her moans throughout the castle, to know that I was the one bringing her that level of pleasure, while also hating that anyone could hear it—wanting those noises to be completely mine. I hadn't hesitated to mark her however I could, even sliding my cum into her after marking her beautiful skin. I should have felt barbaric, and maybe I did, but it also motivated me to end this bullshit more than ever before.

I wanted nothing separating Evera from me—*including her parents.*

Which was what they were doing right now. Rhaegal showed up this morning, before I had a chance to wake her, with the urgent message that we'd received a declaration of war.

Something that Xakery, who'd been waiting for us in the office, didn't give a shit about, instead deciding to once again harp on the topic of Evera's hidden magic. I knew it was hidden; I refused to believe it was gone. I'd almost killed my brother, my silent fury causing him to pale when he'd even suggested the concept of taking another.

Evera was it for me—the only woman I would ever have.

We just had to figure out how to coax her magic out. But I didn't want her stressed about the process, which is why I refused to utter the concern—refused to poison her mind with doubts. All she needed to worry about was adjusting to being back in Vargr and making Nightfall and this castle her home.

There was always something to complicate it, though. Life could never be that easy for us, and this declaration of war was the perfect example.

I stared down at the letter that arrived this morning, the room silent as the council members, Rhaegal, and Captain Arnoux waited for my thoughts on how to move forward.

I didn't have thoughts, though—just a red haze of fury that coated everything like I wanted her parents' blood coating their fallen throne. I had to resist the urge to act immediately.

They wanted to take her from me—they wanted to take *çiçeğim*.

"This has been a long time coming. They're using her as an excuse," Dalziel, one of the oldest council members outside of Marx, pointed out. He paced by the windows, his gaze on the training field below.

The same one that Evera had walked across earlier. My lips almost twitched at the memory of the conflict I'd witnessed and the details her guards had given me after. It didn't surprise me that Evera hadn't risen to Dallina's bait. Dallina was far less tactful than her father, which is probably why he was glaring down at the field with annoyance.

He was a smart man and had realized long ago that I had no interest in marrying his daughter—and therefore never brought it up to me. I appreciated that.

"They want her," Marx argued, looking uncharacteristically serious. "They've waited fifty years. They want their daughter back."

And maybe if they'd treated her kindly—as parents

should treat a daughter—I would consider having peace talks. But they hadn't, so I wouldn't.

"When are they demanding she be returned?" Faybiena asked, her hands folded over her lap as she watched me with speculation. I knew she was waiting for me to do something reactionary, my usual when discussing anything related to the Kingdom of Eventide or Evera.

But I restrained myself, knowing we couldn't afford to fuck this up.

"Two days," I rumbled. "That's not happening."

"Of course not," Jira agreed, her gaze on the letter in my hand. Despite being the youngest of the council members, I trusted her and Marx the most. "We just need to figure out how serious they are."

"Serious," I confirmed. I would've waged war to get Evera back, so their threat of one didn't surprise me in the least. Inhaling, I looked down at the note and made my decision.

"We are *not* returning her. That isn't even in question. Like Dalziel said, we've been expecting a war, and Evera is only an excuse to act. Whether she's the entire reason or only part of it doesn't matter—when she hasn't been returned two days from now, they *will* wage war. Send the courier back with the message that we will not be returning their daughter and *eagerly* anticipate their next action." I smirked and folded the declaration on my desk. "That is my decision."

No one seemed surprised, and all the council members save for Marx left, each with their own assignments on how to enact our plan. Normally Kathleen would have handled crafting the response to the Kingdom of Eventide, but Captain Arnoux had mentioned she wasn't feeling well this afternoon, so I assigned Marx the responsibility instead. I took a seat alongside Rhaegal, the captain, and Marx, leaning back into the chair with a long sigh.

"Well, this is going to be quite the event—Vargr at war once again," Marx said. "I plan on resting tonight; I have a feeling I won't be getting much in the future."

"And I need to find Evera," I murmured to myself in thought. He was right in the sense that we needed to make the most out of tonight, because come morning...

Marx chuckled, interrupting my train of thought. "Yes, but you will not be getting rest, Axel. Neither will the two of you."

"What do you mean?" Captain Arnoux frowned, suddenly on high alert.

"I received word that Evera, Kathleen, and Clari left for one of the nearby villages about two hours ago. I made sure their guards didn't go fetch them—figured you would want to do so."

The room froze as my eyes narrowed on his amused expression. "They're out there alone?"

"You didn't stop them?" Arnoux growled. He stood so abruptly that his chair fell over, striding towards the door. "You didn't even let their fucking guards follow them?"

"Why didn't you stop them?" I asked Marx, Rhaegal standing slowly and moving towards the man. *Shit*. I needed Marx, and as annoying as his fucking actions were, I knew my kingdom was safe for now.

At least I thought it was. Fuck, I needed to go get her.

"That is not my responsibility." He flashed a smile and turned towards Rhaegal. "And you would be smart to not try to kill me—Clari would be very upset."

Rhaegal's gaze narrowed, and Marx chuckled again as he left us. Nodding towards the door, I put my crown on my desk and followed him out. We didn't need to talk about our plan; we were going to go get them and bring them back to the castle.

I knew Evera was confused about everything going on, but I was about to make it extremely simple.

Leaving the castle without fanfare was a lot harder than you would imagine, but having Captain Arnoux with us made a lot of the guards feel better about the concept. Despite being the most terrifying thing in this kingdom, they felt responsible for my safety, and it wasn't something I'd ever purposely tried to quash. I knew it came down to loyalty.

My hood and dark clothing, much like Rhaegal and the captain's, hid me in the shadows as we made our way out of the castle and into the night. Arnoux knew the way to the village, having mentioned it was the one Kathleen had grown up in, so we followed his lead. When we were only about a mile out of the castle boundaries, the forested path grew less dense, revealing a village ahead.

From our distance, I could hear the sound of celebratory cheering, the tune of music, and the scent of food. Fairy lights lit up the night, and I felt a surge of contentment knowing that those living under my rule were able to enjoy themselves like this. I was even glad that Evera was getting to experience it.

I wanted her to fall in love with Nightfall.

What I hated? The idea of her being around men without me—men who didn't realize she was taken. Men who didn't see my mating mark on her neck and assumed she was available. Men who didn't realize she was under my protection—that she was their future queen.

"You're growling," my brother said, his voice flat. As relaxed as he tried to appear, I could tell he was tense—and more than anything, pissed the fuck off. Probably because he and Clari had been going back and forth since she arrived in my kingdom two years ago after having escaped her own problems back in Eventide.

"No shit," I snarled. "My mate is at an event with other men. Unprotected. Unmarked. If she wanted to go to a party, we could've held something at the castle. We're about to wage war—who knows if the courier brought anyone else with him."

It was a consideration that now weighed on me heavily. I knew this hadn't been done with poor intent, but I hated the idea of Evera being out there alone. And while the courier himself was being held comfortably in our dungeon and none of our soldiers had reported seeing anyone traveling with him, it didn't eliminate the possibility of others with ill will in our midst.

"This wouldn't have happened if I hadn't believed Kathleen when she said she was sick," Arnoux grumbled, furious with himself.

"This was Clari's idea," Rhaegal interjected. "I know it. The brat has absolutely no limit. I don't think I can do this anymore."

He said the last part was more to himself, so I didn't comment on it.

"Then just mark her as your mate," Arnoux said simply. I knew he'd marked Kathleen recently, one of his assignments having brought him to a village within castle territory where his mate had been living right under his nose.

"Like it's that simple." Rhaegal shook his head, and I clasped my brother's shoulder in understanding.

As we reached the entrance of the village, my eyes darted around the civilian filled town square as I inhaled, trying to catch her scent. When I did, I moved without holding back, pushing my way through the crowd as people naturally parted for me.

I'd planned on finding Evera, throwing her over my shoulder, and immediately taking her back to the castle, but when we found the women, I stayed rooted to the spot. I found I couldn't interrupt them, not at this moment, because Evera's smile was lighting up the entire damn place. Gold magic seemed to glitter across her skin from the lights above, and her head fell back as she turned, dancing with the other two.

Putting a hand out to stop Rhaegal and Arnoux, we stayed at the edge of the pavilion, my eyes tracking the way Evera moved—the ease and grace, the fluidity. It was perfection, and my wolf rattled inside of me, reaching out for hers.

I swear, for the faintest second I felt her wolf respond, but then the wall she had up collapsed over the connection, making me grunt.

"We should get them," Rhaegal said, his body poised to surge forward to grab his mate—but I didn't remove the physical barrier I had put up.

I knew he was right, but I wanted my girl to enjoy this moment, especially knowing what was coming next. When we woke in the morning, we would be preparing for war with her own damn family.

Right at that moment, a younger group of assholes approached them, and I saw one in particular go straight for Evera. He approached her from behind and went to wrap a hand around her waist, probably thinking he could dance with her, and that was when my patience and tolerance for this laid-back atmosphere ran out. I moved faster than I ever had outside of battle, stopping his hand in an effortless snap, the sound of bones breaking filling the air as the music cut off with a painful screech.

His cry of pain echoed through the square as a sound left my throat that had everyone scattering, my hand going to the back of his jacket and lifting him up so he was choking, trying to grasp for some stability. Evera turned around, wide eyes staring up at me with absolutely no fear, only surprise—her gaze going to the man I was holding before furrowing in confusion.

I had no idea what Arnoux and Rhaegal had done with their mates, but everyone was giving us a clear space, the magic coming off of me making it all too obvious that there was another predator, one far more dangerous than them, in the area. As I looked over the bastard hanging in front of me, my lip drew back in disgust. Either he was drunk or had a death wish.

"Axel…"

"He was trying to touch you," I said simply, the breeze wafting through the clearing surrounding me with her scent as my hood fell back. Instantly, the village square filled with chatter as the man I was holding up paled. Impressive, since the hold I had on his collar was turning him blue.

"I think you should put him down." Evera looked around, nibbling her lip.

I eyed the man once more and spoke in a harsh, rough tone. "You have one chance—one chance before I rip out your throat."

Dropping him, the man scattered away, and I immediately picked Evera up in a bridal hold, sweeping her away from the eyes of everyone there. I briefly heard the captain shout something as the music started back up, but I didn't plan on going far. When we reached a part of the pathway that was darkened by the heavy foliage of the forest surrounding it, I pinned her to a tree, my body holding hers up as her legs tightened around me.

"What are you doing?" she hissed, her eyes darting towards the village as her fingers dug into my shoulders, her sharp nails feeling like claws. I loved the idea of her marking me. I also loved the idea of tearing this dress off. The pale gauzy, material with a slip underneath should have been fucking illegal for her to wear.

I didn't bother wasting the words I would probably fuck up anyway, instead slamming my lips against hers. She let out a small moan that instantly had my cock hardening, and I lifted her up further, pressing my body against hers. I could feel how hot and warm she was, her nipples pressed against the thin material of her dress, and I found myself wanting to get down on my knees to taste the sweet honey between her thighs. The primal demand to possess and mark her, though, had me wanting to do so much more.

"Wait—" She ripped her lips away from mine, and a deep, dangerous noise left my throat.

"Why wait?" I wrapped one of my hands around her throat, keeping the firm grasp that I loved on her, her body subconsciously melting underneath mine. She may have been confused, but her body trusted mine—I could literally feel it.

"We need to talk. We really need to talk, Axel," she

growled, looking frustrated. "If this is going to work between us—"

"There is no *if*," I corrected. "There has never been an *if*. These lips are mine, çiçeğim. Only mine. If they ever even grazed another, I would slaughter the person who thought they could take you from me."

Her eyes dilated as her fingers tightened again on my shoulders, a small noise of concern and something else leaving her throat. I was glad she was understanding that I wasn't fucking around here, but I couldn't help but take it further.

"I will never let you belong to anyone else. It doesn't matter what else existed outside of now—you're here, and you're mine. You better come to terms with that or else I'm going to lock you to me in every fucking way."

I already planned on doing that, but I was more than happy to let her view it as a choice.

Chills ran over her skin, her legs tightening around me once more as she nibbled on her bottom lip. "Except as your mate."

"You are my mate," I told her forcefully, refusing to let her think anything else. "Always have been and always will be."

Immediately I knew I had fucked up because her entire body locked up and the vulnerability on her face gave way to hurt. "You've always known we were mates?"

I nodded sharply, trying to stop myself from saying the words on the tip of my tongue—being mates wasn't the only thing I'd been sure of for some time. Her gorgeous eyes flooded with tears as she put a hand on my chest, trying to push me away.

"Why reject me then? And don't give me some shit about

not being a king—you know I never cared. If I was truly your mate, then you would've wanted to figure it out instead of just letting it be for all those years."

"It was obvious to everyone how I felt—so much so that your own father threatened me, saying that you'd be the one to suffer if I ever did anything, if I ever even talked to you about it. I was okay with living in anguish if it meant you were protected. But then I lost you anyway, because of them, so I spent the last fifty years building an empire and becoming a man that was worthy of you. You are my mate, *çiçeğim*, and that will absolutely never change."

A delicate hope filled her gaze. "And what about now? Why wouldn't you tell me about being your mate? Especially after what your brother said."

My brow dipped as I examined the hurt in her eyes. I had royally fucked this up, and it didn't take a lot of examination to understand why. I was shit at it, but inhaling sharply, I did my best to explain why I struggled with all of this so damn much—not as an excuse as much as wanting her to understand that I would continue to try because I knew it mattered.

"Before I was your guard, it was only my brothers and me. Our parents passed away when we were around one hundred or so, within months of each other. Xakery was the oldest, but somehow I became our leader, and because of that I didn't really have to explain anything to, well...anyone."

"That explains a lot," Evera murmured, and I had to bite back a smile at the slight scowl on her face.

"Right," I continued, "so when I met you and you started asking me a million questions and I found myself wanting to answer them, it threw me for a loop. Still does. It's why I can come off as a bit—"

"Gruff. Broody. Running off on me all the time." There was a small tug playing on her lips that gave me hope that I was managing to handle this just a bit better than before.

"And because I've always wanted to protect you, sometimes it's easier for me to insist that I have something handled and that you don't need to worry about it—"

"Than to explain it," she summarized, her brow dipping. "But Axel, I *need* you to explain it. It's been fifty years. I have lived an entire life without realizing you were here and waiting for me. I need…we need to realize that if we want a future—"

I rumbled at that, hating the idea of 'if' in any context of our future.

"If we want a future," she repeated, hesitating momentarily before continuing, "then we need to focus on the now. Which means talking to me."

I swallowed, pressing my forehead against hers. "And what if you don't like the person I've become, çiçeğim? I have far more blood on my hands than I used to."

"But if you don't show me any of that, I won't even have a chance to fall in love with this version of you."

"Love?"

She made a small embarrassed noise, her cheeks turning pink. "Yes," she whispered.

I nodded, holding her gaze and speaking clearly, "I don't want you worrying about your magic, Evera, because it won't make a difference in what I want between us. I want you as my queen, the mother to our children, and my mate. There has never been another, and there never will be. You will never be some damn—"

"Mistress," she whispered.

"And I know you don't have your magic back yet; I know you can't feel the bond yet... but you are everything, Evera. Fucking everything."

My girl wrapped her arms around my neck and spoke quietly. "But if my magic doesn't come back, we can't form a mate bond. We can't do anything."

"We'll figure it out. We'll figure all of this out—I promise you."

Her gaze filled with so much affection that I nearly groaned, my cock hardening in response as she nodded. "I believe you. I trust you, Axel."

I buried my head against her neck, letting out a deep rumble as I fought the sudden urge to hike up her skirt and pound into her. The need ran like a lightning bolt down my spine, and I had to force myself to pull back, confusion filling her expression.

"What's wrong?"

"Nothing, but if I don't step away, I will pin you to this tree and fuck you in front of everyone."

Her breath caught, her hold on me releasing as she slid down my much larger frame. Her eyes went wide at just how hard I was, and she offered me a small, coy smile.

"Evera..." I warned.

"You said to not run because you don't trust yourself," she drew out.

"Correct." My gaze tracked her as she slipped from my hold and stepped back into the forest, my instincts demanding I pull her back and pin her to the ground. Claim her. Prove to her that we were the only option for mating.

"But I just said I trust you, so I'm running."

Fuck.

She turned and was off, her light footsteps echoing around me. I inhaled, locking onto her scent. Unable to fight the instinct to hunt, I prowled into the woods, completely set on catching my prey. And when I did...

I wasn't holding anything back.

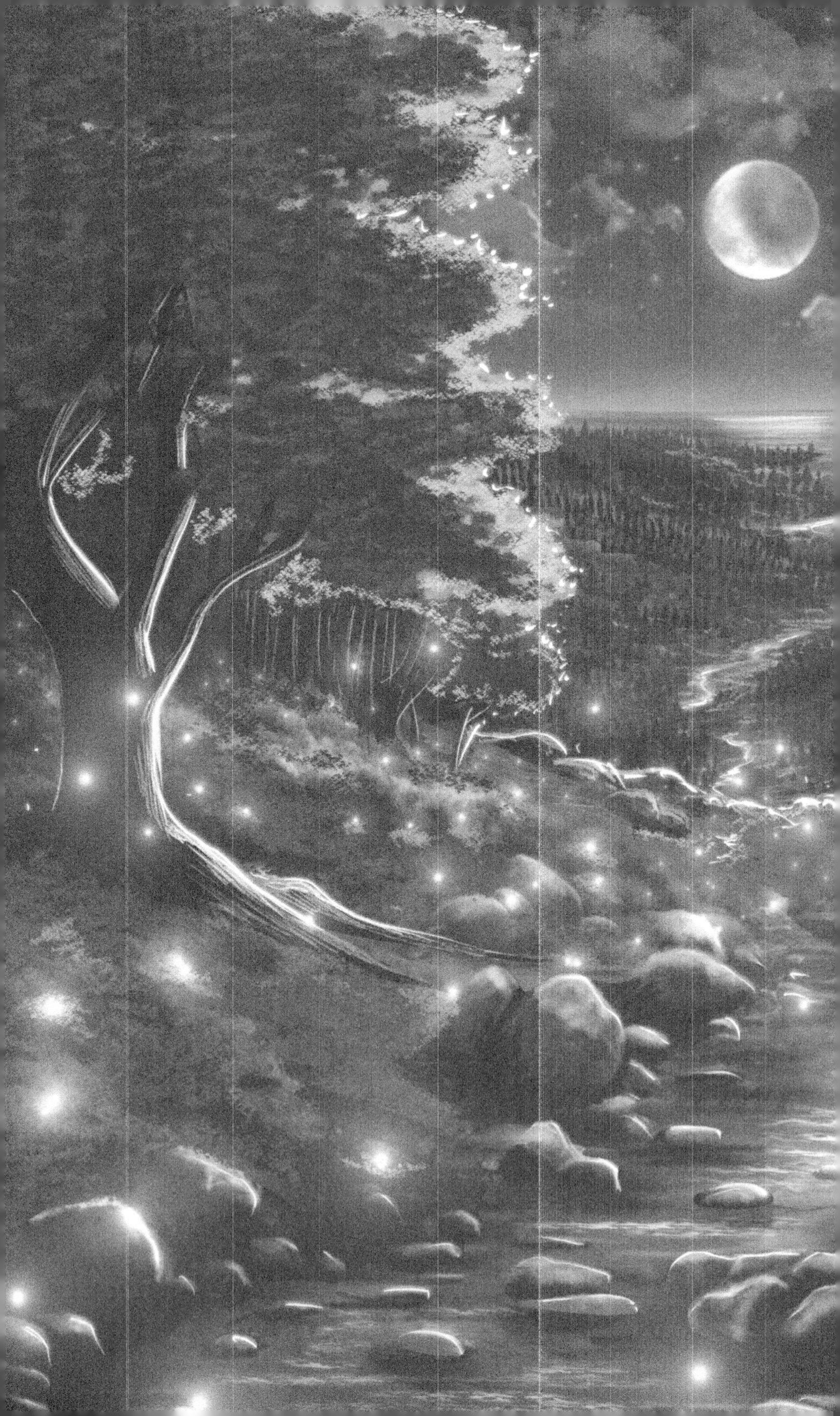

CHAPTER SIXTEEN

EVERA

A dangerous thrill ran up my spine as I sprinted through the forest that spanned for miles off the path in all directions. Adrenaline coursed through me as my muscles worked to swiftly move my frame as quietly as possible, my heart thudding in my ears.

The light of the moons couldn't break through the foliage above, so I was practically running in complete darkness, and when a howl vibrated loudly, a chill rolled over my skin. Desire crashed into me as something shifted deep inside of me, causing my body to break into a flush of heat.

I kept pushing through, my teasing nature giving way to something much more base as I found myself wanting to be truly hunted—to be truly caught. I'd always wanted that from him. I'd run from him time and time again when he was my guard, and this time I needed him to catch me.

When I felt like I finally had run far enough, I paused for a minute, taking a deep breath in. After I caught my breath, I realized that my ribs no longer hurt. In fact, I felt nearly healed. How was that possible?

I didn't have a moment to think before he was practically upon me.

"You can't hide from me, Evera."

Oh shit. Turning and hiding against the back of a tree, I inhaled and tried to slow my breathing, the soft snapping of breaking branches drawing closer.

Almost like a tangible shadow, I felt his magic rush out to greet me. The heat wave of desire only expanded, my legs pressing together at the need pushing over every nerve ending in my body, lighting me up.

I needed to keep running. Lunging forward, I decided to risk it—

Two large arms caught me, and I let out a small scream. Axel's scent invaded my senses as his grip on my throat tightened, the other arm slung across my abdomen. In a singular second, I was pinned to the ground with his massive frame over me, his eyes absolutely wild and filled with a raw, burning heat.

"That didn't count," I whispered, my breathing erratic as his fingers on my hips moved up my dress and, with all the ease in the world, snapped each strap. I squirmed against him, one hand still holding me to the ground as he moved his gaze over my frame. He tugged down the gauzy material of my dress, my breasts on full display for him.

A guttural sound left his throat, and I nearly shot off as his lips wrapped around my hard nipple, the other hand teasing its counterpart. My legs spread automatically to allow more space for his frame as a whimper slipped from my mouth.

"Fuck, I can smell how wet you are from here," he growled. "Do you like running from me, çiçeğim?"

"I like you catching me," I admitted on a gasp as both of

his hands moved to my hips and pushed up my dress, the material snagging and ripping on the branches around us. I flushed as his eyes ran over me before looking up at me with a narrowed gaze.

"No panties?"

"None." My breath caught as an objectively terrifying sound left his chest, one that had my heartbeat pounding in my ears and should have had me running. Instead I nearly climaxed under his touch as his fingers ran over my wet heat. My pussy was absolutely drenched, and I couldn't help the moan that left my throat as he tortuously teased me.

"That deserves a punishment," he warned, leaning down and nipping my lip. I pressed my hips up, hoping for more friction, but he only removed his hand, a dark smirk appearing at the sound of frustration that left me.

When his head dipped down and he buried his mouth against my center, I climaxed immediately, the pleasure nearly blinding me as I jolted against him. His hands tightened on my hips as if I was trying to escape, and my fingers dug into the dirt underneath me as he began to truly devour me.

The pleasure was so intense and his attention to my clit almost painful, my body so extremely responsive that I found myself begging, "*Please*, Axel—."

"What do you need, Evera?"

"You. I need all of you."

Axel didn't hesitate, pulling back and shrugging off his jacket. My gaze ran over the way his shirt clung to him, his arms flexing as he undid his pants and ran a hand over his covered cock. Trying to sit up and reach for him had Axel moving so fast the breath whooshed out of me as I found myself once again pinned underneath him.

"I didn't say you could move," he growled, his lips moving down my throat and nipping the delicate skin. When he sat back again and released his cock, my eyes greedily took in every inch of it—and him—as he began to stroke himself.

"Going to mark you again," he said, his fingers sliding over my pussy as he pushed my legs apart so that I was completely bare to him.

"Inside of me," I whispered. His eyes snapped to mine, an inferno dancing there.

"Say it again. Where do you want me to mark you? Where do you want my cum?"

"Inside of me," I whimpered. "Please, Axel."

"Good girl," he growled, leaning down to brush his lips against mine. I was so enraptured by the kiss that I could only moan when his cock ran against my slit.

Without warning, Axel punched his hips forward, impaling me with half his length at once. I let out a small surprised scream against his lips, a sharp twinge of pain radiating through me. My fingers dug into his muscular arms, which formed a cage around me. A deep, guttural sound left his throat as he pulled back from our kiss and pressed his forehead to mine.

"I know, *çiçeğim*, I know it hurts—you saved yourself for me, didn't you? Just like in your last life. Even though you didn't know it, your body realized it was waiting for me—that it belonged to me." He kissed the few tears running down my cheeks as I nodded, gasping at just how large and thick he was.

"You're already taking so much of me," he growled, running a thumb over my clit and circling it. I tightened around him as my skin broke out into a pleasurable flush. Any residual pain was soon replaced with pleasure as he began to slowly pump in and out, causing my body to loosen. My muscles relaxed as he wrapped a hand around my throat, keeping me pinned to the ground. It was so intense, and when I let out a moan, letting my legs fall open wider, a savage sound left him as he sank the rest of the way inside of me.

"You're so big," I gasped, wanting him to move. *Needing* him to move. "Axel, I need you to move more—please."

"Fuck," he growled, pulling back and pushing back in, the sight of him sliding in and out of me completely mesmerizing. "You are so fucking tight, but you're taking every inch of me. Of course you are—you were fucking made for me."

"More," I urged, tilting my hips up so that he could slide completely inside of me with each pump, a hiss leaving his lips.

"I'm trying to not hurt you."

"I trust you," I reminded him breathlessly and then whimpered as I saw the darkness roll over him, an intense, almost painful dominant surge of magic infecting every part of him. His hand tightened on my throat, and I got exactly what I asked for as his pace suddenly turned demanding and hard.

There was a lethal strength to him, and the way he moved was so deep and intense that I felt like I was being completely drilled into the ground while merging into one with him. He was completely in control, and it allowed me to let go, a sense of pure euphoria filling me. It wasn't the only thing that would be filling me soon, though.

I could practically feel his cock swelling larger inside of me, and I locked my legs around him, loving the sensation of being so connected. I whimpered as he slammed into me again and again, and out of nowhere, an orgasm blasted over me, sending me reeling.

"That's right, milk my cock, çiçeğim. Fuck—"

Axel buried himself inside of me as I felt him explode, a gasp leaving my lips at the pressure building in my abdomen as he seared our lips together. I squeezed around him, and another wave of pleasure rolled over me, causing me to shudder with relief. Tears welled in my eyes once again, feeling so incredibly connected—so incredibly *right*.

"Axel," I whispered as he kissed up my cheek and brushed his lips against my nose.

He was still hard, and he pushed into me again in small movements, his cock pulsing as he let out a deep groan filled with masculine satisfaction. I felt intensely proud that I'd been the one to pull that sound from him.

"Goddamnit," he murmured. "I'm going to spend every day and night buried between these legs. You are so fucking perfect."

I kissed him softly as he pulled out, causing me to wince, and I fought the urge to whisper words that would have made this moment complete. I held back only because he pulled away and instantly wrapped me in his coat before picking me up. Resting my head against his chest, I squeezed my legs together, still feeling him deep inside of me—something I knew wouldn't go away anytime soon.

An hour later I was submerged deep in a tub with Axel against my back, my eyes closed as my head lolled against his muscles. His fingers ran over my skin in a mesmerizing pattern, and the silence between us was perfect, my brain a million miles away. My body was sore in the best possible way, and the only thing I regretted about tonight was not saying goodbye to my friends.

I'm sure they would understand though. We all knew what we were doing when we went out.

"We could have had this for years." His lips brushed against my ear. "I was stupid."

"Not stupid, trying to protect me." I tilted my head back. "Thank you, Axel."

A rumble left his throat as he turned me gently so I was straddling him. "Maybe someone should have been protecting you from me, çiçeğim."

"What do you mean?"

"I mean that the shit I did in the name of protecting you should have earned me the death penalty and a public execution. It was the only thing I had at the time—that and the fact that it was my literal job to keep you safe. It gave me some fucking purpose."

"What did you do?" I asked, nibbling my lip. His eyes narrowed on me.

"You look far too intrigued by this." He ran a hand through my hair and tilted my head back.

"I was obsessed with you, Axel. Hearing that I wasn't alone in it makes me feel less pathetic," I admitted. His eyes filled with understanding as he brushed his nose against mine.

"You are anything but pathetic, Evera. To begin with, I watched you sleep every single night," he drew out, his hand drifting to my waist.

"I know," I teased.

"From next to you in bed," he added. My eyes widened. "I also kissed you goodnight, more than once."

"We had our first kiss and I didn't even know about it? What the hell, Axel?"

"That's the part you're mad about?" He chuckled, the flash of humor making him look younger and more carefree than I was used to. "And yes, çiçeğim, without you knowing—because brushing my lips against yours in passing is not the same thing as truly kissing you. I knew I wouldn't be able to hold back if you kissed me; I would have pinned you down and taken you right there and then…"

Axel shook his head as if trying to clear that thought.

"What else?"

His gaze turned dark. "I took care of anyone that bothered you—permanently."

"Like, how did you take care of them? Like…sleeping with the fishes?" I arched a brow as he offered me a confused look.

"Earth thing—doesn't matter." I brushed past my analogy. "You killed them?" Why didn't that bother me as much as it should have?

Axel offered me a knowing look but just shrugged.

"Anything else?" I bit down on my lip.

"Much more, but nothing I'm willing to tell you. I like how you look at me; I don't want that to change."

"You just freakin' told me that you killed someone! How much crazier could it get?!"

"Multiple someones," he murmured, "and crazier. Trust me on that."

"Tell me one day, then?" I asked.

His smile grew. "Maybe."

"Maybe?" I kissed him quickly. "Well then maybe you won't get anymore kisses—"

Axel's hand came up to my jaw and he kissed me hard,

not allowing me to escape. "That's not your choice anymore, Evera. I told you that you're mine. Besides, I will tell you... just after I've locked you to me in every way possible and you can't leave."

Once again, not nearly as upsetting as it probably should have been.

A knock on the door had Axel frowning, and he motioned for me to sink further into the water and bubbles as Vanessa's voice sounded from behind the door. "I don't want to bother either of you, but the captain needs to speak to you immediately."

Axel tensed. "Tell him to give me thirty."

When he turned back towards me, his face was soft, but I could see something was bothering him. "What's wrong?"

"I don't know," he murmured. "Something must have changed."

"What?"

He shook his head and pressed his forehead against mine. "Something to worry about tomorrow."

"You have a lot to worry about, I feel like." I ran my hands over his shoulder. "I want to help you, Axel. I love what you've built here. It's so different from anything in my parents' kingdom."

"I built it so that you would love it," he admitted. "I knew you wouldn't be happy with how they ruled, so I made damn sure Nightfall would look nothing like Eventide. I didn't want you to have any reason to leave."

"I have no reason to leave—especially if you're here."

"I love the sound of that," he rumbled.

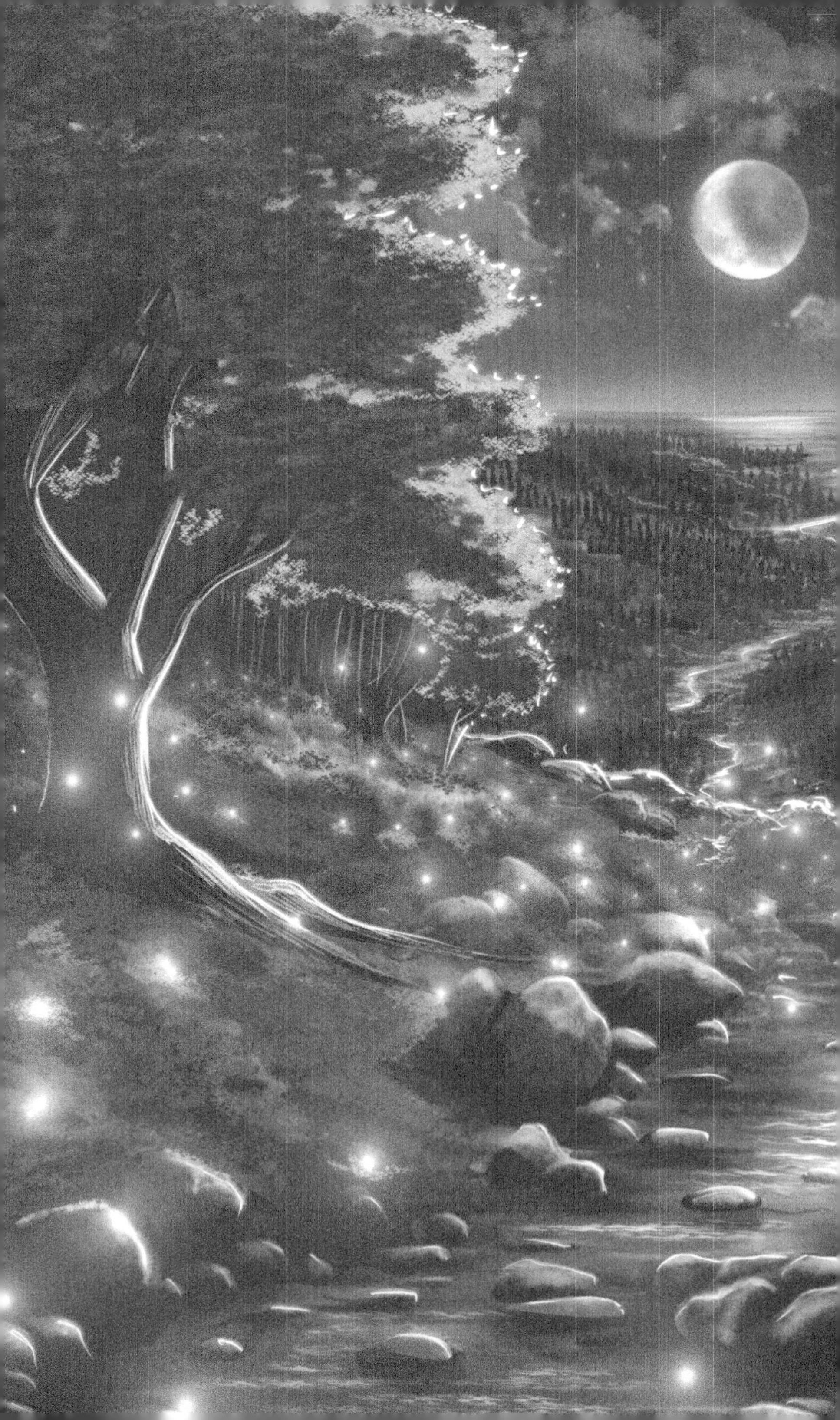

CHAPTER SEVENTEEN

EVERA

"If you keep frowning like that, your face will get stuck," Kathleen pointed out, lounging comfortably on one of the velvet couches in the library, a large text flipped open in her lap. Unlike myself, she seemed the epitome of relaxed, down to her robe, slippers, and her attempt at making light of a situation that was anything but.

Clari made a frustrated noise but didn't comment, her anger practically palpable from where I stood across the room. There was a large book of maps laid out on a nearby table, and the way she was flipping through it so aggressively was honestly a bit scary—so I wasn't surprised she didn't put words to her thoughts. After all, with how long we'd been in here—what else was left to say about the situation?

Apparently, my brain disagreed.

My gaze darted towards the long, thin windows of the library, showcasing the setting sun, and I let out a small snarl of anger. "Forty-eight hours—*two days* that we've been trapped in here. This is ridiculous!"

It wasn't often that I got angry, but it had been building and was now at the point of bubbling over.

"Held prisoner in our own home," Clari spit out, her gaze narrowing on the door. "There will be hell to pay after this."

I would've felt bad for Rhaegal if I wasn't so pissed at Axel.

Although, even I had to admit that this was far from a typical prison. Caz and Vanessa ensured that the space was set up comfortably and that we had everything we needed—except for the freedom and ability to actually leave this damn room.

They seemed to have no problem coming and going as they pleased, though.

After having fallen asleep in Axel's arms completely content and sated, I woke up yesterday morning to not only find myself in a different bed, but with only Clari and Kathleen to keep me company. Apparently, the kingdom was facing a threat so great—not that we'd been clued into said threat—that Axel, Rhaegal, and Arnoux had thought it a good idea to lock the three of us in the library, turning it into a makeshift safe room.

The hallway outside was so heavily guarded that any attempt to escape would fail spectacularly. We would know, since Clari had tried twice now.

All of it felt absolutely ridiculous, and I wouldn't lie—I felt betrayed.

Not because of our imprisonment, but because Axel didn't even extend the courtesy of telling me his reasoning himself—*especially* after the conversation we had about communication. *Instead* he'd left the three of us in the dark, with only the small library windows to give us hints of what was happening outside. Although, considering the amount of soldiers being deployed out of the palace—as well as those guarding the walls—it wasn't difficult to assume.

There was only one major threat in Vargr that would cause him to worry like this—to go to this extreme.

Looking towards the three makeshift beds that had been set up in here, I scowled. No amount of fur blankets, oriental rugs, or soft luxuries could make up for what was going on here.

I sighed and threw myself down on my cot, my dark dress ballooning out around me. How could I be both so damn frustrated and yet miss him so much?

"Think about the positives." Kathleen closed the book on her lap and sat up straight. "You've finally had the time to refresh your knowledge on everything regarding Vargr—that's something you probably wouldn't have had time to do if Axel was around."

"That's easy for you to say," Clari said. "You're used to the captain acting like this, all overprotective. But Rhaegal knows better than to pull this shit."

"Well, that should show you how worried he is," Kathleen pointed out.

She wasn't wrong on either count, but I didn't have to like it.

Despite my memories slowly returning, there was a vast array of topics that I didn't have time to remember naturally—especially if we were facing a threat. So I'd buried myself in books, occupying the long hours by spending the majority of yesterday reviewing elements of our society that were buried somewhere in my subconscious.

One stood out to me for obvious reasons: that the goddess blessed the wolf shifters of Vargr with fated mates. It wasn't something that was made known until you and the other individual were in their early twenties, differing for each person, but then it was extremely obvious.

Clearly not obvious enough for me, though.

I had *thought* Axel and I were mates in my past life, but his consistent rejection of my advances had me second-guessing at the time. There was a small bit of pride associated with knowing I'd been right all along, even though I didn't have access to my magic right now to confirm it.

It was something I would have loved to talk to Axel about...if he were here.

Mates weren't the only focus of my studies, though. No, without my magic, there were far too many questions I had about wolf shifters in general, bits of knowledge that I would have remembered or known instinctively if my magic was present. Luckily, this library contained answers to all of it.

While I didn't have the memories to confirm, our first shifts apparently happened around puberty and were normally due to the moons' heavy pull and influence on us. The greater the lunar cycle—the full moons being the most powerful—the more likely a young shifter would react. It was only after time and practice that you learned to control it. I couldn't remember how powerful I'd been or the control I'd had in my past life, but I really hoped I'd taken the time to practice—especially with how clearly powerful Axel was.

Something that was confirmed as I'd run my fingers over illustration after illustration of our species' mid-shifted form. It was a form that only the most powerful of our kind had, resembling that of a werewolf in modern movies.

As a true heir, I should have had access to that form as well...but that never showed itself in my memories. Instead, I was limited to my fully shifted form that resembled a wolf that you would find in the wild except much larger. I remembered the flashes of pain associated with shifting, especially when I was younger, and the hunger that came with hunting, the sensations slowly trickling into my thoughts and filling me with hope that maybe, just maybe, I would get a chance to feel that way again.

The pain paled in comparison to the sheer amount of power and magic surging through you, and I craved to feel that way again.

As I dove deeper and deeper into the history of our land, I learned of an old lineage, a kingdom older than my parents', that had the added ability of extending their magic out like a shadow self, allowing you insights into the world around you outside of your already heightened senses as a wolf shifter. It was fascinating to learn about, and the dark magic that floated around the illustration was so different from the golden magic I'd seen at the sacrifice.

It didn't appear more powerful, per se, just darker.

Unfortunately, despite every piece of knowledge I devoured, at the end of the day it was all for nothing—information that didn't do me a lot of good since I still *felt* nothing. I kept trying to reach for the sensation I'd felt when I'd first arrived in Vargr, and then again in the river, but it was just gone...or trapped behind the same wall as my memories, at least.

I'd even tried shifting, but the best I accomplished was creating flashes of power under my skin, but those could have easily been my brain remembering what I was supposed to be feeling rather than me actually feeling anything. Never even a whisper of my wolf. It was enough to drive me crazy, and I found myself searching long into the night, rooting through my brain and body for anything, the smallest hint of my wolf's essence...only to end up disappointed.

When I'd talked to the girls about it, they floated the idea that my magic was hiding because it recognized the threat my parents posed when I'd arrived in the Kingdom of Eventide. It wasn't a crazy thought, but it didn't answer the question of how to get it to come out.

Once again, I would have loved to talk to Axel about it, but...

"Evera?" Clari pulled me back into the conversation, making me realize I'd been just staring up at the ceiling, trapped in thought.

"I'm just frustrated," I admitted. "If this is about my parents—if they are the threat out there—then I should be part of the response. Axel should have at least talked to me about it!"

I mean *seriously*, I understood that he was working on his communication, but this was a perfect example of the problem! I had no doubt that he'd worked it out in his head that he was doing all of this to protect me, but I refused to just stay locked up in a tower awaiting my fate. I wasn't...I wasn't that girl anymore.

Maybe that was the true problem. Axel and I had both changed in our time apart, and while it wasn't a bad thing, it would take time to get used to. I was no longer a princess with her head in the sand, blindly relying on her guard to take care of her, and Axel was no longer a mere guard—he had the weight of an entire kingdom on his shoulders.

I wanted him to trust in me, to view me as his partner and not just someone to take care of...as much as I did love that. That wasn't how a healthy relationship worked—well, at least I didn't think it did.

"Unless they aren't willing to talk and instead are calling for violence. Without your wolf, you wouldn't be able to fight," Kathleen said with a small smile, trying to soften the hurt her words caused. She was right once again, but I didn't like feeling useless.

"I don't agree," Clari argued. "Evera is smart; they could have easily found a way for her to contribute, even if not on the battlefield. All of us could have. They should've trusted us to help, to deal with this together."

"Like I said—bullshit."

That would have been ideal. I groaned and rolled over, burying my head in the sheets as a much darker thought went through my head. What if Axel didn't want this anymore? Didn't want *me* anymore? What if that night had been him simply getting me out of his system and now he was using whatever threat we were facing as a way to avoid me? I mean, unless he was away from the castle, what was stopping him from coming in here?

It was a ridiculous thought, heavily lined with my own insecurity, but the timing hadn't been great, and it was causing a chaotic storm of sad and angry emotions to whirl around my head as hours ticked by.

When the heavy doors of the library opened, I rolled onto my back and sat up, then immediately wanted to lay back down and roll over again. Xakery had come to pay us a visit. The hallway behind him was filled with guards, even more than before, and I nearly growled as the doors slammed shut, trapping us with him.

I probably should have used the moment as a chance to try to escape, but if Clari had failed at pushing through them with her magically heightened strength, what were the chances of me being able to get through?

"Ladies." Xakery offered a tight smile, looking over the three of us. "How are we doing this evening?"

"We'd be far better if we weren't trapped in here," I said immediately, hoping that maybe he'd come here to tell us we could leave—but I knew that probably wasn't the case.

"Well, I'm sure it's all in an effort to keep the three of you safe"—Xakery paused while pouring himself a drink from a bar cart and turning towards us once again—"now that war has officially been declared on the Kingdom of Nightfall."

By my parents, no doubt. I shook my head and looked down at my tangled fingers.

"By Eventide?" Kathleen demanded, her soft demeanor disappearing. I often forgot that she was in the military herself, but I shouldn't have. She was extremely rational and probably fit in perfectly, especially when it came to logistics.

"Yes." Xakery sat down in a large armchair as I stood and made my way over, sitting on the couch across from Kathleen.

"Why wouldn't he tell me?" I asked, hurt. I was talking to myself more than anything, so I was surprised when Xakery answered.

"For one, he's not here. At least not anymore. But considering he found out the night before you were all locked in here…well, I would have to say that *maybe* he doesn't trust you. After all, you *are* their daughter."

"I have no loyalty to them," I growled. Axel knew that.

"You're so screwed," Clari pointed out, crossing her arms and suddenly looking amused. "You're going to get booted out of the kingdom for saying shit like that to her."

"Why?" He arched a brow, looking unconcerned.

"You know they're mates," Kathleen sighed, annoyed. I

stayed quiet, not sure what to say in this situation since I wasn't feeling all that sure myself.

"Oh! Do we have confirmation that you two are mates?" Xakery asked curiously, looking me over. "I know you've mated in the human sense...but I don't see a mating mark."

He was an arrogant and patronizing bastard. Unfortunately, he was also right.

"My magic still isn't present," I said evenly.

"Interesting." Xakery took a long drink before adding, "Can I ask you something, Evera?"

"No," Clari answered for me as I sighed and nodded, knowing he would do it anyway.

"Why didn't he at least try to form the bond or place a mating mark? I mean, it could've released your magic and solved all of this, but I'm guessing he didn't even try."

My lack of an answer had him nodding.

"I just think it's odd that Axel never made a move in your past life, and now, despite his claims, he's yet to try to even form the bond. And you can't tell if his claims are valid because of your lack of magic, so instead you're just left to... wait? Is that right?"

Unease churned in my gut, my lips pressed together because I didn't know what to say. He was voicing all of my insecurities aloud, because I had no idea why Axel hadn't tried that.

"And what do you think is going on, Xakery?" Kathleen asked, her face filled with distaste. "Since you seem to know everything."

"Me? Well, if it were me, I'd be careful that he isn't using you to increase his power. Axel has been looking for an excuse to rid this land of his only true rival. Would it be all that shocking if he were using you to further that purpose?"

"Fuck off," Clari snarled. "You're a fucking idiot if you think Axel is anything but obsessed with her. You're just trying to cause problems."

And put doubt in my head. Sadly, it was working.

"Listen, I'm not saying Axel doesn't feel something for her, but is it everything? I'd just be worried that he's keeping you as a toy and a hostage to display for your parents." He made a show of looking around the room, casting a significant glance at the closed door. "This is a bit like a prison, isn't it? It could be protective, but I also wouldn't put it past him to use it as a power move. In the time that you've been away, Evera, he hasn't only been focused on you. His first focus is this kingdom and how to improve its future. That's all I'm saying."

The girls didn't say anything, and as I took in his expression, I realized it was possible that he truly believed what he was saying.

Shit.

"He said he wouldn't take another as his queen or mate," I said in a fragile attempt to protect my feelings.

"Oh, I would believe that—I mean, you *can* still produce heirs without being his mate or queen... They wouldn't be true heirs, but if the man doesn't ever want to give up power, that wouldn't be a negative in his eyes. He'd get the best of everything."

It had, of course, crossed my mind that we hadn't used protection, that there was nothing stopping that from happening, but I hadn't truly thought through the implications. I mean, he'd literally said he wanted me to be the *mother of his children*. God, talk about a delayed reaction in terms of worrying about that now.

How did I even feel about the idea of being pregnant? Let alone with Axel's children...

I stopped those thoughts immediately, my body making it all too clear how I felt about it.

Xakery stood and shrugged, setting his glass down. "Maybe it's better for you to live in ignorance? I suppose that's for you to decide. I just came here to deliver my thoughts and to let you know that Axel, along with Rhaegal and Arnoux, are at the Midnight Keep. There's a meeting going on with your parents in an attempt to negotiate terms for this war...to negotiate your future, Evera. Yet here you are, locked away."

He walked to the door and turned one last time, looking right at me. "Listen, you can ignore everything I've just told you, or you could walk out of here—something you've been able to do this entire time."

"But the guards," I managed to get out, my throat tight with emotion.

"Have been ordered to not touch you, so how will they stop you?"

Interesting. I mean, my own guards had followed my orders before without question...maybe it really was that easy to get out of here.

"Clearly the same rules don't apply to me," Clari snarled.

"Oh, I'm sure they do, but the king's brother isn't as scary as the king," Xakery said with a bitter expression.

"Why do you care? About any of this," I asked, standing up.

"Honestly? Because I don't think Axel realizes what your parents are capable of. What they would do to retain power. I have a lot of issues with him, but he's still my brother, and right now he's being blinded by either his thirst for power...

or possibly his instinct to protect you. I'm not sure. But I think there's only one person who could have real negotiating power at that meeting, and it's you."

The doors shut, leaving us in silence. I inhaled sharply and ran a hand through my hair.

"He's such an ass," Clari scowled.

"Even so...he's not wrong about the meeting. I should be there."

"Then let's go," Clari agreed, standing and pulling our shoes and cloaks from the wardrobe. "We should be there, and I refuse to be a sitting duck. Your parents are the reason I had to leave my home to begin with—I won't let them take this one from me as well."

"My parents? That was why you had to leave Eventide?" I began to pull on my boots, realizing I'd have to walk to the Midnight Keep wearing a dress and cloak...but it wasn't like I had many options in this damn library, and something told me that I didn't have time to go up to my room to change. As it was, Kathleen was angrily lacing up her boots, her expression one of fierce determination.

"Yeah, they killed my father," she said like it was no big deal. "He was a bastard, so no loss there, but I had to go on the run. In Eventide, I would've had to assume all of his gambling debts. I wasn't about to stick around to see what they offered me to get rid of them."

Fair.

"My parents always loved violence, so I don't blame you for running," I murmured. I looked to Kathleen, who'd finished with her boots and was standing, ready to go.

"Let's do this. And remember, we should probably hang onto you, Evera, because they can touch us—just not you."

"This will be fun." I smiled at the picture her words

painted before my mind momentarily dipped to Xakery's words.

Was he right? Were Axel's intentions different than I thought—than what he'd told me? Had he been lying about making me his mate or queen? I didn't think so. I didn't *want* to think so…but I needed to talk to him. I needed to find out the truth for myself.

More than anything, I wanted to handle the one true threat to our future: my parents.

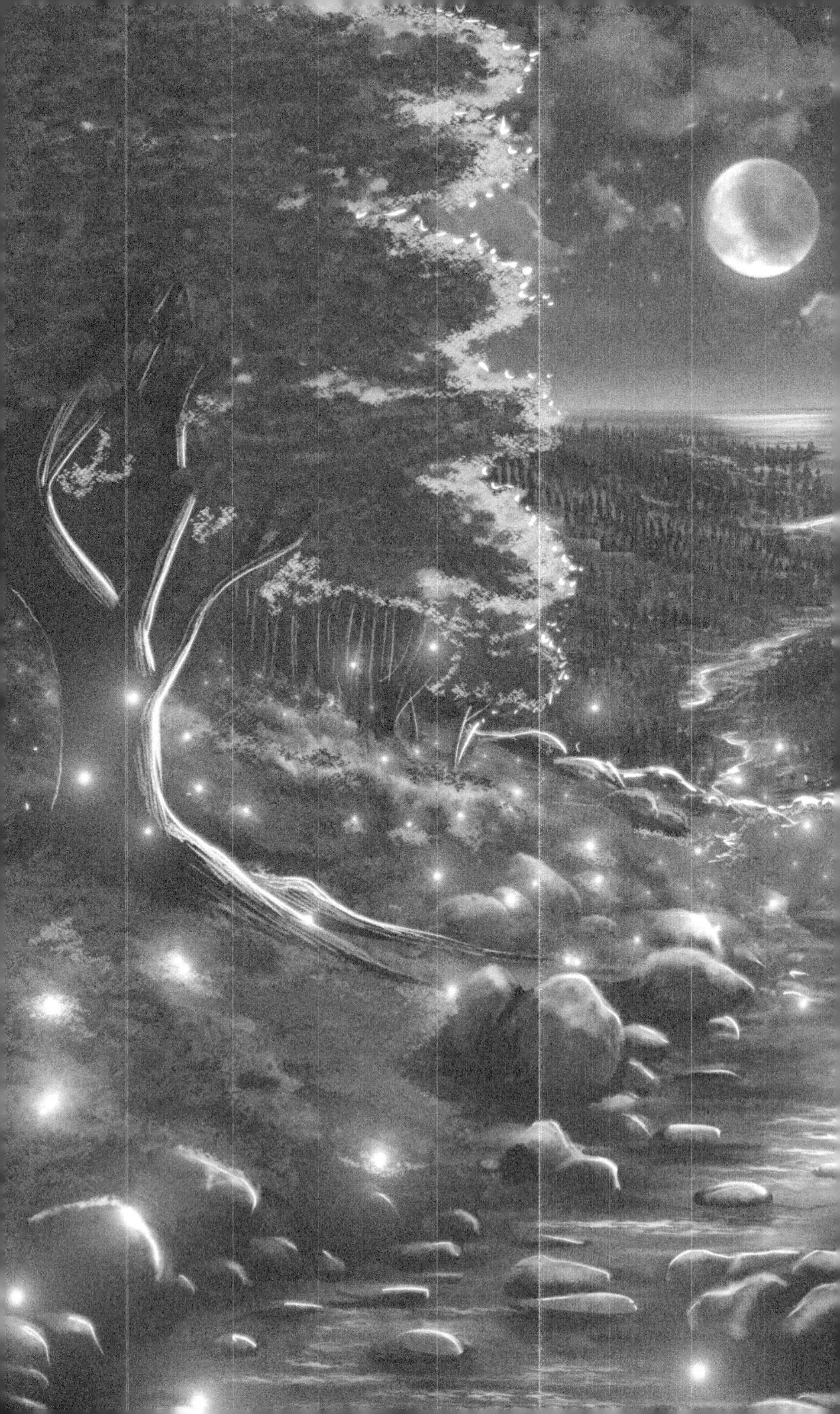

CHAPTER EIGHTEEN

EVERA

"I can't believe that worked!" I nearly laughed again as I looked back at the castle in the distance. Had we already traveled so far? It felt like it had been only moments since we'd snuck out a secret passage Kathleen had led us through, but the distance between us and the castle was impossible to ignore. We were doing this.

Xakery had been telling the truth, at least about one thing.

The guards truly hadn't been able to touch me or the other girls, each of whom had one of my arms thrown over their shoulders. The guards' faces paled when they realized we'd found that loophole, and as soon as we were past them, we broke into a full-on sprint. To their credit, they'd tried to chase us, but after a few quick turns and a jaunt down a secret tunnel, we were free.

Now the sun was extinguished on the horizon, the sky painted lavender and deep blue as we traveled down a main road towards the Midnight Keep. Our group of three was fairly quiet, but at my words Clari offered me a smile.

"It doesn't surprise me. Axel has been very clear about how important you are to him," she said, Kathleen nodding in agreement.

"I get Xakery's point," Kathleen admitted. "And normally I would say that using you for power is exactly what Axel is doing because the logic behind it is solid…but I don't think that's the case here. In fact, every decision he's made regarding you is more on the illogical side. I mean, who orders their guards to protect their mate but also not to put a hand on her, no matter what?"

I couldn't help the laugh that escaped me.

"I'm just glad to not be trapped in there anymore," I sighed.

"Wasn't too bad." Kathleen shrugged.

"Because being locked up is your literal kink," Clari shot back. My eyes widened, but Kathleen just laughed, unbothered.

"I can't deny that," she mused, "but I was talking about us getting to hang out."

"That part was nice," I agreed. "Next time we should just have a sleepover, though, rather than locking ourselves in a room for days on end."

"Unless we're keeping the men out—that could be fun," Clari said with a glint in her eye.

It would be fun to watch the men's reactions…

Well, maybe not Axel's considering how intense he got at that festival we went to…that hadn't been funny, but it had been really hot. It just still baffled me how I could cause such a strong reaction in a man like him. I loved it, but I really didn't understand it.

"But seriously, Evera, don't listen to him," Clari said. "Axel cares about you; everyone can see it."

It was good to hear, but convincing myself was another matter.

"I want to believe that the reason he didn't suggest trying to mark me was because he didn't know how I would react, that it could be dangerous…"

"Which it could be," Kathleen assured. "Humans and wolf shifters aren't compatible, and without your magic…"

"I'm essentially human," I finished. "But that doesn't mean his intentions aren't also focused on my parents and what it would mean to be rid of them. I know he wants them gone… I just don't know if he wants them gone for us or for Nightfall."

"It could be both," Kathleen said, the voice of reason.

"Or not," Clari countered. "He could just be protective over you and wants you to be his mate, his queen, and put babies in you type of thing." My stomach tightened at that thought, and not completely out of nervousness. "Guess we'll find out soon—we're nearly there."

My breath caught at the sight of the military post. It was beautiful against the silhouette of the Darkridge Mountains, lit up by the lanterns of the camps surrounding it.

Had it really been only days ago that I'd arrived here with almost no memories and no understanding of who I truly was? And now I was about to face my parents, the reason I was in this mess to begin with.

Because of who they'd aligned themselves with.

"Are you sure you want to do this? To see them again?" Kathleen asked quietly.

"I don't want this place devolving back into chaos because they want me back. Not after everything I sacrificed."

All of that time lost, away from Axel—decades apart. No.

I wouldn't allow it to be for nothing, and I hoped Axel would understand that—understand why I had to come.

As we made our way through the camps of soldiers surrounding the Midnight Keep, I heard whispers make their way through each group—even the soldiers of Eventide on the other side. Two captains—one from Nightfall and one from Eventide—guarded the doors in stoic silence, their expressions surprised to see us walking up to them. Probably because no one had tried to stop us.

The 'no touching' rule clearly applied here as well.

"Move," Kathleen demanded. The soldier from Nightfall stepped to the side without hesitation, but the soldier from Eventide scoffed.

"I am *not* moving."

"Evera here is King Axel's mate, so I would highly suggest you reconsider." Clari's response was filled with a dark amusement, as if predicting his reaction.

The man's gaze filled with momentary fear, and he stepped to the side, his hands shaking as he pulled open the door. I offered him a small nod, and as we stepped into the Midnight Keep, my senses were immediately assaulted by several unpleasant things.

First, everyone was looking at us—and I mean *everyone*. The only three I didn't mind were Axel, Rhaegal, and Captain Arnoux. The rest made me uncomfortable, their gazes unyielding as we rounded the table in the center of the room.

Second, the familiar scent of my mother's perfume floated through the air, and I could practically hear her hissing my name in annoyance. I didn't look at either her or my dad as I finally reached Axel, his gaze questioning and not mad in the least at our appearance. He did, however, look concerned—maybe even panicked—at me being here.

I knew at that moment that I'd been right in my assumption—he'd locked me away out of fear, scared that my parents would take me away from him. It was probably the only thing that terrified Axel, and had from the start. It didn't make his actions better, but it did relax something in me.

Many of my doubts fell to the side as I slid a hand over his shoulder and squeezed, his fingers wrapping around my waist as he tugged me onto his knee. The room was silent, Kathleen and Clari making themselves comfortable near their mates, as I finally turned my attention to the most unpleasant thing in the room.

My parents.

"Mother. Father."

I took in the two individuals that created me, and I realized that any loyalty I'd had to them died along with me fifty years ago. They looked so similar to back then, a result of the eternal youth wolf shifters received along with their extended life spans, that it was nearly eerie. But there was something drawn and exhausted about them now, their energy tainted with a darkness that had only grown over time.

My gaze moved to Reynor, who was backed up against the wall, his arms crossed defensively. I had to bite back a smile. He didn't seem nearly as bold as he had before, especially in this small space with Axel.

"You came," my mother said softly, the shock on her face mirrored by my father's.

"I did." I leaned further into Axel, his hands possessively holding me as if worried they would just pluck me from his lap. "I figured I should be here for such an important discussion instead of trapped in a castle...figuratively, of course."

Clari coughed, covering a laugh, and from the corner of my eye I saw Kathleen shake her head, smiling. Axel's chest rumbled as he kissed my shoulder, the action causing my father to snap out of his surprise.

"Evera." His voice was cold. "It's good to see you."

I tilted my head. "Is it? Did you miss me these past five decades?"

"Of course we did," my mother snapped, then tried to soften her voice. "It's why we were surprised that you didn't come through the portal with Reynor—that you didn't come home. Now, though, the reason is clear—*Axel has taken you prisoner.*"

"Yes, that's it," Axel drew out, his tone dry.

"An argument could be made..." I murmured so quietly that only he could only hear, my lips pressing into the barest hint of a smile.

"Evera..." His voice was filled with warning that had my face flushing.

I decided to refocus on my parents. "He didn't take me prisoner. In fact, I went to his kingdom willingly even though I originally landed in Eventide. I didn't even want to see either of you again, but here we are. I sacrificed myself to atone for your wrongdoings, and now, once again, you're trying to start a war, to cause chaos—"

"To get you back!" my father insisted, slamming his fist on the table.

"To get your *true heir* back—to get *my magic* back," I countered knowingly. I'd always struggled to stand up for myself, especially when I didn't have the upper hand, but this was my life they were playing with. I knew what they wanted;

their intentions were clear—but I'd already given enough in their name. No more.

"And how do you know he's not doing the same?" my mother asked, nodding towards Axel.

"Because her magic doesn't do anything here." Axel carefully enunciated each word, speaking slowly to make sure they understood. "When I came to this land, I laid claim, and it's absolute."

I ran my hand over the arm wrapped around my center in what I hoped to be a comforting manner.

"Claiming land isn't the same as being a true heir," my father argued.

"I *am* a true heir."

Axel's admission silenced the room, and even I turned to look at him in confusion.

"What?" Clari asked, the only one who hadn't completely frozen at Axel's declaration.

"I'm a true heir."

"That's impossible!" My father stood, his face as red as a tomato.

"It's not, Thomas," Axel leveled. "Two thousand years ago, your family destroyed the old Kingdom of Night and most of my ancestors with it. But the land never accepted its usurpers, which is why you could never lay claim to it. Centuries later my brothers and I were born, our family having hidden the knowledge of our history until I returned to this land. Until I claimed it as mine, as the true heir of our lineage."

Holy crap.

"Prove it," my mother hissed.

Axel removed his arm from my waist and rolled up the sleeve of his right wrist, revealing a dark mark that looked like a jagged scar running up the inside of his arm. My mother cursed as my father sat down slowly, looking dazed. I couldn't help but smile because while this was important for so many reasons, it proved that he didn't need my magic.

Axel had his own magic, and so damn much of it.

"I'm glad to see you understand," Axel drawled. "The land will not accept you, even if you do steal Evera's magic to strengthen yourselves."

I could see my parents were taken aback by his words, not because they were wrong but because they didn't understand how he knew their plan. My brow dipped as I spoke softly, drawing their attention. "It wasn't enough when I sacrificed myself to keep your kingdom? To save our people? You really have to steal my magic as well?"

"That's exactly what they plan to do," a familiar voice said. Oliver pushed away from the wall, making my eyes widen in surprise. I hadn't even noticed him there, and he returned my smile as he took a seat next to Arnoux. "I have confirmation that if she wasn't willing to do their bidding and marry Reynor, they would kill her and steal her magic, transferring the crown to him."

"Are you serious?!" They wanted to *kill* me? I knew they were despicable, but what the actual fuck? I mean seriously, I come back from the dead, essentially—reincarnated after fifty years—and they planned to kill me again?! I was their daughter, their flesh and blood! Clearly that meant *nothing* to them.

My mother stared down at the table, my father glaring at Oliver.

"I never should have trusted you; from the start your allegiance was with him," my father spat.

"It was your father's idea." My mother put her nose up,

looking annoyed. As if she could put the blame completely on him. "I never wanted to put your brother on the throne—after all, he was a mistake."

Reynor shot her a hateful look but refrained from saying anything.

"You have used me your entire life, all three of you," I said, sweeping my finger angrily between them. I was so agitated, so full of adrenaline, that Axel's hands on my waist were the only things keeping me from jumping to my feet. "I gave my *life* to fix what you messed up, and I won't be doing it again—ever. As your power fades and becomes mine, I will take the throne and fix everything you've messed up in Eventide."

That hadn't been my original plan—I had no idea where those words had even come from—but the satisfaction I felt at the horror on my mother and father's faces was enough to make it worth it, no matter what ended up happening.

My father stood, his chair screeching loudly. "You're asking for a war, daughter."

Axel squeezed my waist. "Then that is *exactly* what she will get. My forces have been ready from the start, since the moment I received your letter. Can you say the same about yours? How many will willingly traverse the Darkridge Mountains to face thousands of my men ready to slaughter them? I would think carefully on how you want to proceed."

The image he painted was enough to have my father putting his hands on the table in front of him, his head hanging slightly, looking dazed and yet still furious at his lack of control of the situation.

"Maybe." My mother squeezed my father's hand. "This conversation would be better saved for the morning—rested heads make better decisions, after all."

I didn't trust her for a minute.

"Please consider and choose wisely," Axel said as they stood and left, their soldiers following quickly, looking scared themselves. Reynor hesitated by the door, the group of us staring at him before he finally turned and held my gaze.

"I'd like to talk to you."

"You should run, Reynor. Fast and far." Axel stood, carefully placing me behind him. "I will kill you without a second thought."

Reynor drew his shoulders back and snarled, "I want to talk to my sister."

I really disliked Reynor referring to me as *his* anything, especially his sister.

Rounding Axel to stand by his side, I placed a hand on his chest but kept tucked against him. "I don't want to talk to you, though."

His eyes narrowed on me. "If this war comes to pass, it will destroy everything. Your words and his magic won't save you." Axel's chest rumbled as Reynor continued, clearly having a death wish. "Would it be so horrible to come home?"

He wasn't asking that, though—he was asking if it would be horrible to go home and face the fate that awaited me there.

I moved towards him, speaking in a soft tone that was laced with more venom than I'd ever heard from myself. "That place is not my home. I would never willingly return, and I would never marry you, so you can get that revolting thought out of your mind. I mean, seriously, *what* is wrong with the three of you? Can't you see how messed up all of this is?! Reynor, you are nothing to me, and you certainly are not family. I remember everything you did—how you loved scaring me, threatening me. I don't ever want to see you again."

Reynor's expression morphed into pure malice. "Then everything will be destroyed, and you will face your fate with the blood of thousands on your hands."

The door slammed shut, leaving us in silence.

"Well..." Oliver drew out. "It's great to see you again, Evera. I'm glad you made it."

My lips pressed up slightly as Axel wrapped an arm around me. "It's good to see you again, Oliver."

Now that Oliver had broken the tension, Clari turned to Rhaegal and smacked his chest. "What was all of this about, locking us into a room?".

"It was necessary," he gritted out.

"Hardly," she scoffed.

"Upstairs, now," he commanded. Clari flipped him off, and in an effortless move, he picked her up and stalked upstairs. Kathleen, Arnoux, and Oliver had settled at the table and were opening up a bottle of amber liquor. Axel brushed his lips against the top of my head.

"Interested in a drink?" Arnoux asked.

"No," Axel answered. "Evera and I need to talk."

An understatement if I'd ever heard one.

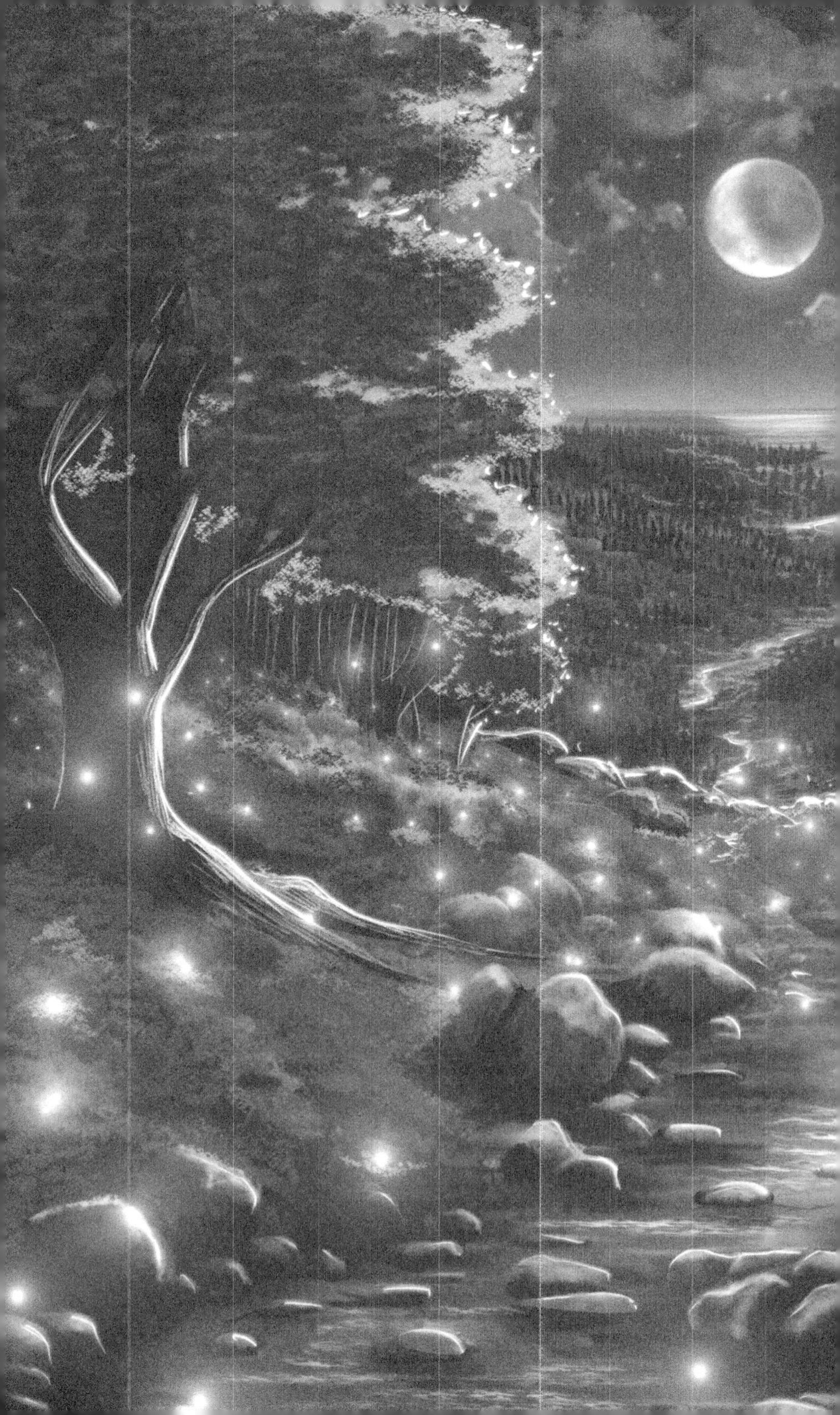

CHAPTER NINETEEN

AXEL

"**G**o upstairs. I'll be right there, *çiçeğim*."

My voice was softer than the heavy emotions I felt as I looked down at my flower, her eyes filled with confusion, affection, and hurt. I wanted to fix that—I *needed* to fix that—but I couldn't until I handled one fucking thing.

More precisely, one fucking individual—one aspect of the much larger problem that had kept me away from Evera these past few days. The reason I hadn't been able to spend the days learning all about the many ways my mate had changed since we were apart. The reason I hadn't been able to spend the nights with her wrapped in my arms. The reason that seeing her smile hadn't even been a possibility until now—although right now she did not look even close to smiling.

"No." She tilted her chin in defiance. "I know you're going to go find Reynor, and we need to talk. He's not worth it."

Oh, but he was. I already had thousands of ideas on how to make him suffer under my wrath, but none of it would be enough. Even if I skinned him alive, it wouldn't be enough.

Not for what he'd tried to do to Evera and what he no doubt still wanted to do.

The minute I found out he was in my kingdom, I felt an overwhelming need to shield Evera from him, not wanting him or her parents to step further than the Midnight Keep. He'd already tried to take her from me once when he tried to pull her through the portal.

An unwelcome memory surged forward and collapsed over me, causing my vision to turn red with fury. The moment when I realized what a threat he actually was to my flower.

"Evera?" I called at her door, wondering if she'd already gone to bed for the night. It wouldn't be unusual considering how tired she'd been recently. Her parents had been keeping her nearly chained to the throne with the duties they'd assigned her. They were trying to make her hate the idea of ruling, but I don't think she viewed it that way.

After only five months, I felt like my grasp on the princess was growing more solid. No longer did I feel like I was drowning in a wave of my desire for her. Desire I shouldn't have had for someone so full of life, with so much ahead of them.

I'd seen too much war and bloodshed to even think about touching her, never mind the fact that she was a fucking princess. Mind you, the desire hadn't disappeared—rather it had grown—but my need to protect her had allowed me to learn how to swim rather than drown in it.

"Evera?" I called out again as I stepped into her bedroom. I heard the sound of her humming from the attached en suite and groaned, knowing that she was in the tub. Fuck.

Shaking my head, I sat down in the chair in the corner of her room, the one I watched her from every night. It wasn't truly part of my job, and she could have told her parents and probably have me killed, but she never seemed to mind.

In fact, she seemed to like it, which was a huge fucking problem.

I didn't need to know what else she liked because I had a problem—a fixation with my flower. And she was exactly that, delicate and untouchable, but something I coveted nonetheless.

If I ever got her under me, I would break her.

Suddenly, her bedroom door opened and I sat back, narrowing my eyes on the entrance. Unless this was Oliver coming to talk to me, although even he shouldn't be fucking walking in here, no matter the reason—

A figure made their way into the room, stopping when they saw me.

"Reynor," I snarled, unable to keep my distaste out of my mouth. This motherfucker. For a half-brother, he sure as fuck had his eyes on Evera a whole lot. His mouth pressed into a grimace as his gaze darted towards the bathroom.

"Why are you here? Trying to get a free show?" he spit out, looking flustered.

"I'm doing my job and guarding her from this exact type of scenario." I stood up and walked towards him, causing him to stumble backwards. "What are you doing in here, Reynor?"

"We often talk at night," he stuttered.

"No you don't."

"Not anymore," he growled. "Not since you got here."

Damn right.

The bathroom door opened, and a surprised noise left Evera's throat at the sight of us. My gaze ran over her, glad she was in a robe. She looked like an angel, her face flushed as steam wrapped around her from the open door.

"Reynor, what are you doing here?" she accused, coming to stand by my side. Victory.

His jaw tightened. "Nothing. I'll tell you at breakfast."

The coward ran, and I looked down as Evera grabbed my hand, causing me to tense. Her gaze filled with worry as the door shut. "I thought he would stop doing that."

"What?" I grit out.

"He used to surprise me after my bath a lot, so much so that I had to start putting something in front of the door to give me warning when he was coming in." Motherfucker. "It stopped when you got here."

"I'll make sure it doesn't happen again." I squeezed her hand and nodded towards her closet. "Go get dressed, Evera." Before I rip off that tiny robe.

Her squeak and disappearing act nearly had me smiling. Nearly.

I didn't hesitate to give into the urge to lay in her bed with her that night, watching from as close as possible—ensuring no one hurt her. It was the first night my fingers ran over her hair and my lips coasted over her forehead. It was the beginning of the end for me.

Knowing that Reynor had threatened her with his mere presence was unacceptable, and it wasn't just that. No, there had been another time were he'd cornered her—

"Axel!" Evera's voice snapped me out of my haze, and I realized a lethal sound was coming from my chest that had her looking at me in concern. The air outside was silent, and I knew everyone had heard the violent sound, including Reynor.

Good. He should know that he would be the first to die

come morning. I wouldn't even hesitate, and we all knew her parents weren't going to solve this in a civil way.

"Upstairs, come on." She tugged on my hand, and it finally sank in that there was no way in hell my flower was going to let me go after him. That was fine, though—I would have my soldiers bring him back to the castle so I could enact the torture that I saw fit.

I nodded and turned sharply, picking her up in a swift movement and carrying her upstairs. There were many rooms at the military installation, but the top floor contained a suite for me. I carried her straight there, desperately needing to be alone with her.

Tossing her onto the bed, I climbed over her, her thighs opening and allowing me to rest between them. I groaned into her neck. "Fuck, *çiçeğim*, I've missed you so damn much."

"Could have fooled me," she said, hurt lacing her tone. I pulled back and captured her face between my hands.

"I didn't want to stay away, Evera. I wanted to show you all of Nightfall. I wanted to show you your new home. I wanted to be in our bed together every night. I wanted to have my hands on you and to hear you screaming my name—"

"Axel," she murmured, her cheeks blasting with heat.

"I'm serious. The last thing I wanted was to be apart," I confessed. Evera's effect on me made me anything but logical, which is why my next words made so little sense. "What you did tonight was dangerous, reckless, and brave. I know how hard it must have been to face them, and I absolutely hated having you in the same room as them. But I'm also fucking thrilled you're here, even if I have to kill my guards for letting you out of their sight."

I was so fucking conflicted on everything right now that the confused look on her face didn't surprise me in the least.

"We would've never had to be apart if you hadn't locked me up. What you did wasn't okay," she said evenly. "You can't keep me out of the loop—we even talked about it the other night! But you *especially* can't do that when it comes to my parents."

"I will always keep you safe," I growled, not willing to give any ground on that front.

"Safe is one thing, but if you want me to be your queen—"

"*If?*" I examined her expression, not liking the hesitancy there. When I'd left her, there hadn't been any question of my intentions...at least I assumed not. "Why the *if?*"

Something in her gaze softened. "You really want me to be your queen? And your mate?"

I offered her an incredulous look before pressing a hard kiss to her lips. "I'm not sure what else I need to do to convince you—"

"No," she whispered, shaking her head. "It's not you. You've reassured me before...it's just Xakery said something that made me wonder."

My jaw tightened. "And what did he say?"

Because anything that cast doubt in her mind was an immediate death sentence—brother or not.

"That you could've tried to mark me to see if it would activate my magic, but you didn't." Evera hesitated for a moment before the words flowed out of her so fast that I had to focus to keep up. "And that you're potentially using me as a pawn for gaining more power. That you could still have me by your side, but if you don't take me as queen or mate, that your power will never be transferred to Nightfall's future true heir, so you'll get to keep it forever. Essentially the best of both worlds."

I would kill him. I would fucking kill him.

Pulling her up with me, I placed her on my lap and kissed the side of her neck softly. "I'll deal with my brother later, but let me assure you, Evera—you will be my queen and my mate, but also the mother to my children, including a future true heir. All of that will be ours. Understand?"

"So this isn't just about taking my parents' kingdom?" she asked, swallowing down the insecurity plaguing her.

"I could have killed your parents decades ago," I admitted, her eyes flashing with a darkness I felt deep in my soul. "I only kept them alive so you could ultimately decide their fate. A war was inevitable, but I wouldn't have killed them without your permission. They are no threat to me or my kingdom—never have been. But they are a threat to you and our future, which makes them my enemy."

Evera let out a long sigh and melted against me. "I think I knew that, I just needed to hear you say it. Xakery has a way about him…"

"I know." I brushed my lips against her forehead. "I know he fucking does."

"He did give me the hint that you ordered my guards not to touch me—that's how I got here." I could see the tiniest bit of amusement in her gaze, and it led me to believe that she may have had more than a bit of fun breaking out of the castle, despite the circumstances.

"I'm going to send him to Eventide or drop him in the ocean," I snarled. My brother's sins were stacking up quickly, from placing doubt in her mind to sacrificing her safety.

"He did it because he thought you were underestimating my parents. I think he was worried," Evera said, causing my brow to furrow. That didn't sound like Xakery, but Evera was extremely perceptive, so I'd be an idiot to dismiss her words entirely.

"He still shouldn't be talking about that to you," I murmured as she suddenly turned to straddle me, a groan leaving my throat.

I let her push me down onto the bed, my cock swelling as her elegant fingers brushed over my chest. Evera tried to fix me with a stern look, but it only managed to turn me on more. I hadn't thought that was possible.

"Why did you leave without a word? Why not say something or leave a note? Especially right after we..." She blushed, and a rogue smiled pulled at my lips. How she could blush after everything I'd done to her was a fucking wonder, yet I found myself loving it, savoring that part of her that was completely for me.

"Because I knew if you protested at all about staying at the castle, or if you told me to stay—that I would in a heartbeat," I sat up on my elbow and brushed my lips against her throat, pulling her tight against me with an arm wrapped around her curved waist.

"I should be a part of this."

"You've been a part of this from the start—you *solved* the problem last time, protected everyone by sacrificing your very life." I pulled back and stared into her gorgeous eyes. "Let me protect you, Evera. Let me handle your parents, this war, and anything else in the way of our future."

A softness invaded her expression as she nibbled on her lip. "I still want to know what's going on, even if it's just information."

"You're right. I'm sorry, çiçeğim." Something about my simple words seemed to have her relaxing, her gaze warming as her hands ran up my shoulders and pushed off my jacket, encouraging me to sit up all the way. I discarded the garment immediately, and when Evera grabbed my wrist and turned it, her long, delicate fingers tracing the mark on the inside of my arm.

Her brow dipped. "I had a mark like this before?"

"It will return with your magic," I promised her, not liking the sadness in her expression. I could only imagine the loss she felt at remembering her magic but not being able to experience it.

Leaning forward, I nipped her bottom lip. A soft moan filtered out of her as she deepened the kiss, my fingers tightening on her waist.

I hoped the door was locked, because there was no way I was leaving this damn bed—not after being away from her these past couple of days.

I should have cared that there were so many around to hear my mate's moans, but instead I relished in it. I wanted them to hear how fucking good I made her feel, how I was the only acceptable option for her mate. That no one could make her feel like I did.

I tugged at her cloak, revealing the flowy dress she wore. My lips trailing down to her collar, the swell of her cleavage making me groan in pain. She smelled so fucking sweet, and I couldn't help but push her dress up to her hips, wanting to feel her ride the hard ridge of my cock as she shifted in my lap. Her skin was so soft and silky, and I could practically scent how wet she was from my simple touch.

I would never get used to how damn responsive she was —the woman was handcrafted to drive me insane.

My lips traced the column of her throat, and I had to fight

back the urge to bite down on her pulse hard enough to leave a mark.

Not yet—not until I could place my mating mark there.

As if her thoughts were in the same place, she whispered, "I want you to try marking me this time, Axel."

A guttural noise left my throat at the imagery her words conjured. That was all I fucking wanted, and I'd considered it the last time we were together—but there was something holding me back, larger than any desire or possessive instinct.

"I don't want to hurt you. I have no idea what will happen without your magic or wolf to help process the magic the mate bond requires."

"I still want to try," she urged, her hands delving into my hair. "Try to mark me. Please. I want everything we talked about—*everything*."

Fuck. Those words had me wanting to slam her down on my cock and fill her up immediately, just to see the ecstasy that I knew I could put on her face. Evera came so fucking pretty, and I planned on toying with her body every day until I had it memorized—until I knew how to make her come from just a teasing touch.

"Everything?"

Because *everything* meant marking her not only on her neck, but inside as well. The beast inside of me had been demanding we take everything from Evera, give her everything we had, for so long that I didn't think I had the will to fight it anymore.

No. I couldn't ignore the primal urge rolling through me anymore, the creature that demanded I bury my teeth in her soft neck as she screamed my name, filling her with enough seed that it was impossible to not breed her. The idea of seeing her carrying my child was so fucking appealing, but I needed to know that she wanted that as well—that she understood what 'everything' meant.

I sucked hard on her neck, sending shivers down her skin. "Everything means you open up your pretty thighs wide enough so that I can breed you, çiçeğim. Everything means having nothing between us so that nothing is stopping me from planting my seed deep inside of you, ensuring an heir. Is that what you want, Evera? Do you want me to hold you down and mark you in every single way? I've come in this pretty pussy once, but if I do it again, knowing you want that, I won't stop—I'll always be inside of you. Always trying to fill you up."

The urge would be impossible to ignore, knowing that she wanted it as much as I did.

"I want that," she moaned, turning her neck as I ran my tongue down her throat. "I really want that. I never want anything between us either. Please?"

"Fuck, you never need to beg for that." I flipped her on the bed so she was underneath me, deciding that her answer was enough to justify giving in to my obsession. There'd been nothing between us before, no protection, and I'd been aware of that—but her giving me permission now was going to unleash something I wasn't capable of controlling.

A rip sounded through the room as her dress fell apart from the center, revealing her dark green bra and panties—the delicate lace barely hiding her perfection from me.

"Your clothes too," she said, her eyes filled with so much heat that I couldn't find it in me to tell her no. Instead I sat back and tugged off my shirt and then my pants, letting them slide to the floor before kicking them away. My hand wrapped around my cock as a concerned noise left her throat, my smirk dark as she watched me with both worry and pure desire.

"There is no way that fit into me last time," she whispered, her thighs trying to press together. I instantly stopped her, opening her legs back up to me.

"Don't close your legs to me, ever," I growled softly. "And it did fit—completely—and it will fit again, Evera. You're going to take all of me."

"Okay." She gasped as I tugged her forward so that her hips were at the edge of the bed, my cock running along her wet slit. "I want it to—I want you to fit."

She was made for me; of course I would fit.

As much as I wanted to impale myself into her, I wanted to make sure she was in a nearly euphoric state before I tried to mark her—I wanted her to only remember the good and not any potential pain. I knelt down between her legs and brushed my lips over her thighs, inhaling her delicate scent.

So fucking sweet.

Like a wild animal, I began devouring her, her perfect taste rolling over my tongue as her fingers strung through my hair and tugged hard. I groaned against her soft skin as she moaned my name, her thighs trembling at the need to come against my mouth. I stiffened my tongue and pressed into her tight hole as she arched off the bed, whimpering as my thumb rolled over her clit. She was so fucking wet, and I was close to coming myself, but I couldn't allow myself to until I was buried inside her.

Any other time, though, I could have spent all night down here, buried in pure heaven.

"Axel!" Evera cried out before climaxing hard, her grip in my hair turning painful—which only turned me on more.

"Good girl," I snarled, standing and grabbing her hips to

stop her from squirming against me. There was a dreamy, dazed look on her face as I lined up the tip of my cock with her entrance and watched with pleasure as I impaled her in one *hard* push.

I roared her name as I was enveloped in her tight warmth, pure satisfaction filling me at claiming her so deeply. Her nails clawed at my back as her thighs squeezed around me, and I felt like I was seeing stars at how damn tight she was. I had to still myself to keep from coming on the fucking spot. This woman had the power to instantly unman me.

If I wasn't so fucking obsessed, I would have probably hated it. But I couldn't. I craved her touch; I craved everything about her.

"You're so big," she groaned, reaching up to grab the sheets above her head.

"That type of comment won't make me any smaller," I assured her with a dark chuckle followed by a groan, matching the way I slowly pulled out of her before pushing in hard and deep once more.

"Faster," she begged, and the call to satisfy my mate made me snap. My pace was relentless and demanding as Evera screamed my name, my cock hitting that perfect place inside of her every time I impaled her with my length as I claimed her perfect body again and again.

I wanted to meld the two of us together into one, and my hands were possessive on her skin as I brought my lips to her ear, telling her how perfect she was and how I wanted to fucking wreck her. How I planned on filling her up with my cum. About needing her so damn bad that I'd spent the past two days dreaming about being back with her, being able to touch and take what was mine.

After climaxing three times around my cock, I pulled back and flipped her onto her stomach, knowing I couldn't hold back anymore. My lips grazed the back of her neck as I continued to pound into her, my hands on her hips shifting into something much more lethal. My claws dug into her skin as my cock swelled in size as Evera arched back into me. The creature inside of me roared to life and broke out, our only thought that we needed to mark her completely.

"Tell me what you need, çiçeğim," I demanded, my voice thick and rough because of my transformation.

"You. Your mark. Your cum," she whimpered, and victory coursed through me.

Her words were enough to end me, and with one final slam, I buried my cock as deep as I could while sinking my teeth in the side of her throat. Her scream nearly burst my eardrums as I let go and released into her, the world around me spinning at the relief rolling through me.

The Midnight Keep suddenly shook, and a deep sound vibrated the very air around us as magic sparked along our skin. The air in the room began to crack and pop as Evera tensed and then gasped, her body shuddering and giving out. I felt her magic before I saw it, the explosion of it rushing over me as a floral vine began to appear on her left arm, replacing the jagged scar there. I needed to know when that was from and how it happened—but I knew right now wasn't the moment to discuss what I assumed wasn't a good memory. Her body trembled, and I instantly felt our magic connect. Through it all I held her tight against me, refusing to let go of her as the world shifted.

Her magic—it was back.

"I can feel it," she gasped. "I can feel my magic and my wolf."

My teeth released her as my form shifted back to normal, my tongue rolling over her mating mark as cum leaked from the place where we connected. As I pulled back, I felt a swell of pure rightness at the sight of my mating mark on her neck, which turned gold as I watched. Proof that no matter how long it took for her to shift or use her magic again, she did have magic.

Like an infinity loop, the two of us were intertwined for eternity now.

Carefully, I lifted Evera into my arms and brought her to the bath. After I took care of her, I would pull her into my arms and rest knowing we were completely mated. I could deal with Xakery and Reynor later.

All that mattered right now was my mate.

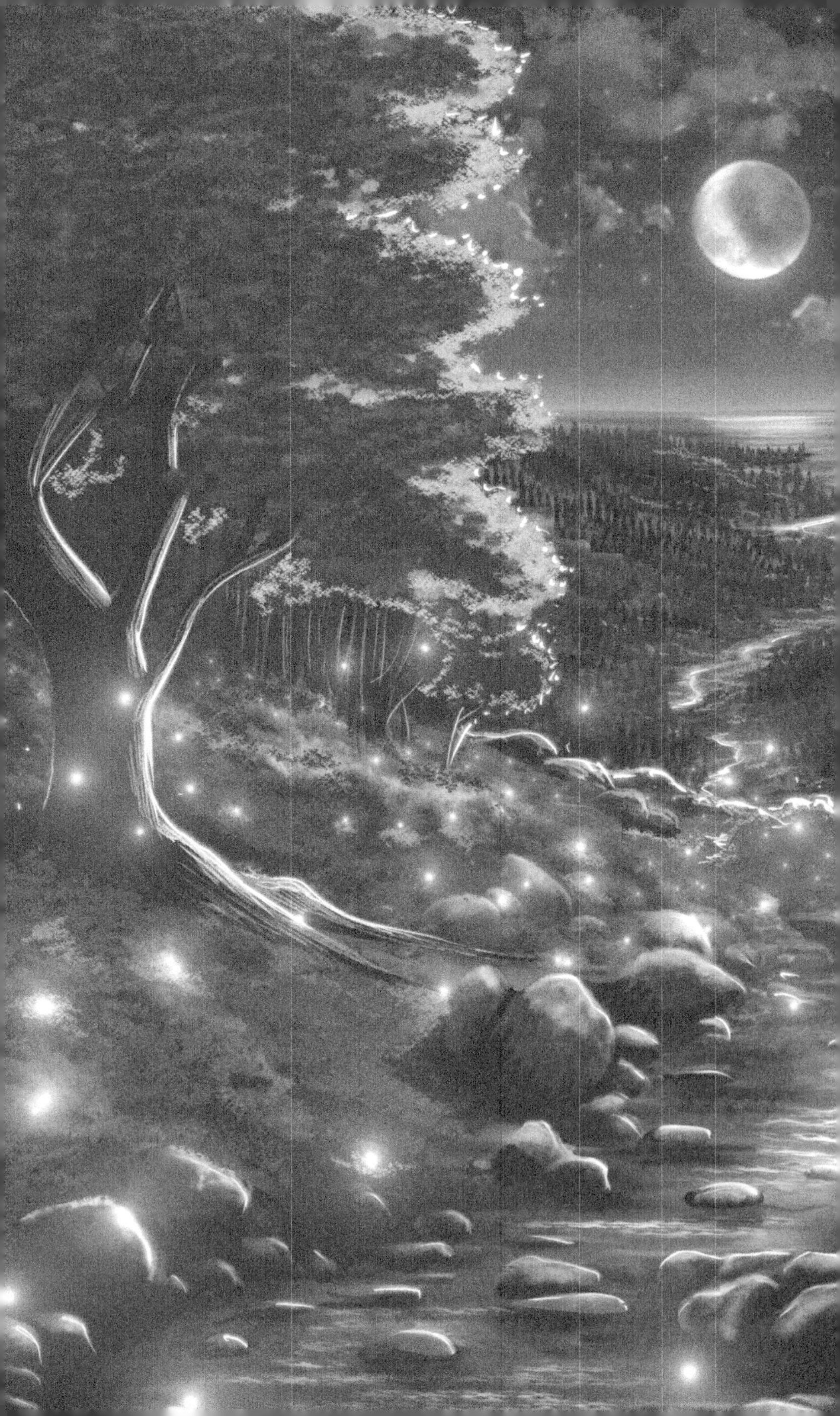

CHAPTER TWENTY

EVERA

My eyes were heavy as I finally managed to open them and look around, finding that I was in the same clearing as when I'd first arrived in Vargr. Where this entire journey had begun.

Across the way, lit beneath the light of two moon-like moons, was a massive black wolf nearly double the size of myself. Yet I was anything but scared.

Slowly, I stood, realizing that I had not two legs underneath me but four. Brown fur covered my legs down to my paws. My paws. I was a wolf—an actual wolf. There was a part of my brain that recognized how insane this was, but at the same time it felt so incredibly natural and right.

I was so trapped in my thoughts that I'd forgotten about the other wolf, and when I snapped my head back up, I found that he'd moved closer while I was distracted. I had no idea how I knew it was a 'he,' but somehow it was obvious to me. His glowing silver eyes ran over me as well, as if drinking me in. A whimper left my throat, and I had to fight the sudden urge to throw myself at him.

Why did I need to restrain myself, exactly? I couldn't remember.

My tail started to move around like crazy as I tried to back away, the deep rumble that emanated from the wolf's chest causing an intense reaction within me. My control shattered, and any thought of holding back fled as I launched myself towards him. I wasn't sure what my intention was until I crashed into the massive creature...and then I realized who he was.

My mate. Axel.

"Welcome back, çiçeğim." Axel's voice floated through my head as I buried my nose against his throat. Then a yip of excitement escaped me, a thrill of excitement coursing through me, and I could feel Axel's amusement through our bond.

Our mating bond.

"I missed this," I said, trying to employ the same tactic he'd used to communicate as we sank into the grass of the clearing. My tail wrapped around my body as I buried my nose against him once more.

"It hadn't crossed my mind that marking you would release your magic. I was far too worried about the potential of hurting you—I suppose I owe Xakery."

I didn't even care anymore; I was just thrilled that I could be in this form, even in a dream.

"I hope I can shift in real life."

"I know you can, Evera."

A happy, purr-like sound left my chest at his belief in me, and I fought back the words I desperately wanted to say to him—words I knew needed to be said in person.

"What is it?" His snout tapped my nose as I tried to look up at him.

Before I could tell him, the world shook around us. A whimper left me as pain shattered everything—

. . .

"Fuck! We don't have much time—let's go!"

I groaned as my head smacked against a wall, my body bound and hanging uncomfortably over someone's shoulder. I whimpered as I tried to look around and realized my mouth and nose were covered—I couldn't make a noise even if I wanted to. My fingers and toes were going numb from being restrained, and terror began to crawl up my throat.

"He's going to be awake in no time," a female voice said, panicking.

I wasn't positive if it was from my head being hit around or what, but I was finding it difficult to focus on anything, let alone determine who was around me. I groaned as my head smacked against another wall, the person carrying me clearly not caring if I got banged around. Somehow it didn't surprise me, though, and a part of me recognized whose voice it was even though I couldn't put a name to it.

"The others should be out for some time—the drink was powerful," the man argued, "but you're right about Axel. If we don't get her out of here, we're fucked."

Suddenly, the cold air from outside slapped against my skin and the pieces began to click together, Axel's name ringing clear. It was at that exact moment that I realized in horror that I was being kidnapped, stolen from the Midnight Keep right under Axel's nose. *Shit.*

Adrenaline pumped through my veins, and I began to try to scream and throw my body around, the man holding me cursing and gripping me tighter. The voices around me pitched in fear, and I thought that just maybe I had a chance of gaining someone's attention…but then someone pressed a cloth over my nose.

Suddenly, the world got very small and tight, suffocating, and my eyelids grew heavy.

My magic surged under my skin to try to protect me, but before I could even put it to good use, it was lights out.

Darkness warped around me, tilting the space underneath my feet and making me stumble as I tried to grab hold of something. When bright lights suddenly lit up the world around me, a scream lodged in my throat. I was on a wall, hanging sideways, the drop thousands of feet below me. Digging my nails into the stones underneath my fingers, blood began to seep from my fingertips, a howl echoing in the distance.

There was something underneath the stone, something the wall was holding back. I found myself wanting to shake it, to pull down the very foundation. To see what was behind it. At the same time, I feared the possibility, terrified of what I'd find.

It didn't matter if I was scared, though. The walls had heard me, and they began to crumble.

I cried out as stone by stone, the wall shattered around me, my body flailing until I fell backward. I watched the sky grow distant as the rocks below became my new destination.

I expected pain, but right as I slammed into the ground, everything disappeared—

"The troops are surging through the mountain pass right now. The temporary bridge worked," a sharp voice called, the jostling of my body causing my stomach to churn. "We'll ensure that none of the enemy combatants come through here—his soldiers will have to eliminate each and every one of ours, and by then it'll be too late."

Too late? Too late for what? I hated everything that had come out of the individual's mouth, and the idea of soldiers rushing into Nightfall made me sick. This mountain pass was both the kingdom's greatest defense because it almost guaranteed no one would try to get in any other way, but it was also its greatest flaw for the same reason. It was essentially the only way out, making Axel's path to me predictable.

My head throbbed, but my heart hurt far worse. Was Axel okay? Given they'd managed to take me from our bed, I couldn't imagine so.

A scream of frustration tried to leave my throat, but whatever they'd had me inhale left me limp and barely able to rouse the energy to move, let alone talk. At least I wasn't slung over a shoulder anymore, but the cold, hard floor of whatever vehicle they'd thrown me in wasn't much better.

I tried to shift subtly like I was sleeping, but when I opened my eyes, all I could see was darkness, the cloth over my eyes making it impossible to tell where we were going. The voices were silent at the moment, but I could feel eyes on me.

"She has a mating mark." The anger in that voice was unmistakable—*Reynor*.

My body was sore and limp, my mind fuzzy and my magic weak, but that didn't stop the absolute fury from surging through me. My wolf was restless under my skin, waiting for the moment to break out. To fight, to kill if we had to.

Not yet. I had to be patient.

I should have been scared by the violent thoughts circulating through my head, but I was only fiercely determined. I would do whatever it took to escape and get back to Nightfall, where I belonged.

"Axel's mark," a soft voice agreed—my *mother's* voice. Why had I still thought there was something redeemable about the woman? It caused nothing but pain, that false hope for something better from her, but now? *Now it was gone.*

"Who she is mated with won't matter soon," my mother added. "The ceremony will kill her and transfer her magic to you. You'll take the throne, and Evera will remain the martyr princess of memory that she should have remained when she died fifty years ago."

It wasn't until that moment that I realized my magic wasn't the only thing that had returned. My memories—*all* of them—had come back to me as well, and they revealed clearly what Axel had been trying to protect me from. I was naive last time, blinded by family loyalty, but as I looked over each slight, each shady dealing I witnessed, each creepy comment Reynor made...

Well, it was all too obvious that Axel truly had been the only one protecting me from them.

And nothing would protect them from Axel's wrath when he found them.

Axel, who I loved. Axel, who loved me.

We hadn't said the words yet, but I recognized that truth down to my soul—a love that had always been there, that had spanned two lifetimes—just like the pain I could feel through our bond the farther and farther we were pulled apart. Tears welled in my eyes as I found myself regretting not telling him how I felt.

"Her arm," Reynor growled. "The true heir mark."

"Has her magic returned to her in one night?" my mother hissed.

"The mating may have triggered it," my father said. I think I'd known he was here, but I still hated his voice, wishing he would've stayed silent. "No matter, the ceremony is just a more assured success."

"Unless she overpowers us," my mother murmured. "She's not the controllable girl she once was."

Damn straight.

I did my best to remain still as silence once again filled the cabin. Some time later—it could have been minutes or hours—we came to a stop, and a small groan left my throat as the sudden change in momentum nearly made me roll onto my face.

"Holy shit," I whispered as my blindfold was ripped off. Reynor's face was black and blue, one of his eyes swollen shut.

I was physically feeling worse for wear after enduring the bumpy ride on the unforgiving floor, but clarity was returning to my mind, and I didn't need to ask how he'd gotten that way. Somewhere between falling asleep in Axel's arms and him being knocked out, this had happened.

Reynor looked horrible.

"Shut up," he snarled, grabbing my hair and pulling me forward across the floor of the carriage. I didn't bother protesting as Reynor put me over his shoulder and spoke in a low, threatening tone. "This could have been much easier. You could have been mine, but now you have to die. What a fucking waste."

"Or you could drop this and ask for forgiveness," I spit.

Reynor came to a hard stop, hauling me off his shoulder and holding me in front of him so that my feet dangled off the ground, his eyes filled with pure malice. "You are a stupid, stupid little girl—as you have always been. You won't live to see morning, and Axel won't be coming for you, especially since *you* are responsible for the slaughter of so many in his kingdom. He's probably already dead at this point anyway.

"I will give you one chance to hand yourself over to me—"

"Never," I hissed. *Didn't he understand the word 'no'?! Clearly not.*

Rage filled his expression, but I didn't fear it. Instead I only felt guilt at the idea of being the cause for war—the cause of so much death.

Before he could respond, a savage howl broke through the night air. The moons themselves seemed to grow brighter, the entire realm shifting and creaking beneath the power associated with the noise. My skin broke into shivers as everyone locked up at the sound, Reynor's face paling to a sickly green.

My smile grew as my mating bond surged to life, making it clear that Axel was awake and aware of what happened. My voice was calm and filled with victory as I rejoiced in Reynor's fear.

"Axel isn't dead. He's coming for me—and you better be gone by the time he does, because I won't save you from his wrath."

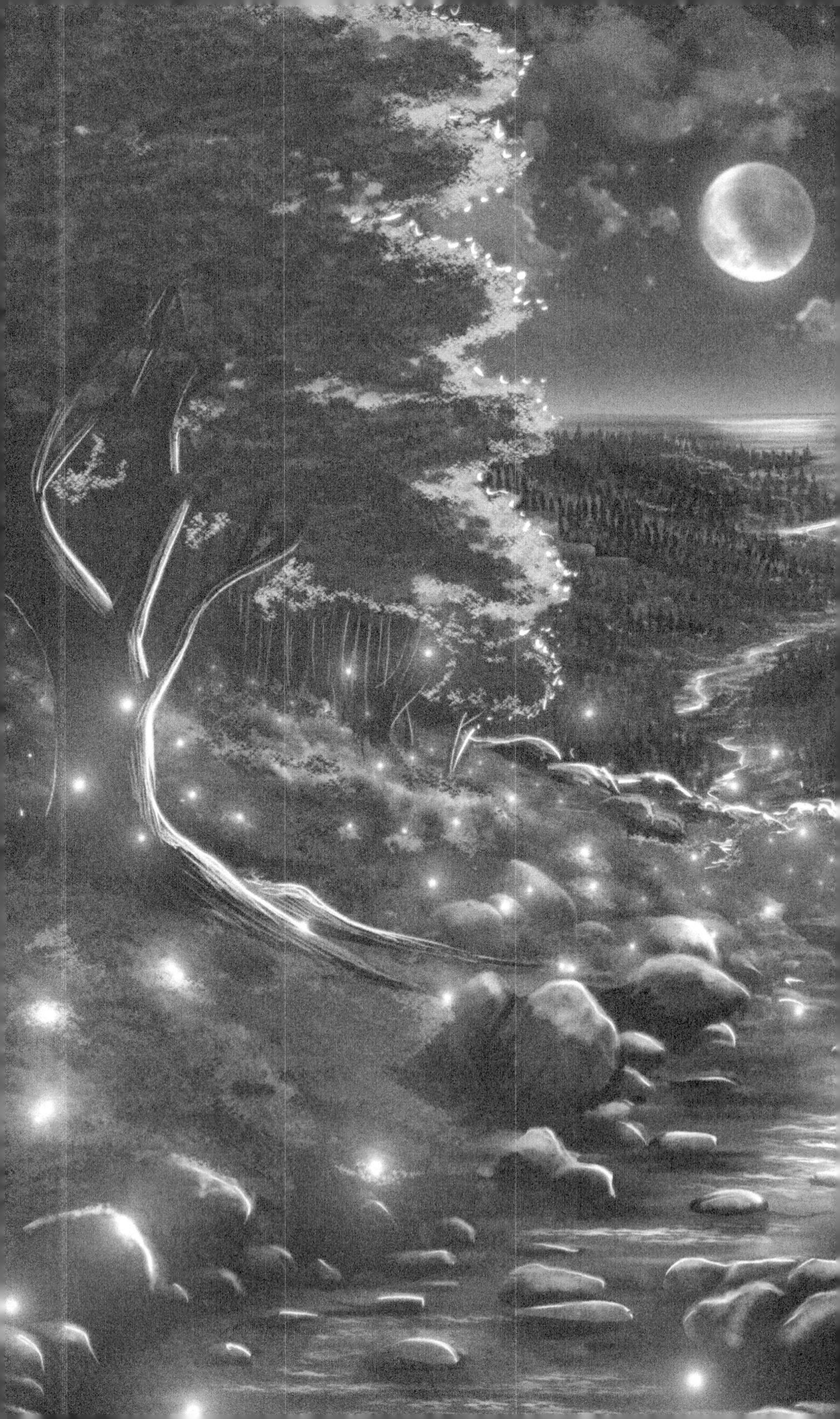

CHAPTER TWENTY-ONE

EVERA

I'd thought I understood the connection between mates—but now I knew that I'd only truly had a small inkling of the reality.

Without confirmation of our bond, I'd assumed after a while that the intensity of my emotions for Axel in my previous life were like a school girl's crush. The analogy had never felt right, but without him ever acting differently toward my advances, it was the only conclusion I'd been left with.

But this entire time I'd been right—those intense feelings weren't just those of a crush. They had been so much more than that, and the feeling of *rightness* I felt around him had been completely correct—*we were right for one another*. Meant for one another, destined for one another.

We were literal mates, and now that I was aware of that, it put everything I'd ever felt and everything we'd ever experienced into perspective. It also explained what I was feeling now—how much I was suffering.

The collision of my experiences in this life and the resurgence of memories from my past life were creating an energy inside of me, a glowing orb that was ever-expanding with the knowledge of my relationship and emotions for Axel.

It was a source of comfort and light that should have sustained me, but it was being drained by withdrawal—all because of our quick separation following the formation of our mating bond.

The withdrawal was like nothing I'd ever experienced before, my chest aching with acute pain, feeling like I couldn't take a full breath, my head spinning as the echoes of his howl rolled through my ears again and again.

Axel. I needed him. I needed him to come here.

The two days we'd spent apart before the bond was solidified were nothing compared to the twenty-four hours I'd spent locked in this cell, the silence around me screaming loudly as my skin turned raw and bloody from trying to break out of the metal cuffs wrapped tightly around my wrists.

I had to get out of here; I had to break free.

I had no doubt that the soldiers of Eventide were weaker than Axel's forces, but my wolf didn't care about that or about Axel's military and leadership experience. No, she was demanding that I be there on the battlefield to ensure our mate's safety. That I prioritize it over everything.

If *I* felt this protective, I couldn't imagine how Axel felt... actually, it was completely possible that some of the emotions I was feeling were because of him and our bond.

The sudden jostle of chains drew my attention to the far corner of the dungeon, where the only other prisoner was—a woman who'd yet to speak to me.

I distinctly remembered this dungeon being full when I lived here. It had even been a point of pride for my parents.

Yet right now it was empty, and the only reasoning I could come up with was that the prisoners were sent to the front lines for battle. It seemed like something my parents would do.

So why had this woman been left here? Her head had been down this entire time, and despite the dark she was shrouded in, I could see every detail of her slight form. I had a feeling she was tall, but I couldn't tell because of how she was curled up. Her dress was dirty and aged, making me wonder how long she had been down here, especially since her cell looked clean and untouched. Something I didn't remember being the norm from the few times I'd walked through.

From what I could tell, the dungeon hadn't changed much since I'd lived here, but the rest of the castle had. Even in the short glimpse I'd gotten while being led down to the dungeon, I'd noticed the changes. Or maybe it wasn't that things had changed, the decor frozen in time, but that nothing had been maintained or taken care of.

The gleaming castle I'd grown up in was no more, a dark shadow blanketing the estate with a depressive, heavy energy.

It was something I would've explored more, but Reynor and his men hadn't wasted any time before throwing me into a cell. My bound hands had been transferred to a pair of metal cuffs attached to a spike on the ground, not allowing for much movement. I had cried out in frustration several times now, but considering the staff had averted their eyes as I walked through, I knew I wouldn't gain anything from my outbursts except for a small outlet for my frustration.

In fact, the only assistance I'd received was from the guards and female staff who came by a few hours ago to lead me to the bathroom to relieve myself—apparently a small courtesy for me being a princess. *Thoughtful of them.* Still, I knew that'd be the limit of their helpfulness.

And I needed help getting out of here because I felt like I was slowly losing my sanity in such an awful place, the cold water on the stone floor chilling me to the bone, the silence damn near repressive.

My legs were numb from where I sat leaning against the bars of the cage, and the turning and twisting of my wrists in an attempt to slip my hands out had left my skin raw, frustration surging through me now that their drugs had worn off. The only light, which shone from a singular window near the top of the wall, told me it was mid-afternoon.

Far too much time had passed for me to be comfortable with it, and the quiet outside only threatened to depress me further. If there was no noise, it meant he wasn't here yet. My mate was too far from me—much too far.

"I know you probably don't want to talk," I called out to the woman, having already tried before, "but I want you to know that we're going to get out of here. They'll be here soon. I promise."

Putting my head down, I was shocked when a curious voice responded, "Who will be here?"

Snapping my head over, I stifled a surprised noise at the woman looking up at me. Her eyes were a bright green, almost neon, and her white-blonde hair, while notably dirty, surrounded her face in a long veil. I could instantly tell that, despite her youthful appearance and power being weakened, most likely a result of exhaustion, she was far older than she appeared. Probably several hundred years old.

"My mate," I said. "The king of Nightfall."

"Ah, the new kingdom." She nodded, tilting her head

while looking me over. "I heard about that right after I first was put down here."

Horrified, I asked, "You've been down here for fifty years?"

"Something like that," she whispered. "I stopped counting after the first few years."

"Why?" I demanded, knowing she'd understand I wasn't asking why she'd stopped counting.

"The King didn't like it when I refused his proposition." She offered a cynical grin, seemingly amused...or maybe angry? I honestly couldn't tell but, it was obvious she had an edge to her. I wouldn't want to be this woman's enemy.

"Ah, that makes sense." I sighed. A minute passed in comfortable silence before I asked, "Why did you decide to answer me this time?"

"Oh, have you tried to talk to me before this?" she asked, wincing as I nodded. "I apologize, then. I tend to go into long meditative sleep states, but something woke me...I can sense something coming."

My smile grew at her words—that's exactly what I wanted to hear.

"Why are you down here?" she asked, returning my question. "You had to have arrived recently, right? I was confused when they cleared the dungeon, but I'm now seeing that a battle is taking place."

"Yes. And because my parents suck," I lamented, not bothering to explain past that. I didn't want her knowing who my parents were lest she think I was anything like the man responsible for putting her in here.

Suddenly, the door upstairs opened, and I knew immediately who it was. The woman went quiet, but this time I knew she was alert and watching. I had a feeling that no matter what I wanted, Reynor was about to make it all too clear who I was. The smarmy asshole appeared at the bottom of the stairs.

"There she is—the lady of the hour," Reynor chuckled, the scent of liquor coming off of him. "I was annoyed when Mother and Father made me stop celebrating our success in battle to come check on you, but to see you looking so pathetic? I'm glad they did."

Success in battle? Or more the realization that he was screwed? I honestly doubted the first, but I wasn't willing to ask him—I knew it wouldn't garner any real answer. I didn't bother responding to him as he came to crouch down in front of me, causing me to lean back slightly, a hiss leaving my lips at the metal cutting into my wrists.

Reynor narrowed his eyes on my wrists. "You dumb bitch. You would rather bleed than be close to me?"

"Absolutely," I leveled.

"You know," he hissed, gripping the cage, "the staff has been talking about your return, about how much they fucking missed you. I had to remind them—hurt them—until they remembered they *didn't* miss you. Already had to kill three of them."

I thought I knew hate, but it was nothing compared to the intensity of my abhorrence for this man.

"You're a fucking monster."

"I am," he agreed with a dirty smirk. "And soon I'll be even more of one once I take away your damn magic. You *know* this ceremony could have been a wedding...instead I'll be watching you get slaughtered. It's a fucking pity."

I had to fight down the bile threatening to rise. I'd only just gotten my magic back, and I refused to lose it again.

Plus, "Dying is preferable to marrying you. I have a mate, and it's not you, Reynor."

"Yes," he responded with a look of disgust. "Well, your mate, who unfortunately survived the night, will not be showing up here—he's been informed that if he attacks, you will die immediately. So don't think that it's only a matter of time until he rescues you."

"Except that's bullshit, and he probably knows that. I mean, you already said you were going to kill her with this ceremony, so if you're doing it either way..." the woman said with a mocking bite that had me nearly smiling, causing Reynor to jump in surprise.

"Who the fuck are you?" he demanded, standing up.

"Gwyndolyn. Or Gwyn, if you're my friend—which you are not," she mused. "In fact, I can't figure out why you're still down here."

"You fucking bitch—"

"Reynor," my mother's voice sounded as two pairs of footsteps echoed down the stairway. *Shit.* Reynor may have been idiotic, but my parents were a true threat.

Running my gaze over their expensively dressed forms, I noticed how tired both of them looked, my mother not even holding my gaze as my father looked at Reynor in distaste. Why the hell would he make him the ruler of Eventide? I didn't understand it.

But I actually did.

"Reynor," I drew out, deciding to point it out to him. "You've probably put it together by now, but you realize why they want you to be the true heir over me, right? Especially now." Now that I wasn't willing to be their puppet.

"Evera, shut up," my mother snapped.

"Because I'm the best." Reynor flashed me a smile.

Oh god. He really didn't know. I almost felt bad for him... but not really.

"Because you're controllable."

"Fuck you," Reynor hissed. "When I rule Eventide, it will be with—"

"The ceremony is set for two hours from now," my father said, interrupting him and squeezing his shoulder so hard that Reynor hissed. "Prepare yourself, Evera."

A surge of anger rolled over me as I narrowed my eyes at him.

"I have nothing to prepare for," I said evenly, not allowing him to diminish my confidence in Axel. I knew without a doubt that he would come for me.

"So eager to die," my mother scolded. "You had everything here—*everything*."

"I had nothing." I made my expression go blank, refusing to let them know how much it had hurt me back then. "I remember *everything* about how you treated me, so don't fucking lie to me."

My father shook his head. "There's no convincing her. Let's go."

As they turned towards the stairs, a sound blasted through the lands that had my smile growing once more—a series of war horns that caused my skin to break out in chills. All of them froze in their tracks as I spoke the words that came to me with joy.

"He's here."

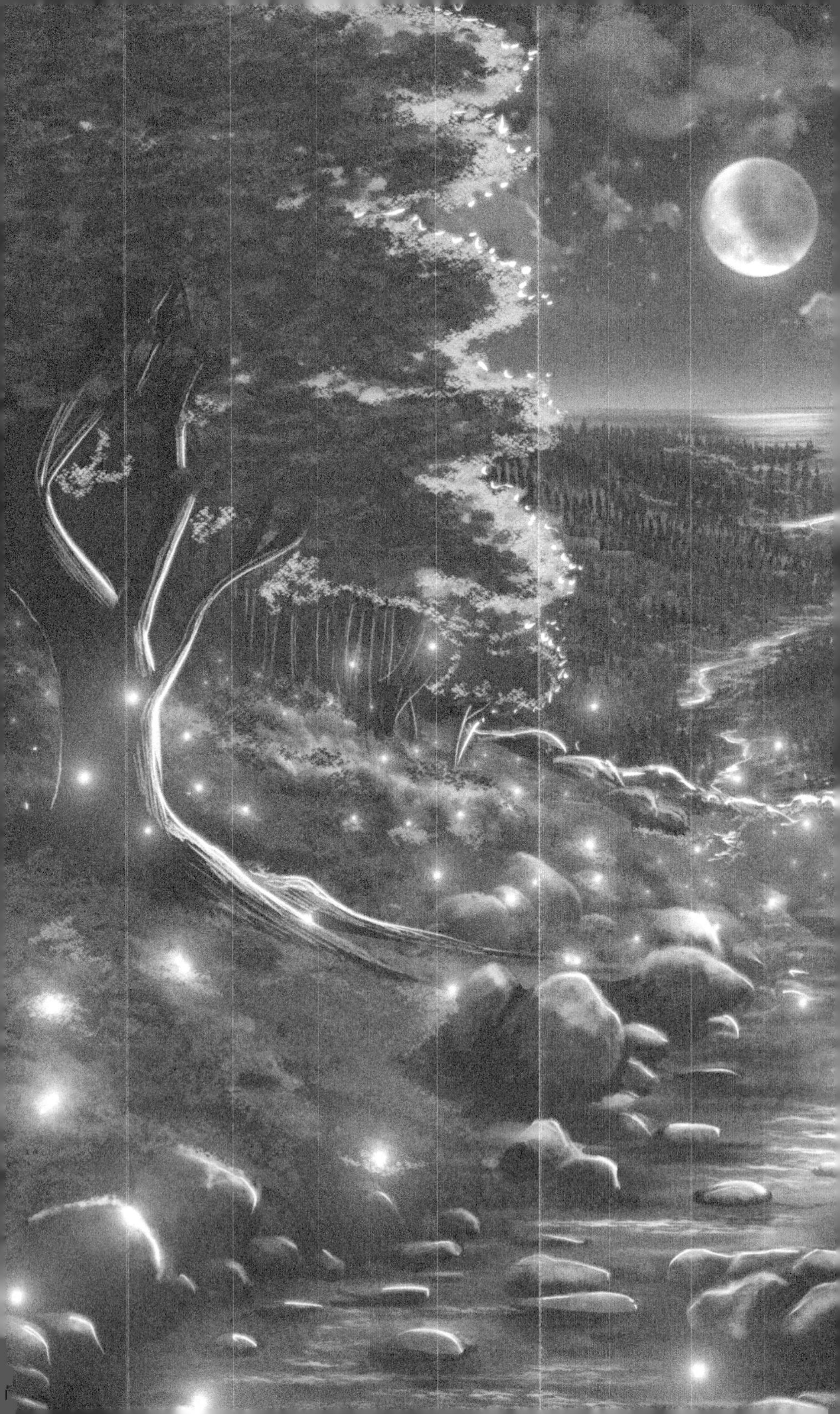

CHAPTER TWENTY-TWO

AXEL

"Where is she, Oliver?"

I knew my voice was far sharper than it should have been, portraying my panic. My friend's brows shot straight up, amusement filtering into his expression.

Bastard.

My posture was rigid as I looked around the gardens once again, my senses open to any sound that would lead me to Evera. How was she always escaping my grasp?

It was driving me mad.

"She told me not to tell you. Royal orders." Oliver shrugged while putting his hands up in a 'what the fuck can I do' gesture.

My chest produced a rumble that had his eyes narrowing in frustration. He cursed and nodded toward the hedge-covered riverbank without saying a word. Probably because he knew she would hear whatever he said, even at a distance.

Muttering a curse, I made my way past the gardens and down the hill towards the river. It was a sunny day, but the wind that rushed over the lands made it a bit more dangerous than normal to *be on the water. As it was, I'd told her it wasn't safe down here, especially by herself, time and time again.*

Not that it ever stopped her, obviously.

The scent of blood that suddenly hit my nose had me breaking into a full sprint. "Evera! Where are you?"

"Over here!" she called before a small hiss left her lips. "Crap, this was a bad idea."

"Yes it was," I agreed, a slight growl to my voice as I scooped her up from the rocky shore of the river.

The bottom of her dress was soaked from standing in the shallows, the material ripped at the knee where she'd fallen and hurt herself. I squeezed her tighter against my chest, ignoring the frantic pounding of my heart.

It was my job to keep her safe, even from her own clumsiness.

At least that was what I continued to tell myself.

Carrying her back up the hill, she offered me a scowl. "You know it's impossible for me to live my entire life without injury, right?"

"That's not true." My voice was hard with the conviction I felt down to my soul. It was absolutely possible for her to live her life without injury. I would make it my personal fucking mission.

"How's that?" she asked, her eyes filled with a soft light.

"Because I won't allow it, çiçeğim."

But I had allowed it. I'd broken the vow I'd made to protect her when I didn't stop her from sacrificing herself. When I didn't stop her from being taken—from being ripped from our bed by her mother and Reynor.

Seething fury ran over me like a hot, molten wave as I tried to contain the anger—tried to contain the unfettered emotions coursing through me. I was barely restraining myself from shifting, barely restraining the urge to slaughter every single Eventide soldier I came across. It wasn't that I didn't want to—rather the opposite, considering—but it wasn't my focus.

My focus was getting to Evera, and I was nearly there.

It hadn't taken much to piece together what had happened last night. How they'd conspired and drugged the drink that my comrades and I consumed.

After Evera had fallen asleep, I'd been eager to hunt down Reynor and end him right there and then. Unfortunately, he'd hidden behind a wall of soldiers and his parents, so I had settled for a drink with the others while considering how I could make him suffer. The war was inevitable, and at this point I was just waiting for them to make a move, willing to stay up until dawn so I could be there when it began.

I should have been suspicious when I was hit with a wave of sleepiness that had me trailing upstairs to return to bed and my mate, but I just assumed that I was exhausted from both the stress associated with protecting my kingdom and the relief that came from mating with Evera.

I'd heard Evera's screams while trapped in a drug-induced stupor, unable to move. It was a sound that would haunt me forever, one that would reside heavily in my soul until we died. It hadn't taken long before I was able to break out of it, though by that point their soldiers had attacked and blocked the mountain pass. We'd been left with no other option but to slaughter those who tried to stop us from retrieving Evera and capture those who surrendered.

Unlike the soldiers of Nightfall, Eventide didn't rely on loyalty to keep its forces strong—rather they used prisoners for their front lines and paid the rest of their forces. It was why it had been so damn appealing to my brothers and I when we were young. Having that knowledge also made it far too easy to convince the Eventide soldiers to surrender upon capture.

It had taken hours, though it felt more like days, but we finally fought our way into Eventide. They'd dedicated most of their forces to defending the pass, leaving very few for us to fight once we were on the other side. I stood at the base of the mountain, looking over the kingdom of Eventide and narrowing my eyes on the castle where Evera was being held prisoner. Her once home.

"The castle is being guarded minimally. Most of their forces were moved forward for the attack, and our scouts have gone ahead to warn the towns to not get involved if they value their lives," Rhaegal said, his body rigid with tension. I knew that both he and Arnoux were bothered by the concept of leaving their mates back at the Midnight Keep, but I needed them completely focused, and there was no way that would happen if they were here.

"Let's go." I signaled to Oliver to join my brother and myself as I shifted into my wolf form. Captain Arnoux would join us later, currently in the thick of battle. As soon as my paws hit the ground, they ate up the space between us and the kingdom. Carnage soaked the land around us, and I easily avoided soldier after soldier, not wanting to waste my time fighting pawns. The pull to get to my mate was so intense that I was certain she could feel me coming for her—that I would extinguish this final threat to our future.

As we approached the castle, I noticed the significant lack of guards, many of the normal stations deserted. My gaze ran over the familiar facade as I instantly clocked a large window in the ballroom, meeting her father's gaze. His face turned ashen, and he backed out of sight as I shifted into human form and strode forward. I had no intention of going after him first, though.

No, my full focus was on getting to Evera.

Reaching the entrance hall of the castle, I looked around the once familiar space, Oliver and Rhegal at my side. Eyeing the terrified staff, I noticed none of them were bothering to run, all of them holding household items close to their chests as if they were going to use a pillow or broom to defend themselves from us.

"I have no intention of hurting any of you if you don't attack first," I announced, my voice echoing in the terrified silence. "I'm looking for where Princess Evera is being held."

The staff exchanged looks, some of the younger members keeping their heads down in submission, causing a frustrated sound to leave my throat. Fear was useful for getting information, but it could also be the reason why someone wouldn't speak up.

Finally, an older woman stepped forward, wringing her hands anxiously. "The princess has been locked away in the dungeon—"

A lethal noise left my chest at the concept of who else might be down there with her. My brother's hand on my shoulder had the noise cutting off as I tried to restrain my fury, not wanting to scare the woman who'd been so helpful.

"I can show you the way," she continued hesitantly.

"We know where it is—thank you."

I began striding across the space, but her voice rang louder. "Thank *you*, King Axel. Please take her from here. The ceremony is set to happen soon, and none of us want to see her hurt."

"Or for Reynor to take over," another man spoke up.

"Neither of those will be happening," I spit out with venom while moving toward the dungeon. There had been only a few times that Evera had gone down to the dungeon, and each time I had fucking hated it.

"Why are there so many down here?" Evera asked quietly. "I didn't realize my parents were so harsh."

That was an absolute understatement.

The cold, damp air of the dungeon was far too rough for her skin, but she'd asked to see it and I knew if I'd denied her, she probably would've found a way down here on her own anyway. Plus, her elegant arm wrapped around mine as she leaned against me made me feel far better, as I was able to shield her from the vision of many that we passed.

I was pretty sure I knew who she was looking for, and it wasn't any of the bastards gawking at her.

"Your parents are harsh," I agreed. "They believe a slight against them is a slight against the crown." And I was extremely critical of that. It wasn't my place to say that to her, but I could see how she felt. Even my own brothers thought the crown was far too reactionary, and our father had been a lead advisor before his death.

"There she is," Evera said, slipping past me and going to a cell where a young girl, no more than fourteen, sat huddled against the bars. Evera knelt down in her silk dress, the others around the girl staring in silent shock.

My assumption on why she'd wanted to come down here had been correct, then—this was the girl who'd been taken in for theft only a few hours ago. She'd stolen food, no doubt for her family, and I'd been too late to intervene before other guards got involved—

ones far less likely to look past an opportunity to lock someone up for the hell of it.

Their conversation was quiet as I kept an eye on the others in the cell with the girl, and when Evera finally stood, I wondered what her plan was.

"Axel, I would like her freed tonight. Can we do that?" she whispered as we walked up the stairs, looking hesitant to ask. "And...and I want food delivered to their home. Her father died a few months ago, so no one is able to work except for her. She has five younger siblings."

"Of course." I nodded, knowing that even if I didn't have the power, I would find a way to make it happen. I would make anything happen for this woman.

The echo that followed us as we made our way down the stairs would no doubt alert Evera we were here. I could hear her heartbeat, loud and strong, and my wolf immediately surged forward to connect with hers.

Rhaegal and Oliver followed me but then turned and went to a far cell in the back, the only other one occupied. A faint heartbeat caught my ear, but I couldn't focus on that—no, my entire attention was on Evera.

"Axel," she whispered, almost in awe. Her hands were wrapped around the bars on the cage and she looked exhausted, bruises covering her exposed skin. I kneeled down on the ground and reached forward, trying to gather as much of her as possible against me. I knew I needed to grab the keys and let her out, but I gave into the desire just to hold her as close as I could—needing to assure myself that she wouldn't disappear the minute I turned away.

My throat felt thick with emotion that I'd allowed this to

happen. I had no idea what to say, so I just buried my nose against her hair, assuring myself that she was here and in my arms.

"They will die for this, *çiçeğim*."

Evera pulled back and looked up at me, her eyes filled with a fierce determination and anger, tears welling as she nodded sharply. "Help me get Gwyn out of here before we leave. She's been down here for fifty years—"

A sharp growl sounded from Oliver down the way, and my head snapped over. The sound hadn't been made in response to my mate's words, but something going on between the three of them. Rhaegal was backing up a bit, giving Oliver and Gwyn space, but I didn't like looking away from Evera long enough to figure it out more than that. Refocusing my attention on my mate, I was confused to see her attention focused there as well, her brow furrowed.

"What's wrong?"

"Nothing. I think the two of them—"

The sound of voices upstairs instantly had me standing and striding towards a compartment where spare keys were kept for the dungeon. They were hidden, but I'd worked here long enough to know exactly what stone to pull out to retrieve them.

We could deal with everything else later. Right now we just needed to get Evera out of here so that I could hunt down her parents.

Tossing a set of keys toward my brother, I knelt down in front of Evera's cell and unlocked the door before turning my attention to her wrists. She hissed as I released the metal there, fresh blood dripping from her skin as I pulled her against me. My mate's body melted against mine as I kissed her hard, a whimper slipping from her lips.

I pulled back and grasped her face gently. "I love you, Evera. I am absolutely never letting you go, çiçeğim."

A spark of joy filled her gaze as she brushed her lips against mine, whispering, "I love you too. So incredibly much."

It shouldn't have been a perfect moment, trapped in the confines of this dungeon with my mate bleeding, but her sweet words were everything...until it was darkened by something far more dangerous.

A sharp sensation pierced through me as a guttural sound broke from my chest, feeling like my body had been burned by a brand that had buried itself in my heart.

Evera gasped and immediately pulled back, blood covering her dress. She didn't seem injured, so where had the blood come from? Her gaze darted behind me, her expression filling with horror. I couldn't move, my body frozen as pain eclipsed everything.

"Reynor," Evera hissed as I looked down at my chest, finding the tip of a blade sticking through it. *Fuck.*

"This is for thinking you can have her." He plunged his sword deeper into my back, the blade slicing through my sternum. I coughed, struggling for breath, as blood poured from my mouth. The swipe of a blade at the back of my neck had my eyes shutting as I fell forward, bracing myself at the last minute on my forearms, my entire body void of feeling except for pain.

Evera's scream echoed around me.

It was the only thing I could hear before everything went dark.

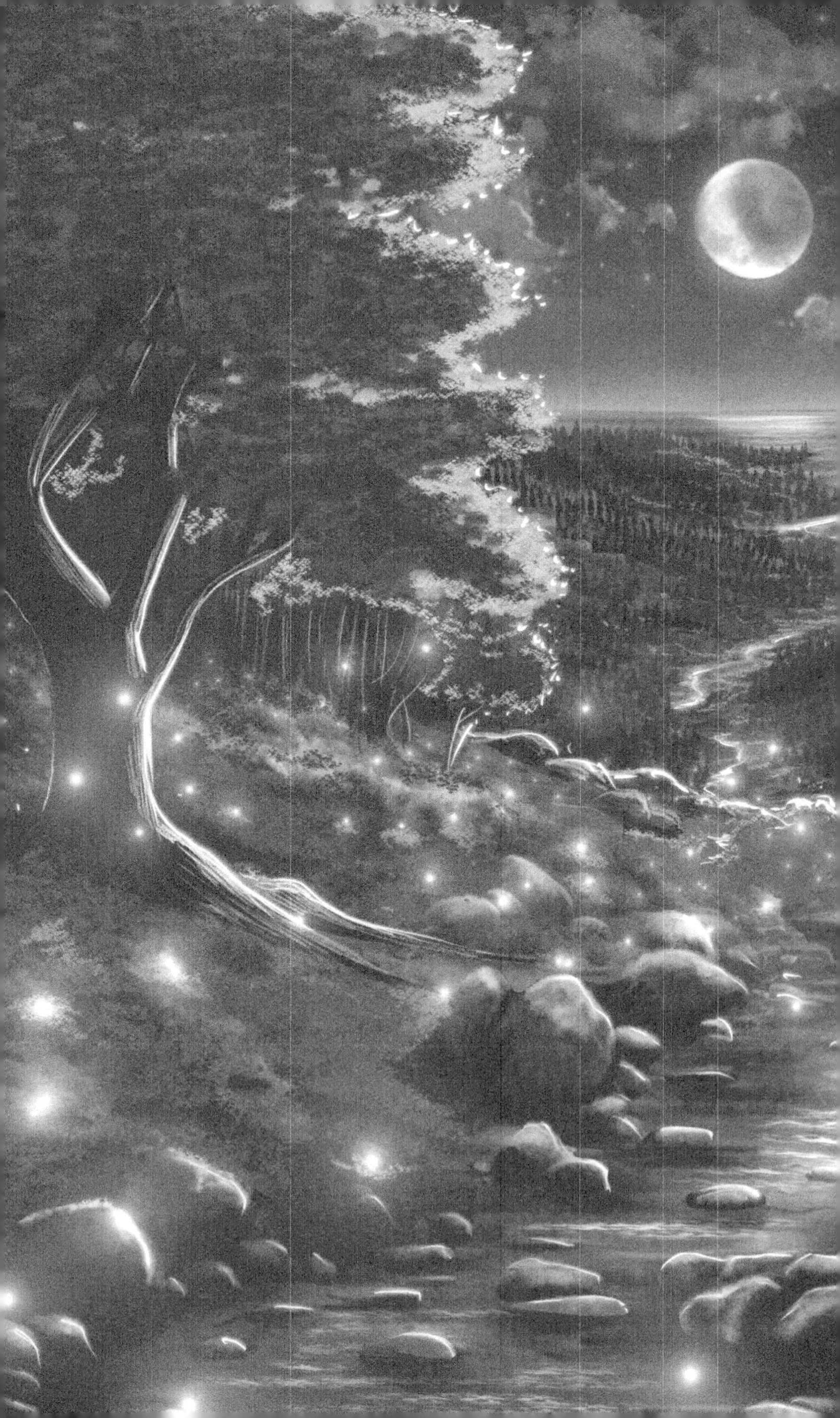

CHAPTER TWENTY-THREE

EVERA

All at once, every single moment and experience with Axel collided in my memory as horror rushed over me, blood coating me from where he'd been pierced through—stabbed in the back.

By a coward.

My mate fell forward, landing on his forearms, and I tried to help him up, supporting him with as much of me as possible. Reynor smirked as he withdrew his sword and put away the dagger he'd used to cut the back of his neck. I held onto my mate, his breath raspy as if a lung had been punctured, his eyes closed. A dangerous growl sounded from somewhere in the dungeon as I began to shake, a red haze filtering over my vision as I kept my gaze on the sole threat here.

"Don't fucking move." Reynor pointed his sword toward the others. The sound of boots filled the air as soldiers rushed down to the dungeon, separating me, Axel, and Reynor from Rhaegal, Oliver, and Gwyn. Their silence spoke volumes for what they would allow to happen down here at Reynor's hand.

"If you move or try to fight them," he said in warning, "I'll kill her."

"You fucking sniveling, low-life *coward*." My voice was a low hiss that had Reynor snapping his gaze to me. "You stabbed him—in the *back*."

"Call me whatever you want; I don't care what I have to do to rid this realm of him. Maybe now that he's almost dead you'll see the benefits of your remaining options." Reynor looked smug as I gently put Axel down on his side, letting his heavy frame rest.

Straightening up, my body shook with rage as I stood in front of my mate protectively. "I see the truth—I see that you are a coward. A fraud. A worm so terrified of Axel you could only kill him by surprise instead of in an honorable way."

"Honor?!" Reynor scoffed. "He's no different than I am. He slayed hundreds of men outside—those that used to serve under him—and for what? We would have left his kingdom alone. He did this only for you. Where's the honor in that?"

"There's always honor in doing things for the ones we love," I retorted, unable to even begin unpacking that backward logic.

While we'd been arguing, my mother and father joined us, apparently believing there was no more threat. My gaze darted to Axel, whose breathing was slowing. This was bad… but shouldn't he be healing? Why wasn't he?

"Poison." Reynor said as if he'd guessed my thoughts, his voice laced with amusement. My spirits sank with dread. *Fuck.*

"You finally managed to do something right," my father drew out, my mother staring at me with nothing but contempt and disgust.

"Come now, Evera. Your mate bond is broken—or will be soon…"

"Shut up!" I screamed, my body shaking. "He will *not* die. I will not allow it. The only ones dying will be the three of you."

Before they could react to my words, my magic sparked like wildfire—and I shifted.

Pain radiated through every nerve ending as my skin split open, and a savage howl broke from my throat, filling the space with a deadly energy blast. Throwing my head back, I howled again, bloodlust and fury like I'd never experienced infecting every single part of me. I was a predator, and the prey standing in front of me wouldn't make it out of here alive.

I absolutely snapped.

I didn't hesitate to lunge right for Reynor, flattening him to the ground before burying my teeth in his throat and tearing. The bloody gurgle that left him as I spit his skin from my mouth was satisfying, my blood pumping loud in my ears.

This was for Axel. This was the least Reynor deserved for what he'd done to my mate.

My mother's scream pierced the air—until my father slit her throat. Fast, efficient, his face filled with annoyance at her fear. This was far from the first time he'd killed, but no matter how skilled, he was next.

I stalked forward, baring my teeth as her body went limp, my father's eyes widening as he realized he was cornered. I let out a dangerous growl as he put his sword out in front of him, his grip shaky at the prospect of facing me.

"I'm warning you, girl, you will not survive this. You'll end up just like your mate—*dead*."

It was the wrong thing to say.

Lost in a haze of rage, I poured every ounce of heartbreak and fury into what I did next. I may have ripped out Reynor's throat, but I absolutely ruined the king of Eventide, ripping pieces off of him one by one until he was no longer recognizable. He deserved it for everything I'd watched him do in my previous life and now this one. My mother and Reynor had played their parts, but I knew who held the power, who was truly responsible for this—and my magic, my wolf, demanded that I destroy him.

I hated every drop of blood I tasted in my mouth, not wanting anything belonging to him. When his heart stopped beating I felt relieved, felt safe enough to back away slowly and shift.

I stood on shaky legs and looked over my slain enemies. I'd been right from the start—my magic had been hiding, waiting for the right moment to reveal itself. Waiting for the opportunity to eliminate the true threat to myself, my magic, and my mate.

Which was why I couldn't believe it was too late to save Axel, poison or not.

Plus, I'd finally shifted, and I needed...I needed to tell Axel that. He would be so excited for me, I absolutely knew it. So why couldn't I move my eyes from the three corpses around me? Why did I feel numb with terror at the idea of looking at my mate? Why did our connection feel almost... invisible now?

No. He wasn't dead. *They* were dead.

They were finally dead. Blood coated my hands, Reynor's dead eyes staring at me from where he lay on the ground. My mother's form was crumbled against the stone wall, and my father's body was...somewhere. I couldn't see past the blood around me. Voices filled the dungeon, but there was only one that stood out to me. Gwyn.

"They're dead," she said loudly, walking forward. None of the soldiers even tried to stop her. "I promise you, they're dead, but your mate—"

My head snapped toward Axel and I sped to him, kneeling in the blood pooling around his body. His eyes were closed, and his breathing was labored and so incredibly slow. His life force was dwindling. Rolling him onto his back, I clasped his face gently.

"Axel," I whispered, my voice so faint it was nearly inaudible. "You can't…you can't die."

There was no answer, and I could feel tears streaming down my cheeks. I'd heard his brother call for medical aid, but we couldn't move Axel in this state, and help wouldn't make it in time. I could feel how long he had left, and it wasn't enough.

"Please don't leave me," I begged louder, sobbing as I rested my forehead against his own.

Axel's voice rumbled under my ear, and I tightened my hold on him. "I could never leave you, whether in this life or the last."

Hot tears dropped onto his face as I kissed him softly, feeling desperate and lost. My entire body was trembling, and something in the center of my chest shuddered at the thought of losing our other half. The man we loved. *Our mate.* The castle around me creaked as the stone underneath me shook, the power from the land pushing upward, its golden threads reaching for my magic.

This land was mine. This kingdom was mine. *Axel* was mine.

The threads wrapped around the two of us, pulling on

our magic and pulsating its own into us in waves. The realm recognized us, and I refused to let him be taken from me. We were the rightful heirs of the entire territory, and I knew the magic here would recognize that. That it would help me right the wrong that had been done.

Reynor's selfish action was nothing compared to our love, which had transcended the confines of life. Memories of our time together flashed before my eyes, and his own memories fueled mine, showing me how he viewed us.

Showing me how much he'd always loved me.

Like a movie reel, they played behind my closed eyes that were hot with tears. I valued each and every one, the moments like precious stones I wanted to collect and keep forever. Axel had known from the start what was between us, that a mate bond could easily form for us—but instead of pushing for that, he'd promised me his protection and nothing else. He had pledged his life to me...and now he'd given his life to save mine.

A heart-wrenching sound left my lips as his breathing became shallow and slowed to almost nothing, his heartbeat barely there.

"No," I growled, squeezing him. "No. You cannot leave me—"

My words exploded my magic, and all at once gold power streamed through my hands and into him, the threads from the realm wrapping us in a golden cocoon. Shadows of wolves, like faint gold whispers that sparkled, ran across my skin as the world shook underfoot. My skin felt flushed and hot, and my eyes fluttered shut as I poured every ounce of intention I had into keeping Axel alive.

I would not lose him. I refused.

I would protect him this time—for once *I* would be the one to save *him*.

As if hearing me, my magic continued to build, flooding our mate bond. It wrapped around the tether and solidified it in a metal casing, completely untouchable to anyone outside of us. Thousands of howls echoed in my ears as the rushing wind and ocean surrounding Vargr celebrated the union, my body shielding Axel protectively from the rest of the world as a faint smile pressed onto my lips.

The hole in his chest was healing.

My magic was being drained, but I couldn't have cared less. I would give every ounce of my magic and love for him.

Finally, my arms gave out completely, as I sank against him. His heartbeat grew stronger as mine became softer, and I heard a whisper of my name as my heavy eyes began to close, Axel's hands tightening on me. It was everything I could hope for, contentment soothing my despair.

As darkness closed around me, there was one thought that eclipsed everything. No matter what, no matter what happened to me…*he would live.*

My mate would live.

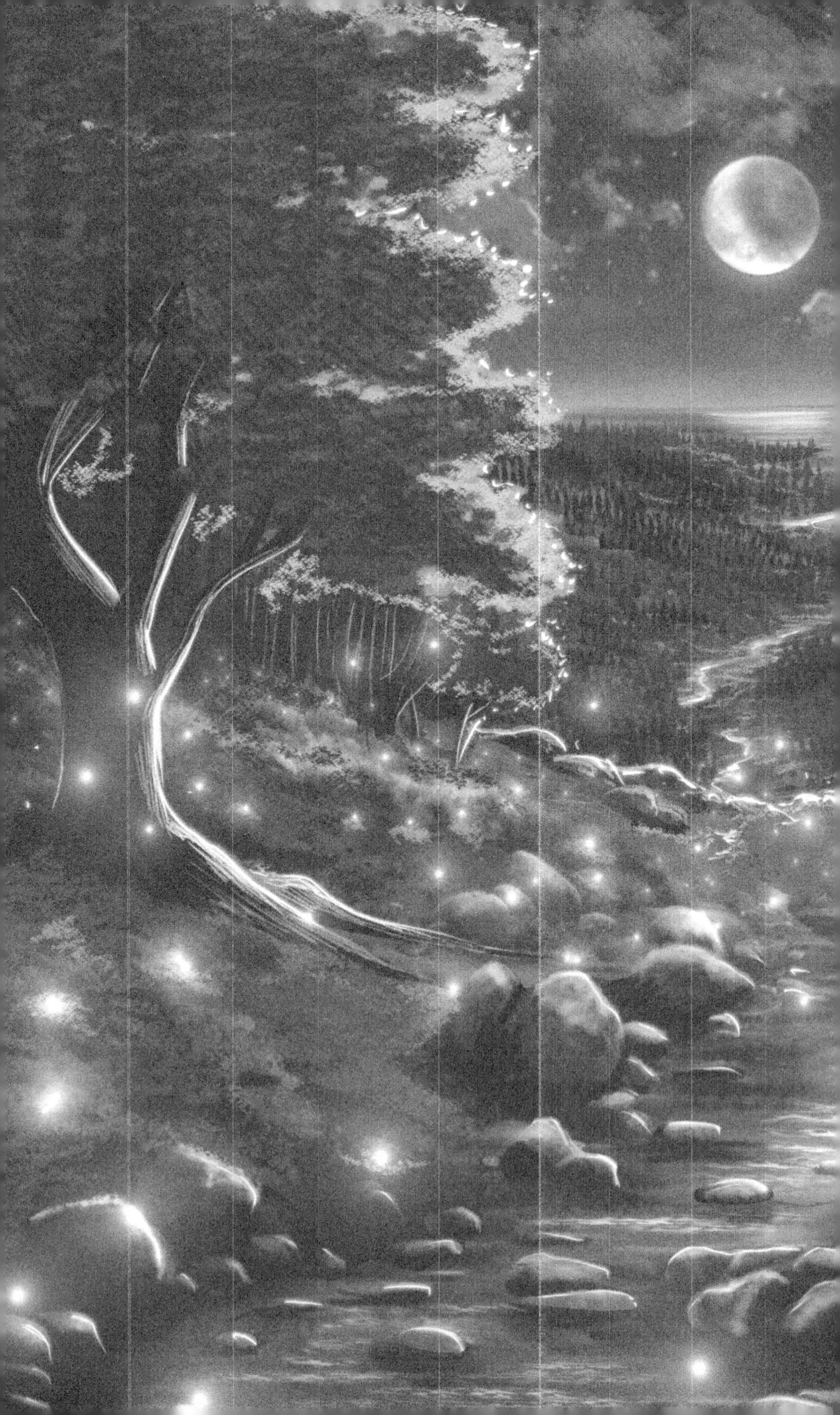

CHAPTER TWENTY-FOUR

AXEL

Raw, unfiltered agony lanced through me as the tether between Evera and me began to unravel, the thread fraying into tiny pieces that blew away in the gale wind that ravaged Vargr. The sky above us cracked with thunder, and the ground shook with the power of what was taking place within the Sacred Temple.

I knew Evera was there—I knew she'd gone, and I'd been too late to stop her.

Now I knelt outside of Var's empty temple with no way to reach her, her anguish echoed in every single one of my nerve endings. A furious howl ripped through my chest as my skin burst, and I found myself shifted into my half-form.

The torment spiraling through me was a mixture of Evera's torment and my own, knowing that my mate was being put through hell. My heart was shattering, being ripped from my chest, as her life force weakened, her soft voice in my head repeating my name again and again.

I would willingly rip out my heart, bloody and raw, and give it right to her if it meant saving her. Evera was sacrificing everything for Vargr, and for the first time in my life I felt helpless. I couldn't stop her.

I couldn't stop my mate, the woman I loved, from giving her own life for her people.

A tortured sound ripped from my throat as I felt her heartbeat slow and her whisper of my name grow fainter.

I regretted so much. I should have told her we were mates. That I loved her. That I needed her.

It was too late, though. Far too late.

A tormented howl broke from my throat as the connection with Evera broke. Silence drowned me as my body gave out, my knees going weak, and everything seized up in the realization that we'd lost her.

Evera was dead.

"You should be resting."

I offered Vanessa a blank expression from where she and Caz stood near the end of the bed, both of them knowing damn well that I wasn't moving. Not until Evera opened those stunning eyes. Currently, her dark lashes hadn't moved, still resting against her flushed cheeks as she occasionally turned her head or buried herself further under the covers.

I could hear her heartbeat far stronger now that we were back at the castle. I could feel her magic and wolf coursing with energy after only twenty-four hours of expending it all...yet she hadn't woken. Only her soft breathing made me feel moderately better, but even that did very little. Inhaling, I let out a frustrated groan and ran a hand over my face. What was I going to do with this woman?

Love her—for the rest of eternity, if Marx was to be believed.

In the dungeon, Evera had done something unexpected and completely unheard of. My brilliant mate had bonded our life forces, as the two recognized true heirs, to Vargr itself—ensuring that as long as the land was here, we would be as well. That our bloodline would continuously rule for centuries to come.

It made it so that we were not only immortal, but that our mate bond was completely unbreakable. Not even death could separate us again.

Which is why, of course, I shouldn't have been worried about her health, but instead I felt more anxious than I had in a very long time.

"I'm fine," I promised the two of them, who were still looking at me expectantly.

Marx scoffed from the doorway, and as I looked over, I noticed the documents tucked under his arm. Medical staff trailed in after him, and I stood to let the physician take over—though I only moved two feet away, enough so they could do what they needed but I could still watch her every breath.

"Join me." Marx nodded toward two armchairs positioned further from the bed. They were only a few feet away from my current position, but I'd gone far enough. I grabbed both of them and shifted them closer. Marx shook his head as Vanessa glared at me.

"What?" I asked, rubbing a hand across my bandaged chest. She worried too much; I was fine. More fine than I would have been if it wasn't for Evera. I wasn't sure how I wanted to punish her for doing something so reckless and self-sacrificing, but I was sure I'd manage something.

Scratch that—I knew exactly what I'd be doing when she woke, and it had nothing to do with punishment.

Letting out a frustrated rumble at her still not being up, I sat down and motioned for Marx to join me. I knew he had updates on the state of the realm outside these walls, and despite how troublesome he could be, I'd never been so thankful for him and my brothers.

Yes, *brothers*—both blood and not.

In the wake of what happened, I was surprised to find Xakery concerned about our wellbeing—not only mine and Evera's, but Rhaegal's as well—his normal problematic disposition absent as he stood by my side while the medical staff attended to our injuries.

In the long hours of the night as I watched over Evera, he'd taken the time to stop by to see how she was doing, which led to a long-overdue conversation. It probably hadn't been the best timing...or maybe it was perfect, because we'd finally gotten to the core of the problem—*why he was always trying to start shit.*

"I know you've always wanted the crown," I leveled at him. I wasn't sure why he thought he was entitled to it, but it had always been his focus. Or at least I assumed so, considering his commentary on my leadership, and more often, the position he was in compared to my own.

Xakery shook his head, letting out a long sigh. "I don't want your crown, brother. I don't always agree with your choices, but I know this is your land."

"So what's the problem then?"

"I feel useless," he admitted. "Rhaegal works with Captain Arnoux every single day, aiding in the progress of our military—

he's useful to you. I'm not. I do nothing. I'm labeled as an advisor, but I'm sure it's only because of nepotism. You've never once asked me for my advice, and when I offer it, you ignore it. I mean, unless I was being an asshole you acted like I didn't exist in the first place."

Was that true? My brow dipped. "Is the military—"

"Goddess, no." He chuckled. "No interest in that, but I would like my advice to be taken seriously. I'm not trying to cause problems, but the more you've ignored me over the years, the more I've assumed you don't want me here. Thank the goddess she sent you Evera because at least she was willing to listen to me—what were you thinking, going to meet her parents without a plan?"

Shock radiated through me at the obvious concern in his voice.

Inhaling, I considered his words. "I assumed your criticisms of my leadership and your position were implying something else."

"I wouldn't know the first thing about being king," he admitted. "But I also can't continue on for the next several hundred years feeling useless."

Nodding, I offered him a look of understanding. "Take your pick of what you'd like to do, Xakery. I don't want to lose you."

The resolution between us had gone a long way to remove a heavy weight on my shoulders that I hadn't realized had been there. One that had grown heavier at the concept of losing my brother because of our inability to live in peace. Now I understood that neither of us were communicating what was necessary.

Marx had suggested he work as the ambassador to Eventide as we mended Vargr and figured out what to do following the short-lived conflict. Apparently in our absence, he and Marx had worked to keep the citizens of Nightfall calm and to keep things running smoothly. Xakery had been on board, deciding to immediately travel there with two of the council members to ensure no uprising or coup took place in the absence of leadership. Especially before Evera woke up.

I was extremely grateful for the help from him, because I wanted Vargr to thrive, and for that to happen I needed Evera by my side—so I wouldn't leave hers until she woke.

Rhaegal and Arnoux were handling the aftermath of the conflict and the military fallout of both kingdoms—from injuries, to lives lost, to the prisoners that surrendered to our kingdom mid-battle. It wasn't going to be an easy process. People were angry at the loss of lives, and with Evera's parents dead, there wasn't anyone for the people of Eventide to place the blame on except us.

Still, I had a feeling that once Evera was able to travel to Eventide to announce her status as true heir, things would go smoother. I had no idea how we were going to rule both kingdoms since I didn't plan to be away from my mate for more than a few hours—at most—but I was positive we could find a solution. Until then, we planned to focus on recovery and putting the pieces of Eventide back together.

"Oliver sent word that he'll be arriving shortly," Marx said. "There was a group of shifters living in the mountains in fear of both kingdoms, and there's a woman with him that's from there—Gwyndolyn, I believe?"

"Yes." I should have known there was another reason for Oliver to have stayed in Eventide for all those years—something that became obvious when he made a beeline for Gwyndolyn when we got to the dungeon.

I didn't know the woman personally, but from the short

conversation I'd had with Rhaegal, two things were clear. First that she was his mate, and second that something had been stopping him from getting her out of that cell. I didn't understand the nature of it, whether it was her magic or something from Evera's parents, but Rhaegal had been the only one that could even touch the bars. When Oliver tried, he'd been brought to his knees by the power surging through them.

The two of them had all but run off together following the incident. I was just curious to hear the full story and to have them back.

"Make sure to give them and the wolves they're bringing back with them access to whatever they need. We don't want them to fear us."

Marx nodded and made a note for himself. Taking care of these things would normally be something Kathleen and Arnoux would handle, but they along with Rhaegal and Clari were still traveling back to the castle.

The physician completed his exam and turned to give us his report. "Evera is healing remarkably fast compared to last time. Right now she's sleeping, but I would expect her to wake very soon."

Thank fuck.

After discussing a few more pertinent topics with Marx, everyone cleared the room and left me to my vigil. Moving to the bed, I stretched out next to her and stared down at my beautiful mate, wanting to pull her into my arms but finding myself fearful of hurting her.

Muttering a curse, I closed my eyes and let my mind drift in and out of plans for the future. I was half asleep, finally feeling the extent of my injuries now that I was slightly more relaxed, when movement next to me had my eyes snapping open. Evera stared up at me with wide eyes, a smile breaking onto her lips.

"Axel," she whispered, running her hand up my chest and resting it on my heart. Our mate bond thrummed happily as I gently pulled her closer. She sighed happily and melted against me, her nose against my throat.

"How is this possible? Or am I dreaming? I thought…I thought I died back there."

She nearly had.

Pulling back and clasping her jaw, I looked over her expressive face that was filled with so much hope and the tiniest bit of concern. "No, *çiçeğim*, this isn't a dream. We're here, both of us, because of you. Because of how strong you are. You saved us, Evera."

Tears welled in her eyes as she surged forward and kissed me hard. I monitored my grip on her, making sure to not squeeze her too tightly as she fit her body perfectly against my own. When she pulled back, I could see a sea of emotion in those stunning eyes, and not for the first time I felt so damn lucky that after all this time I could have Evera as mine. Forever.

"I love you, Axel."

"I love you, *çiçeğim*," I rumbled, picking her up and carrying her toward the bath. I didn't even bother fighting the urge to take care of her, and frankly, I didn't trust myself in bed with her.

Considering the coy look on her face, I had a feeling she was well aware of that.

Evera

"You're going to be the death of me," Axel grumbled against my neck, my body filled with a liquid satisfaction, my skin flushed, and my hair damp from our bath.

I was laid out on the bed underneath him, and despite trying to convince me that I should have been focused on recovery, it hadn't taken much to persuade him that what I actually needed was for him to be inside of me.

"You didn't seem *that* against it," I teased, his hips pushing forward as a moan left my throat, his length still buried deep inside of me. I couldn't express the relief and joy I felt at seeing him when I opened my eyes—I hadn't expected to survive what happened in the dungeon, let alone wake up in bed with my mate.

"Just worried about you, çiçeğim. Trying my damn best to take care of you," he said, staring at the place we were connected as he slowly pulled out. My body instantly felt the loss.

Dipping his head, Axel traced his lips down my throat and nipped my neck right on his mating mark. A shiver of delight raced over my skin as a happy sigh of his name left my lips.

Biting down on my lip in thought, I realized there was something else I wanted…our mating bond was fully in place, only taking one bite to do so, but I still wanted my bite on him. I wanted my mark on his neck, a clear marker that I owned him as much as he owned me. It was possessive, but I had a feeling he wouldn't mind…

Wrapping my legs around his hips, I rolled us, Axel easily adjusting to the new position and pulling me on top of him, a deep rumble rolling from his chest as he ran his gaze over every inch of me.

"Fuck, you're perfect," he murmured. I could feel how

much he meant that, considering how hard he was against my ass. Leaning down, I brushed my lips against his neck and slid back so that his length was sliding right against my center. A pained sound left him as I rolled my hips and the tip of his length pressed into me.

"Axel," I murmured, "I want to mark you—"

"Yes," he growled instantly, his cock pulsing as I slid further down on him, both of our releases making it easy for him to push inside of me. Offering him a heated look, my wolf and magic rolled over my skin before I surged forward and bit down on his pulse.

Our wolves connected and our mating bond lit up, our magic thrilled with the additional marker, creating a golden glow around our bond.

The action also landed me back on my back as Axel pushed into me in a hard thrust, his full length impaling my center as I gasped out his name. Somehow the man managed to dominate me while keeping his weight off my body, ensuring I only felt complete pleasure. One of his hands gripped my hip, the other pulling my hands above my head as he began to slide in and out of me, my mark on him turning gold as a wave of satisfaction ran through me.

"This feels amazing," I whimpered, my legs opening further to account for his large frame as he slammed his hips forward, continuously pounding inside of me.

"This—*you*—feel like home." He leaned down to nip my lip, a moan slipping from my mouth.

"I am home with you," I whispered.

"Forever."

I couldn't help but smile up at him.

"Forever."

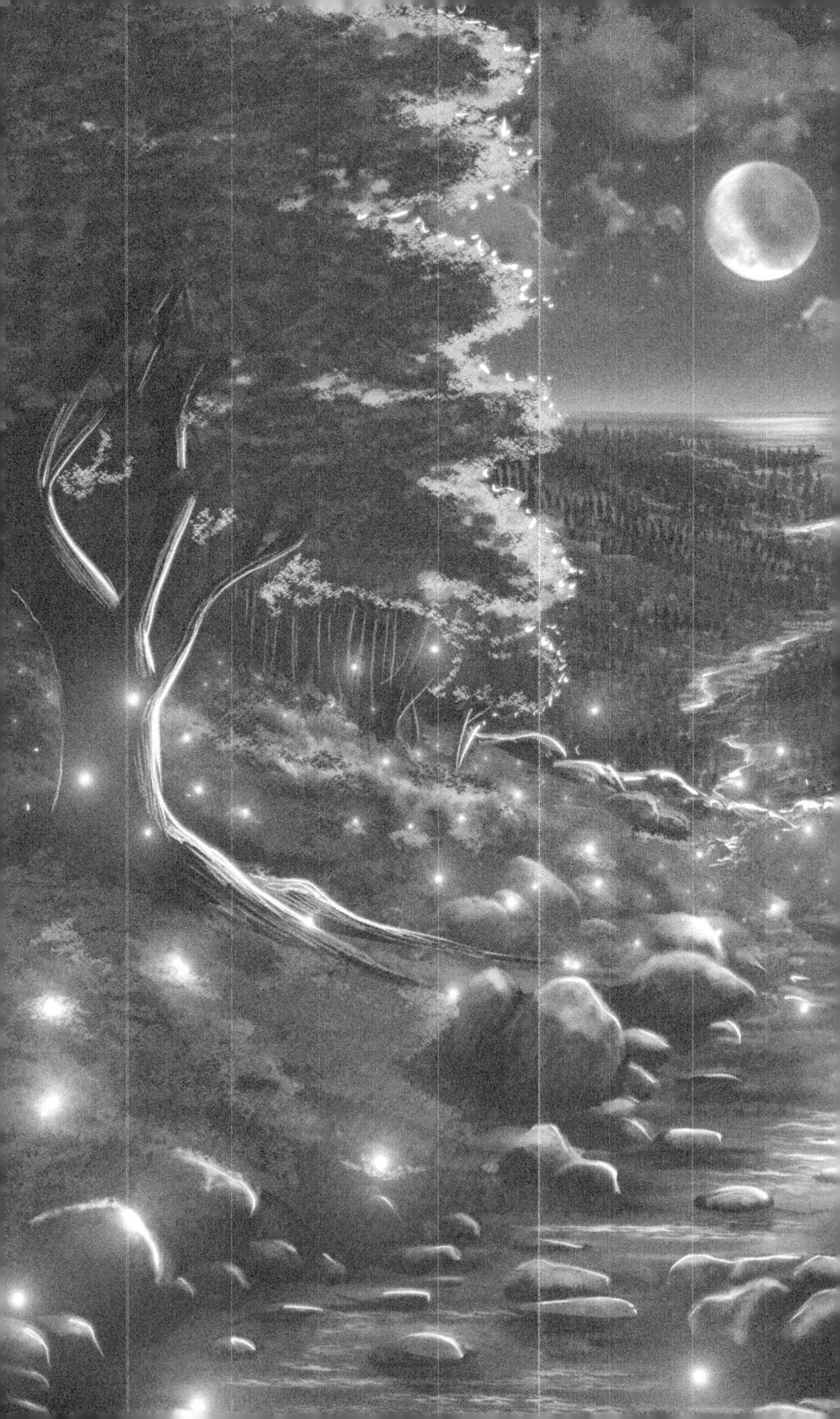

EPILOGUE

EVERA

TEN YEARS LATER...

"Mom!" a frustrated call of one of my many titles had me snapping my head to the right as my nine-year-old daughter practically threw herself into my arms.

I caught Missandei easily, spinning her around and savoring the hug before placing her back on the ground. I swear, the girl was getting far too old far too fast.

"What's up, honey?" I examined her expression, a scowl etched into her pretty face. Despite looking every bit the princess she was, wearing a copper-colored dress with a bronze crown covered in moonstones over her bouncy brown curls, there were telltale signs of the little girl I saw every day.

The little girl who was normally covered in dirt, hair messy after spending all day running through the forest with one of her playmates or cousins. Today she'd insisted on the dress though, thrilled to dress up like me, which was why her expression and disposition was more than a bit alarming.

"He's doing it again," she growled, her green eyes filled with a fierce light.

"Your brother?" He was my first suspect since the two fought like cats and...wolves? Sure.

I looked over her shoulder to the path that led from the party. Vanessa shook her head from next to me, going through her checklist with Caz as if we weren't dealing with a *very* dramatic problem right now. One I was still unclear on.

"No." She put her hands on her hips. "Rozen."

Ah, that explained it.

Rozen was only a month older than Missandei and the firstborn son to Captain Arnoux and Kathleen. They had twin girls as well, only two years old.

If I had to guess, Rozen would be here any moment. He'd always been right at my daughter's side from the time they could walk.

"What did he do?"

"Nothing!" Rozen growled, right on cue. He was quite worked up for a nine-year-old. As if realizing his tone, he snapped his head up to me and blushed. "Sorry, Queen Evera. I just meant...I just meant that it wasn't a big deal."

"Yes it is! You embarrassed me," my daughter growled.

"What happened?" Vanessa asked as Caz walked away, returning to the celebration. I shrugged as I continued to watch the two kids, knowing they would sort it out. They were best friends, after all, and well...I had a prediction of their future, but my husband wasn't a huge fan of my theory.

He hated the idea of our kids ever having mates or future partners, especially our two daughters. Speaking of which...

Axel flashed me a knowing smile, approaching us with our youngest, Laurain, clinging to his back like a little monkey. Her three-year-old smile was bright as she waved to me while continuing to look around the forested canopy above us and humming under her breath.

When naming our youngest daughter, there hadn't been a doubt in my mind who I wanted to name her after—whose memory I wanted to honor. Laurain had been one of the bright spots of my time on Earth, so I'd commissioned an artist to create an oil painting based on the picture I'd brought from Las Vegas, which now hung in my office in Eventide.

Every time I looked at it, I was reminded of everything I'd gone through—the strength I'd gained from those experiences, enough so to stand up to my parents—and the kindness she had shown me. The way she'd shown me that, in a world filled with darkness, compassion still existed.

So it only made sense that I honored her memory in a fitting way.

"I was dancing with Jeremy and then Rozen literally pushed him away!" Missandei exclaimed, the boy in question not looking upset or apologetic in the least.

"Good job," Axel commended, clapping Rozen on the shoulder before looking down at our daughter. "You don't need to be dancing with boys, let alone a twelve-year-old. There are plenty of other people to dance with."

"See!" Rozen said, making me want to roll my eyes.

Missandei scowled and threw her hands up before stalking away, Rozen following after. Vanessa offered us an amused look and trailed behind, looking over her clipboard.

I offered Axel a knowing look. "You know you commend him, but I think we're both aware why—"

"No" Axel rumbled and put a hand around my waist, leading me toward the party.

Laurain jumped down from his back and skipped ahead of us, dressed head to toe in a bright pink frilly dress with massive bows on her head. To say she was obsessed with the color was an understatement—I rarely saw her in anything else.

I completely blamed Clari.

She and Rhaegal had all boys, so she'd decided that any girls Kathleen, Gwyn, or myself had would be completely at the mercy of her fashion choices. Laurain loved it, while Missandei felt...well, half the time—like today—she loved it, and the other half she hated it.

Suddenly, rambunctious yelling echoed through the space and five shorter frames darted onto the path, nearly knocking over Laurain. Axel shot forward and grabbed our son, who groaned in defeat.

Seifer was nearly six and best friends with his cousins—Clari and Rhaegal's gaggle of sons—who all stopped, offering Axel a sheepish look. Each of them had armfuls of sweets, and my son's face was covered in cake.

"Watch out for your sister, you nearly knocked her over," my husband warned. Laurain flashed a smile and continued humming, having already moved on. Listen, she was only three, so I knew it wasn't on purpose—but *man* did she come off as sassy...well, almost *all of the time.*

"I promise, I promise!" he growled, and Axel dropped him. He ran off, and Axel pulled me back into his side as we continued down the path. Running off with candy was the least of our concerns when it came to the five of them. Plus, it was a celebratory day, so if it kept them occupied I would take it.

"How are you feeling?" he asked. He knew I hadn't slept

well last night, but that had way more to do with what I'd been doing and not my ability to sleep.

"I'm just happy she's okay," I said quietly.

Despite the events of today, I'd been in the medical center all night because Gwyn, who was on her third pregnancy, had fallen while out in the training yard overseeing one of the new squadron units. She was completely fine, but she was being monitored. Oliver had been by her side since she went in, their two kids under our watch for the day. Well, not *only* our watch.

"No." Lavender, Gwyn's oldest daughter, was glaring at Xakery and Rhaegal. I almost laughed at Xakery's expression, looking completely taken aback, as his wife—Gwyn's sister Pandi—shot me a smile. "I will absolutely not be nice to them."

"I'm just saying, exchanging pleasantries—"

"They don't deserve it," her twin brother, Erik, agreed. They were the same age as Missandei and were so incredibly dangerous together. Probably the funniest but biggest troublemakers out of all the kids.

"Plus, you aren't nice to people just because," Lavender pointed out as Xakery's mouth dropped open in shock. Pandi burst out laughing as Rhaegal offered an amused smile.

I knew Pandi was worried about Gwyn, dark circles under her eyes from staying up all night as well, but she was doing her best to keep it together for her niece and nephew. I wished I could do more to ease their worry, but I knew that Gwyn would be okay. It just would take a few more days until everyone felt better after such a scare.

While Pandi and Xakery had never had kids, they were naturals at handling them. I could tell they were working hard today to keep Lavender and Erik distracted, even if it meant arguing about useless stuff.

"Can't argue there," I murmured as Laurain went to sit on Pandi's lap. Axel and I made our way to the head table, knowing that they would continue back and forth for a while. The twins *loved* fighting and arguing.

"This is beautiful," I said, looking over the massive celebration laid out before me.

The autumn had turned the Darkridge Mountains red and orange, like they were on fire beneath the setting sun, as citizens from both kingdoms gathered to celebrate Havestia. A day that always reminded me of when I'd come back here —come back *home*. When everything in my life had changed, setting a new course for Vargr's future.

It had taken about three months following my kidnapping and the events that ensued, but we'd been able to clear house in the Kingdom of Eventide. We removed problematic individuals who threatened the future of both kingdoms while offering positions and land to those I knew I could trust.

It had been easy to tell who mourned my parents because they'd almost immediately acted out.

Something we squashed.

It had been a long time since Vargr had experienced true peace, and we knew the only way it would happen was if change was enacted—radical change.

Luckily, with Axel's help we'd been able to craft a way to move forward with the Kingdom of Eventide based on a new structure that was not only far more democratic but encouraged independent commerce and trade with the other territories in Terrea.

It was a concept my parents would have never allowed

for, concerned that if their citizens gained too much financial power they would revolt against them. A valid concern since they never did anything that wasn't self-serving.

I didn't worry about a revolt.

In large part because both kingdoms had adopted the policy of having citizen-elected representatives serving on our councils to aid in decision-making. I was proud to say that had been my idea.

In a decade, we had come so incredibly far.

I could still remember how proud Axel had looked when I'd stood in front of all of Eventide during my coronation. I'd been scared, worried I wasn't ready for such a massive responsibility, but something about vowing to protect the land and its people felt so right. Vowing to remove my parents' shadow from where it hung threateningly over Vargr.

No trace of them or Reynor existed—even the crown I wore was different from the ones worn by my parents. Made of gold and moonstone, it was elegant, simple, and representative of the land. It had been crafted for me by the same individual who made Axel's crown, and I absolutely loved it.

While the responsibility of being a monarch was heavy, I wasn't scared. With my mate ruling by my side, I knew there would be no shortage of prosperity and peace. Something I was personally celebrating tonight, considering it had been ten years to the day that I'd arrived.

Axel also liked to consider it our anniversary, along with several other dates—he pretty much looked for any excuse in the book to celebrate the two of us. Following the incident with my parents, Axel stayed true to his word and continuously worked at being better about not only communicating with me but having me be a part of everything in his kingdom—just how he was a part of everything within my own. I hadn't thought it was possible to love the man more than I did, but every single day he gave me more and more reasons to fall in love with him.

Our actual wedding anniversary was a month from now—we even planned a trip to visit several of Terrea's territories with our kids. While I hadn't had the opportunity to host many of the leaders from the other territories, outside of visiting and having Stella here, I'd been in correspondence with most of them. It was the first step in my plan to foster better communication throughout Terrea, and considering all the rulers were the same women who stood by my side when we sacrificed ourselves to save the Sacred Tree, I had high hopes.

The first kingdom on our itinerary would be Isramaya to see Queen Rhodelia and King Varan. We'd heard so many fascinating tales about the Courts of Blood and Nightmares that I knew we couldn't leave it off our list, and I'd been happily surprised when Rhodelia and Varan accepted our invitation to come and celebrate with us tonight. I'd extended the offer to all of the kingdoms, though I hadn't really expected anyone to come since many already had celebrations planned within their territories—so I was thrilled to have Rhodelia and Varan as guests.

I wasn't positive what reaction I'd expected from our people, but the foreign royals had been received with a warmth that made me feel proud of our kingdom. We'd come a long way since Valandril almost destroyed all of us, and most of Terrea had been hesitant to trust his son following the incident—understandably so. But in the ten years since he took over, King Varan had proved over and over that he was nothing like this father.

Right now, Varan was watching his wife from the edge of the dance floor with a wide smile on his face. Queen Rhodelia danced in circles with about a dozen little girls, the group of them all quite obsessed with her long silver hair and even more so with the floor-length gown that seemed entirely made out of diamonds, sparkling as it moved. No one cared about their long, sharp fangs—they were just new and interesting friends.

And I truly did consider them friends. My thoughts drifted to when they had first arrived yesterday, Axel and I immediately greeting them within the throne room.

"It looks like this is quite the celebration you're having tomorrow." King Varan's amber eyes were warm and friendly, and he smiled down at Rhodelia who was looking around the throne room with interest. After their initial arrival, it quickly became apparent that formalities weren't necessary between the four of us, and we found ourselves talking as if we'd been close friends for years.

"Not just tomorrow, either," Axel explained, looking down at me with amusement. "Several days. We've already set up accommodations for you two to stay as long as you want."

"We appreciate that." Varan squeezed Rhodelia's waist, and she moved her attention back to us.

"I couldn't believe everything we passed on the way here!" Rhodelia exclaimed. "The entire mountain was lit up with tents and flooded with people. It looks like it's going to be amazing."

"I hope you enjoy it," I told them honestly. "It's not very often that we get to host other territories."

"I don't think enjoying it won't be a problem," Varan admitted. "Although my wife insists that I can be a bit of a grump who prefers to brood in dark corners and make everyone nervous."

Rhodelia offered him an amused smile. "I mean, I'm not exactly wrong."

Axel chuckled at that, his laugh momentarily making me smile up at him, loving the warm nature of it. I looked back at the two of them. "Do you not host parties in Isramaya?" The way they were talking, it almost seemed to be the case.

Before he could respond, a small body collided with Rhodelia's long dress, Laurain letting out a squeak. She nearly fell to the ground, but Rhodelia scooped her up before she could crash onto her butt.

"Who is this?" Rhodelia asked as Laurain stared at her wide-eyed before taking her pudgy three-year old hands and tugging on Rhodelia's silver hair. I winced but relaxed when Rhodelia just broke out into a laugh.

"Our youngest, Laurain," I explained, and when Laurain wiggled out of Rhodelia's arms and pulled her toward a window nearby, I couldn't help but appreciate how friendly she was being toward our little tot.

"We do," Varan said, answering our question about celebrations. "Though not like this. We may have to make some adjustments to our events moving forward."

"What are celebrations like for your people?"

"My father didn't allow them unless they involved bowing at his feet. In hindsight, we should've seen it for the red flag that it was." He smirked before motioning to his wife. "Rhode has made it her mission to bring joy and happiness back to Isramaya these last ten years."

"But?" I asked curiously. "I sense a 'but' in there."

King Varan grinned as his wife took his hand and joined us, Laurain running back toward her nanny that was waiting nearby. "But our kingdom forgot how to relax under my father's reign. Vampires by nature are not as free-spirited, unfortunately, so the *adjustment isn't the fastest. Luckily, my lovely wife is stubborn and refuses to give up."*

Queen Rhodelia sighed, but she was still smiling. *"Both of our Courts needed a little structure to help them find their footing. But now I know how we're going to party next time."*

"If you need any ideas, let me know—I love party planning," I admitted, excited at the prospect of coordinating something within another territory.

"And I love celebrating and dancing." Queen Rhodelia grinned, her silver eyes sparkling bright. "When you come visit, we'll hold a celebration, and then you'll have to let me know how we did."

"I'm sure it will be amazing—maybe we'll convince all the other very serious vampires to dance with us," I teased.

Rhodelia snort-laughed before looking toward her husband. "The moment they see Varan on the dance floor, they'll flock to him like moths to a flame."

"I'm sure it wouldn't be that extreme..."

"Mark my words, I shall only get to wave to you from across the hall. I'll have to ensure you have proper footwear with padding, as I doubt you'll have the opportunity to sit."

Axel laughed. "I sure hope you're a good dancer."

King Varan's amber eyes flashed a bright, glowing red. His gaze slid down to his wife as he gave her a crooked smirk. "Perhaps we should practice tomorrow, my love?"

And it appeared they were getting more than enough practice since they'd yet to leave the dance floor—it made me so extremely happy.

"It *is* beautiful," Axel agreed, responding to my comment about the party before dropping a kiss on top of my head. "And so are you."

"So romantic," I teased.

"Only for you, çiçeğim," he said seriously, his gaze warming on me before a sound tugged his attention toward the dance floor.

The celebration spread for miles in each direction, groups camping out with tents and vendors setting up shop for the next few days, but the heart of the event was right here in our back yard.

The view of the kingdom of Eventide was gorgeous from here, and lights began to glow brighter from the chandelier hanging from the tent above us, casting shadows throughout the space. Citizens of all status danced together, and while it was crowded, it felt comfortable and everyone seemed in fantastic spirits.

Then again, this was both mine and many of our citizens' favorite time of year—how could it not be with such an exciting celebration? Plus, each year we held the harvest festival in a different location, so we were always changing it up—holding it in either Nightfall, Eventide, or the Isle of Wildcrest.

Wildcrest was an island off the Eventide coast where our family spent its summers. I'd never been able to explore it as a young girl, my parents having used it for military training. We'd transformed it into a place our kingdoms could enjoy, and I loved that my kids could play freely there.

We split the rest of the year by staying the fall and winter in one kingdom and the spring in the other—usually choosing to stay in Eventide during the harsher weather since it was easier to manage. Although, considering the bridge we'd built across the mountain range, there really wasn't much separation between the two kingdoms anymore.

It was my favorite part about being a leader in Vargr—having the ability to bring the two kingdoms together.

"Shit," Axel cursed, standing as a scuffle broke out on the dance floor. He was down there so fast that even though I was right behind him, I wasn't even sure what had happened until he pulled Rozen away from a group of kids.

Messandei stood slightly to the side of them, looking shocked as Rozen essentially exploded in a burst of magic, shifting on the spot.

Oh shit.

The other kids near them backed away in fear as my daughter grabbed my hand, not looking scared but worried for her friend. Axel put him down, maintaining his ground as Rozen let out a low, dangerous growl, first at him and then the other kids.

"Rozen, I need you to calm down." Axel's voice, while gentle, held a dominant thread of energy that would force him to comply. My head reared back slightly as Rozen continued to growl and Messandei slipped from my side, going to stand next to Axel.

"Where's Arnoux and Kathleen?" I asked Axel as he kept his gaze on Rozen.

"I'm not sure, but this is a potential problem," he admitted. That was an understatement. Rozen wasn't supposed to shift this young. The earliest I'd heard of was twelve, and while it wasn't impossible…it seemed extreme.

"Come on, Rozen." Messandei's voice was pitched, sounding hesitant. "Let's go hang out somewhere else."

His head snapped toward the kids whispering, and a lethal sound left Rozen that even had some of the adults looking worried. My daughter shifted foot to foot, looking unsure on how to handle this.

I was glad Axel and I were here. I knew that Rozen would never hurt our daughter, but I could practically feel the anxiety rolling off of her.

"What happened?" Axel asked quietly.

"Some kids were making fun of me, it doesn't matter," she said, unbothered. "Seriously, Rozen—"

Out of nowhere, Arnoux appeared, crouching down to get his son's full attention before speaking to him in low tones. After a moment, Rozen let out a frustrated sound before shrugging him off. With that, the boy took off.

Kathleen approached us, the crease between her brows telling me she was worried. I could see my daughter wanted to follow, but for whatever reason she stayed.

"Give him a few minutes," Kathleen said softly to her, offering both of us a tight smile.

"How long?" Axel asked Arnoux.

"Two weeks," Arnoux said. "We don't know why."

"Let's walk." Axel nodded in the direction Rozen went.

"I know why," Kathleen murmured, shooting me a meaningful glance.

Messandei squeezed my hand, and I nodded, understanding her silent question. "You can follow if you want."

She sped off as I walked back to the table with Kathleen, comforting my friend. "Don't worry, they're going to be totally fine—he's just protective."

"I have a feeling it may be hard for a while," she confessed. "He's very temperamental, and while I understand he's protective over her, I don't want Messandei to miss out on having friends."

I smiled, loving that she was protective, even over my daughter. But that was how all of us were—it was like a massive family.

"Messandei is very strong-willed," I mused. "You know she'll tell Rozen if she doesn't like what he's doing—she did so earlier. This was a bit different of a situation."

"You're right." Kathleen sighed. "I went to go check on Gwyn—she's feeling really good. Clari is going to come join us out here soon."

"Good. I'm planning to go check on Gwyn myself in an hour or so."

"Let me know when you go." Kathleen squeezed my shoulder as I sat back down at the table. Axel returned a few minutes later, wrapping an arm around me. I smiled, noticing Rozen and Messandei playing with the twins, completely calm and smiling. As if nothing had happened.

"How did you do that?" I asked.

"Calm him down? That was all Arnoux, actually. Although I'm sure our daughter being there helped. He's going to be very strong if he's already shifting."

"Not a bad thing if he goes into the military like Arnoux," I pointed out.

Axel hummed in agreement, and I let out a squeak of surprise as I was tugged onto his lap. As if she'd been waiting for an opening, Laurain climbed onto my chair at the head of the table. I offered Pandi a heads up, her gaze tracking our fast-moving daughter, to let her know that I had eyes on her again.

"Mommy, look!" She showed me the candy in her hand, melted chocolate getting everywhere. I arched a brow at Seifer, who was walking over.

"She gave me the look," he growled in annoyance, making me laugh. I knew the exact pout he was accusing his little sister of. The girl was going to be a force to be reckoned with when she was older.

I let out a small happy sigh as I leaned into my husband, feeling a sense of contentment amongst the chaos of our little family. It was messy, and everyone was everywhere, but it made up for every bit of loneliness I'd felt in my life on Earth.

Despite having to traverse an entire lifetime, I was *finally* home with my mate and the family we'd built.

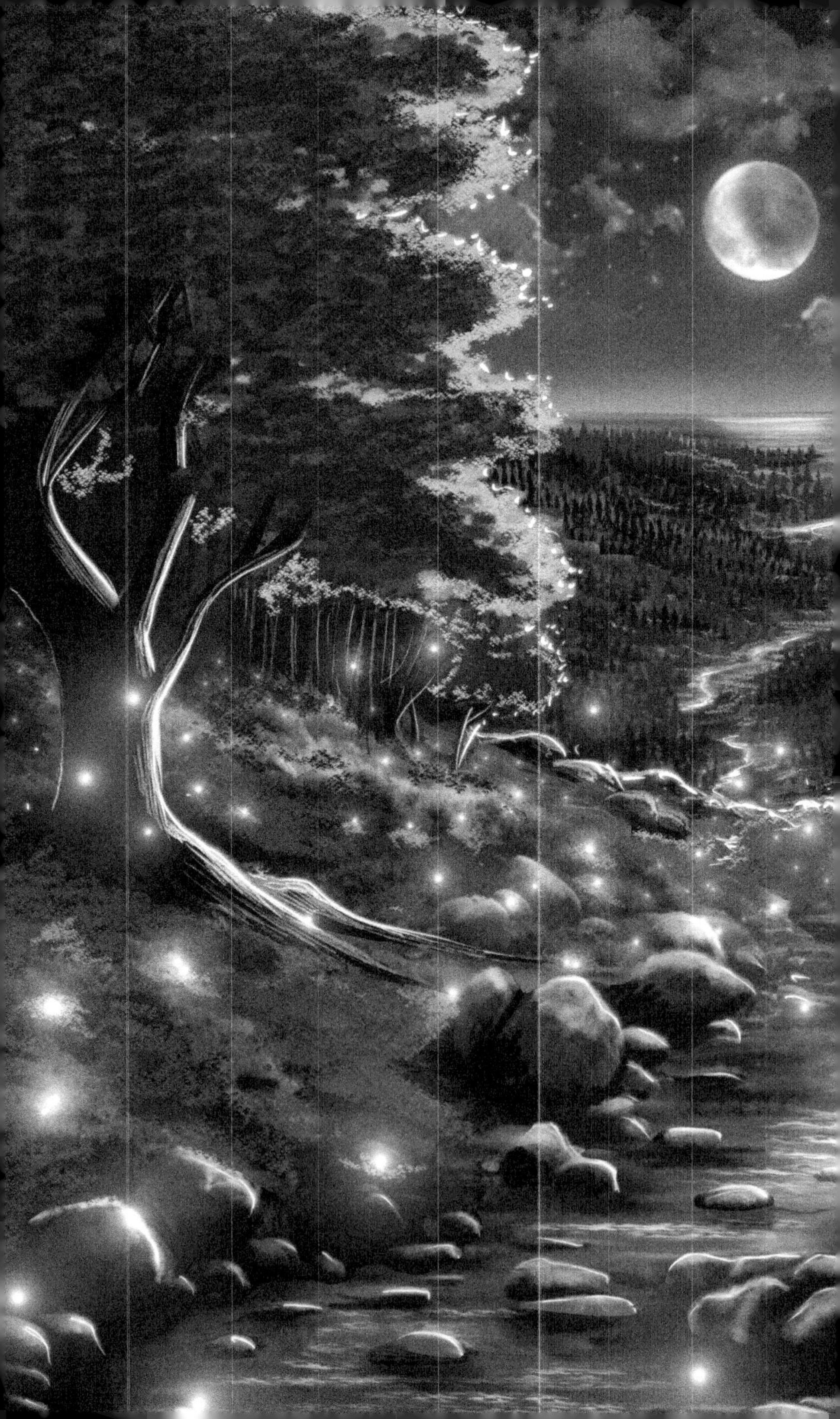

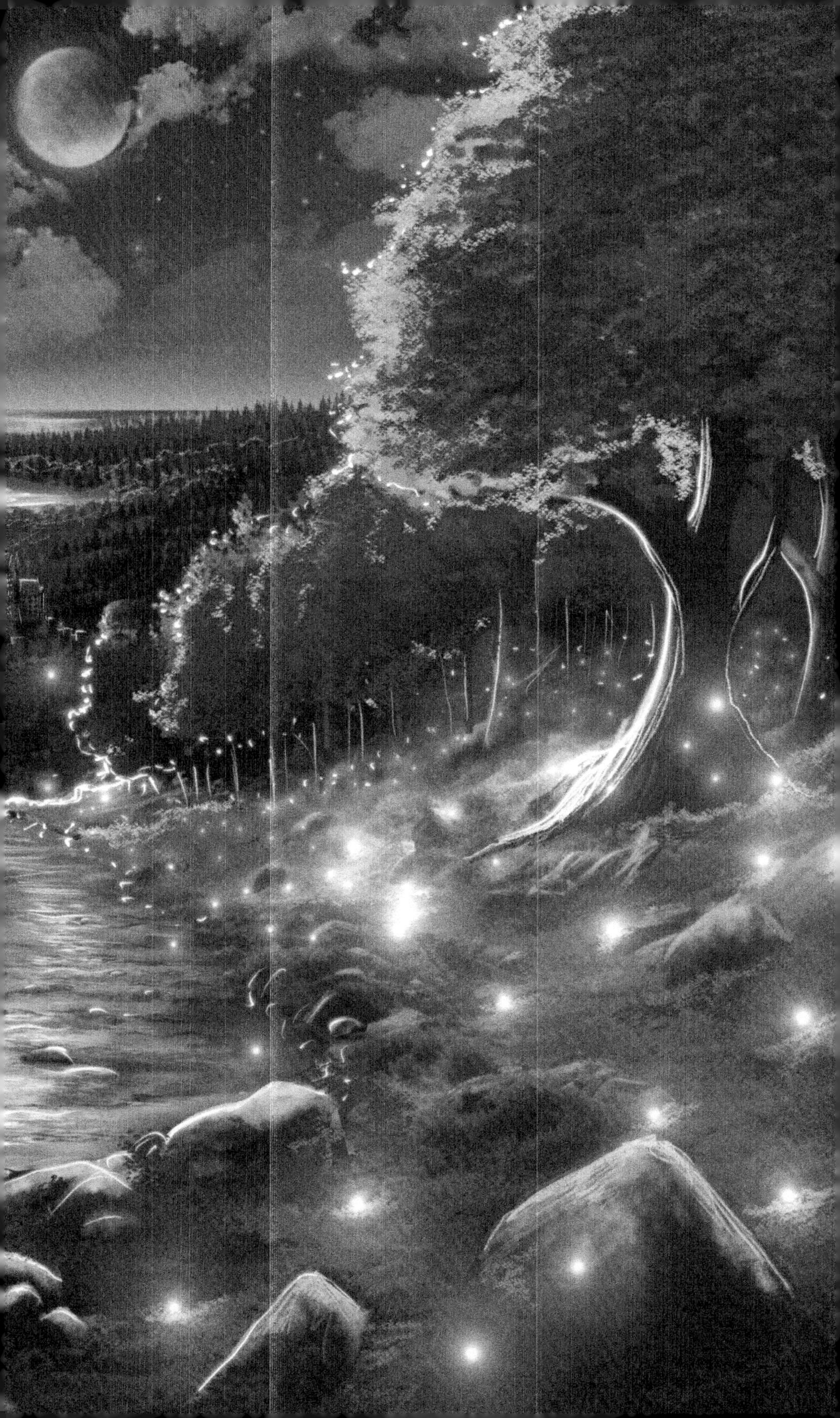

AUTHOR'S NOTE

I want to thank each one of you for giving Evera and Axel a chance. It has been a very exciting process writing my first M/F dynamic fantasy-romance novel and plan to do many more in the future. Come by Sinclair's Ravens for any announcements, cover reveals, or teasers!

Did you enjoy Evera's story? Loved how possessive and protective Axel was? Check out my backlist for similar stories!
    The Storm Dragons' Mate - Blitz
    Reborn - Reborn In Flames
    Silver Falls University - Lost

M. SINCLAIR

M. Sinclair is a USA Today Best-Selling Author who can be found writing or thinking about her characters and plots nearly every moment of the day. With over 65 published works since her debut in 2019, her work spans from paranormal to contemporary romance rooted in extensive world-building and deep character development. M. Sinclair believes there is enough room for all types of heroines in this world, and that being saved is just as important as saving others.

Just remember to love cats... that's not negotiable.

PUBLISHED WORKS

M. Sinclair has crafted different universes with unique plotlines, character cameos, and shared universe events. As a reader, this means that you may see your favorite character or characters... appear in multiple books besides their own storyline.

UNIVERSE 1

Established in 2019

VENGEANCE

Book 1 - Savages

Book 2 - Lunatics

Book 3 - Monsters

Book 4 - Psychos

Complete Series

Vengeance : The Complete Series

THE RED MASQUES

Book 1 - Raven Blood

Book 2 - Ashes & Bones

Book 3 - Shadow Glass

Book 4 - Fire & Smoke

Book 5 - Dark King

Complete Series

A Raven Masques Novel - Birth of a Raven

Tears of the Siren

Book 1 - Horror of Your Heart

Book 2 - Broken House

Book 3 - Neon Drops

Book 4 - Snapped Strings

Book 5 - Fractured Souls

Book 6 - Shattered Galaxies (TBA)

Descendant

Book 1 - Descendant of Chaos

Book 2 - Descendant of Blood

Book 3 - Descendant of Sin

Book 4 - Descendant of Glory

Book 5 - Descendant of Pain

Book 6 - Descendant of Victory (TBA)

Reborn

Book 1 - Reborn In Flames

Book 2 - Soaring In Flames

Book 3 - Realm Of Flames

Book 4 - Dying in Flames

Book 5 - Ruling in Flames

Complete Series

The Wronged

Book 1 - Wicked Blaze Correctional
Book 2 - Evading Wicked Blaze
Book 3 - Defeating Wicked Blaze
Complete Series
The Wronged: Completed Series

LOST IN FAE
Book 1 - Finding Fae
Book 2 - Exploring Fae
Book 3 - Freeing Fae
Book 4 - Loving Fae (TBA)

UNIVERSE 2

Established in 2020

AMONG SHADOWS
Book 1 - Court of Betrayal
Book 2 - Court of Deception (TBA)

PARANORMAL & FANTASY SERIES

THESE SERIES ARE NOT CURRENTLY AFFILIATED WITH A SPECIFIC M. SINCLAIR UNIVERSE.

HUNTER'S MOON RITUAL

Book 1 - Howling Love (TBA)

Book 2 - TBA

Book 3 - TBA

Phases of the Moon

Book 1 - Lunar Witch

Book 2 - Blood Witch

Book 3 - Shadow Witch

Book 4 - Unblessed Witch (TBA)

The Storm Dragons' Mate

Book 1 - Blitz

Book 2 - Flicker

Book 3 - Surge

Book 4 - Flash (TBA)

The Dead and the Not So Dead

Book 1 - Queen of the Dead

Book 2 - Team Time with the Dead

Book 3 - Dying for the Dead

Complete Series

The Dead and the Not So Dead: Completed Series

Silver Falls University

Book 1 - Lost

Book 2 - Forgotten

Book 3 - Discovered

Book 4 - Pursued

Book 5 - Found

Complete Series

I.S.S.

Book 1 - Soothing Nightmares

Book 2 - Defending Nightmares

Book 3 - Defeating Nightmares

Book 4 - Loving Nightmares

Universe Standalone Novel - Mating Monsters

Complete Series

CONTEMPORARY UNIVERSE

Established in 2021

THE SHADOWS OF WILDBERRY LANE

Book 1 - Perfection of Suffering

Book 2 - Execution of Anguish

Book 3 - Carnage of Misery

Complete Series

Complete Collection: The Shadows of Wildberry Lane

THEIR POSSESSION

Book 1 - Sheltered

Book 2 - Searched (TBA)

STANDALONE NOVELS

Peridot (Jewels Cafe Series)

Time for Sensibility (Women of Time)

Of Claws & Chaos (Forgotten Kingdoms)

WILLOWDALE VILLAGE COLLECTION

A collection of standalone novels about the women of Willowdale Village.

Voiceless

SEASONS OF THE HUNTRESS

Winter Huntress

COLLABORATIONS

MONARCHS OF HELL

(M. SINCLAIR & R.L. CAULDER)

BOOK 1 - INSURRECTION

BOOK 2 - IMBALANCE

BOOK 3 - INHERITANCE

Complete Series

FALLEN DESTINY

(M. SINCLAIR & R.L. CAULDER)

BOOK 1 - WINGS OF STARS

BOOK 2 - TBA

Book 3 - TBA

The Vampyres' Source
(M. Sinclair & R.L. Caulder)

Book 1 - Ruthless Blood

Book 2 - Ruthless War

Book 3 - Ruthless Love

Complete Series

Rebel Hearts Heists Duet
(M. Sinclair & Melissa Adams)

Book 1 - Steal Me

Book 2 - Keep Me

Complete Duet

Printed in Great Britain
by Amazon